I0768989

CULTIVATION IS A GAME

BOOK ONE

CULTIVATION IS A GAME

IS A

GAME

BOOK ONE

Kalzara

Podium

All rights reserved. No part of this publication may be reproduced, stored in a retrieval system, or transmitted in any form or by any means electronic, mechanical, photocopying, recording, or otherwise without prior written permission from Podium Publishing.

This is a work of fiction. Names, characters, places, and incidents are either products of the author's imagination or used fictitiously. Any resemblance to actual events, locales, or persons, living, dead, or undead, is entirely coincidental.

Copyright © 2025 by Kalzara

Cover design by Dalia and Sam

ISBN: 979-8-89539-424-3

Published in 2025 by Podium Publishing
www.podiumentertainment.com

CULTIVATION IS A GAME

BOOK ONE

CHAPTER ONE

The soft glow from three twenty-seven-inch monitors lit up Kai's face as he frantically mashed the buttons on his keyboard.

On his central monitor, his character—a heavily-armored dwarf warrior—desperately parried blows from a giant boss monster. The creature, a grotesque fusion of machine and flesh, loomed over the battlefield, its metallic tentacles lashing out at Kai's team.

"Shit, shit, shit!" Kai muttered, his eyes darting between his health bar and the boss's attacks. "Sarah, I need a heal!"

A golden light enveloped Kai's character as Sarah's priestess cast a healing spell. But it wasn't enough. The boss's next attack sent Kai's dwarf flying, his health bar depleting to zero.

[YOU DIED]
Character: Grimbold the Dwarf
Time alive: 8:42
Damage dealt: 145,623
Experience lost: 2,500

"Not again!" Kai slammed his hand on the desk. His eyes darted to the party status indicators as two more messages popped up in rapid succession.

[PARTY MEMBER DEFEATED: Shadowblade]
[PARTY MEMBER DEFEATED: LightBringer]

The Discord channel erupted with groans and curses.

"That's it. I'm done," Sarah's defeated voice came through. "Six hours and we can't even get it below 40% health."

"Yeah, man," Jake chimed in, sounding exhausted. "Maybe we should call it."

Kai leaned back, running his hands through his disheveled brown hair. His blue eyes burned from staring at the screens for so long. Empty energy drink cans, crumpled snack wrappers, and a forgotten slice of pizza cluttered his desk—typical for a Friday night marathon gaming session.

Kai was about to agree when something spurred a thought. Leaning forward, he replayed the boss fight in his head, focusing on its attack patterns.

"Wait," he said, excitement creeping into his voice. "Guys, I think I've got something."

Jake groaned. "Dude, come on. It's four a.m."

"No, seriously," Kai insisted, pulling up the boss's stats on his second monitor. "Look at this. Every fourth attack, it does that big AOE slam, right?"

"Yeah, so?" Sarah asked, curiosity overtaking her fatigue.

Kai's fingers flew across the keyboard, pulling up his team's character stats. "So, what if instead of spreading out, we stack for that attack? Jake, if you pop your evasion right before it hits, and Sarah, if you time your group shield . . ."

He laid out the plan, pointing out how they could use the boss's own attack pattern to create a window for massive damage.

There was a moment of silence, then Jake let out a low whistle. "That's . . . actually a good idea."

"It's risky," Sarah added, but Kai could hear the spark of hope in her voice.

Kai grinned, cracking his knuckles. "High risk, high reward. That's how we play, right? One more try. If it doesn't work, the next time we meet, beers are on me."

"You're on," Jake chuckled. "Let's do this."

They respawned, making their way back through the neon-lit cyberpunk cityscape to the boss arena. Kai's dwarf took point, shield raised as they entered.

The fight began, and Kai called out the attacks. "AOE coming in three . . . two . . . one . . . Now!"

They stacked. Jake's rogue shimmered, becoming nearly invisible. Sarah's priestess threw up a light barrier. The boss slammed down, but this time, they were ready.

"Go, go, go!" Kai shouted.

Jake's rogue appeared behind the boss, daggers flying in a flurry of critical hits. Sarah's priestess unleashed a torrent of holy fire. Kai's dwarf charged in, his war hammer glowing with level seventy-two enchantments.

The boss's health bar plummeted—75%, 50%, 25%.

"Holy shit, it's working!" Sarah yelled, her priestess dodging a retaliatory strike.

With a final, coordinated assault, they brought the mighty creature down. It collapsed in a heap of sparking metal and oozing flesh.

[VICTORY ACHIEVED]
Boss Defeated: Cybernetic Abomination
Time: 14:23
Damage dealt: 1,543,267
Experience gained: 50,000
Rare loot unlocked!

"We did it!" Jake whooped. "Kai, you beautiful bastard!"

Kai leaned back, a wide grin spreading across his face. "See? Told you we could— Wait, what the hell?"

A small glitch appeared in the corner of his main screen, pixelating the edge of the victory banner. It spread rapidly, consuming the image.

"Guys, are you seeing this?" Kai asked, frowning as he leaned in for a closer look.

"Seeing what?" Sarah asked, still celebrating. "Kai?"

The glitch exploded across all three monitors. The game world dissolved into a swirling chaos of code and fragmented images. At the center, a trident-like symbol pulsed with an eerie red glow.

"What the fu—" Kai started, reaching for the power button.

An overwhelming surge of energy burst from the screens. It wasn't just visual—Kai could feel it crackling over his skin, seeping into his very being.

He tried to move, to call out to his friends, but found himself paralyzed. The strange energy enveloped him as the world began to fade.

The last thing Kai heard was Jake's voice, distant and distorted: "Kai? Kai, you there, man?"

Then darkness claimed him, the red trident symbol burning in his mind as consciousness slipped away.

His last coherent thought was, *God, I really hope this is just some weird dream . . .*

The first thing Kai noticed as he regained consciousness was the smell. Gone was the familiar scent of his room: a mix of coffee, electronics, and the faintest hint of sweat from long gaming sessions. Instead, his nostrils were assaulted by the nauseating smell of manure.

Did someone leave my window open again? he wondered groggily.

Kai's eyes fluttered open, then immediately widened in shock. Instead of the familiar sight of his bedroom ceiling, he found himself staring up at the evening sky.

"What the . . ." Kai muttered, pushing himself up to a sitting position. His head swam with the movement, and he took a moment to steady himself.

As his vision cleared, Kai took in his surroundings with growing disbelief. He was in the middle of a forest. Towering trees stretched as far as the eye could see. The ground was carpeted with a thick layer of moss and ferns, dotted here and there with overgrown mushrooms.

This has to be a dream, Kai thought, pinching his arm hard. The sharp pain did nothing to dispel the scene before him.

"Okay, stay calm," he said aloud, his voice sounding oddly muffled in the large forest. "Think this through logically."

Kai stood up, brushing leaves and dirt from his clothes. He was still wearing the T-shirt and sweatpants he had on while gaming, but his feet were bare.

First step, assess the situation, he thought, falling back on his analytical instincts.

He patted his pockets, finding only his phone and wallet. The phone, unsurprisingly, had no signal.

"Great," Kai muttered. "No shoes, no food, no idea where I am. This is just perfect."

As he continued his self-assessment, Kai noticed something strange on his right wrist. A faint, glowing mark pulsed just beneath his skin. It resembled the symbol he had seen on his computer screen just before . . . whatever this was had happened.

"Okay, that's new," he said, prodding at the trident-like mark. It didn't hurt, but he could feel a subtle warmth emanating from it.

Focus, Kai, he chided himself. *Weird glowing tattoos can wait. I need to figure out where I am and how to get back home.*

Kai picked a direction at random and started walking. As he moved through the forest, he couldn't shake the feeling that something was off. The air felt different—thicker somehow, charged with an energy he couldn't quite explain.

It's like I can almost feel the life in this place . . . Stop it. That doesn't make any sense. You're just disoriented.

After what felt like hours of walking, Kai's ears perked up at a sound that didn't belong to the forest. Voices, human voices.

Finally, some answers, he thought, quickening his pace.

As he pushed through a particularly dense patch of undergrowth, Kai found himself at the edge of a small clearing. His jaw dropped at the sight before him.

A small village nestled at the foot of a towering mountain, its architecture unlike anything Kai had ever seen outside of historical documentaries or fantasy games. The buildings were wood and stone, with sweeping, tiled roofs that curved upward at the corners. People milled about, dressed in robes and carrying baskets of what looked like herbs and vegetables.

"No way," Kai breathed. "This can't be real."

He watched from the tree line for several minutes, his mind racing. The villagers spoke a language he couldn't understand, but their mannerisms and the general layout of the village reminded him of something . . .

It's like I've stepped into one of those xianxia novels, he thought. *But that's impossible. Right? This must be some sort of prank?*

Deciding that standing in the forest wasn't going to get him any answers, Kai steeled himself and stepped out into the open. Almost immediately, several villagers noticed him and began pointing and talking excitedly.

Here goes nothing, Kai thought as he approached the nearest person, a bald old man.

"Excuse me," Kai said, trying to keep his voice steady. "Can you tell me where I am?"

The old man's eyes widened in surprise. He replied in a language Kai didn't understand, gesturing animatedly.

"I'm sorry, I don't . . ." Kai began, but he trailed off as he realized something incredible. While he couldn't understand the man's words, their meaning was somehow becoming clear in his mind.

"Young man," the old man was saying, "are you lost? This is Misty Waterfall Village. If you don't know where that is, we're at the foot of Mount Celestial Ascent."

Misty Waterfall Village? Mount Celestial Ascent? I've never heard of either place. The names sounded like something out of a fantasy game, not real locations.

Kai struggled to keep his face neutral, not wanting to alarm the old man. Where on Earth was he? Or was he even on Earth anymore? The thought sent a chill down his spine.

"Yeah . . . I think I am lost," Kai said. "I'm not sure how I got here. Everything's a bit . . . fuzzy."

The old man's expression softened. "Ah, a troubled mind. Come, come. Let's get you something to eat and drink. Perhaps that will help clear your thoughts."

As Kai followed the elder into the village, he couldn't help but feel a twinge of guilt at his deception. But he pushed the feeling aside, knowing that before he found out what was going on, caution was necessary.

It's not really lying, he rationalized. *I am confused and lost. I'm just . . . omitting some details.*

The old man led Kai to a small teahouse near the center of the village. As they walked, Kai took in every detail he could, cataloging information for later analysis. The villagers went about their daily routines, but many paused to stare curiously at the newcomer in his odd clothing.

Inside the teahouse, the air was scented with herbs and spices. The old man gestured for Kai to sit at a low table, then spoke quietly to the proprietor. Soon, a steaming cup of tea and a plate of dumplings were placed before Kai.

"Eat, drink," the elder encouraged. "Then we can talk about your situation."

Kai nodded gratefully and took a sip of the tea. The flavor was unlike anything he'd tasted before—complex, earthy, with an underlying energy that seemed to invigorate him.

Focus, he reminded himself. *Gather information. But be careful what you reveal.*

"Thank you for your kindness," Kai said, setting down the cup. "I'm afraid I don't remember much. My name is Kai, but beyond that . . ." He trailed off, shrugging helplessly.

The old man nodded sympathetically. "I am Chen Lao. It's not unheard of for cultivators to experience memory loss after a particularly intense breakthrough or battle. Perhaps that is what happened to you?"

Kai's ears perked up at the familiar term. *Cultivators. So, this really is a xianxia world . . .*

"Cultivators?" he asked, feigning ignorance. "I'm not sure what that means."

Chen Lao's eyebrows rose in surprise. "You don't know of cultivation? But surely, with your level of qi . . ." He trailed off, studying Kai more closely. "Fascinating. It seems your memories are more damaged than I thought. Tell me, young man, what do you know of qi?"

Kai pretended to concentrate, as if trying to recall something just out of reach. "Qi . . . it sounds familiar. Something about energy? Life force?"

The elder nodded encouragingly. "Yes, yes. Qi is the energy that flows through all living things. Cultivators are those who have learned to harness and strengthen their qi, gaining great power in the process."

As Chen Lao spoke, something extraordinary happened. A translucent window suddenly appeared in Kai's field of vision, hovering in the air like a holographic display. Kai managed to keep his expression neutral, but internally, his mind was racing.

A status window. Just like in the games. Either I've taken too many mushrooms again or I'm really in a new world . . .

The window displayed his name at the top, followed by a series of stats.

> Name: Kai Thorn
>
> Level: Qi Refining Stage 1
> Qi: 10/10
> Strength: 10
> Agility: 12
> Durability: 10
> Intelligence: 10
> Wisdom: 9

Kai's eyes widened slightly at his stats.

"Is something wrong?" Chen Lao asked, noticing Kai's distraction.

Kai quickly refocused on the conversation. "No, sorry. Just . . . trying to process everything. You said cultivators can gain great power? How does that work?"

As the old man launched into an explanation of the basics of cultivation, Kai listened intently while also experimenting with the status window. He found that he could interact with it using his thoughts, expanding different sections and viewing more detailed information.

This is a game-changer, Kai realized. *With this interface, I can optimize my growth in ways others can't even imagine.*

"And that's why many young cultivators join sects," Chen Lao was saying as Kai tuned back in. "The major sects provide resources and training that can greatly accelerate one's cultivation journey."

Kai nodded, filing away this crucial information. "These sects, are there many of them?"

"Oh, yes," the elder replied. "The largest in our region are the Azure Sky Sect, known for their righteous path, and the Dark Moon Sect, who . . . well, they have a reputation for being more pragmatic in their pursuits."

Righteous path versus pragmatism. I'll need to learn more about these sects before making any decisions.

"Thank you for explaining all this," Kai said, bowing his head slightly. "It's helping to clear some of the fog in my mind. I'm still not sure how I got here or where I came from, but at least I have a better understanding of where I am now."

Chen Lao smiled. "You are welcome, young man. Now, we should consider your next steps. Without your memories, you are vulnerable. With your talent, perhaps we could arrange for you to meet with one of the sect recruiters when they next visit our village?"

Kai considered the offer. It was tempting—a direct path into this world's power structure. But he also knew he needed more information before committing to anything.

"That's very generous," he said carefully. "But I think I need some time to . . . find myself first. Is there somewhere I could stay for a few days? I'd be happy to work in exchange for lodging."

"Hmm, yes, that could be arranged," the old man stroked his beard thoughtfully. "My nephew runs the village granary. He could always use an extra pair of hands during the harvest season. And we have a small guesthouse where traveling cultivators sometimes stay. It's yours for as long as you need."

Kai bowed deeply, genuinely grateful for the man's kindness. "Thank you, Chen Lao. Your generosity is overwhelming."

As they stood to leave the teahouse, Kai caught his reflection in a polished metal surface. He still looked like himself—short, dark hair, lean build, blue eyes—but something seemed different. There was an energy about him that hadn't been there before.

Welcome to your new life, Kai, he thought to himself. *Time to start playing the game.*

CHAPTER TWO

Kai's eyes fluttered open as he was greeted by the unfamiliar ceiling. He blinked, memories of the previous day flooding back. The forest, the village, Chen Lao's kindness, it all felt surreal.

He sat up slowly, taking in his surroundings. The guesthouse was small but comfortable, with simple furnishings and a window looking out onto the village.

It wasn't a dream. I'm really in another world.

As he stretched, Kai realized something surprising. He didn't feel the pang of homesickness he'd expected. Earth, with its familiar routines and technology, seemed like a distant memory.

It's like I've stepped into one of my games. Except now I'm the main character . . .

Kai had always been more at home in virtual worlds than in reality. His friends were mostly online gaming buddies, their interactions limited to voice chats, strategy discussions, and the occasional meetup. As for family . . .

Mom, he thought, a brief wave of sadness washing over him. She had passed away shortly after he finished college, leaving him alone in the world. His father had never been in the picture.

Kai shook his head, pushing away the thoughts. *No use dwelling on the past. This is a fresh start, cultivation is just another game system to master. I've got my status window, and now I need to level up.*

Name: Kai Thorn
Level: Qi Refining Stage 1 Qi: 10/10 Strength: 10

Agility: 12
Durability: 10
Intelligence: 10
Wisdom: 9

His eyes lingered on his Agility stat, slightly higher than the others. A small smile tugged at his lips as he remembered the countless hours he'd spent in the kickboxing gym. It had been his escape, a way to stay fit and work out his frustrations. It seemed those years of training had followed him to this new world.

If this is anything like the games I've played, those stats are going to be crucial. Time to start grinding.

A knock at the door interrupted his thoughts. "Kai?" Chen Lao's voice called out. "Are you awake?"

"Yes, I'm up," Kai replied, quickly pulling on the simple robes that had been provided for him. He opened the door to find the old man smiling warmly.

"Good morning," Chen Lao said. "I hope you slept well. My nephew is ready to show you around the granary if you're still willing to help out."

"Of course," Kai nodded. "I'm grateful for your hospitality. It's the least I can do to repay you."

The granary was a large, sturdy building on the outskirts of the village. A young man with a friendly face was waiting outside, waving as Kai approached.

"You must be Kai," he said with a warm smile. "I'm Liang. Uncle Chen told me about you. Welcome to Misty Waterfall Village!"

Kai smiled back and stuck out his hand. Liang looked at it oddly, seeming confused. Kai quickly realized his mistake: This wasn't how people greeted each other here. He lowered his hand and gave a small bow instead.

"Thanks for having me," Kai said. "I'm ready to work."

Liang returned the bow with a laugh. "Eager, I see! Well, we've got plenty to do. Come on, I'll show you around."

The next few days passed in a blur of activity. Kai threw himself into the work, helping to sort and store the newly harvested grains, repair damaged storage containers, and assist with inventory.

It was hard, physical labor—something Kai wasn't used to. But as the days went by, he found himself growing stronger, more agile. His status window reflected that.

Name: Kai Thorn

Level: Qi Refining Stage 1

> Qi: 10/10
> Strength: 11
> Agility: 13
> Durability: 11
> Intelligence: 10
> Wisdom: 9

Not bad, Kai thought, studying the screen during a brief break. *But I need to start working on my qi if I want to make real progress in this world.*

As if the universe had heard his thoughts, an opportunity presented itself that very afternoon. Kai was carrying a heavy sack of grain when he noticed an old man struggling with a similar load.

"Here, let me help you with that," Kai offered, setting down his own sack and moving to assist the elder.

The old man's eyes widened in surprise. "Oh, thank you, young man. These old bones aren't what they used to be."

As Kai picked up the sack, he noticed something odd. The old man's frail appearance seemed at odds with the way he moved—there was a fluidity, a subtle grace that spoke of hidden strength.

There's more to this guy than meets the eye . . .

"I'm Kai," he said, introducing himself as they walked. "I'm new to the village."

The old man nodded. "Ah, yes. I've heard about you. The young man with no memories. I am Zhang Wei."

There was something in Zhang Wei's tone that made Kai pause. A hint of . . . curiosity? Suspicion?

"That's right," Kai said carefully. "I'm afraid I don't remember much about my past."

Zhang Wei hummed thoughtfully. "Memory is a fickle thing, young Kai. But the body remembers what the mind forgets. Tell me, have you ever heard of qi?"

Kai feigned ignorance, shaking his head. "Chen Lao mentioned it, but I'm not sure I understand."

"Ah," Zhang Wei nodded. "Memory loss can be a tricky thing, especially for cultivators. Sometimes a particularly intense breakthrough or battle can scramble one's mind." He leaned forward. "Would you allow me to sense your qi? It might help me understand your situation better."

Kai hesitated for a moment, but, realizing there was no downside, he nodded. "Of course, Elder."

The old man reached out, placing a hand on Kai's wrist. Kai felt a strange tingling sensation, as if something was probing gently at his core.

After a moment, Zhang Wei sat back, his expression a mix of surprise and intrigue. "Fascinating," he murmured. "Your qi . . . it's at the level of Qi Refining stage one, but there's something unusual about it. Almost as if . . ." He trailed off, lost in thought.

Kai leaned forward, genuinely curious. "What is it, Elder Zhang?"

The old man shook his head. "It's hard to say for certain. But your qi feels . . . pure, untainted. As if you've never used any cultivation techniques at all, despite clearly having a strong foundation."

"I see," Kai said. "Is that . . . unusual?"

Zhang Wei nodded slowly. "Quite. Most cultivators at your level would have already begun shaping their qi according to specific techniques. Yours is like a blank slate." He studied Kai intently. "Tell me, young man, would you be interested in relearning some basic cultivation methods? It might help jog your memory."

Bingo. This is exactly what I need. Kai kept his expression neutral. "I would be very grateful for your guidance, Elder Zhang."

And so, after finishing his work at the granary, Kai found himself following Zhang Wei to a small clearing just outside the village.

"Now," Zhang Wei said, his voice taking on a more authoritative tone, "qi is the energy that flows through all living things. Cultivators learn to harness this energy, to strengthen their bodies and perform incredible feats."

Kai listened intently, pretending to absorb this information for the first time.

Zhang Wei continued, "Close your eyes, young Kai. Try to feel the energy within you. It may be faint at first, but with practice, you can learn to sense and control it."

Kai did as instructed, closing his eyes and focusing inward. To his surprise, he could indeed feel something: a warm, tingling sensation that seemed to flow through his body.

Is this qi? It feels . . . familiar somehow.

"I . . . I think I feel something," Kai said hesitantly, opening his eyes.

Zhang Wei nodded, a satisfied smile on his face. "Good, good. Now, try to gather that energy. Imagine it pooling in your lower abdomen."

Kai concentrated, visualizing the energy as a glowing orb. To his amazement, he could feel the qi responding to his will, slowly gathering as directed.

Zhang Wei's eyebrows shot up in surprise. "Impressive! You're a natural, young Kai. Or perhaps . . . you're remembering skills you once knew."

Kai feigned confusion. "What do you mean?"

"Your control is too refined for a complete novice," Zhang Wei explained. "I suspect you were once a cultivator of some skill. Your current level seems to be that of Qi Refining stage one, but it's likely it was previously higher."

Higher? You couldn't be more wrong, old man, Kai thought with a smile. Aloud, he said, "I . . . I'm not sure. It does feel somewhat familiar."

Zhang Wei nodded sagely. "The mind may forget, but the body remembers. Now, let's try something more advanced. Channel your qi to your hand."

Kai complied, focusing on directing the energy as instructed. As he did so, he felt a strange tingling in his right wrist. Glancing down, he saw the mysterious mark glowing faintly.

What the . . .

Suddenly, the qi in his hand seemed to solidify, taking on a vaguely sword-like shape.

Zhang Wei's eyes widened in shock. "By the heavens! Y-You're condensing qi!"

Kai stared at the shimmering energy construct in his hand. *This . . . this could be a game-changer.*

"I've never seen anything quite like it," Zhang Wei continued, his voice filled with awe. "Young man, your background must be extraordinary. You must come from a powerful sect indeed!"

Kai hesitated for a moment before nodding slowly. "I . . . I suppose I must." *Better to let them think that. It might keep me safer in the long run.*

"We must continue your training," Zhang Wei said eagerly. "Your talent is too great to waste. Meet me here again tomorrow, and we'll work on developing this ability further."

As Kai made his way back to the guest house that evening, his mind was buzzing with possibilities. *Qi Condensation . . . I can create weapons out of pure energy. The tactical advantages are enormous.*

He spent the next few hours experimenting with his new ability, forming various weapons and tools from his qi. Swords, spears, shields—each came with its own advantages and drawbacks.

I need to plan for every scenario. In close combat, a sword would be ideal. For ranged attacks, maybe I can form something like a bow. And a shield for defense . . .

As he practiced, Kai couldn't help but feel a sense of exhilaration. *This really is the ultimate game. And I intend to master it.*

The next morning, Kai woke up early, eager to continue his training with Zhang Wei. As he made his way to the clearing, he ran through potential scenarios in his mind.

If I encounter a stronger cultivator, I'll need to rely on strategy rather than brute force. Maybe I can use the environment to my advantage . . .

"Ah, young Kai," Zhang Wei greeted him as he arrived. "Ready to continue your training?"

"Absolutely," Kai nodded, a determined look in his eyes. "What's next?"

Zhang Wei smiled approvingly. "Let's work on refining your Qi Condensation skill. Try forming different shapes, focusing on stability and detail."

For the next few hours, Kai practiced diligently under Zhang Wei's guidance. He formed swords, spears, shields, and even attempted more complex shapes like chains and grappling hooks.

"Remarkable," Zhang Wei muttered, watching Kai create a detailed dagger of pure qi. "Your progress is astounding. Almost like this all comes naturally to you. Are you sure you don't remember any of your past training?"

Kai shook his head, maintaining his facade of confusion. "No, it's all still a blank. But this . . . it feels right somehow."

"Your ability, your rapid progress . . . these are not traits of an ordinary sect," Zhang Wei nodded thoughtfully. "I suspect you may have connections to one of the major powers in our world. Perhaps even one of the hidden bloodlines!"

Outwardly, Kai maintained a look of confused interest. "Hidden bloodlines? What do you mean?"

Zhang Wei lowered his voice, glancing around as if afraid of being overheard. "There are whispers of powerful cultivation families that operate in secret, away from the politics and conflicts of the major sects. They are all born with an ability unique to that family. This could explain your Qi Condensation skill. If you really do come from such a background, young Kai, you must be very careful. Such connections can be both a blessing and a curse."

Despite knowing he didn't hail from such a family, Kai nodded. "I understand. Thank you for the warning, Master Zhang."

I can convince others that I have a powerful backing, it might deter potential enemies. But I'll need to be careful not to attract too much attention. It's a delicate balance.

Over the next few days, Kai split his time between working at the granary and training with Zhang Wei. His progress was rapid, impressing even the old cultivator.

"Your talent is truly remarkable," Zhang Wei commented one afternoon as they took a break from training. "In just a few days, you've advanced to Qi Refining stage two. At this rate, you'll be ready for Foundation Establishment in no time."

Kai nodded, allowing a small smile of satisfaction to cross his face. His status window now showed:

Name: Kai Thorn
Level: Qi Refining Stage 2

Qi: 25/25
Strength: 15
Agility: 17
Durability: 15
Intelligence: 10
Wisdom: 10

Not bad. But I need to keep pushing, I'm barely scratching the surface. In this world, power is everything.

"Master Zhang," Kai said, an idea forming in his mind. "You mentioned Foundation Establishment. I don't know much about it; can you tell me more?"

Zhang Wei's expression grew serious. "Ah, Foundation Establishment. It's a critical step in a cultivator's journey. It involves solidifying your qi foundation, creating a stable base for future advancement. But it's also incredibly dangerous. Many cultivators fail at this stage, their foundations crumbling under the pressure."

"What happens to those who fail?"

A shadow passed over Zhang Wei's face. "Best-case scenario? They're left unable to advance further, their cultivation stagnating. Worst case . . . their cultivation can backfire, crippling or even killing them."

A high-risk, high-reward scenario.

"Is that what happened to you, Master Zhang? If you don't mind me asking."

Zhang Wei sighed. "Yes, it is. I was once a promising disciple of the Azure Sky Sect. But when I attempted Foundation Establishment, my foundation crumbled. I was lucky to survive, but the sect had no use for a crippled cultivator. They cast me out, and I've been living here ever since. Now, I'm no better than a Qi Refining stage five cultivator at best . . ."

The sects aren't as benevolent as they might want people to believe. Kai's eyes narrowed slightly. *I don't blame them though; even the righteous sects have to be pragmatic.*

"I'm sorry to hear that, but thank you for sharing that with me." He gave a slight bow.

Even though the decision to expel the old man was logical, Kai still felt genuinely bad for him.

Zhang Wei nodded, a sad smile on his face. "Learn from my mistakes, lad. Don't rush into Foundation Establishment until you're absolutely ready. And be wary of the major sects. They can offer great opportunities, but their favor is fickle."

* * *

As Kai made his way back to the village that evening, his thoughts were focused on advancement.

I need to get stronger, fast. This village feels like a typical starting point in a game. If it follows gaming logic, I'd bet anything this village is going to face some kind of threat that is just above my current level. A monster attack, a bandit raid, or maybe a rival cultivator causing trouble. That's how these things always go in games.

But I can't rush this. No point in pushing for Foundation Establishment if it might kill me. I need to be smart about my training. Find that sweet spot where I'm as strong as possible without taking stupid risks.

He spent the next few hours practicing his Qi Condensation skill, forming shapes and testing their durability. *If I can create solid, lasting constructs, it could give me a significant advantage in combat.*

As he trained, Kai felt fatigue creeping in. His qi reserves were dwindling, arms growing heavy, and a dull ache spread through his head. Despite the discomfort, he pushed on, determined to make progress.

Gritting his teeth, Kai focused his remaining energy on one final exercise. He poured his qi into creating a perfect replica of a longsword. As the construct solidified, a wave of exhaustion washed over him. His vision swam as the glowing weapons dissipated before him. Kai's legs buckled and he sank to the ground.

"I need to be careful," he sighed between labored breaths. "Using too much qi is dangerous. I should rest."

As he caught his breath, Kai's mind wandered to his new circumstances. *It's strange. A week ago, I was just a gamer, living a normal life on Earth. Now, I'm training to become a cultivator in a world straight out of a fantasy novel.*

But despite the strangeness of it all, Kai felt no real desire to return to his old life. *What was there for me back on Earth, really? No family, no real friends . . . just games and a dead-end job. Here, I have the chance to become truly powerful. To make a real difference.*

This is my reality now. I have to accept it.

CHAPTER THREE

The sun dipped toward the horizon as Kai trudged back to the village, his muscles aching from another day of intense cultivation practice. Three weeks had passed since he found himself in this new world, and the rhythms of village life were becoming comfortingly familiar to him.

As he entered the village, the sounds of the day winding down greeted him: children's laughter echoing between houses, the metallic clangs of farmers storing their tools, and the enticing sizzle of evening meals being prepared.

Kai paused, a wave of conflicting emotions washing over him. Part of him wanted to cling to the idea that this was just an elaborate game. If it was a game, then the brutal realities of what he knew the cultivation world was really like wouldn't weigh so heavily on him. The dangers, the violence, the constant struggle for power—it would all just be part of the gameplay he was looking forward to.

It's easier this way, a voice in his head whispered. *They're just NPCs. Don't get attached.*

"Kai! You're back!" a small voice called out, interrupting his thoughts. Mei Li, a bright-eyed girl of about eight, came running up to him. "Did you do more cool qi stuff today?"

Kai felt a pang in his chest. Mei Li's enthusiasm, her innocence—it all felt too real. He ruffled her hair, trying to maintain some emotional distance. "I sure did. Want to see something new?"

As he created a small qi butterfly for Mei Li, Kai found himself torn. The joy on her face, the wonder in her eyes—it was hard to dismiss that as mere programming.

But if she's real, then she could get hurt. She could die. And I'd have to live with that.

The thought sent a chill down his spine. It was so much simpler when he first arrived, when he could pretend it was all just a game.

He continued towards the center of the village, where Auntie Chen's food stall was located. The smell of her famous dumplings made his stomach growl.

"Ah, Kai!" Auntie Chen beamed as he approached. "Right on time. I was worried you'd miss out on the last batch."

"I wouldn't dream of it, Auntie Chen," Kai replied with a grin that didn't quite reach his eyes. "Your dumplings are the best motivation for training hard."

She laughed, loading up a bowl for him. "Flatterer. Here, I added a few extra. A growing cultivator needs his strength."

As he ate, Kai noticed Lin, the miller's daughter, giving him a shy smile. His heart skipped a beat, and he quickly looked away. *No,* he told himself firmly. *Don't go there. It's safer if she's just an NPC.*

"You know, Kai," Auntie Chen whispered, "Lin has been asking about you. Maybe you should talk to her father about—"

"Auntie Chen!" Kai protested, his face reddening. "I'm just focusing on my cultivation right now."

She patted his arm, chuckling. "Of course, of course. But don't focus so hard you miss out on life, young man."

As the evening wore on, Kai found himself drawn into conversation with several villagers. Old Man Liu wanted to know if Kai could use his qi to help fix a leaky roof. Zhang Wei's wife asked if he'd escort her to the neighboring town for the market day next week. Even the village head stopped by to discuss Kai's progress and what it might mean for the village's future.

With each interaction, Kai felt his image of them being "NPC" break apart. These weren't just background characters in his story. They were people: complex, flawed, wonderful people who had welcomed him into their lives.

"We're lucky to have you here, Kai," the village head said. "It's been years since we had a promising young cultivator in our midst. You give us hope for better times ahead."

Kai felt a lump in his throat. The sincerity in the village head's voice made it hard to maintain his emotional walls. "I . . . thank you."

As night fell and Kai headed back to his hut, he felt mentally exhausted from his internal struggle. Just before reaching his door, he paused, looking back at the peaceful village bathed in moonlight.

If this is real, then I have so much to lose. But if it's just a game . . .

He couldn't finish the thought. Deep down, he knew the truth. These people, this village, they had become more than just background characters in his story. But accepting that meant accepting all the fear, pain, and responsibility that came with it.

Kai entered his hut, his mind still churning. He knew he'd have to confront these feelings eventually. But for now, it was easier to let the uncertainty linger, to exist in the space between game and reality.

The next morning, Kai sat cross-legged on a mossy rock in the forest, his eyes closed in concentration. He took slow, deep breaths, following the cultivation technique Zhang Wei had taught him. The cool air filled his lungs as he focused on the flow of qi within his body.

Breathe in, hold, breathe out. Feel the energy circulating.

He'd been practicing diligently these past few weeks, gradually strengthening his qi and advancing through the early stages of cultivation. Physical labor no longer affected his stats, he would need to cultivate if he wanted to grow stronger.

As he continued the breathing exercise, Kai felt a subtle shift within him. The energy flowing through his meridians seemed to pulse more strongly, gathering and condensing in his dantian.

This feeling . . . could it be?

Kai opened his eyes, a smile tugging at the corners of his mouth. He pulled up his status window, confirming his suspicion.

Name: Kai Thorn
Level: Qi Refining Stage 3 Qi: 50/50 Strength: 20 Agility: 22 Durability: 20 Intelligence: 11 Wisdom: 10

"Qi Refining stage three," Kai murmured, satisfaction in his voice. "Not bad for a few weeks of work."

He stood up, stretching his limbs and feeling the increased vitality coursing through his body. While he knew he still had a long way to go in terms of cultivation, each advancement felt like a significant milestone.

Some would assume it was mainly the physical stats that caused the disparity between the different stages in the Qi Refining Realm, but Kai didn't think so.

"It's the qi." Kai nodded. "The quality and quantity make the real difference."

He compared his current qi to when he was at stage two. It felt denser, more potent. He could sense it flowing through his meridians with greater force.

Kai approached a tall tree. He took a stance and threw a punch, channeling qi into his fist. The bark cracked, leaving a noticeable indentation.

"If I was still at stage two, that same punch would've barely scratched the surface," he mused. "The physical difference isn't huge, but the impact of the qi is night and day."

Holding out his hand, Kai's thoughts turned to his unique skill in this world. *Time to practice Qi Condensation.*

He focused, drawing upon his qi and willing it to take shape. A faint glow emanated from his palm as the energy coalesced into a simple dagger. Kai studied the construct critically, noting its strengths and weaknesses.

The blade looked sharp enough, but he could see minor imperfections in its form. More importantly, he could feel the drain on his qi as he maintained the construct. After about thirty seconds, the dagger flickered and dissipated.

"Hmm, better than when I started," Kai mused aloud. "But still a long way from being combat ready."

He spent the next hour practicing, forming various shapes and testing how long he could maintain them. Swords, shields, even simple tools like hammers—each presented its own challenges.

The bigger or more complex the shape, the faster it drains my qi, Kai noted. *And the strength seems directly tied to how much qi I put into it. At my current level, when facing a higher-stage cultivator, it is more of a parlor trick than a weapon.*

Still, he couldn't help but feel excited about the potential of this skill. With enough practice and as his cultivation base grew stronger, Kai knew this ability could become a formidable asset.

As the sun climbed higher in the sky, Kai decided to call it quits for the morning. His stomach growled, reminding him that he hadn't eaten yet.

Maybe I should bring something back for the village. A little hunting practice couldn't hurt.

Kai moved deeper into the forest, his footsteps nearly silent thanks to his improved agility. He kept his senses alert, listening for any signs of prey. After about fifteen minutes, he heard a rustle in the underbrush ahead.

Crouching low, Kai peered through the foliage. A plump pheasant pecked at the ground, unaware of his presence.

Perfect, Kai thought, a plan already forming in his mind.

He focused his qi, forming a thin, razor-sharp blade in his hand. Taking careful aim, Kai threw the qi construct like a throwing knife. The ethereal blade whistled through the air, striking the pheasant before it could react.

"Got it." Kai grinned, retrieving his prize. "Let's see how the villagers like this for breakfast."

With the increase in his stats, he had made sure to set aside some time to practice the basic skills of survival since he didn't have the luxury of living in a developed nation anymore.

My aim's not perfect yet, but it's improving.

Feeling quite pleased with himself, Kai made his way back toward the village. As he neared the outskirts, however, his smile faded. Something was wrong. The usual peaceful atmosphere was shattered by sounds of distress—crying, shouting, and the general chaos of panic.

Kai quickened his pace, bursting into the village square. The scene that greeted him was one of devastation. Several buildings showed signs of damage, with broken windows and splintered doors. Villagers milled about in confusion and fear, some nursing injuries while others comforted crying children.

"What happened here?" Kai demanded, approaching a group of villagers.

An older man with a bandaged arm turned to him, his face pale with shock. "Bandits," he spat. "They came about an hour ago, like a pack of wolves. We tried to fight them off, but . . ." He gestured helplessly at the destruction around them.

A woman nearby let out a wail of despair. "They took them! My daughter, my sweet Lin . . . they took her and the other girls!"

"Kidnapped?" Kai's blood ran cold. "How many?"

"At least a dozen," the injured man replied grimly. "Mostly young women and girls. We couldn't stop them."

Damn it. I should have been here. Maybe I could have . . . The guilt and fear threatened to overwhelm him. *This is why I didn't want to get attached. This is why I wished it was just a game.*

He shook his head, pushing away the useless thoughts. What mattered now was what he could do about it. These weren't NPCs. They were real people who needed his help.

"Where's Zhang Wei?" Kai asked, scanning the crowd for the old cultivator.

"Over by the well," someone called out. "He's hurt pretty badly."

Kai hurried over, finding the elder slumped against the stone well, his robes stained with blood. Zhang Wei looked up as Kai approached, his face scrunched in pain.

"Kai," the old man croaked. "You're all right. I feared . . ."

"I'm fine," Kai assured him, kneeling beside his mentor. "What happened? How badly are you hurt?"

Zhang Wei grimaced. "Nothing fatal, just my pride. I tried to stop them, but . . ." He shook his head, frustration evident in his voice. "I'm useless. Can't manipulate qi past stage-five Qi Refining anymore. Years ago, those bandits wouldn't have stood a chance."

"What stage were the bandits at?" Kai's eyes narrowed. "Were they all cultivators?"

"Most were just mortal thugs," Zhang Wei replied. "But there were a few cultivators among them. Their leader . . ." The old man's voice dropped to a whisper. "He was at least stage six Qi Refining. Maybe even stage seven."

Stage six or seven? That's at least three whole stages above me, Kai thought, his mind already calculating odds and possibilities. *In gaming terms, that's like an experienced player versus a newbie. But . . .*

"We can't just let them take those women," Kai said firmly. "There has to be something we can do."

"Kai, no," Zhang Wei looked at him sharply. "I know what you're thinking, but it's suicide. You can't hope to defeat a stage seven cultivator. Not at your level."

Kai stood up, his jaw clenched. "Maybe not in a straight fight. But I've always specialized in taking down opponents way above my level. It just takes the right strategy."

He looked around the village, taking in the devastation. Children huddled in corners, crying for their missing mothers and sisters. Men nursed injuries, their faces full of shame and helplessness. Kai thought of Auntie Chen, who always slipped him extra treats after training, and young Mei Li, who had watched wide-eyed as he showed off his qi skills.

They don't deserve this. These people took me in, helped me when I had nothing. I can't abandon them now.

"I'm going after them," Kai announced, his voice leaving no room for argument.

Zhang Wei struggled to his feet, grabbing Kai's arm. "Please, don't throw your life away! You're talented, yes, but talent means nothing against raw power at that level!"

Kai gently but firmly removed the old man's hand. "I appreciate your concern, Master Zhang. But I'm not going to charge in blindly. Trust me, I have experience with this sort of thing."

Maybe not in real life, Kai admitted to himself. *But how different can it be from raid planning?*

"I'll scout their location, assess their defenses, and come up with a plan," Kai continued. "If it looks impossible, I'll come back and we'll figure out something else. But I have to try."

Zhang Wei stared at him for a long moment, then sighed heavily. "I can see there's no talking you out of this. At least take some supplies with you. And for heaven's sake, be careful!"

Kai nodded, a grim smile on his face. "Always am. Don't worry, I'll bring them back."

As he gathered some basic supplies—food, water, and a sturdy knife—Kai's mind was already making plans.

First step, tracking. Then reconnaissance. Find their weaknesses, create a diversion, and extract the hostages. Simple in theory, but the execution will be tricky.

He paused at the village gate, looking back at the worried faces of the villagers.

I won't let you down, he silently promised. *Time to put all those hours of gaming to real-world use.*

With a deep breath, Kai set out on the bandits' trail. Whatever challenges lay ahead, he was ready to face them. After all, he'd come to this world with nothing. Now he had a chance to prove his worth.

Let the hunt begin, Kai thought as he disappeared into the forest.

CHAPTER FOUR

Kai crouched low in the underbrush, his eyes scanning the forest floor. Broken twigs and trampled vegetation marked the bandits' trail clearly. He allowed himself a small smile.

Tracking in real life isn't so different from following quest markers. Just have to pay attention to the details.

Kai knew he was severely outmatched in terms of raw power, but that had never stopped him before. In his gaming days, he'd led raid groups to take down bosses twenty levels above them.

This is just another raid. Gather intel, form a strategy, execute flawlessly. Simple.

After a few hours of careful tracking, Kai heard voices ahead. He slowed his pace, moving as silently as possible. Through the trees, he caught glimpses of a small clearing with several crude tents.

Bingo. Bandit camp located.

Kai found a secluded spot with a good view of the camp. He settled in, preparing for a long stakeout. As he watched, he counted at least a dozen bandits milling about. Most looked like common thugs, but a few carried themselves with the confidence of cultivators.

Okay, let's see. Two guards on rotation, three by the main fire, four near the prisoner tent . . .

His eyes narrowed as he spotted a large, muscular man barking orders. The other bandits seemed to defer to him.

That must be the leader. Stage six or seven Qi Refining, according to Zhang Wei. Way out of my league in a direct fight.

As Kai continued his reconnaissance, he overheard a heated argument breaking out among a group of bandits near the prisoner tent.

"I say we have some fun with the girls now," a scruffy-looking man growled. "Why wait?"

Another bandit, taller and leaner, shook his head. "You idiot. They'll fetch a higher price if they're untouched. Think with your head, not your d—"

"Enough!" The leader's voice boomed across the camp. He strode over, his presence silencing the argument immediately. "We stick to the plan. No one touches the merchandise. Anyone who disobeys answers to me. Understood?"

The bandits mumbled their agreement, though some looked less than pleased.

Kai felt a surge of disgust. *These bastards want to sell these women and children as slaves. I can't let that happen.*

He continued observing, gathering every scrap of information he could. Guard rotations, sleeping arrangements, the layout of the camp—Kai committed it all to memory.

As the sun began to set, Kai retreated deeper into the forest to plan his next move. He found a small clearing and sat cross-legged, closing his eyes to focus.

Okay, let's break this down. I'm outnumbered and outpowered. A direct assault is suicide. I need something to even the odds.

He opened his eyes, gazing at the darkening forest around him. An idea began to form.

In games, when you're up against a tough boss, sometimes you can use environmental hazards to your advantage. What if . . .

Kai's eyes widened as the plan crystallized in his mind.

A spiritual beast. If I could lure a powerful beast to the camp, it would cause chaos. The bandits would be distracted, maybe even thinned out. That could be my opening.

He nodded to himself, a smile spreading across his face. It was risky, borderline insane even. But it was the best shot he had.

Now, where to find a stage-seven qi beast?

Kai closed his eyes again, recalling everything he'd learned about this world's ecology. He thought back to countless hours spent studying monster spawns and boss locations in his old games.

In games, powerful monsters usually inhabit specific biomes. They need territory, food sources. If I were designing this world, where would I put a stage-seven beast?

He opened his eyes, scanning the forest with new purpose. The terrain sloped upward to the east, towards rockier ground.

Higher elevation, more dangerous terrain. That's where I'd put the tough mobs.

With a nod, Kai set off towards the rocky slopes. As he hiked, he kept his senses alert for any sign of a powerful presence. After walking for a while, he saw something moving in the bushes. Kai got excited, but when he looked closer, it was just a small fox-like creature.

A little window popped up in his vision.

Name: Forest Quickfox
Level: Qi Refining Stage 2 Type: Wood Attribute Beast Danger Level: Low

"Dang, too weak," Kai muttered. He kept going.

A bit later, Kai heard a loud bird call. He looked up and saw a big eagle circling overhead.

Name: Windwing Eagle
Level: Qi Refining Stage 4 Type: Wind Attribute Beast Danger Level: Moderate

"Better, but still not strong enough," Kai said to himself.

As the day went on, Kai found more creatures. A spiky boar, a sneaky shadow panther, even a group of flame-tailed monkeys. But none were above stage five.

"Come on, there's gotta be something bigger out here," Kai grumbled.

He decided to climb higher into the mountains. The trees got thinner, and the ground got rockier. Just as he was beginning to doubt his theory and wonder if game logic didn't apply to this world, he felt it—a prickle of energy on the back of his neck.

There's something up ahead. Something powerful.

Moving cautiously, Kai crept forward. As he peered around a large boulder, his breath caught in his throat.

There, in a small valley below, stood a creature straight out of legend. It resembled a tiger, but far larger than any earthly feline. Its coat glowed with an otherworldly blue-green light, and Kai could see sparks of energy crackling around its massive paws.

As Kai focused on the beast, a translucent window suddenly appeared in his vision.

Name: ???

> Species: Thunderclaw Tigress
> Level: Qi Refining Stage 7
> Type: Lightning Attribute Beast
> Danger Level: High

Holy sh—

Kai's thoughts were cut short as the tigress's head snapped towards him. Its eyes, glowing with electric-blue light, locked onto his position.

A wave of pressure washed over Kai, nearly driving him to his knees. The beast's aura was overwhelming, far beyond anything he'd encountered in this world so far.

Oh, shit, Kai thought, his heart racing. *Why did I think this was a good idea?*

The Thunderclaw Tigress let out a bone-shaking roar, electricity arcing between its fangs. Kai's mind raced, searching for a way out of this potentially fatal situation.

Okay, don't panic, he told himself, trying to steady his breathing. *Think this through. What would I do if this was a game?*

The massive beast began stalking towards him, each step sending small shockwaves through the ground. Kai's eyes darted around, looking for any advantage he could use.

I can't outfight it, and I probably can't outrun it for long. Need to outsmart it somehow.

He spotted a narrow crevice in the giant rock face behind him. It looked just big enough for him to squeeze through, but far too small for the tigress.

That's my out. But I need to time this perfectly.

Kai took a deep breath, steeling himself for what came next. He locked eyes with the approaching beast, then made a show of stumbling backward in fear.

"Nice kitty," he said, voice quavering. "Good kitty. You don't want to eat me. I'm all skin and bones, see?"

The tigress growled, lightning crackling along its flanks. It crouched low, preparing to pounce.

Almost there. Just a little closer . . .

At the last possible second, as the beast launched itself towards him, Kai dove to the side. He rolled to his feet and sprinted for the crevice, hearing the thunderous impact of the tigress landing behind him.

Kai squeezed into the narrow opening, jagged rock scraping his sides. He pushed deeper into the crevice, his heart pounding in his ears.

A deafening roar echoed through the rocks, followed by the sound of massive claws scrabbling at the entrance. Kai pressed himself as far back as he could, watching sparks fly as the beast tried to force its way in.

After several tense minutes, the tigress finally withdrew, letting out a frustrated growl. Seeing the giant rock hold, Kai allowed himself a breath of relief.

If this beast was at Foundation Establishment or above, it could probably have changed the landscape to get to me. Lucky for me, it's not quite that powerful.

Okay, step one complete. I've found a stage-seven beast. Now I just need to figure out how to lure it back to the bandit camp without getting myself killed in the process. No pressure.

He peeked out of his rocky shelter, watching the Thunderclaw Tigress pace back and forth. Its eyes were fixed on the crevice where Kai had hidden.

This might take a while, Kai thought, settling in for a long wait. *But hey, at least the hard part's over, right?*

As he huddled in the cramped space, Kai's mind was already working on the next phase of his plan. He'd need to be smart, cautious, and more than a little lucky to pull this off.

Just another day in the life of an isekai protagonist.

CHAPTER FIVE

Kai's heart raced as he sprinted through the forest, the thunderous footsteps of the beast echoing behind him. Branches whipped at his face, leaving stinging scratches, but he didn't dare slow down.

He'd waited in the crevice for hours, carefully observing the tigress's patterns. When it finally wandered far enough away, distracted by a low-level spiritual beast that accidentally wandered into its territory, Kai had seized his chance. He'd slipped out of the rocky shelter and taken off running, purposely making noise to draw the beast's attention.

This is just like kiting a high-level mob, Kai thought as he ran. *I need to keep it chasing me without letting it catch up.*

The beast roared, the sound reverberating through Kai's bones. He risked a glance back and immediately wished he hadn't. The creature was massive, easily twice his height, and it was quickly gaining on him.

Okay, time to use that Qi Condensation skill. Let's see how creative I can get with this.

As the beast lunged forward, Kai focused his qi, willing it to take shape beneath his feet. A glowing platform materialized in midair just as he leapt upward. He landed on the ethereal surface, wobbling slightly but managing to keep his balance.

The beast skidded to a halt below, confusion in its glowing red eyes. It swiped at Kai with its massive paw, but he was just out of reach.

"Not so tough now, are you?" Kai taunted, allowing himself a small grin. *Taunting giant monsters probably isn't the smartest move but I have to admit, it is fun!*

The beast roared in frustration, rearing up on its hind legs. Kai's eyes widened as he realized it could almost reach him at this height.

Time for a little parkour, he thought, focusing his qi once more.

Just as the beast's claws were about to connect, Kai leapt sideways. Another qi platform materialized, providing a brief foothold. He pushed off immediately, creating a series of glowing stepping stones in the air.

The beast gave chase on the ground, its massive form crashing through the underbrush. Kai kept moving, alternating between running on the ground and creating aerial platforms when needed.

Every few moments, the tigress would launch itself into the air, massive paws swiping at Kai as he leapt. Each time, Kai barely managed to twist away or create a new platform just out of reach.

"Too slow!"

The beast roared in frustration, electricity crackling along its fur. It redoubled its efforts, closing the gap inch by inch.

This is actually kind of fun, Kai mused as he vaulted over a fallen log. *In a terrifying, might-die-at-any-moment kind of way.*

As they neared the bandit camp, Kai noticed a change in the beast's behavior. Its pursuit became less focused, its head turning towards the scent of the camp.

Looks like it worked, Kai thought, relief flooding through him. *Time to let this oversized furball be their problem.*

He created one last qi platform, using it to propel himself onto a nearby tree. From his perch, Kai watched as the beast stalked towards the camp, its earlier chase forgotten.

Now, let's have a good look at what we're dealing with, Kai thought, his breath finally steadying as he observed the bandit camp below. The bandits continued their celebration, oblivious to the danger lurking at the edge of their camp.

"Hey, Wang Jun! Pass me another bottle!" one bandit called out, his words slurring slightly.

A burly man with an ugly scar across his cheek tossed a bottle to his companion. "Here ya go, Liu. But don't blame me when your head's pounding tomorrow!"

Liu caught the bottle clumsily, nearly dropping it. "Ah, who cares? We've got plenty to celebrate! That village was a gold mine!"

Another bandit, a thin man with a bow slung across his back, chimed in. "Yeah, and the ladies ain't bad either. Bet we can fetch a good price for 'em in the city."

Near the fire, a group of bandits had started a dice game. Shouts of triumph and groans of defeat mingled with the crackling of the flames.

"Ha! Read 'em and weep, boys!" a bandit with an eyepatch crowed, scooping up a pile of coins.

His opponent, a younger man with a wispy mustache, slammed his fist on the ground. "Dammit, One-Eye! You've got to be cheating!"

One-Eye grinned, revealing several missing teeth. "Ain't my fault you can't spot a good bluff, kid. Maybe you should stick to robbing grannies."

The other bandits roared with laughter, causing the young man's face to flush red with embarrassment and anger.

As the night wore on, the bandits' revelry grew louder and more boisterous. Some began to argue over trivial matters.

"I'm tellin' ya, I'm the one who knocked out that old geezer in the village!" a heavyset bandit insisted, swaying slightly on his feet.

His companion, a man with a long braid, scoffed. "In your dreams, Fat Zhang! You were too busy stuffing your face with stolen food. I saw the whole thing!"

Fat Zhang's face contorted with anger. "You callin' me a liar, Braid-boy?"

"Maybe I am! What you gonna do about it?" Braid-boy taunted, puffing out his chest.

Just as it seemed the two might come to blows, a voice cut through the noise, "Enough! Save your energy for something useful, you idiots."

The bandits immediately fell silent, turning to face the speaker. A tall, imposing man stepped out of the largest tent, his presence instantly demanding respect. Even from his hiding spot, Kai could sense the power radiating from this man.

It's him again. Their leader.

The leader surveyed the camp with cold eyes. "We move out at first light. Make sure the prisoners are ready for travel. And keep your wits about you. We're not out of the woods yet."

As the bandits scrambled to follow their leader's orders, a low, menacing growl suddenly echoed through the camp. The beast Kai had led there had finally made its move.

In a blur of blue-green fur, the creature burst into the clearing, its massive jaws snapping shut around the nearest bandit before anyone could react. Screams of terror and pain filled the air as chaos erupted.

"It's a Thunderclaw Tigress!" someone yelled. "Quick, get your weapons!"

Kai watched as the battle unfolded. The Thunderclaw Tigress was a whirlwind of destruction. Its glowing coat lit up the night, sparks flying with each movement. Long, curved fangs crackled with electricity, and its claws left scorched gouges in the earth with each step.

The bandits, caught off guard and many still drunk, struggled to mount an effective defense. Some swung wildly with swords or axes, while others fired arrows that mostly missed their mark.

This is my chance, Kai thought, his eyes darting between the battle and the group of prisoners. *While they're distracted, I can free the women and get them out of here.*

Keeping low to the ground, Kai began to make his way around the edge of the camp.

As he approached the prisoners, Kai couldn't help but continue observing the battle. The Thunderclaw Tigress moved with a fluid grace that belied its massive size. It effortlessly dodged most attacks, retaliating with swift, brutal strikes of its own.

I am glad I never engaged it in battle. I wouldn't have stood a chance. Kai let out a sigh of relief.

The bandit leader had joined the fray, he wielded a long, curved blade that glowed with an eerie blue light. Each swing left trails of frost in the air, and where it struck the Thunderclaw Tigress, patches of ice formed on its fur.

Interesting. Some kind of ice-attribute weapon. Definitely need to watch out for that.

Finally reaching the group of prisoners, Kai quickly ducked behind the tent they were tied to. He peeked around the corner, making sure the coast was clear before calling out to the women.

"Psst! Over here!" he whispered urgently.

The women's heads snapped towards him, eyes wide with a mix of fear and hope.

"Kai?" a small voice gasped. It was Mei Li, her eyes big and round in the darkness. "Is that really you? Did you come to save us like a hero?"

Kai's heart clenched at the child's words. He nodded, pressing a finger to his lips and offering a gentle smile. "Shhh. Yes, it's me, Mei Li. I'm here to help you all, but we need to be very quiet, okay? Like we're playing a secret game."

The women and Mei Li nodded, the little girl's face looking very serious.

Kai quickly set to work, using a small qi-blade to cut through their bonds. As he worked, he kept one eye on the ongoing battle, ready to create a distraction if needed.

"All right," he whispered once they were all free. "We're going to sneak out of here while the bad guys are busy. Remember how we play hide-and-seek in the village? It's just like that. Stay low, move quietly, and go straight home. Can you do that for me, Mei Li?"

Mei Li nodded vigorously, but then her lower lip trembled. "But what about you, Kai? I'm scared. Can't you come with us?"

Kai knelt to her level, placing a hand on her shoulder. "Hey, it's okay to be scared. But you know what? You're one of the bravest kids I know. I need you to be brave for just a little longer and help the others get home safely. Can you do that for me?"

Mei Li sniffled but squared her small shoulders. "O-Okay. I'll be brave."

Kai managed a reassuring smile. "I promise I'll be right behind you. Now go, quickly and quietly!"

As the women began to slip away into the darkness, with Mei Li holding tightly to one of their hands, Kai turned his attention back to the battle. The Thunderclaw Tigress was holding its own, but the bandit leader was proving to be a formidable opponent.

Suddenly, the leader's eyes flickered towards the escaping prisoners. His face contorted with rage.

"The prisoners! They're escaping!" he roared, parrying a swipe from the Thunderclaw Tigress. "Feng Lei! Go after them!" he ordered, pointing at one of the bandits who had been hanging back from the main fight.

Damn it. So close.

Kai turned to the fleeing women. "Go! Run as fast as you can! I'll hold them off!"

As the women disappeared into the forest, Kai turned to face the approaching bandit.

Okay. Time to put all that gaming experience to the test. Let's see what we're up against.

As he focused on the bandit, a familiar translucent window appeared in his vision.

Name: Feng Lei
Level: Qi Refining Stage 4
Qi: 75/75
Strength: 27
Agility: 23
Durability: 25
Intelligence: 13
Wisdom: 12

Huh, not as tough as I thought. But still a level above me. This is going to be tricky. I just hope all those years kickboxing comes in handy . . .

CHAPTER SIX

Kai's eyes narrowed as he assessed his opponent. Despite strength being his greatest stat, Feng was lean and wiry.

"Well, well," Feng sneered, twirling his daggers. "Looks like we've got a little hero here. You really think you can take me on, boy?"

Kai forced a confident smirk onto his face, even as his mind raced through possible strategies. "Why don't you come find out?"

Feng's eyes flashed with anger. "Cocky brat. I'm going to enjoy cutting you down to size!"

With that, Feng lunged forward, his daggers a blur of motion. Kai barely managed to dodge, feeling the wind from the blades as they passed inches from his face.

He's fast, Kai thought, his heart pounding. *But speed isn't everything. I need to outsmart him.*

As the bandit's right dagger came slicing down in a horizontal arc aimed at Kai's midsection, Kai focused his qi, channeling it into a thin, translucent barrier just as the blade descended. The dagger struck the barrier with a shower of sparks, deflecting harmlessly away.

Not wasting a moment, Feng followed up with his left dagger, stabbing straight for Kai's chest. Kai quickly formed another barrier, this one angled. The blade glanced off, throwing the bandit slightly off-balance.

Now's my chance! Time to go on the offensive.

Kai focused his qi into his right hand, quickly forming a dagger of his own. Without hesitation, he lunged forward, aiming for the bandit's throat.

Feng's eyes widened and he tried to jerk his head back, but Kai's attack was too fast. The dagger sliced through the air, catching Feng across the face.

A thin, glowing cut appeared from chin to cheekbone, the edges sizzling with residual qi.

"What kind of technique is this?" Feng stumbled backward, his hand flying to his face. "I-I've never seen anything like it."

Kai smirked. "Let's just say I've got a few tricks up my sleeve."

And a whole lot of gaming experience to draw from, he added silently.

"But want to try again?" he continued, his tone purposely nonchalant to rile up his opponent.

Feng's face contorted with anger, the cut on his cheek making his expression even more menacing. "Oh, I'm going to do more than try," he growled, tightening his grip on his daggers. "I'm going to carve you up piece by piece!"

Good, he's angry, Kai thought. *Angry fighters make mistakes. But I need to be careful, condensing qi drains my energy fast. I need to end this as quickly as possible.*

Feng snarled and charged again, both daggers raised. He brought them down in a powerful overhead strike. Kai crossed his arms, channeling qi to form a thick barrier above him. The daggers crashed against the barrier with a resounding clang. The impact sent vibrations through Kai's arms, but the barrier held.

As Feng recoiled from the failed strike, Kai noticed the bandit's eyes flick to his right side.

There it is, Kai thought. *He's telegraphing his next move. Just like an NPC with a predictable attack pattern.*

When Feng's right arm whipped out in a wide slash, Kai was ready.

Predicted and countered, Kai thought with satisfaction as he ducked under the blade. *Now to capitalize on this opening.*

He formed a quick qi platform at his feet, propelling himself to Feng's left side.

He'll have a harder time defending from this angle. Time to press my advantage.

But before Kai could attack, Feng spun, his left dagger coming around in a backhand slash. Kai created a small, disc-shaped barrier in his palm and used it to parry the strike. The clash of qi against metal rang out, and Feng's arm was knocked wide.

Perfect, Kai thought, his eyes narrowing as he spotted the opening. *He's off-balance. Time to counter-attack and combo into my next move.*

Kai formed a spiked gauntlet around his right fist and delivered a right hook. The qi-spikes raked across Feng's jaw, leaving thin, glowing scratches. The bandit stumbled back, spitting blood.

Seizing the opportunity, Kai formed a long, flexible whip of qi. With a flick of his wrist, he wrapped it around Feng's ankle and yanked. The bandit crashed to the ground with a heavy thud.

"You son of a—" Feng began, his face twisted with rage. His curse was cut short as the qi-whip tightened around his leg, sending a jolt of energy through his body. "Argh! How in the nine hells are you doing this?!"

Feng thrashed on the ground, trying to free his trapped leg. His daggers scraped against the floor as he attempted to cut himself free, but the qi-whip held firm.

"Damn you, boy!" Feng snarled, his eyes wild with a mixture of pain and fury. "I'll gut you for this! I'll—"

But before Feng could finish his threat, Kai was already moving. His hands glowed with concentrated qi as he shaped his energy into a new weapon. A large hammer began to form above his head.

As Feng's eyes widened in fear, Kai shifted his stance and swung the massive qi-hammer in a powerful, horizontal arc.

Just like swinging a giant war hammer in an RPG, Kai thought, his muscles straining with the effort.

"Oh, shi—" Feng's curse was cut short as the hammer connected with his midsection. There was a dull thud, followed by a whoosh of air forcibly expelled from the bandit's lungs.

The impact lifted Feng off the ground, the qi-whip around his ankle dissipating. He flew back several feet, his body limp as a rag doll, before crashing into a nearby tree with a sickening crack.

Feng slumped to the ground, his daggers clattering uselessly beside him. His eyes rolled back in his head, and a final, weak groan escaped his lips before he fell silent.

Kai stood up, breathing heavily but grinning from ear to ear. *I did it. I actually won my first real fight!*

His gaze turned to the bandit's unconscious form, and he formed a sharp qi-blade, his hands trembling at the thought of what he was about to do.

I should end this. In the games, it's so easy. Just click a button and your enemy disappears.

But as he raised the blade, Kai hesitated. The reality of taking a life hit him hard. This wasn't a game character made of pixels. This was a living, breathing person.

Can I really do this? Am I ready to cross that line?

Images flashed through Kai's mind—the terrified faces of the kidnapped villagers, the casual cruelty of the bandits' conversation. He thought of what would happen if he let Feng live. How many more people would suffer at his hands?

It's not just about me. It's about protecting others.

Kai closed his eyes, took a deep breath, and plunged the qi-blade down. He felt a sickening resistance, then nothing. As the life drained from Feng, Kai's eyes widened in shock. The trident mark on his wrist suddenly blazed with an intense golden light. One of its sharp prongs shifted from black to a deep, blood red, while the other two remained dark.

A translucent message appeared in Kai's vision.

> Experience gained: 100 XP
> Level up!
> You are now Qi Refining Stage 4!

Kai stared at his blood-stained hands and the glowing mark on his wrist. His whole body trembled. The metallic smell of blood filled his nostrils, threatening to make him retch.

What have I done? As much as I wish it was, this isn't a game. I just . . . I just killed someone. And what's happening to my mark?

Yet, even as his mind reeled from the shock, something else stirred within him. A detached, analytical part of his brain—the part honed by countless hours of gaming—took over.

Loot the body, it whispered. *Don't waste resources.*

Moving as if in a trance, Kai knelt beside Feng's corpse. His hands, operating on autopilot, began to search the dead bandit's clothes.

He found a small pouch of coins, which he mechanically counted and pocketed. Next, he removed Feng's daggers, noting their superior quality compared to his own weapons. A small vial of greenish liquid—poison, perhaps?—joined the other items in Kai's inventory.

A deafening roar suddenly tore through the air, causing Kai to flinch. The sound snapped him back to reality.

No time for anything else. I need to make sure the villagers are safe.

With one last glance at Feng's body and a worried look at his changed mark, Kai turned and ran in the direction the freed prisoners had fled. As he disappeared into the forest, the sounds of battle faded behind him, but the weight of what he'd done settled heavily on his shoulders.

This was no longer a game. The stakes were real, and Kai had just learned the hardest lesson of all: in this world, survival often came at a terrible cost.

And usually, it was a life.

CHAPTER SEVEN

Kai stumbled into the village, his mind reeling from the events of the past few hours. The once-quiet village now buzzed with activity as families reunited and tended to the wounded. He spotted familiar faces among the rescued prisoners—women and girls he'd come to know during his short time here.

"Kai! You really did it!" Mei Li rushed towards him with tears in her eyes. "You saved us all!"

Before he could respond, Kai found himself surrounded by a crowd of grateful villagers. They patted his back, shook his hand, and showered him with praise.

"Our hero!"

"We knew you'd come for us!"

"How can we ever repay you?"

Their words washed over him, but Kai barely registered them. His mind kept replaying the moment he'd taken Feng's life. The feeling of the qi-blade sinking into flesh, the light fading from the bandit's eyes . . .

It's not like in the games. There's no respawn. No reset button. He's just . . . gone.

"Kai?" Mei Li's childish voice cut through his thoughts. "Are you all right? You don't look too well."

"I'm fine," Kai forced a smile. "Just tired, I guess."

Keep it together, he told himself. *You did what you had to do. It was him or you.*

But the logical part of his brain couldn't quite silence the voice of doubt gnawing at him.

Suddenly, he remembered the danger wasn't over. "Listen, everyone," Kai raised his voice. "The bandits might still be alive. We need to prepare in case they come back."

A hush fell over the crowd. Zhang Wei stepped forward, his face dark. "You heard him. We'll need some men to keep watch. Volunteers?"

Several villagers raised their hands, and Zhang Wei quickly organized them into shifts.

"Thank you, Kai," Zhang Wei said, placing a hand on his shoulder. "Your warning may save lives."

But Kai could see the worry in the old man's eyes. He knew what Zhang Wei was thinking—if the bandit leader had survived, the village stood little chance against his wrath.

"Come with me," Zhang Wei said quietly. "I think we need to talk."

Kai nodded, grateful for the excuse to escape the crowd. He followed Zhang Wei to a secluded corner of the village, away from the noise and commotion.

The old man studied Kai's face for a moment before speaking. "You had to take a life today, didn't you?"

Kai's eyes widened in surprise. "How did you—"

Zhang Wei held up a hand. "I've seen that look before. On my own face, many years ago."

Kai slumped against a nearby wall, suddenly exhausted. "I didn't think . . . I mean . . . but this . . ."

"Was very real," Zhang Wei finished for him. "And now you're wondering if you did the right thing. If you're still a good person."

Kai nodded, unable to find the words.

Zhang Wei sighed heavily. "Let me tell you something, Kai. For those of us who walk the path of righteousness, it never gets easier. Taking a life should never be done lightly, and it should never stop affecting you."

"But what if it does?" Kai asked. "What if I get used to it?"

The old man's eyes hardened. "Then you risk becoming the very thing you're fighting against. Those who say it gets easier, who can kill without remorse . . . they're the ones who become monsters."

Kai didn't respond. He thought about the games he used to play, how easily he'd racked up virtual body counts without a second thought. Now, faced with the reality of taking a single life, he felt shaken to his core.

Maybe I'm not cut out for this world after all. But what choice do I have?

Zhang Wei seemed to sense his inner turmoil. "Go rest, Kai. What you're feeling . . . it's normal. It's human. Don't try to push it away."

Kai nodded, grateful for the old man's wisdom. "Thank you, Master Zhang."

As he made his way back to his room, Kai's mind continued to race. The villagers' gratitude, Zhang Wei's words, the memory of Feng's death—it all swirled together in a confusing mix of emotions.

Once inside, Kai collapsed onto his bed, staring at the ceiling. Suddenly, he remembered something: the system notification he'd received after defeating Feng.

That's right . . . I leveled up.

With a thought, Kai pulled up his status window.

<table>
<tr><td>Name: Kai Thorn</td></tr>
<tr><td>Level: Qi Refining Stage 4
XP: 0/400
Qi: 75/75
Strength: 25
Agility: 27
Durability: 25
Intelligence: 18
Wisdom: 15</td></tr>
</table>

Huh. Nice boost across the board, he thought, his gamer instincts kicking in despite his emotional turmoil. *But wait . . . XP?*

Kai sat up, frowning at the screen. He'd never seen an XP bar before. Since arriving in this world, he'd assumed experience points weren't a thing here. Cultivation had seemed to be the only path to growth.

So, I do gain XP after all. But how? Just from fighting? Or completing tasks? This changes things. I might be able to level up faster than I thought.

Kai's gaze then drifted to his right wrist, where the mysterious trident mark glowed faintly. One of its prongs now shone a deep, blood-red color.

What are you? Kai wondered, tracing the mark with his finger. *And what will happen when the other two turn red?*

Curious, Kai focused his qi, forming a simple dagger construct in his hand. He studied it carefully, looking for any changes or improvements.

Seems about the same. Maybe a bit more stable? Hard to tell.

Kai dispelled the construct and flopped back onto the bed.

If it took one life to turn the first prong red, does that mean I need to kill two more people to complete it? And then what? Will I unlock some new skill?

He shook his head, trying to clear the thoughts away. "No point in speculating," he muttered to himself. "I'll cross that bridge when I come to it."

If I come to it, a small voice in the back of his mind added.

Exhaustion finally began to overtake Kai. His eyelids grew heavy as the events of the day caught up with him.

Maybe sleep will help, he thought as he drifted off. *Maybe I'll wake up and this will all have been a bad dream . . .*

But Kai's sleep was far from peaceful. As soon as he closed his eyes, he found himself back in the forest, reliving the fight with Feng.

The dream-forest was darker, more ominous than reality. Shadows seemed to move of their own accord, and every rustle of leaves sounded like whispered accusations.

Dream-Kai faced off against Feng, but the bandit's features were distorted, almost demonic. His eyes glowed red, and his mouth was filled with sharp fangs.

"You think you can defeat me, little hero?" Dream-Feng taunted, his voice echoing unnaturally. "You're nothing but a pretender. A fraud playing at being a warrior."

Kai tried to respond, but no words came out. He reached for his qi, trying to form a weapon, but nothing happened.

Feng lunged forward, his daggers flashing in the dim light. Kai dodged desperately, feeling the blades whistle past his face.

"What's wrong?" Feng sneered. "Can't use your little tricks here? This isn't a game anymore, boy. This is real!"

Kai stumbled backward, his heart pounding. He knew it was a dream, but the fear felt all too real.

Suddenly, the scene shifted. Kai found himself standing over Feng's defeated body, a qi-blade in his hand. But this time, Feng looked human—scared, vulnerable.

"Please," Dream-Feng begged, his eyes wide with terror. "I have a family. Children. Don't do this!"

Kai tried to lower the blade, to show mercy, but his arm moved of its own accord. He watched in horror as the qi construct plunged into Feng's chest.

The bandit's face contorted in pain and betrayal. "Monster," he gasped. "You're no better than us."

As Feng's life ebbed away, Kai felt a burning sensation on his wrist. He looked down to see the trident mark glowing brightly, its first prong turning blood-red.

The scene shifted again. Kai stood in the village square, surrounded by the people he'd rescued. But their grateful smiles had turned to looks of fear and disgust.

"Murderer," Mei Li hissed, backing away from him.

"We trusted you," another villager accused.

"He's dangerous," someone else whispered. "A killer."

Kai tried to explain, to defend himself, but once again, no words came out. He looked down at his hands and saw they were covered in blood.

The villagers began to close in around him, their faces twisted with anger and fear. Kai frantically tried to wake himself up, to escape this nightmare, but he remained trapped.

Suddenly, a new voice cut through the crowd. "This is what you are now, Kai Thorn."

Kai turned to see a figure emerging from the shadows. It was . . . himself. But this version of Kai looked different—colder, harder. His eyes glowed with an eerie red light, matching the fully crimson trident mark on his wrist.

"This is what you'll become," Dream-Kai said, his voice devoid of emotion. "A killer. A monster. It's the only way to survive in this world."

"No," Kai tried to say, but still, no sound came out.

Dream-Kai smirked. "Oh, yes. You've taken your first step down this path. And deep down, you know it felt good. The power. The rush of victory."

Kai shook his head frantically, trying to deny it. But a small part of him, buried deep, knew there was truth in those words.

"Embrace it," Dream-Kai urged. "Stop fighting what you're becoming. In this world, only the strong survive. And to be strong, you must be willing to do whatever it takes."

The scene shifted once more. Kai found himself standing atop a mountain of bodies, his hands dripping with blood. At his feet lay the corpses of Feng, Zhang Wei, Mei Li, and countless others.

"This is your destiny," Dream-Kai's voice echoed around him. "This is the price of power."

Kai wanted to scream, to run, to wake up. But he remained frozen in place, forced to confront the nightmarish vision before him.

In the sky above, the trident mark appeared, massive and glowing. Its three prongs pulsed with a sickly red light.

"Three lives to unlock your true potential," Dream-Kai whispered in his ear. "How many more to become a god?"

Kai felt his resolve weakening. The temptation of power, of safety in this dangerous world, pulled at him.

Maybe this is the only way, a traitorous part of his mind whispered. *Maybe I have to become the monster to survive.*

But then, cutting through the darkness, came another voice. Warm, familiar, full of wisdom.

"It never gets easier," Zhang Wei's words echoed in his mind. "Those who say it does . . . they're the ones who become monsters."

Kai clenched his fists, fighting against the nightmare's pull. "No," he finally managed to say, his voice growing stronger. "This isn't who I am. This isn't who I want to be!"

The nightmarish landscape began to crumble around him. The mountain of bodies dissolved into mist. Dream-Kai's mocking laughter faded away.

"You can't fight it forever," his doppelganger's voice called out as it faded into nothingness. "Sooner or later, you'll give in. It's the only way . . ."

Kai sat bolt upright in bed, gasping for air. Sweat drenched his clothes, and his heart raced as if he'd run a marathon.

For a moment, he sat there in the darkness, trying to calm his breathing. The nightmare's images still danced behind his eyelids, vivid and terrifying.

It was just a dream, he told himself. *Just a dream. I'm not that person. I won't become that.*

But as his gaze fell on the trident mark, its single red prong glowing faintly in the moonlight, Kai couldn't quite shake the lingering doubt.

What if the dream is right? What if this is the path I'm on?

He shook his head, trying to clear the dark thoughts away. "No," he muttered aloud. "I make my own choices. My own destiny."

> You have successfully faced your inner demon!
> Reward: 100 XP

Kai blinked, reading the notification twice to make sure he understood. A weak smile tugged at his lips.

"So even my nightmares are worth XP now?" he muttered. "I guess that's . . . good?"

> New Skill Unlocked: Mental Fortitude

Kai's eyes widened, not expecting to unlock a skill.

> Mental Fortitude (Passive): This skill grants the user increased resistance to emotional trauma and mental stress. It helps maintain a calm and logical state of mind in high-pressure situations, reducing the impact of fear, anxiety, and other negative emotions. While it doesn't completely eliminate these feelings, it allows the user to process them more effectively, preventing them from overwhelming rational thought.

This could be really useful, Kai thought feeling a subtle shift in his mind as the skill took effect. The lingering fear and doubt from the nightmare seemed to recede, becoming more manageable. *Especially if I have to face more situations like today.*

CHAPTER EIGHT

A loud knock jolted Kai from his now peaceful sleep. He blinked, disoriented, as the pounding continued.

"Mister Kai! Please help!" a child's voice cried out between sobs.

Kai scrambled out of bed, his mind instantly alert. He yanked open the door to find little Ming, the baker's son, tears streaming down his face.

"What's wrong?" Kai asked, crouching down to the boy's level.

"Bad man . . . in the village . . ." Ming hiccupped. "He's hurting people!"

Kai's blood ran cold. He let out a heavy sigh, his shoulders slumping. What he had been dreading had happened—the bandits had survived.

"Stay here," he told Ming. "I'll handle this."

As Kai sprinted towards the village center, his mind raced. *I need to assess the situation fast and form a strategy.*

The scene that greeted him made his stomach churn. Villagers huddled in terrified groups, many openly weeping. At the center of it all stood a man Kai recognized instantly: the bandit leader.

The man was a mess. His clothes were torn and bloody, deep gashes visible across his arms and torso. One eye was swollen shut, and he swayed on his feet as if a strong breeze might topple him.

But what made Kai's breath catch was the sight of old man Zhang. The elderly cultivator lay prone on the ground, the bandit's foot pressed firmly on his neck.

"Please," a woman near Kai whimpered. "We've given you everything. Just leave us in peace!"

The bandit leader's head snapped towards her, his one good eye blazing with fury. "Peace?" he snarled. "There will be no peace! That little bastard," he gestured wildly with his free hand, "lured a stage-seven beast to our camp! My men . . . my entire operation . . . destroyed!"

His gaze swept the crowd, finally locking onto Kai. A twisted smile spread across his battered face.

"There you are," he growled. "The boy who thinks he's clever."

Kai met the man's gaze steadily. *After being put in this state, how is this guy even alive right now?*

"I don't care about money anymore," the bandit leader continued, pressing down harder on Zhang's neck. The old man wheezed painfully. "All of you . . . every last one . . . will die!"

Kai's eyes narrowed, and he focused on the bandit leader. A translucent window appeared in his vision.

Name: ??? (Injured)

Level: Qi Refining Stage 7 (Fluctuating)
Optimal State: Qi Refining Stage 7 (Low)
Current State: Severely Weakened
Qi: ???/???
Strength: ??? (Unstable)
Agility: ??? (Impaired)
Durability: ??? (Critical)
Intelligence: 10
Wisdom: 8

So, he really is stage seven, Kai thought, a chill running down his spine. *No wonder he was able to survive. But he must be on the lower end of that stage if the beast was still able to do this to him.*

For a brief, shameful moment, Kai considered running. *I'm outmatched, even with him injured. I could slip away, start over somewhere else . . .*

But then he looked at the terrified villagers. At Mei Li huddled with the other children. At Auntie Chen, looking at him with hope. At old man Zhang, still fighting for breath under the bandit's boot.

These people helped me. I can't abandon them now. I'm not that kind of person.

Taking a deep breath, Kai stepped forward. "Let him go," he said, his voice steadier than he felt. "Your problem is with me."

The bandit leader's eye gleamed with malice. "Oh, it's with all of you now. But you . . . you I'll save for last."

He's injured, unstable. That's my only advantage. I need to keep him off-balance, use the environment . . .

"Big words from a man who can barely stand," Kai taunted, hoping to provoke a rash move.

Surprisingly, it worked. With a roar of rage, the bandit leader charged, abandoning his hold on Zhang. The old cultivator gasped for air as Auntie Chen and another villager quickly dragged him to safety.

Kai dodged the initial rush, but the bandit was faster than he expected. A wild swing caught Kai across the ribs, sending him stumbling back with a grunt of pain.

Damn, even injured he hits like a truck, Kai thought, wincing. *Can't take too many of those.*

He focused his qi, forming a shield construct just in time to deflect another blow. The impact still rattled his bones, but it was better than taking the hit directly.

"Coward!" the bandit leader spat. "Fight me like a man!"

Kai allowed himself a small smirk. "Sorry, I prefer to fight smart."

He created a series of qi-platforms, using them to leap and bound around the village square. The bandit leader gave chase, growing more frustrated with each missed swing.

"Stop running!" he bellowed.

"Make me," Kai shot back, channeling his inner troll. *Keep him angry, keep him sloppy.*

As they weaved through the village, Kai heard the murmurs of the watching villagers.

"Look at him go!"

"But can he win?"

"He's so brave . . ."

"I want to marry him!"

"The boy's going to get himself killed!"

Marry me? Kai shook his head as he tuned out the chatter, focusing entirely on the fight. He created trip wires of solidified qi, causing the bandit to stumble. He formed slippery patches beneath the man's feet, throwing off his balance.

But for all his tricks, Kai couldn't land a decisive blow. The bandit leader, for all his injuries, was simply too tough. Nothing like the bandit he had fought.

This isn't working, Kai realized after several minutes of cat-and-mouse. *I need a new strategy.*

He glanced around, looking for any advantage. His eyes fell on a stack of empty barrels near the village well.

Perfect.

Kai darted towards the well, the bandit hot on his heels. At the last second, he leapt up, using a qi-platform to vault over the barrel stack.

The bandit leader, unable to stop his momentum, crashed straight into the barrels. They toppled, several smashing over his head and shoulders.

For a moment, Kai dared to hope it might be enough, even though he knew that wouldn't be enough to kill any cultivator. A roar of rage proved him right as the bandit leader burst from the wreckage.

"I'll kill you!" he roared, his remaining eye blazing with murderous intent.

Before Kai could react, the bandit shot forward with some sort of dash skill. A massive hand closed around his throat, lifting him off the ground. Kai gasped for air, clawing desperately at the iron grip.

"Not so clever now, are you?" the bandit sneered, squeezing tighter.

Black spots danced at the edges of Kai's vision.

Can't . . . breathe . . .

In desperation, he focused every ounce of his remaining qi into his right hand. A blade of pure energy formed, wickedly sharp.

With the last of his strength, Kai plunged the qi-blade into the bandit's shoulder.

The man howled in pain, his grip loosening just enough for Kai to squirm free. He fell to the ground, gulping in precious air.

But his reprieve was short-lived. The bandit leader, driven by pain and fury, lashed out with a vicious kick. It caught Kai square in the ribs, sending him flying back several feet.

Kai hit the ground hard, the impact driving the air from his lungs. He tasted blood.

Get up, he told himself. *Get up or you're dead.*

Gritting his teeth against the pain, Kai staggered to his feet. His vision swam, and he could feel warm blood trickling down his side.

This is bad. Really bad.

The bandit leader advanced, a predatory grin on his battered face. "I'm going to enjoy this," he growled.

Kai tried to form another qi construct, but his reserves were dangerously low. The energy blade flickered and died in his hand.

No, no, no, Kai thought, panic rising. *I'm out of options. I'm out of—*

His train of thought was cut off as the bandit's fist connected with his jaw. Kai's head snapped back, and he tasted more blood.

Another blow to his stomach doubled him over. A knee to the face sent him sprawling.

Through the haze of pain, Kai heard the villagers crying out.

"Someone help him!"

"He's going to die!"

"We have to do something!"

But no one moved. They were too afraid, too weak to make a difference.

Can't blame them, Kai thought as another kick caught him in the side. *This guy's way out of their league. Out of my league too, apparently.*

The bandit leader grabbed a fistful of Kai's hair, yanking his head back. "Any last words, boy?" he sneered.

Kai spat blood. "Yeah," he rasped. "Your breath stinks."

The bandit's face contorted with rage. "Die!" he roared.

Kai saw the glint of steel as the bandit drew a wicked-looking dagger. Time seemed to slow.

So, this is it? Game over. No respawns in this world.

He closed his eyes, bracing for the killing blow.

This time, it came.

Kai felt a searing pain across his neck, and then . . . nothing. The world spun dizzyingly, and he had the strangest sensation of falling.

When he opened his eyes, he was staring at the ground. But something was wrong. His perspective was all off. Why was he looking up at his own body?

With dawning horror, Kai realized the truth. His head was no longer attached to his body.

I've been . . . decapitated? The thought was surreal, almost comical in its absurdity. *This can't be happening. This isn't how the game is supposed to end!*

But as he watched his own body crumple to the ground, a lifeless heap, the reality of the situation hit him like a punch to the gut. Or rather, where his gut used to be.

I'm dead. Actually dead.

The villagers' screams seemed distant, muffled. The bandit leader's triumphant laughter barely registered. All Kai could focus on was the bizarre sight of his own headless corpse.

This isn't fair, he thought desperately, his fear fighting against the effects of the mental fortitude skill. *There has to be a way to reload, to try again. There's always a way in games.*

As his consciousness began to fade, Kai clung to one final thought:

Respawn in three . . . two . . . one . . .

Then the world went dark.

CHAPTER NINE

Kai opened his eyes to darkness. An endless void stretched in every direction, devoid of light or sensation. He floated in nothingness, unable to see or feel his own body.

Is this . . . death? An eternity of emptiness?

As the reality of his situation sank in, frustration and regret washed over him.

I underestimated him, even injured. I should have found a way to quickly end it instead of playing around. And my qi reserves were too low—I need to work on that if I get another chance.

He paused, struck by the absurdity of planning for a future that likely didn't exist.

If I get another chance? Who am I kidding? This is it. Game over.

Just as despair began to set in, a familiar shape materialized before him. The trident-like mark that had appeared on his wrist glowed softly in the darkness. As Kai watched, transfixed, the red prong flickered, its crimson hue fading to black.

What the—

Before he could complete the thought, a message appeared before him.

Respawn will occur in 30 seconds!

Holy crap, Kai thought, a wave of relief washing over him. *There really is a respawn feature! I'm not perma-dead after all!*

As the implications sank in, Kai's mind raced. *But it seems connected to the trident mark somehow. The red prong turned black just before the respawn message appeared . . .*

He pieced it together quickly. *So, respawning uses up a prong? That means I've got no more lives left . . .*

He barely had time to process this revelation before another notification popped up.

Player death has unlocked all game features!

All game features? What does that mean?

As if in response to his unspoken question, a flood of information filled his vision.

Unlocked Features:

Detailed Stats Window
Skills List
Inventory System
Quest Log
Achievement Tracker
Faction Reputation
Crafting Menu
Map Function

This changes everything! It's like the full game just unlocked. But why now? Why did I have to die first?

He didn't have long to ponder. The endless void began to shift and warp around him. Darkness gave way to familiar shapes—buildings, trees, people. The village materialized, but everything was frozen in place, as if time had stopped.

It's like the game is paused. I can see everything, but nothing's moving.

His gaze fell on the scene of his death. His own headless body lay crumpled on the ground, a pool of blood spreading beneath it. The bandit leader stood triumphant, a cruel grin twisting his features.

A new message appeared before Kai.

New Quest Available: Kill the Bandit Leader
Reward: 300 XP, Increased Reputation with Village
Failure: Permanent Death, Village Destruction

Now we're talking! With the full game features unlocked, I can actually do quests to grind for XP and track my progress!

He glanced at the countdown timer hovering in the corner of his vision. Ten seconds left before respawn.

Okay, think. I've got the element of surprise. He won't be expecting me to come back from the dead. I need to end this fast—no playing around this time.

Kai formulated a quick plan. *Materialize behind him. Use Qi Condensation to create a blade. Go for the heart, one clean strike.*

As the final seconds ticked away, Kai steeled himself. *This is it. No mistakes this time.*

One second.

Game on.

The world lurched back into motion. In the blink of an eye, Kai's consciousness snapped back into a physical form. He materialized silently behind the bandit leader, his body whole and unmarked, as if the brutal decapitation had never happened.

Without hesitation, Kai focused his qi. A razor-sharp blade of pure energy formed in his hand. With all his strength, he drove the ethereal weapon into the bandit's back, aiming for the heart.

The bandit leader's laughter turned into a choked gasp. He staggered forward, spinning around to face his attacker. His eyes widened in disbelief as he saw Kai standing before him, very much alive.

"H-How?" the bandit wheezed, blood bubbling from his lips. "I killed you . . ."

Kai met his gaze coldly. "You did," he replied. "I got better."

The light faded from the bandit's eyes as he collapsed. Kai watched dispassionately as the man's body hit the ground with a dull thud.

Quest Completed: Kill the Bandit Leader
Rewards:
300 XP
Village Reputation increased
Level Up! You are now Level 5

Well, that was anticlimactic. But effective.

Feeling a sudden warmth on his wrist, he glanced down and noticed one of the prongs on his trident mark turn red.

I've got one respawn left if another boss decides to show up out of nowhere. Kai released a quiet sigh, feeling a bit more secure. He then turned to face the stunned villagers, who stared at him in slack-jawed amazement. For a moment, nobody moved or spoke.

Then, as if a spell had been broken, chaos erupted.

"He's alive!" someone shouted.

"It's a miracle!" cried another.

"The Heavens have blessed him!" an old woman proclaimed.

Kai raised his hands, calling for quiet. *Time to think fast. I can't tell them the truth, but I need some kind of explanation.*

"It's . . . complicated," he began, choosing his words carefully. "What you saw was an illusion technique I've been working on. It made it appear as if I had been killed, but I was actually able to escape and strike back at the right moment."

Zhang Wei hobbled forward, studying Kai intently. "An illusion so perfect it fooled even my old eyes? Remarkable. I've heard of such techniques, but to see one used so flawlessly by one so young . . ."

Great, now they think I'm some kind of cultivation prodigy. Well, no harm in rolling with it.

"I'm still perfecting it," Kai said with a shrug. "But right now, we need to focus on cleaning up this mess and making sure there aren't any more bandits lurking around."

The villagers nodded, seemingly accepting his explanation for the moment. They began to disperse, some tending to the wounded while others started the grim task of dealing with the bodies.

Little Mei Li pushed through the crowd. "Kai!" she squealed, running up to him. "You're alive! But how? We saw the bad man . . ." She stopped, her little face scrunching up as she tried to make sense of what had happened.

Kai knelt down to her level. "It's okay, Mei Li. What you saw wasn't real. It was like . . . a trick."

"A trick?" Mei Li repeated, her eyes widening with wonder.

Kai nodded, smiling. "That's right. I made it look like the bad man hurt me, but I was actually hiding. Then, when he wasn't looking, I was able to stop him."

"Wow!" Mei Li exclaimed. "Can you teach me how to do tricks, too?"

Kai chuckled, patting her head. "Maybe when you're a bit older. For now, can you help me? We need to make sure everyone in the village is okay."

Mei Li nodded eagerly. "I can do that!" She paused, then suddenly threw her arms around Kai in a tight hug. "I'm really glad you're not gone forever," she mumbled into his shirt.

Kai hugged her back, feeling a lump in his throat. "Me, too, Mei Li. Me, too."

As Mei Li ran off, Kai took a moment to assess his situation. He pulled up his newly unlocked stats window.

Name: Kai Thorn
Level: Qi Refining Stage 5 XP: 0/500 Qi: 100/100

Strength: 31
Agility: 33
Durability: 32
Intelligence: 23
Wisdom: 20

Skills:
Qi Condensation (Level 2)
Basic Cultivation Technique (Level 3)
Unarmed Combat (Level 2)
Deception (Level 3)
Mental Fortitude (Passive)

Quests:
Completed: Kill the Bandit Leader
Active: None
Reputation:
Misty Waterfall Village: Respected (50/100)

Not bad. That level up from killing the bandit leader gave me a nice boost. But I've got a long way to go if I want to survive in this world.

The unlocked game features opened a whole new world of opportunities. He could track his progress, manage an inventory, even take on proper quests now.

It's like the tutorial is finally over, and the real game has begun.

As Kai studied his status window, a frown appeared on his face, something was nagging at him.

It's strange. Even though the full game features have been unlocked, I still can't allocate my own stat points when I level up. The system seems to do it automatically.

He pondered this for a moment, his gamer instincts kicking in. In most RPGs he'd played, reaching a certain point usually meant gaining the ability to customize your character's growth more directly.

Is this a limitation of this world's system? Or is it intentional?

A theory began to form in his mind. *Maybe it's to prevent someone from becoming too overpowered too quickly. If I could allocate all my points into a single stat, I might be able to max it out early on.*

Kai imagined the possibilities—and potential problems—of having one incredibly high stat while the others remained low. It could create significant imbalances.

It makes sense, in a way, he reasoned. *This world seems to value balanced growth and gradual improvement. The automatic allocation keeps me well-rounded.*

Still, a part of him couldn't help but feel a twinge of disappointment. The ability to fine-tune his stats would have given him more strategic options.

I guess I'll have to rely on skills and techniques to specialize, rather than raw stat allocation. It's not ideal, but I can work with this. I'll just have to be smarter about how I train and which skills I prioritize.

With that thought, Kai closed his status window as a commotion near the village entrance drew his attention. Several men were dragging something—or someone—into the square.

"We found one!" one of the men shouted. "He was hiding in the forest!"

They dumped their captive unceremoniously at Kai's feet. It was a young man, barely out of his teens, wearing the tattered remains of bandit gear. He looked up at Kai with terrified eyes.

"P-Please," the young bandit stammered. "I didn't want any part of this! They forced me to join them. I never hurt anyone, I swear!"

Kai studied the trembling figure before him. *This could be interesting. A chance to test out some of these new game mechanics.*

He turned to the villagers who had gathered around. "What do you think we should do with him?"

The crowd erupted as they all began to give suggestions.

"Kill him!"

"Make him pay for what his friends did!"

"Show mercy! He's just a boy!"

"Put him to work rebuilding what they destroyed!"

Kai held up a hand for silence. He focused on the young bandit and a small information window appeared.

Captured Bandit
Name: ???
Level: Qi Refining Stage 2 Qi: 20/25 Strength: 13 Agility: 17 Durability: 15 Faction: Broken Fang Bandits (Dissolved) Status: Terrified, Remorseful
Possible Actions: Execute (Gain: 50 XP, -10 Village Reputation) Imprison (Gain: 25 XP, +5 Village Reputation)

Recruit (Gain: 100 XP, +1 Follower, -5 Village Reputation)
Release (Gain: 0 XP, -5 Village Reputation)

Now this is more like it. Real choices with clear consequences.

He considered his options carefully. Execution seemed needlessly cruel, and he didn't want to risk losing village reputation. Imprisonment might be the safe choice, but it didn't offer much benefit. Releasing the boy would be the "good" thing to do, but Kai wasn't sure he could afford to be so altruistic in this world, especially when there was no benefit in doing so.

That left recruitment. It was risky, but the potential rewards were tempting.

"Listen up," Kai addressed the young bandit. "I'm going to give you a choice. You can either face the village's judgment for your crimes . . ." He paused for effect, noting how the boy's face paled even further. "Or you can swear loyalty to me. Serve me faithfully as a servant, and I'll ensure you have a chance to redeem yourself. What's it going to be?"

The young bandit's eyes widened. He looked around at the angry faces of the villagers, then back to Kai. Without hesitation, he prostrated himself on the ground.

"I swear it!" he cried. "I'll serve you with my life, Master! Thank you for your mercy!"

Follower Gained: Liu Wei

Level: Qi Refining Stage 2
Loyalty: 50/100
Qi: 20/25
Strength: 13
Agility: 17
Durability: 15
Intelligence: 11
Wisdom: 7

Skills:
Basic Cultivation Technique (Level 1)
Stealth (Level 2)
Lockpicking (Level 1)
Dagger Proficiency (Level 1)

Interesting. He's got some useful skills. This could work out well.

Kai said, "Stand up, Liu Wei. You're a member of my party now. Betray me, and you'll wish I'd let the villagers deal with you. Serve me well, and you may be able to redeem yourself."

The villagers muttered among themselves, clearly not entirely happy with this turn of events. Kai turned to address them.

"I know this might seem strange," he said, projecting confidence he didn't entirely feel. "But trust me. Having an insider's knowledge of the bandits could prove invaluable if we face similar threats in the future. I'll take full responsibility for him."

Zhang Wei stepped forward, stroking his beard. "The boy isn't wrong, and he did just save us," the old cultivator proclaimed. "We should trust in his judgment."

Slowly, the villagers nodded their acceptance, though some still eyed Liu Wei with suspicion.

As the crowd dispersed, Mei Li ran up to Kai, her eyes wide with a mixture of confusion and awe. "Kai! You were dead and now you're not!" she exclaimed. "And you're friends with the bad man now? How come?"

Kai couldn't help but smile at her innocent curiosity. He knelt to her level, speaking gently. "Sometimes, Mei Li, people who did bad things can change and become good. We're giving Liu Wei a chance to do that."

Mei Li scrunched up her face, thinking hard about this new idea. "Like in the stories where the villain becomes a hero?"

"Something like that."

The little girl's expression suddenly turned serious. "But you won't get hurt again, will you? Promise?" Her lower lip trembled slightly.

"I promise I'll be as careful as I can. I have too many friends here to protect."

This seemed to satisfy Mei Li, and she skipped off to join her friends, occasionally glancing back at Kai with a mix of admiration and lingering worry.

As Mei Li left, Kai turned his attention to his new follower. Liu Wei stood nervously nearby, fidgeting with the hem of his torn shirt.

"All right, Liu Wei," Kai said. "First things first. Tell me everything you know about the Broken Fang Bandits. Their hideouts, their contacts, everything."

Liu Wei nodded eagerly. "Of course, Master. I'll tell you everything I know."

As the former bandit began to spill his secrets, Kai's mind was already racing ahead, plotting his next moves.

This is it. Time to start building my power base.

With a small smile, he turned his full attention to Liu Wei's information. Every bit of knowledge was power in this world, and Kai intended to gather as much as he could.

The sun began to set on the village, casting long shadows across the square.

As the villagers went about the depressing task of burying their dead and tending to the wounded, Kai stood apart, his mind whirling with plans and possibilities.

I need to get stronger. Fast.

He pulled up his skills list, studying it intently.

Skills:
Qi Condensation (Level 2)
Basic Cultivation Technique (Level 3)
Unarmed Combat (Level 2)
Deception (Level 3)
Mental Fortitude (Passive)

Not bad, but not great either. I need to diversify.

Kai turned to Liu Wei, who was still hovering nervously nearby. "Tell me about the cultivation techniques the bandits used. Did they have any special skills or abilities?"

Liu Wei's eyes lit up, eager to prove his usefulness. "Oh, yes, Master! The leader, he knew this technique called 'Iron Skin.' Made him really difficult to hurt. And there was another guy who could do this thing with wind—made his movements super fast."

Interesting. Defensive and speed techniques. Those could be useful.

"Do you know how they learned these skills?" he pressed.

"Not really," Liu Wei shook his head. "I think they got some scrolls from a raid on a merchant caravan. But I never saw them myself."

Kai nodded. *So there really are skill scrolls in this world. I wonder if I can absorb them . . . I'll need to keep an eye out for those.*

He turned his attention to his newly unlocked map function. To his surprise, it showed not just the village and immediate surroundings, but a vast expanse of terrain. Most of it was shrouded in fog, but he could make out the general layout of the land.

Looks like I've got a lot of exploring to do. I guess the bandit camp, or what's left of it, is as good a place to start as any.

CHAPTER TEN

Kai and Liu Wei made their way through the forest, their footsteps muffled by the thick carpet of fallen leaves. The air was heavy with the scent of damp earth and vegetation. Kai's eyes flicked constantly to the translucent map hovering in his vision, a feature he was still getting used to seeing in real life.

Red dots of varying sizes pulsed on the map, indicating potential threats. Kai steered them clear of these danger zones, much to Liu Wei's bewilderment.

"Master," Liu Wei said, breaking the silence. "It's strange. We haven't encountered any spiritual beasts yet. Usually, the forest is teeming with them."

Kai shrugged, careful to keep his face neutral. "Maybe we're just lucky."

Or maybe having a video game mini-map is the ultimate cheat code, he thought with amusement.

"Still," Liu Wei continued, "when I was with the bandits, we'd get into skirmishes with beasts almost daily. It's a bit scary with how quiet it is now."

Kai nodded, only half-listening as he focused on a particularly large red dot on his map. It dwarfed the others, pulsing ominously.

Wonder what that could be. A boss monster, maybe? Foundation Establishment beast sounds about right for this level of the game. Need to stay far away from that area.

"We should remain vigilant," Kai said aloud, more for Liu Wei's benefit than his own. "Just because we haven't seen any beasts doesn't mean they're not out there."

"Of course, Master," Liu Wei nodded eagerly. "You're so wise."

As they walked, Kai's mind raced with possibilities. *I need to level up fast if I want to survive in this world. But how? Grinding low-level mobs would take forever. Cultivation is even slower. There has to be a more efficient way.*

He glanced at Liu Wei, who was nervously scanning their surroundings. *And what am I going to do with him? Having a follower could be useful, but can I really trust someone with forced loyalty?*

"So, Liu Wei," Kai said casually, "tell me more about your time with the bandits. How'd you end up with them in the first place?"

Liu Wei's shoulders slumped. "It's not a proud story, Master Kai. My family . . . we were poor. Barely scraping by. When the bandits came to our village, they offered a choice: join or die. I was young and scared. I chose to live."

Kai nodded, filing away the information. *Tragic backstory. Classic NPC stuff. But it could be useful leverage later.*

"And what did you do for the bandits?" Kai pressed.

"Mostly scouting and lockpicking," Liu Wei admitted. "I was never much good in a fight, but I could sneak around and get into places others couldn't."

Interesting. Those could be valuable skills.

They continued their journey in silence, Kai expertly navigating them around the threat indicators on his map. After a few hours of travel, they finally reached the clearing where the bandit camp had been.

Kai let out a low whistle as he surveyed the destruction before them. The once-bustling camp was now a scene of carnage and chaos. Tents lay in tatters, supplies were scattered everywhere, and the ground was scarred with deep gouges and scorch marks.

"By the heavens," Liu Wei breathed, his eyes wide. "I remember it being bad, but this . . ."

Kai nodded. "The Thunderclaw Tigress did quite a number on your friends."

As they picked their way through the wreckage, Kai's eyes landed on a massive form lying motionless at the edge of the clearing. A slow grin spread across his face.

No way. Did they seriously leave the beast's corpse behind?

He approached the fallen beast, marveling at its size. Even in death, the Thunderclaw Tigress was an impressive sight.

This has got to be worth a fortune. And it's just sitting here, free for the taking.

Without hesitation, Kai reached out and touched the tigress' corpse. In an instant, it vanished, absorbed into his inventory.

Liu Wei's jaw dropped. "Master! Did you . . . did you just store that entire beast in your storage ring?"

Kai turned, hiding his amusement. "Something like that. Now, let's see what other treasures these bandits left behind, shall we?"

Liu Wei nodded, still looking a bit shell-shocked. "R-Right. The treasure vault is this way, Master."

As they made their way to the bandits' stash, Kai's mind raced with possibilities. *A high-level monster corpse, plus whatever loot these bandits had squirreled away. This is turning into quite the profitable expedition.*

Liu Wei led him to a large tent that had somehow survived the destruction relatively intact. Inside, Kai found a treasure trove of stolen goods, spirit stones, and various cultivation resources.

"Last time I was here, I only had time to grab a few things for the villagers, but now . . ." He grinned, cracking his knuckles. "Let's see what we've got here."

As Kai began systematically looting the tent, stuffing everything of value into his inventory, Liu Wei watched with a mix of awe and trepidation.

"Master," he said cautiously, "some of these items . . . they're quite valuable. Are you sure it's wise to take everything?"

Kai paused, fixing Liu Wei with a stern look. "Are you questioning my decisions, Liu Wei?"

The young man paled. "N-No! Of course not, Master. I just . . . I mean . . ."

Kai softened his expression slightly. "Look, these bandits stole all this stuff in the first place, right? We're just . . . redistributing the wealth. Besides, we'll need resources if we're going to get stronger."

Liu Wei nodded quickly. "You're right, of course."

As Kai continued his methodical looting, his eyes fell upon a small, ornate box tucked away in a corner. Curious, he opened it to find three ancient-looking scrolls inside.

Jackpot! Skill scrolls, if I'm not mistaken.

He carefully unrolled the first scroll, and a translucent window immediately popped up in his vision.

Skill Scroll Discovered!
Name: Iron Skin Technique
Description: A defensive cultivation technique that hardens the user's skin, providing increased protection against physical attacks.
Would you like to learn this skill?

This must be the technique Liu Wei mentioned earlier. The one that made the bandit leader so difficult to hurt.

Kai glanced at the other two scrolls.

Skill Scroll Discovered!
Name: Swift Wind Step
Description: An agility-focused cultivation technique that allows the user to move at greatly increased speeds for short bursts.

Would you like to learn this skill?

Skill Scroll Discovered!
Name: Flame Palm Strike
Description: An offensive cultivation technique that imbues the user's strikes with fiery energy, dealing additional burn damage.
Would you like to learn this skill?

Three new skills, just like that. This is almost too easy.

Kai glanced over at Liu Wei, who was busy sorting through a pile of spirit stones. Making sure the young man wasn't paying attention, Kai stepped behind a large crate for privacy.

I have a feeling this might look a bit weird to an outside observer.

Taking a deep breath, Kai focused on the iron skin technique and selected "Yes."

Instantly, the scroll in his hand began to glow. It grew warm to the touch, then hot, before suddenly crumbling to dust. Kai felt a rush of knowledge flood his mind, as if he'd just speed-read an entire textbook on the technique.

A new notification appeared.

Skill Acquired!
Iron Skin Technique (Level 1)
Your Durability increases by 10% when activated

Grinning from ear to ear, Kai repeated the process with the other two scrolls. Each time, he felt that same rush of knowledge, followed by a notification of his new skill.

Skill Acquired: Swift Wind Step (Level 1)
Your Agility increases by 10% when activated
Skill Acquired: Flame Palm Strike (Level 1)
Your Attack increases by 10% when activated

Kai couldn't help but do a little victory dance. *Three new skills, just like that! This is exactly the kind of power-up I needed.*

He pulled up his status window to admire his newly expanded skill list.

Skills:
Qi Condensation (Level 2)
Basic Cultivation Technique (Level 3)

Unarmed Combat (Level 2)
Deception (Level 3)
Iron Skin Technique (Level 1)
Swift Wind Step (Level 1)
Flame Palm Strike (Level 1)
Mental Fortitude (Passive)

Not bad at all. Of course, they're all at level one for now so the increase isn't that significant, but that just means I've got room to grow.

Lost in his thoughts, Kai didn't notice Liu Wei approaching until the young man called out.

"Master! Master, come quick! I've found something!"

Kai quickly closed his status window and turned to face his follower.

"What is it, Liu Wei?"

CHAPTER ELEVEN

A map, Master!" The young man was practically bouncing with excitement. "I think it might lead to a hidden treasure!"

Kai raised an eyebrow, his interest piqued but his suspicion immediately aroused. *A conveniently discovered treasure map? Handed over willingly by someone whose loyalty is forced? This screams "trap."*

"Let me see it," Kai said, keeping his voice neutral.

Liu Wei handed over a worn piece of parchment. As Kai unfolded it, his eyes widened. The map was intricately detailed, showing a vast expanse of forest with various landmarks and paths marked.

"This is the Whispering Woods," Liu Wei explained, his finger tracing a winding path through the trees. "It's rumored to house beasts above the Qi Refining Realm."

Kai studied the map carefully, noting the various symbols and notations scattered across it. There were markings for dangerous areas, potential water sources, and what looked like ruins or abandoned structures.

"It won't be an easy journey," Liu Wei continued. "The forest itself is said to be alive, constantly shifting and changing."

Once Kai finished studying the map, he noticed his own map function updating, a new location appearing as a glowing marker. At the same time, a quest notification popped up.

New Quest: The Bandits' Hidden Hoard
Description: Follow the map to uncover a secret treasure vault hidden in the woods.
Reward: Unknown
Would you like to accept this quest?

Kai's mind raced, weighing the potential risks and rewards. *On one hand, this could be a huge payoff. On the other, it's almost certainly a trap of some kind. But then again, what's an RPG without a good dungeon crawl? Accept!*

He looked up at Liu Wei, who was watching him expectantly. "Where did you find this, exactly?"

Liu Wei's enthusiasm dimmed slightly under Kai's scrutiny. "It was hidden in a false bottom of one of the chests, Master. I . . . I remembered seeing the boss consulting it sometimes, but he always kept it secret from the rest of us."

Kai nodded slowly, his eyes narrowing. "And you're just handing it over to me? Just like that?"

Liu Wei's face fell, and he dropped to his knees. "Master, I swore my loyalty to you! I would never betray you. I thought . . . I thought you'd be pleased . . ."

Kai studied the young man's face, looking for any signs of deception. His deception skill was high enough that he was pretty good at spotting lies, but Liu Wei seemed genuinely distraught.

Either he's telling the truth, or he's an even better actor than I am.

After a moment, Kai softened his expression. "Stand up, Liu Wei. I'm not accusing you of anything. I'm just being cautious. In this world, things that seem too good to be true usually are."

Liu Wei stood, relief evident on his face. "Of course, Master. Being cautious is good. I just . . . I want to prove my worth to you."

Kai nodded, allowing a small smile. "And you have. This could be very valuable information. Good work."

Liu Wei beamed at the praise, and Kai felt a twinge of guilt. *I should probably work on increasing his loyalty stat. Having a devoted follower could be incredibly useful.*

"So," Liu Wei asked eagerly, "shall we go after the treasure, Master?"

Kai folded the map carefully, tucking it away in his inventory. "Not just yet. We need to finish up here first and then head back to the village. We'll need to prepare properly before we tackle something like this."

Liu Wei nodded, looking slightly disappointed but not arguing.

As they resumed their looting of the bandit camp, Kai's mind was already racing with plans. *A hidden dungeon, new skills to level up, and a follower to train. Things are finally starting to get interesting in this world.*

He glanced at Liu Wei, who was happily sorting through a pile of stolen jewelry. *I'll need to be careful, though. I can't afford to let my guard down, even for a moment. In a world like this, trust is a luxury I can't afford.*

As the sun began to set, casting long shadows across the ruined camp, Kai and Liu Wei finished their scavenging. They had gathered an impressive haul of spirit stones, cultivation resources, and valuable trinkets.

"I think that's everything of value," Kai said, surveying the picked-over camp. "We should head back to the village before it gets dark."

Liu Wei nodded, shouldering a heavy sack. "Yes, Master. Though . . . are you sure we shouldn't at least start towards the treasure map location?"

Kai shook his head firmly. "No, like I said before, we need to prepare first. Besides, I have some business to take care of in the village."

The walk back to the village was quiet, both Kai and Liu Wei lost in their own thoughts. Kai periodically checked his map function, ensuring they steered clear of any dangerous areas. The massive red dot that he suspected represented a Foundation Establishment beast still loomed ominously at the edge of his vision.

I wonder what kind of creature it is. In games, high-level bosses usually guard equally high-level loot. But taking on something like that now would be suicide.

Kai glanced at Liu Wei, who was nervously scanning the forest as they walked. The young man's earlier confusion about the lack of beast encounters seemed to have been forgotten in light of their discoveries at the bandit camp.

"Liu Wei," Kai said, breaking the silence. "You mentioned earlier that the bandits often encountered spiritual beasts in these woods. What kind of creatures are we talking about?"

Liu Wei's eyes widened slightly, as if surprised by the question. "Oh, um, all sorts, Master Kai. Mostly lower-level beasts: shadow wolves, thornback boars, that kind of thing. But occasionally we'd run into something more dangerous."

"And how did the bandits deal with these creatures?" Kai pressed.

Liu Wei shrugged. "Depends on the beast. The weaker ones, we'd hunt for food or materials. The stronger ones . . . well, we usually tried to avoid those. Unless the leader thought there was something valuable to gain."

Smart. Risk versus reward. Basic gaming logic.

As they continued walking, Kai's mind turned to the newly acquired skills burning a hole in his pocket. He was itching to try them out, to see how they worked in this world.

I need to find some time alone to practice. Can't let Liu Wei see me fumbling around with new abilities, that would just be embarrassing.

Just then, Liu Wei stumbled on a root, nearly falling face-first into the dirt. Kai instinctively reached out to steady him, his hand closing around the young man's arm.

To Kai's surprise, a small window popped up.

Liu Wei
Loyalty: 55/100 (+5)
Mood: Grateful

Interesting, Kai thought as he helped Liu Wei regain his balance. *So his loyalty can increase through such a simple action . . . good to know.*

"Thank you, Master Kai," Liu Wei said, his cheeks flushing slightly with embarrassment.

Kai waved it off. "Don't mention it. We need to look out for each other out here."

As they neared the village, Kai's thoughts turned to the quest notification he'd received. The promise of unknown rewards was tantalizing, but the potential dangers couldn't be ignored.

I need more information before I commit to anything, he decided. *Maybe there's someone in the village who knows about this "Dragon's Hoard" place.*

The sun was beginning to set as they finally reached the outskirts of the village. The familiar sights and sounds of Misty Waterfall Village were a welcome change from the eerie quiet of the forest.

"Liu Wei," Kai said as they approached the village gate, "You've done well today. We'll talk more tomorrow about our next steps. Go speak to Zhang Wei about a place to stay, he'll sort something out for you."

The young man nodded eagerly. "Thank you for giving me this chance, Master."

As Liu Wei scurried off, Kai let out a long breath. *Now, time to process everything that's happened and figure out my next move.*

He made his way to the small hut he'd been given, nodding politely to the villagers he passed. Once inside, Kai collapsed onto his bed, the events of the day finally catching up to him.

What a day, he thought, staring up at the thatched roof. *New skills, a mysterious map, a follower with questionable loyalty . . .*

Kai closed his eyes, focusing on his internal qi. He could feel it flowing through his body, a comforting warmth that pulsed with potential. With a thought, he pulled up his status window.

Name: Kai Thorn
XP: 0/500
Level: Qi Refining Stage 5
Qi: 100/100
Strength: 31
Agility: 33
Durability: 32
Intelligence: 23
Wisdom: 20

> Skills:
> Qi Condensation (Level 2)
> Basic Cultivation Technique (Level 3)
> Unarmed Combat (Level 2)
> Deception (Level 3)
> Iron Skin Technique (Level 1)
> Swift Wind Step (Level 1)
> Flame Palm Strike (Level 1)

Kai couldn't help but smile as he looked at his new skills. *Not bad for a day's work. But I've got a long way to go if I want to survive in this world.*

Kai yawned widely, feeling the weight of the day settle into his muscles. He stretched, wincing slightly at the soreness.

I should probably get some rest, he thought, glancing out the window at the night sky. *It's been a long day, and there's still so much to do tomorrow.*

CHAPTER TWELVE

Kai woke up early, his mind buzzing with excitement. Today was the day he'd start training his new skills. He stretched, feeling the qi flowing through his body.

Time to level up, he thought with a grin.

He stepped outside his hut, breathing in the crisp morning air. The village was just starting to stir, a few early risers tending to their daily chores.

Kai made his way to a secluded clearing on the outskirts of the village. He didn't want an audience for his first attempts at these new techniques.

Okay, let's start with Iron Skin. In games, defensive skills are always a good foundation.

He took a deep breath, focusing on the knowledge that had flooded his mind when he absorbed the skill scroll. He channeled his qi, directing it to flow just beneath his skin.

At first, nothing happened. Kai frowned, concentrating harder. *Come on, work!*

Suddenly, he felt a tingling sensation across his body. He looked down at his arms, eyes widening as his skin took on a faint metallic sheen.

"Whoa," he whispered. "It actually worked!"

He poked his arm experimentally. It felt solid, almost like wearing invisible armor.

Now, how long can I maintain it? He held the technique, feeling his qi slowly draining. After about a minute, the metallic sheen faded, and Kai let out a breath he didn't realize he'd been holding.

"Not bad for a first try," he murmured. "But I need to work on efficiency."

He spent the next hour practicing the technique, activating and deactivating it repeatedly. Each time, it became a little easier, a little more natural.

> Skill Leveled Up!
> Iron Skin Technique (Level 2)
> Your Durability increases by 20% when activated
> You have gained 50 XP!

Kai grinned at the notification. *Progress already! This is way more satisfying than grinding mobs in an MMO.*

He moved on to Swift Wind Step next. This one proved trickier. The first few attempts left him stumbling awkwardly, his body moving faster than his mind could keep up.

"Oof!" he grunted, picking himself up after a particularly clumsy attempt. "I should have known, increased speed doesn't automatically mean increased coordination."

But Kai was nothing if not persistent. He kept at it, gradually learning to control the bursts of speed. By the time another hour had passed, he could dash short distances with reasonable accuracy.

> Skill Leveled Up!
> Swift Wind Step (Level 2)
> Agility increases by 20% when activated
> You have gained 50 XP!

"Nice," Kai said, wiping sweat from his brow. "Now for the fun one."

He turned his attention to Flame Palm Strike. This offensive technique required careful qi manipulation, channeling the fire element into his strikes.

His first attempt produced only a faint warmth in his palm. "Come on," he muttered. "I'm going for 'devastating fire attack,' not 'slightly toasty handshake.'"

He kept at it, gradually increasing the heat and intensity. Soon, small flames were dancing across his fingers.

"Now we're talking!" he exclaimed, throwing a few practice punches at the air. Each strike left a brief trail of fire in its wake.

> Skill Leveled Up!
> Flame Palm Strike (Level 2)
> Your Attack increases by 20% when activated
> You have gained 50 XP!

As Kai admired the flames flickering around his hand, he heard a gasp behind him. He turned to see Liu Wei standing at the edge of the clearing, eyes wide with awe.

"M-Master Kai!" Liu Wei stammered. "That was incredible! I've never seen anyone master new techniques so quickly!"

Kai quickly extinguished the flames, hiding his momentary panic. *Right, I'm supposed to be some kind of cultivation prodigy. Play it cool.*

He shrugged nonchalantly. "Oh, Liu Wei. I didn't see you there. Just doing some morning practice."

"Forgive my intrusion, Master," Liu Wei bowed deeply. "I was looking for you and heard sounds of training."

Kai waved off the apology. "No need for that. Actually, your timing is perfect. I could use a sparring partner to test these skills in combat."

Liu Wei's face paled slightly. "M-Me? But Master, I'm only at Qi Refining stage two. I'd surely be no match for you . . ."

Kai considered this. *Right, I'm supposed to be way stronger than him. But I need realistic combat experience at a lower level . . .*

"Don't worry," Kai said, an idea forming. "I'll suppress my cultivation to match yours. It'll be good practice for both of us."

Liu Wei looked both honored and terrified. "If . . . if you're sure, Master."

Kai nodded, then focused inward. *Okay, how do I suppress my cultivation? There's usually some kind of limiter in games for this sort of thing.*

He experimented, trying to mentally "dial down" his qi output. After a few attempts, he felt something click into place. His energy levels dropped, matching what he sensed from Liu Wei.

"There we go," Kai said. "Now we're on even footing. Shall we begin?"

Liu Wei nodded nervously, taking up a basic fighting stance.

As they squared off, Kai noticed movement at the edge of the clearing. Mei Li had arrived, watching them with curiosity.

"Oh, don't mind me," she called out. "I just came to see what all the commotion was about. Please, continue!"

Kai shrugged. *An audience, huh? Might as well put on a good show.*

He turned back to Liu Wei. "Ready when you are."

Liu Wei hesitated for a moment, then lunged forward with a straight punch. Kai sidestepped easily, but he was impressed by the speed.

Not bad. He's got some skill.

They exchanged a flurry of blows, neither landing any clean hits. Kai was surprised to find himself working up a sweat. With his cultivation suppressed, the fight was more even than he'd expected.

"You're doing well, Liu Wei," Kai said, blocking a kick. "But you're telegraphing your moves too much. Try to be less predictable."

Liu Wei nodded, adjusting his stance. His next attack came from an unexpected angle, nearly catching Kai off guard.

"Better!" Kai praised, countering with a swift jab.

As the spar continued, Kai found himself genuinely enjoying the challenge. It was one thing to practice techniques alone but applying them in combat was a whole different experience.

He activated Iron Skin just as Liu Wei landed a solid punch to his ribs. The impact was dulled, but Kai still felt it.

Note to self: Iron Skin reduces damage, doesn't entirely negate it.

Kai retaliated with a Swift Wind Step-enhanced dash, closing the distance faster than Liu Wei could react. He followed up with a Flame Palm Strike, pulling back at the last second to avoid burning his sparring partner.

Liu Wei's eyes widened as he felt the heat pass just inches from his face. "Incredible, Master!" he exclaimed. "Your control is amazing!"

"Thanks," Kai said as he allowed himself a small smile. "You're not doing too badly, yourself."

The spar continued for several more minutes, with Kai mixing in his new techniques while Liu Wei fought the best he could.

Finally, Kai saw an opening. He feinted left, then used Swift Wind Step to dash right. As Liu Wei turned to block, Kai swept his legs out from under him.

Liu Wei hit the ground with a thud, the wind knocked out of him. Kai stood over him, hand extended.

"Do you give up?" Kai asked.

"Yes, Master. That was . . . incredible," Liu Wei said, accepting the hand up. "I've never had a spar like that before. Usually the other bandits just use sparring as an excuse to use me as a punching bag."

Kai helped him to his feet, feeling uncomfortable. He didn't know what to say about Liu Wei's past. "Uh . . . right. Well, that's not how we do things here."

He noticed little Mei Li skipping towards them and felt relieved for the distraction.

"Wow, Kai!" Mei Li exclaimed, her eyes wide with excitement. "That was so cool! You were like whoosh and pow!" She made exaggerated martial arts movements with her arms, nearly losing her balance in the process.

Kai couldn't help but chuckle. "Oh, you liked that, huh?"

Mei Li nodded enthusiastically. "Uh-huh! Where did you learn to do that? Can you teach me?"

"Oh, I picked up a few tricks here and there," Kai replied, ruffling her hair. "Maybe when you're a bit older, okay?"

"Aww," Mei Li pouted, but quickly brightened up. "Okay! I'll practice really hard until then!" She turned to Liu Wei, grinning. "You did good too, mister! You almost got Kai a couple times!"

Liu Wei looked surprised at the praise from the little girl, but smiled warmly. "Thank you, little one. I still have much to learn from Master Kai."

As the two chatted amongst themselves, Kai mulled over the experience. *That was tougher than I expected. If I want to be one of those overpowered isekai protagonists, I've got a long way to go.*

He thought back to the novels and anime he'd consumed back on Earth. Those heroes always seemed to breeze through fights against higher-level opponents.

But that's not realistic. At least not yet. For now, I need to focus on outsmarting my opponents rather than overpowering them.

"Liu Wei," Kai said, "whilst you did do well, there's still room for improvement. Want some tips?"

Liu Wei nodded eagerly. "Yes, please, Master!"

Kai spent the next few minutes breaking down the spar, pointing out areas where Liu Wei could improve his technique or strategy. The young man listened intently, soaking up every word.

As Kai gave Liu Wei some tips, Mei Li tried mimicking their movements.

A small notification appeared in the corner of Kai's vision as he finished giving the tips.

> Liu Wei Loyalty: 60/100 (+5)

He smiled inwardly. *Progress on multiple fronts. Not a bad morning's work.*

"All right," Kai said, stretching. "I think that's enough for today. Liu Wei, why don't you go get some rest? We'll train again tomorrow."

Liu Wei bowed deeply. "Thank you, Master. I look forward to it!"

"Big brother Kai," she piped up suddenly, "are you gonna teach more people? Like a real teacher?"

"Oh, I don't know about that," Kai chuckled. "I'm still learning myself."

"But you're so good!" Mei Li insisted. "You could have a whole school, and I could be your first student!"

Kai chuckled, amused by her enthusiasm. "A whole school, huh? That's a big responsibility."

"Uh-huh!" Mei Li nodded vigorously. "But you'd be great at it! You could teach everyone to be heroes like you!"

"I'm not sure I'm a hero," Kai said, rubbing the back of his neck.

Mei Li looked at him with wide eyes. "But you saved us from the bad guys! That's what heroes do!"

"Well, when you put it that way . . ." Kai smiled, touched by her simple logic.

"So you'll teach me?" Mei Li asked hopefully, bouncing on her toes.

"Tell you what, how about I show you a few simple moves sometime? Nothing dangerous, just some basics. But you have to promise to be careful and only practice when grown-ups are around, okay?"

"Really?" Mei Li's face lit up. "I promise! I'll be super careful!"

Suddenly, Mei Li's expression turned serious, and she tugged on Kai's sleeve. "Kai, are you going to leave us now that you're so strong? Papa says heroes always go on big adventures."

Kai knelt to meet Mei Li's eyes, surprised by her question. He took a deep breath, knowing he needed to be honest but gentle.

"Mei Li, I don't have any plans to leave anytime soon. This village is my home now, and I care about everyone here very much." Mei Li's face brightened, but Kai continued carefully, "But . . . someday, I might have to go on a journey. Not because I want to leave, but because there might be important things I need to do to keep everyone safe."

Mei Li's smile faded, her lower lip starting to tremble. "But . . . but I don't want you to go! Can't you stay forever?"

"I know it's hard to understand. Think of it like this. Remember when your dad had to travel to the big city to get medicine when people were sick last winter?"

Mei Li nodded slowly.

"He didn't want to leave, but he had to go to help everyone. It's kind of like that. If I ever have to go, it would be to protect you and everyone else. But I promise, this village will always be my home, and I'll always come back."

Mei Li sniffled a bit, but seemed to be considering his words. "You promise you'll come back? Really, really promise?"

"I really, really promise," Kai smiled. "And you know what? While I'm gone, you can practice those moves I'm going to teach you. Then you can show me how much you've improved when I return."

This seemed to cheer Mei Li up a bit. "Okay," she said, her voice small but a little more hopeful. "But you have to teach me lots before you go anywhere!"

"Deal," Kai chuckled, ruffling her hair.

Mei Li gave him a quick hug, then ran off, occasionally glancing back at him as if to make sure he was still there.

Kai stood up slowly, watching her go with a mix of emotions. He couldn't help but feel touched by how much his presence meant to this little girl and the village as a whole.

Who am I kidding? Kai shook his head, sighing. *This village is the tutorial area, I'll have to leave sooner or later.*

* * *

Back in his hut, Kai took a moment to review his status window.

Name: Kai Thorn
XP: 150/500 Level: Qi Refining Stage 5 Qi: 100/100 Strength: 31 Agility: 33 Durability: 32 Intelligence: 23 Wisdom: 20
Skills: Qi Condensation (Level 2) Basic Cultivation Technique (Level 3) Unarmed Combat (Level 2) Deception (Level 3) Iron Skin Technique (Level 2) Swift Wind Step (Level 2) Flame Palm Strike (Level 2) Mental Fortitude (Passive)

He nodded in satisfaction. *Solid progress. But I can't get complacent. There's always room for improvement.*

Kai sat cross-legged on his bed, closing his eyes to meditate. As he focused on circulating his qi, he reflected on the morning's events.

The spar with Liu Wei was . . . enlightening to say the least. Even with my cultivation suppressed, I had an advantage thanks to my previous kickboxing experience and strategy. But in a real fight against a stronger opponent, those alone won't be enough, I need to learn more qi techniques.

A knock at his door interrupted his thoughts.

"Come in."

CHAPTER THIRTEEN

The door creaked open, revealing Zhang Wei. The old cultivator looked remarkably better than the last time Kai had seen him. The wounds from his encounter with the bandit leader had all but vanished.

Looks like he got his hands on a healing pill or something. I've got to figure out how to get some of those for myself. The bandit camp had none remaining, most likely they used the little they had during the battle.

"Good afternoon, Kai," Zhang Wei said, his voice carrying a hint of excitement. "I hope I'm not interrupting anything important."

Kai shook his head, gesturing for the old man to enter. "Not at all. I was just finishing up some meditation. What brings you here?"

Zhang Wei settled himself on a small stool. "I have some news that might interest you, given your . . . unique circumstances."

"Oh? What kind of news?" Kai raised an eyebrow, intrigued.

"Well," Zhang Wei began, stroking his beard, "I know you mentioned to Chen Lao before that you weren't quite ready to join a sect. And given your mysterious background, I can understand why these local sects might not catch your interest."

He's not wrong there, Kai thought. *Most of the sects I've read about in xianxia novels are either comically evil or frustratingly rigid.*

Zhang Wei continued, "However, I thought you should know that the Azure Sky Sect is conducting their yearly recruitment soon. It's likely that an Outer Elder will arrive in our village within the next few weeks."

Kai leaned forward, his interest piqued. "The Azure Sky Sect? That's the one you used to be part of, right?"

Zhang Wei nodded, a mix of emotions flashing across his face. "Indeed. And while my time there didn't end as I'd hoped, I still believe it's a great opportunity for talented young cultivators like yourself."

"What makes you think they'd be interested in me?" Kai asked, genuinely curious.

Zhang Wei chuckled. "My boy, your talent is obvious to anyone with eyes to see. The purity of your qi, the speed at which you've advanced, that Qi Condensation skill . . . trust me, you'll catch their eye."

Kai mulled this over. *A recruitment drive, huh? That's pretty standard for xianxia stories. But . . .*

"Wait a minute," Kai said, voicing a thought that had just occurred to him. "These immortal cultivators . . . they don't just, you know, kidnap mortals with potential, do they?"

Zhang Wei burst out laughing, the sound filling the small hut. "Kidnap mortals? Heavens, no! Where did you get such an idea?"

Kai shrugged, trying to look nonchalant. "Oh, you know . . . just stories I've heard."

Stories I've read, more like. But I guess those authors took some creative liberties. Thank goodness for that—I'm not in the mood to get kidnapped anytime soon.

"No, no," Zhang Wei said, wiping tears of laughter from his eyes. "As strange as cultivators can be, that would be counterproductive. The Azure Sky Sect, like most respectable sects, values willing disciples. Forced recruitment only leads to resentment and betrayal."

"I see." Kai nodded. "So, tell me more about this Azure Sky Sect. What are they like?"

"Ah, the Azure Sky Sect," Zhang Wei's expression grew thoughtful. "They are one of the most prominent righteous sects in this region. Their main compound is located at the top of the highest peak of the Azure Mountains, surrounded by clouds that are said to be filled with spiritual energy."

"Sounds impressive," Kai commented.

"Oh, it is," Zhang Wei agreed. "The sect is known for its mastery of wind and lightning techniques. They value honor, discipline, and the pursuit of immortality through righteous means."

Kai nodded, encouraging the old man to continue.

"The sect is divided into Outer, Inner, and Core disciples," Zhang Wei explained. "New recruits start as Outer disciples, of course. But those with exceptional talent can advance quickly. The sect provides resources, training, and protection to its members."

"What about their cultivation resources?" Kai asked, recalling the importance of such things in xianxia settings.

Zhang Wei nodded approvingly at the question. "The Azure Sky Sect is known for its rich spirit veins and well-maintained herb gardens. Outer disciples receive a monthly allowance of spirit stones and access to basic cultivation manuals."

Resource management, check. Probably some kind of currency or point system for higher-level stuff.

"And what about missions or quests?" Kai inquired, trying not to sound too game-like in his terminology. Despite knowing most of this stuff already, he didn't see any harm in hearing the old man's experience, perhaps he may learn something that is different from the stories.

"Ah, you mean sect assignments," Zhang Wei said. "Yes, disciples can take on various tasks to earn merit points and resources. These range from gathering herbs to exterminating monsters plaguing nearby villages."

Fetch quests and monster-slaying. Classic.

"And what about the downsides?" Kai asked, knowing there had to be some.

Zhang Wei sighed. "Well, like any large organization, there can be politics and infighting. The competition can be fierce, especially for those seeking to advance to Inner or Core disciple status. And of course, there are strict rules and expectations that all disciples must follow."

Kai absorbed this information, weighing the pros and cons in his mind.

Pros of joining a righteous sect like Azure Sky:

- Access to resources and training

- Protection from other cultivators and sects

- Potential for rapid advancement if I play my cards right

- A "good guy" reputation, which could be useful

Cons:

- Strict rules and expectations

- Internal politics and competition

- Possible limitations on my freedom

- Might make enemies of rival sects

As Kai pondered this, a thought struck him. "What about the Dark Moon Sect? How do they handle recruitment?"

Zhang Wei's face darkened at the mention of the name. "Ah, the Dark Moon Sect. They are . . . a different matter entirely."

Kai leaned back, surprised by the venom in the old man's tone. "I take it you're not a fan?"

Zhang Wei sighed, visibly trying to calm himself. "Forgive me. I should not let my personal feelings cloud my judgment. You asked, and you deserve an unbiased answer."

Taking a deep breath, Zhang Wei continued, his voice carefully neutral. "While righteous cultivators won't kidnap you, the same cannot be said for demonic cultivators like those in the Dark Moon Sect. They are known for their . . . aggressive recruitment tactics."

"You mean they *do* kidnap people?" Kai asked, his eyebrows raised.

Zhang Wei nodded. "Among other things. The Dark Moon Sect is one of the most powerful demonic sects in the region. They're known for their mastery of yin energy, blood cultivation techniques, and other . . . darker arts."

"But surely they must have some appeal," Kai mused aloud. "Otherwise, why would anyone join them willingly?"

"Well, to be fair, they do offer certain advantages," Zhang Wei said, stroking his beard. "Demonic cultivation techniques often promise faster power growth, and the Dark Moon Sect is less restrictive in terms of personal conduct. They also have access to rare and forbidden techniques that righteous sects won't even think to touch."

Kai nodded, mentally cataloging this information.

Pros of joining a demonic sect like Dark Moon:

- Potentially faster power growth

- Access to forbidden techniques

- Less restrictive rules

- Might suit my more . . . pragmatic approach

Cons:

- Reputation as "evil" could cause problems

- Aggressive recruitment tactics (I'll probably get kidnapped)

- Probably even more cutthroat internal competition

- Higher risk of dying or being used as a sacrifice by some evil elder

As Kai weighed his options, he came to a sobering realization. As much as he valued his independence, he couldn't ignore the realities of this world. His cultivation would soon hit a plateau without proper resources and guidance. Not to mention, he'd need powerful backers for protection in this dangerous realm.

I'd be a fool to think I could make it on my own, he realized. *This isn't a single-player game. I need a faction.*

Remembering the cutthroat nature of the xianxia worlds he'd read about in novels, Kai made a decision.

"I think I'll entertain the idea of joining the Azure Sky Sect," he said aloud. "It seems like a solid opportunity, at least for now."

Zhang Wei's face lit up. "A great choice, Kai! I'm sure you'll do well there."

As Zhang Wei stood to leave, Kai had one more question. "What kind of tests can I expect during the recruitment?"

The old cultivator paused at the door. "Ah, well, that can vary. But typically, they'll test your cultivation level, your aptitude for their techniques, and your character. Be prepared for anything from qi-sensing exercises to combat trials."

Kai nodded. "Thank you, Zhang Wei. This has been helpful."

As Zhang Wei rose to leave, he placed a hand on Kai's shoulder. "Whatever you decide, know that you have my support. You've done much for this village, and I believe you're destined for great things, boy."

After Zhang Wei left, Kai lay back on his bed, staring at the ceiling as he thought about the upcoming recruitment.

Typical xianxia recruitment tests, huh? Let's see . . .

Qi sensing: *Probably something like finding hidden objects or navigating a maze using only qi perception. I'll need to practice that.*

Combat trials: *Could be anything from one-on-one duels to surviving against multiple opponents or even spirit beasts. With my small qi capacity, I'll have to be clever and use my skills strategically. I wouldn't be surprised if the other potential recruits are the later stages of Qi Refining.*

Technique aptitude: *They might have me try to perform basic wind or lightning techniques. I should experiment with my qi to see if I have any natural affinities.*

Character tests: *These can be tricky. Could be moral dilemmas, tests of courage, or even hidden tests to see how I treat others when I think no one's watching. I'll need to be on my guard at all times, don't want to scare them off with my "pragmatic" approach . . .*

Written exams: *Some sects test knowledge of cultivation theory or general intelligence. I might have an advantage here with my Earth education and the stories I've read, but I should brush up on local knowledge too, I'm still not certain this world is exactly the same as the cultivation novels.*

Alchemy or forging tests: *Probably not for initial recruitment, but it's possible. I should at least learn the basics.*

Endurance trials: *Withstanding pain, resisting poisons, or cultivating for long periods. This could be rough, but I'll have to tough it out.*

As he continued to brainstorm potential challenges, a notification popped up in his vision.

New Quest Available: Join a Cultivation Sect
Description: Successfully pass the recruitment trials and join either the Azure Sky Sect or the Dark Moon Sect.
Reward: Sect Membership, 1,000 XP, 3 Random Cultivation Resources
Failure: Remain Sectless, Limited Future Growth

Now we're talking, Kai grinned for a second before his smile faltered slightly. *Wow, I didn't think I'd get an opportunity to leave the village so soon. Just yesterday, I was telling Mei Li I had no plans to leave anytime soon, and now . . .*

He sat up, running a hand through his hair as he contemplated the implications. The village had become a sort of safe haven, a place where he'd learned the basics of this new world. But he'd always known that it was just a starting point.

This is it; the tutorial area is coming to an end. The real game is about to begin.

The thought was both thrilling and daunting. On one hand, joining a sect would open up vast new opportunities for growth and adventure. On the other, it meant leaving behind the familiar faces and relative safety of the village.

I'll have to be careful how I break this news to Mei Li and the others. But this is a chance I can't pass up. If I want to survive and thrive in this world, I need the resources and protection a sect can offer.

CHAPTER FOURTEEN

Kai stepped out of his hut, squinting in the bright morning sunlight. The village bustled with activity, but his mind was focused on one task, finding Liu Wei. He had important news to share about the upcoming sect recruitments.

He made his way to the outskirts of the village, where Liu Wei usually trained. As he approached the small clearing, he saw his servant sitting cross-legged on the ground, eyes closed in deep meditation.

Kai paused, not wanting to interrupt. Interrupting a cultivator's training was considered taboo, in worst cases it could even lead to qi deviation.

As he watched, Kai noticed a subtle change in the air around Liu Wei. The young man's qi, usually a gentle ripple, suddenly surged like a wave.

Is he . . . breaking through? Kai thought, eyes widening.

Sure enough, Liu Wei's eyes snapped open, glowing with power. The air around him shimmered for a moment before settling back down.

Kai couldn't help but smile. *Not bad, kid. You've hit Qi Refining stage three.*

Liu Wei blinked, seeming to come back to himself. He noticed Kai standing nearby and scrambled to his feet, bowing deeply.

"Master Kai! I . . . I didn't realize you were here," Liu Wei stammered, his face flushing.

Kai waved off the formality. "Relax, Liu Wei. And congratulations on your breakthrough."

Liu Wei rubbed the back of his head awkwardly. "Thank you, Master. I've been pushing myself hard since . . . well, since you took me in."

"It shows," Kai said, genuinely impressed. He pulled up Liu Wei's stats.

Liu Wei
Level: Qi Refining Stage 3

Qi: 50/50
Strength: 20
Agility: 24
Endurance: 20
Intelligence: 13
Wisdom: 10
Loyalty: 60/100

Skills:
Basic Qi Gathering technique
Stealth (Level 2)
Lockpicking (Level 2)
Dagger Proficiency (Level 2)

Not bad at all. He's progressing faster than I expected. Maybe taking on a follower wasn't such a bad idea after all.

"So," Kai said aloud, "I actually came to find you because I have some news."

Liu Wei perked up. "News, Master?"

Kai nodded. "It seems the Azure Sky Sect and the Dark Moon Sect will be recruiting in the next few weeks."

At the mention of the Dark Moon Sect, Liu Wei's face paled visibly. Kai noted the reaction with interest.

"Don't worry," Kai continued, "I'm planning to join the Azure Sky Sect."

Liu Wei's shoulders sagged with relief. "Oh, thank the heavens," he muttered.

Kai raised an eyebrow. "Something wrong with the Dark Moon Sect?"

Liu Wei fidgeted nervously. "Well . . . they have a reputation, Master. I was . . . I was worried you might be considering them. And that I'd have to follow you into a demonic sect."

"And that would be a problem?" Kai pressed, curious.

Liu Wei nodded vigorously. "Being forced to be a bandit was torture enough, Master. I'm not cut out for the demonic path. The things they do . . . the cultivation methods they use . . ." He shuddered.

He's got a strong moral compass, Kai noted. *That could be useful, or it could be a liability. I'll need to be careful how I use him.*

"Well, you don't have to worry," Kai reassured him. "The Azure Sky Sect seems like a better fit for us."

Liu Wei's face lit up. "Really, Master? You'll let me come with you?"

Kai shrugged. "Why not? You've shown good progress, and I could use a trustworthy assistant in the sect."

Liu Wei bowed deeply again. "Thank you, Master! I won't let you down!"

Kai waved him off, still uncomfortable with the excessive formality. "All right, all right. We'll need to prepare thoroughly."

Liu Wei nodded eagerly. "Of course, Master! What should we focus on first?"

Kai thought for a moment. "Let's do some qi-sensing exercises. We'll both benefit from this."

Liu Wei nodded eagerly. "Yes, Master. What did you have in mind?"

Kai smiled, an idea forming. "We'll take turns. One of us will hide, masking our qi, while the other tries to find them using only qi sensing. It'll help us both improve our concealment and detection skills."

As Liu Wei darted off into the woods, Kai considered his options. A small icon in the corner of his vision caught his attention—his map function. For a moment, he was tempted to use it to locate Liu Wei easily.

No. Kai shook his head. *That would be cheating. Besides, I can't rely too heavily on the map function. What if I face an enemy with an ability to hide from it? I need to hone my natural sensing abilities just in case.*

When Liu Wei was ready, Kai began his search. He moved quietly through the forest, trying to extend his senses to detect any trace of qi. At first, he felt nothing but the natural energy of the forest.

This is harder than I thought. But I can't give up.

Pushing himself, Kai focused harder. After several minutes, he noticed a slight disturbance in the natural qi of the forest, a spot where the energy flow seemed just a bit too smooth.

Smirking, Kai approached the area. As he got closer, he could sense the faintest trace of Liu Wei's qi.

"Found you," Kai said, touching the trunk of a hollow tree. Liu Wei emerged, looking impressed.

"How did you find me so quick, Master?"

Kai explained his process, watching as understanding dawned on Liu Wei's face.

They spent the next few hours taking turns hiding and seeking, each time discussing their strategies and mistakes. By the time the sun was high in the sky, both were sweating and tired, but satisfied with their progress.

As they finished their final round, Kai felt a sudden rush of insight. It was as if something had clicked into place in his mind, a new understanding of qi and how to manipulate it.

Two notifications popped up.

New Skill Unlocked
Name: Qi Concealment (Level 1)

Description: Allows the user to mask their qi presence, making them harder
to detect through qi sensing.
At higher levels, this skill can completely hide the user's qi signature.
Current effect: Reduces detectable qi signature by 10%
New Skill Unlocked
Name: Qi Detection (Level 1)
Description: Enhances the user's ability to sense and identify qi signatures
in their surroundings.
Current effect: Increases qi sensing range by 10 meters and improves accu-
racy by 10%

Kai's eyes widened. *Now we're talking!* he thought excitedly. Before unlocking the skill, he had been using a crude method of spiritual sense to detect
nearby beings but now, he was able to sense qi from greater distances and with
more precision.

"Liu Wei," Kai said, unable to keep a grin off his face, "I think we've made
some real progress today."

Liu Wei nodded enthusiastically, wiping sweat from his brow. "I feel like
I've learned so much, Master. Thank you for this training."

This kind of practical training is simple but incredibly effective, Kai thought.
*And having Liu Wei here to practice with makes all the difference. I never would
have unlocked these skills so quickly on my own. Plus, I'm getting better at relying
on my own senses rather than game mechanics. That could be crucial in the future.*

As Kai was lost in his thoughts, a small window popped up.

Liu Wei
Loyalty: 65/100 (+5)

And there's the other bonus with training with Liu Wei, Kai smiled.

After drinking some water, Kai remembered the other reason he had
sought out Liu Wei.

"Oh, before I forget," he said casually, "prepare yourself. Tomorrow morning, we're going to scout out that treasure location."

Liu Wei's eyes widened. "Really, Master? You mean the map we found in
the bandit camp?"

Kai nodded. "That's the one. It's time we checked it out."

Liu Wei could barely contain his enthusiasm. "This is amazing, Master!
Do you think we'll find great treasures? Ancient cultivation techniques? Maybe
even . . ."

Kai held up a hand, chuckling at Liu Wei's reaction. "Calm down, Liu

Wei. We're just scouting for now. We don't know what kind of dangers might be guarding the treasure."

Liu Wei's face fell slightly, but he nodded. "Of course, Master. You're right, as always. I'll prepare carefully."

As they wrapped up their training session and headed back to the village, Kai's mind wandered to the last time he had returned from the bandit hideout. The memory brought a smile to his face.

The villagers had been overjoyed when he produced some of their stolen belongings seemingly out of thin air. Their eyes had widened in amazement, having never seen anything like a storage ring before, let alone the concept of an inventory.

That was quite the scene, Kai recalled. *I felt like a magician pulling rabbits out of a hat.*

He remembered the looks of awe on their faces, the tears of joy as families were reunited with precious heirlooms. It had been a good day.

As they entered the village proper, Kai noticed the way the villagers greeted him. There was respect in their eyes, gratitude in their smiles. Some even bowed slightly as he passed.

I guess saving the village from bandits and giving them back their belongings really boosted my reputation. In game terms, I'd say I've almost maxed out my starting zone rep.

Curious, he pulled up his status window.

> Reputation: Misty Waterfall Village—70/100 (Well-Liked)

Not bad. They've basically given me the role of village protector at this point.
As if on cue, a new notification popped up.

> New Title Acquired: Village Protector
> Effect: While in Misty Waterfall Village, gain +5 to all stats
> Note: This title is temporary and will be lost upon leaving the village permanently

Titles with buffs? Now that's interesting. I wonder what other titles I can earn. I bet there are all sorts of titles I could earn in the sect, Kai thought eagerly. *"Top Disciple," "Sect Champion," that sort of thing. Each one could give me an edge over the competition. I'll need to keep an eye out for opportunities.*

As they neared the center of the village, Kai's excitement faded slightly as he remembered a potential problem.

The Azure Sky Sect focuses on wind and lightning techniques, he recalled.

I only have one wind technique. As for lightning techniques, the affinity itself is quite rare according to the locals, I doubt I could get access to any techniques before joining the sect.

He remembered his conversation with old man Zhang, who had confessed to Kai that he couldn't teach him any sect techniques. Breaking such an oath would have dire consequences in this world.

Kai sighed, running a hand through his hair. *I'll have to hope I can pick up a few more elemental skills on our treasure hunt tomorrow. Or pray the Azure Sky Sect doesn't test us on that specifically.*

He shook his head, pushing the worry aside. *I know I have the talent to enter the sect. But I want more than that. I want to be the best, to catch the sect master's eye.*

A familiar fire of ambition burned in his chest. *If I can do that, I'll get a prestigious title with some fat buff, access to the best resources . . . everything I need to dominate in this world.* Kai's lips curved into a small, determined smile. *After all, what kind of gamer would I be if I didn't aim for the top spot on the leaderboard?*

As they reached the village square, Liu Wei turned to Kai with a questioning look. "Master, is there anything else you need me to do to prepare for tomorrow?"

Kai considered for a moment. "Make sure you have any equipment you might need for exploration. We don't know what we'll encounter."

Liu Wei nodded eagerly. "Of course, Master. I still have some tools from my . . . previous occupation that might be useful."

"You mean your bandit days?" Kai raised an eyebrow.

Liu Wei flushed, looking down. "Yes, Master. I'm not proud of it, but . . ."

Kai waved off his embarrassment. "Hey, those skills could come in handy. No shame in using what you've got."

Liu Wei looked up, surprise and gratitude in his eyes. "Thank you, Master. You're very understanding."

More like pragmatic. In games, every skill has its use. No point in handicapping ourselves because of some misplaced sense of morality.

Aloud, Kai said, "Just be ready at dawn. We've got a long day ahead of us tomorrow."

We need to be at our best tomorrow. Who knows what we'll encounter on this treasure hunt, but it'll probably be a boss-level beast . . .

CHAPTER FIFTEEN

K ai and Liu Wei set out at dawn, the cool morning air nipping at their faces as they made their way into the forest surrounding the Misty Waterfall Village.

Kai kept his eyes on the map floating in his vision, carefully guiding them along the path indicated by the treasure map they'd found in the bandit camp. The digital overlay showed their position as a blue dot, slowly moving across the terrain.

This is just like following a quest marker. Except the graphics are a lot more realistic.

Liu Wei trudged along beside him, occasionally casting nervous glances at the shadowy undergrowth. The young man's hand kept drifting to the dagger at his belt, as if reassuring himself it was still there.

After about an hour of walking in silence, Liu Wei cleared his throat awkwardly. "So, um, Master Kai . . . where are you from originally?"

"To be honest, Liu Wei, I don't really remember much," Kai said, keeping his eye on the map. "I must have hit my head or something because a lot of my past is fuzzy."

Liu Wei's face fell slightly, and he looked down at his feet. "Oh . . . I'm sorry, Master. I didn't mean to pry. You probably don't want to talk about it."

Kai laughed, trying to lighten the mood. "No, no, I'm being honest. I really don't remember much."

Liu Wei perked up a bit at Kai's laughter. "Is Kai Thorn even your real name? It's . . . kind of strange, if you don't mind me saying."

Kai shrugged, keeping his expression neutral. "That's all I remember. It might be a nickname for all I know. Why? Does it mean something funny in your language?"

Liu Wei shook his head quickly. "No, no! It's just . . . unusual. I've never heard a name like that before."

"Well, maybe I'm just an unusual guy," Kai said with a wink. "It keeps things interesting, don't you think?"

Liu Wei nodded, a small smile forming on his face. "I suppose it does, Master."

Better to keep things vague. The less I have to lie about, the easier it'll be to keep my story straight.

Sensing Liu Wei's disappointment, Kai decided to change the subject. "What about you, Liu Wei? Where are you from? What happened to your family when you joined the bandits?"

Liu Wei's face clouded over, a mix of sadness and uncertainty in his eyes. "I . . . I don't know what happened to them. I haven't seen my family in five years, since I was thirteen."

Kai raised an eyebrow, "Did the bandits promise to leave your family alone if you joined?"

"Yes, the bandit leader promised that if I joined, they'd spare my family. I'm sure they kept their word. They didn't kill them."

Kai kept his face carefully neutral, not wanting to dash Liu Wei's hopes. But inwardly, he was far less certain. *Bandit leaders aren't exactly known for their honesty. But there's no point in telling him that now.*

"It'll be nice to see them again someday," Liu Wei said, a small smile tugging at the corners of his mouth.

"Have you tried to find them since then?" Kai asked gently.

Liu Wei shook his head. "I was afraid . . . afraid of what I might find. Or what they might think of me, after all I've done."

Kai placed a hand on Liu Wei's shoulder. "Hey, you were just trying to survive. I'm sure they'd understand that."

"You really think so?" Liu Wei asked, a glimmer of hope in his eyes.

Kai nodded. "I do. And you know what? After we've entered the Azure Sky Sect, we'll pay a visit to your village. You can show your family how you've become an immortal cultivator."

Liu Wei's face lit up, his eyes shining with hope and excitement. "Really, Master? You'd do that for me?"

Kai nodded, smiling. "Of course. What's the point of gaining power if you can't use it to help the people you care about?"

Plus, having a loyal follower with strong motivations is always useful in these kinds of stories. Who knows, maybe Liu Wei is secretly a protagonist, he's got the tragic backstory after all . . .

"Thank you, Master," Liu Wei said, bowing deeply. "I . . . I don't know what to say."

As they continued walking, Liu Wei peppered Kai with questions about cultivation and the Azure Sky Sect. Kai answered as best he could, drawing on his knowledge of xianxia novels and games to fill in the gaps.

"Master, is it true that the Azure Sky Sect compound is always surrounded by clouds?" Liu Wei asked, his eyes wide with wonder.

Kai nodded sagely. "That's what I've heard from Zhang Wei. They say the clouds are filled with spiritual energy that helps cultivators advance faster."

At least, that's how it usually works in these kinds of settings. I hope I'm not setting us up for disappointment.

Liu Wei's face scrunched up in confusion. "But how do they see where they're going if they're always in the clouds?"

Kai chuckled. "I'm sure they have ways of navigating. Maybe they can sense the spiritual energy, or they have special techniques for parting the clouds."

Or maybe it's just for dramatic effect and they actually live below the cloud line. Fantasy worlds don't always make perfect sense.

"It's beautiful here," Liu Wei remarked, looking at the forest around them. "I never really appreciated nature when I was with the bandits. We were always too busy . . . well, you know."

Kai nodded. "It's amazing what you can see when you're not constantly looking over your shoulder. But stay alert—beauty can hide danger in this world."

Liu Wei's hand drifted to his dagger again. "You're right, Master. I'll keep my guard up."

As they walked, Kai kept one eye on his map display, watching for any signs of danger or points of interest. The forest around them seemed peaceful enough, with birds chirping and small animals scurrying through the underbrush.

This is almost too easy, Kai thought, a hint of suspicion creeping into his mind. *In games, when things seem this calm, it usually means something big is about to happen.*

As if on cue, a red dot suddenly appeared on Kai's map, rapidly approaching from the east.

I knew it, Kai thought, his body tensing.

"Liu Wei," Kai said sharply, cutting off the young man's latest question about sect life. "Get up in that tree and cover me."

Liu Wei blinked in surprise but didn't hesitate. Years of following orders as a bandit had honed his reflexes. He scrambled up the nearest tree with impressive agility, positioning himself on a sturdy branch with a clear view of the area.

"What is it, Master?" Liu Wei whispered.

Kai took a deep breath, centering himself as he prepared to face whatever was charging towards them. He ran through his available skills mentally, trying to guess what would be most effective against an unknown enemy.

Iron Skin for defense, Swift Wind Step for mobility, and Flame Palm Strike for offense, Kai decided. *But I'll have to be careful with my qi usage. I don't have an infinite mana pool here.*

"Something's coming," Kai replied, his eyes scanning the underbrush. "Something big. Be ready with those daggers of yours."

The sound of snapping branches and rustling leaves grew louder. Kai could hear heavy breathing and the thud of something large moving through the forest.

Please don't be a boss monster, Kai thought, a bead of sweat forming on his brow. *I'm not nearly high enough level for that yet.*

"Master," Liu Wei whispered urgently from above, "I think I see something moving in the bushes to your right!"

Kai nodded, shifting his stance to face the direction. "Good eye, Liu Wei."

Suddenly, the bushes in front of them exploded outward. Kai's eyes widened in shock and disgust as a massive, cockroach-like beast burst into view. It was easily the size of a school bus, its body glowed with a sickly, greenish-black sheen.

Oh, come on! Kai thought, fighting back a wave of revulsion. *I hate insects, and definitely those bigger than me!*

"By the heavens!" Liu Wei shouted, his voice a mix of awe and terror. "What even is that?"

As the monstrous cockroach skittered towards him on its numerous legs, a message popped up in Kai's vision.

Giant Scavenger Roach
Level: Qi Refining Stage 6 HP: 500/500 Strength: 40 Agility: 37 Endurance: 43 Special Ability: Acidic Spit Weakness: Fire

"It's a Giant Scavenger Roach," Kai called out. "And it doesn't look like it's here to make friends!"

CHAPTER SIXTEEN

Okay, this is just like a boss battle. Assess the enemy, figure out its weaknesses, and exploit them.

A notification popped up.

New Quest: Exterminate the Giant Scavenger Roach
Reward: 150 XP, Rare Item Drop
Failure: Death

He quickly compared his physical stats to the beast's.

Kai Thorn

Level: Qi Refining Stage 5
XP: 150/500
Qi: 100/100
Strength: 31
Agility: 33
Endurance: 32

It outclasses me in raw stats, but I have more skills and Liu Wei as backup. Plus, it's weak to fire. I can work with this.

"Liu Wei!" Kai called out, his voice steady despite the deadly threat. "It's weak to fire. Use any fire-based skills you have!"

"I-I don't have any fire skills, Master!"

Right, of course not. That would be too easy, Kai thought.

The roach charged forward, its mandibles clicking ominously. Kai activated his Swift Wind Step skill, darting to the side just as the creature's massive form barreled past.

"Aim for the joints in its legs!" Kai shouted. "We need to slow it down!"

Liu Wei nodded, pulling out a handful of throwing knives, he threw them at the creature's leg joints. Two found their mark but the creature's tough exoskeleton deflected most of the damage.

This is just like that giant beetle boss in Forest of Doom, Kai thought. *We need to find its weak points.*

The roach spun around with surprising speed, its antennae twitching as it faced Liu Wei. A glob of greenish liquid shot from its mouth, narrowly missing the young man.

"Watch out for its spit!" Kai warned. "It's acidic!"

Liu Wei nodded, ducking behind a tree. "Master, what's the plan?"

Kai's mind raced, recalling countless gaming strategies. "We need to kite it!" he shouted, then quickly corrected himself. "I mean, we need to keep it moving, tire it out. You aggro it, and I'll look for weak spots!"

Liu Wei looked confused but nodded. "I'll keep it busy!"

He then darted out from behind the tree, waving his arms. "Hey, you overgrown bug! Over here!"

The roach turned, its multifaceted eyes gleaming with hunger. It scuttled after Liu Wei, who led it in a zigzag pattern through the trees.

Kai took advantage of the distraction, circling around behind the creature.

Wait a second. My Qi Condensation skill . . . I wonder . . .

Kai focused, drawing on his qi and channeling it through his Qi Condensation skill. He visualized flames, willing the energy to take that form.

To his amazement, a small orb of condensed fire formed in his hand.

Holy crap, it worked! This is just like crafting a spell in an RPG.

"Liu Wei!" Kai called out. "I'm going to try something. When I give the signal, hit it with everything you've got! We need to maximize our DPS!"

"Understood, Master!"

Kai began to circle the roach, condensing more and more fire qi into the orb in his hand. The creature tracked his movements, its eyes gleaming with malice.

Just a little closer . . .

When he was directly in front of the roach, Kai shouted, "Now!"

He hurled the condensed fire orb straight at the roach's face. At the same moment, Liu Wei leaped from his perch, daggers in hand, aiming for the creature's back.

The fire orb exploded on impact, engulfing the roach's head in flames. It thrashed wildly, nearly catching Liu Wei in midair. But the young man managed to twist his body, landing on the roach's back and plunging his daggers deep into a gap in its armor.

The roach bucked and writhed, trying to dislodge Liu Wei. Kai saw his chance and charged in, activating his Iron Skin for protection. He aimed a powerful Flame Palm Strike at the roach's underbelly, where the armor looked thinnest.

The strike connected, and Kai felt the satisfying crunch of chitin giving way under his fiery palm. The roach let out another piercing screech, this time tinged with pain and desperation.

"Liu Wei, get clear!" Kai shouted.

His support didn't need to be told twice. Liu Wei vaulted off the roach's back, rolling as he hit the ground.

Kai pressed his advantage, unleashing a flurry of Flame Palm Strikes on the roach's wounded underside. Each hit caused the creature to shriek and flail, its movements becoming more erratic.

This is it, Kai thought. *Time for the finishing move.*

He gathered his remaining qi, condensing it into the most powerful fire orb he could manage. The effort made his head swim, but he pushed through the discomfort.

Skill Leveled Up!
Flame Palm Strike (Level 3)
Your Attack increases by 30% when activated
You have gained 75 XP!

Perfect timing!

"Hey, ugly!" Kai taunted, backing away from the roach. "Over here!"

The creature turned towards him, mandibles clicking in fury. It reared up, preparing to bring its full weight down on Kai.

Wait for it . . .

Just as the roach lunged forward, Kai hurled his condensed fire orb straight into its gaping maw.

For a moment, nothing happened. Then the roach's eyes bulged, and its body began to swell. A muffled boom echoed from within its carapace, and flames burst from every joint in its armor.

The Giant Scavenger Roach collapsed, twitching a few times before finally going still.

Quest Completed: Exterminate the Giant Scavenger Roach
Reward: 150 XP, Rare Item Drop: Roach Carapace Fragment

> You have received a bonus reward for defeating your first beast!
> 150 XP!
> Level Up! You are now Qi Refining Stage 6

Kai let out a long breath, the tension draining from his body. He turned to Liu Wei, who was staring at the roach's corpse with a mixture of awe and disbelief.

"Are you okay?" Kai asked.

Liu Wei nodded slowly. "That . . . that was incredible, Master. The way you controlled the fire, it was like nothing I've ever seen."

Kai grinned, trying to hide how drained he felt. "Just a little trick I've been working on. You did great, too, by the way. Those knife throws were spot on."

Liu Wei beamed at the praise. "Thank you, Master. But . . . what do we do now?"

Kai glanced at the roach's smoking corpse. "Well, first things first. Let's see what we can salvage from this thing. In games— I mean, in stories I've heard, monster parts can be valuable."

They approached the dead roach cautiously. Kai reached out and touched its carapace, surprised to find it warm to the touch. A small piece came away in his hand, glowing faintly with residual qi.

This must be the Roach Carapace Fragment, Kai thought. He slipped it into his inventory, making a mental note to examine it more closely later.

"Master," Liu Wei said hesitantly, "do you think there are more of these . . . things out here?"

Kai frowned. It was a good question. "Possibly. We should stay alert. But hey, look on the bright side. If there are more, that just means more experience for us, right?"

Liu Wei gave him a puzzled look. "Experience?"

Right, not a gamer term here, Kai reminded himself. "I mean, more opportunities to test our skills and grow stronger," he clarified.

"Ah, I see," Liu Wei nodded. "You're right, Master. Every challenge is a chance to improve."

As they continued their journey, Kai couldn't help but feel a mix of excitement and apprehension. The forest around them seemed more alive now, every rustle in the bushes a potential threat . . . or opportunity.

This is way more intense than any game I've played, he thought. *But the principles are the same. Adapt, overcome, and level up.*

They walked in silence for a while, both lost in thought. Kai used the time to review his new stats and skills.

<table>
<tr><td>Name: Kai Thorn</td></tr>
<tr><td>
Level: Qi Refining Stage 6
XP: 0/1000
Qi: 150/150
Strength: 41
Agility: 43
Endurance: 40
Intelligence: 25
Wisdom: 22
</td></tr>
<tr><td>
Skills:
Qi Condensation (Level 3)
Basic Cultivation Technique (Level 3)
Unarmed Combat (Level 2)
Deception (Level 3)
Iron Skin Technique (Level 2)
Swift Wind Step (Level 2)
Flame Palm Strike (Level 3)
Mental Fortitude (Passive)
</td></tr>
</table>

Not bad for one fight. But I'll need to get a lot stronger if we're going to face whatever's guarding that treasure.

"Master," Liu Wei's voice broke into his thoughts. "Can I ask you something?"

"Sure, go ahead."

Liu Wei hesitated for a moment before speaking. "During the fight, you said some . . . strange things. Like when you shouted 'aggro' and 'kite.' What does that mean?"

Kai winced internally. He'd been so caught up in the moment, he'd slipped into gamer lingo without realizing it.

"Ah, that," he said, trying to sound casual. "Aggro is just a term I picked up . . . from some mercenaries I met. It means to attract attention, to make the enemy focus on you."

Liu Wei's eyes widened with interest. "I see! That's sounds useful. And what about when you said 'DPS' when you were hitting it with those fire strikes?"

Crap, Kai thought. *I really need to watch my language.*

"That's, uh, short for 'deliver powerful strikes,'" he invented on the spot. "It's just a way to remind myself to hit hard and fast."

"Fascinating," Liu Wei said. "The way you think about combat is so . . . structured. Is that how they train in your homeland?"

Kai tensed slightly at the question, it seems Liu Wei was still curious about his background, problem was, he still hadn't come up with a solid backstory for himself.

"Something like that," he said vaguely. "From what I can remember, I'm used to . . . analyzing battles a lot. Break them down into components, you know?"

Liu Wei nodded eagerly. "That makes sense. It clearly works well for you, Master. Do you think you could teach me more of these concepts?"

Kai considered for a moment. On one hand, explaining game mechanics to someone from a non-gaming world could be tricky. On the other hand, having Liu Wei understand his strategies better could be a huge advantage.

"Sure," he said finally. "I can try to teach you some basics. But remember, these are just ways of thinking about combat. The most important thing is to stay adaptable and trust your instincts."

"Of course, Master," Liu Wei said, bowing slightly. "Thank you."

As they continued walking, Kai began explaining some basic gaming concepts to Liu Wei, translating them into terms the young man could understand. He talked about "tanking" as deliberately drawing enemy attacks to protect allies, "kiting" as a way to damage enemies while staying out of their reach, and "crowd control" as techniques to limit an enemy's actions.

Liu Wei listened intently, asking thoughtful questions that forced Kai to really think about how these concepts applied to real combat.

"This is amazing, Master," Liu Wei said after a while. "It's like you have a whole system for understanding battles. No wonder you were able to defeat that roach so easily."

Kai chuckled. "Well, I wouldn't say easily. That thing was tough. And remember, all the strategy in the world doesn't matter if you can't execute it. Your skills were just as important in taking that thing down."

Liu Wei beamed at the praise. "Thank you, Master. I'll keep practicing to improve my skills."

As they walked, Kai noticed Liu Wei practicing some of the movements he'd used during the fight, mimicking the way Kai had dodged and struck.

He's a quick learner, Kai thought approvingly. *That'll come in handy.*

The sun was high in the sky now. Kai checked his map, noting that they were getting close to the area marked on the treasure map.

"We should be nearing our destination," he told Liu Wei. "Stay alert. If there was one monster guarding the path, there might be more ahead."

Liu Wei nodded, his hand moving to his dagger. "Do you think we'll face more of those roach creatures, Master?"

Kai shook his head. "I doubt it. In ga— I mean, in my experience, challenges tend to vary. We should be prepared for anything."

As if on cue, a rustle in the bushes ahead caught their attention. Both Kai and Liu Wei dropped into defensive stances, ready for another fight.

But instead of a monster, a small, furry creature scampered out onto the path. It looked like a cross between a rabbit and a squirrel with large, curious eyes and a fluffy tail.

"Oh," Liu Wei said, relaxing slightly. "It's just a forest critter."

Kai, however, kept his guard up. *In games, cute creatures are often more dangerous than they appear*, he thought. He quickly checked his map function, expecting to see a marker for the creature.

His blood ran cold when he saw . . . nothing. The map showed the surrounding area, but there was no indication of the being right in front of them.

What the hell? Kai thought, sweat beading on his forehead. *Is my map function broken? Or is this thing so powerful it doesn't even register?*

Suddenly, a system notification flashed in Kai's vision.

Unknown Entity
Level: ???
Unable to identify. Entity's level exceeds your perception ability by a significant margin.

Holy crap. The map function isn't broken, this thing is just too OP! It could probably sneeze and accidentally wipe us out.

The creature tilted its head. Then, to Kai's surprise, it spoke.

"Greetings, travelers," it said in a high-pitched voice. "What brings you to this part of the forest?"

Liu Wei's jaw dropped. "It . . . it talks?"

A talking animal NPC. Maybe, it's friendly, let's see where this goes. Kai bowed deeply, nudging Liu Wei to do the same.

"We're on a . . . quest," Kai said carefully. "Looking for a treasure that's supposed to be in this area. Do you know anything about that?"

The creature's whiskers twitched. "Treasure, you say? Hmm . . . there are many valuable things in this forest. But not all treasures are what they seem."

Cryptic NPC dialogue. Check, Kai thought wryly.

"Can you give us any more specific information?" he bowed again.

The creature scratched its ear thoughtfully. "I might be able to . . . for a price. Do you have any spirit fruits on you? They're quite tasty, you know."

Kai glanced at Liu Wei, who shook his head. "Sorry, we don't have any spirit fruits," Kai said.

The creature sighed dramatically. "Oh, well. In that case, I can only offer you this advice. Beware the guardian of the hollow tree. Its bark is worse than its bite, but its bite is still pretty bad."

With that cryptic warning, the creature scampered back into the bushes, leaving Kai and Liu Wei staring after it in confusion.

"Master," Liu Wei said slowly, "what just happened?"

Kai exhaled slowly, finally relaxing. "We just had an encounter with a being far beyond our current level. We're lucky it was feeling benevolent."

Liu Wei nodded, still looking bewildered. "A guardian in a hollow tree . . . what do you think it means?"

"I'm not sure," Kai admitted. "But if we're unlucky, we'll find out soon enough. Come on, let's keep moving."

As they resumed their journey, Kai thought about what it could be. *A guardian in a hollow tree . . . could it be some kind of plant monster? Or maybe the tree itself is alive? I'd rather not face a demonic tree!*

He glanced at his wrist, where only one prong was red. *Still no change. I guess killing monsters doesn't count towards giving me respawn lives.*

A thought occurred to him, making him frown. *It would probably be good to find a few bandits and . . . deal with them. Just to be prepared for whatever is at that treasure spot.*

The idea made him uncomfortable, but he pushed the feeling aside. *This is a xianxia world. It's kill or be killed. I need every advantage I can get.*

CHAPTER SEVENTEEN

Only when they were far enough from that unfathomable being did Kai's mind wander to the System.

1,000 XP to break into stage seven. . . the XP needed to level up is increasing faster than I expected. Soon, I'll need to take down multiple high-level beasts just to make a dent. And one day, killing might not even give me meaningful XP at all.

He shook his head, pushing the worrying thoughts aside. *No point dwelling on that now. Who knows if I'll even make it that far?*

Liu Wei's voice brought him away from his thoughts. "Master, do you think we're getting close to the treasure?"

Kai was about to respond when something on his map caught his eye. Three red dots surrounded a single green dot not too far from their position.

Red usually means hostile, Kai thought. *But green . . . that's new. Could it be a friendly NPC? Or maybe a quest giver?*

Without warning, Kai grabbed Liu Wei's arm, cutting him off midsentence. "Quiet," he whispered. "Follow me. Stay low."

Liu Wei's eyes widened, but he nodded, falling into a crouch as they moved through the underbrush.

As they drew closer, Kai could make out voices. They crept to the edge of a small clearing, peering through the foliage.

Three figures stood in the clearing, two men and a woman. At first glance, they appeared to be cultivators, but something about them seemed . . . off. Their clothes were a mishmash of styles, lacking the uniform appearance of sect members.

Rogue cultivators, Kai realized. *Like me, but probably not isekai'd.*

The trio surrounded what looked like a shell the size of a dinner plate.

They seemed to be trying to lift it, but no matter what they did, the small thing just wouldn't budge.

"Dammit, Chen Yan!" one of the men growled, wiping sweat from his brow. "You said this would be easy money!"

The woman—Chen Yan, apparently—scowled. "How was I supposed to know the stupid thing would be so heavy? It's just a baby!"

"Some 'rare beast expert' you are," the other man grumbled. "Can't even tell how strong a tortoise is."

"Oh, like you're any help, Huang Lei!" Chen Yan snapped. "All that muscle, and you can't even budge it!"

The first man sighed. "Both of you, shut up. We need to figure this out before someone comes along and steals our prize."

Kai leaned in closer, straining to hear their conversation. Liu Wei shot him a confused look, but Kai held up a hand, motioning for him to stay quiet.

"Look, Guo," Huang Lei said, addressing the first man. "Maybe we should just give up. This thing clearly doesn't want to move."

Guo shook his head. "No way. Do you know how much a Spirit Shell Tortoise is worth? We could live like kings for a hundred years off this haul!"

Chen Yan nodded. "He's right. We can't give up now. Maybe if we all lift together?"

"We already tried that," Huang Lei pointed out.

"Well, what's your bright idea then?" Chen Yan challenged.

Huang Lei scratched his head. "I don't know . . . maybe we could dig it out?"

Guo rolled his eyes. "Great plan. Let's spend hours digging while any cultivator in the area senses the commotion and comes to investigate."

"At least I'm trying to come up with ideas!" Huang Lei protested.

"Yeah, terrible ones," Chen Yan muttered.

"Oh, like you're one to talk!" Huang Lei shot back. "This whole mess is your fault!"

Chen Yan's eyes flashed dangerously. "What did you say?"

"You heard me!" Huang Lei growled. "If you hadn't insisted on chasing this 'sure thing,' we could be back at the tavern by now, drinking our troubles away!"

"Oh, so sorry for trying to improve our lot in life!" Chen Yan said, her voice dripping with sarcasm. "Next time, I'll be sure to run all my ideas by the great and powerful Huang Lei first!"

"Enough!" Guo shouted, stepping between them. "This bickering isn't helping anyone. We need to focus on the task at hand."

Chen Yan took a deep breath, visibly calming herself. "You're right. I'm sorry, Huang Lei. I . . . I shouldn't have snapped at you."

Huang Lei's shoulders slumped. "No, I'm sorry. This isn't your fault. We all agreed to come out here."

Guo nodded approvingly at the two childhood friends. "That's better. Now, let's think this through logically. What do we know about Spirit Shell Tortoises?"

Chen Yan's brow furrowed in concentration. "Well, they're incredibly rare. Their shells are prized for their defensive properties—they say even Foundation Establishment cultivators have trouble breaking them."

"Which explains why we can't lift the damn thing," Huang Lei muttered.

"Right," Guo said. "What else?"

"They're intelligent," Chen Yan continued. "Some say they can understand human speech, even from a young age."

Huang Lei's eyes widened. "Wait, are you saying we should try talking to it?"

Chen Yan shrugged. "It's worth a shot, isn't it? We've tried everything else."

Guo nodded slowly. "All right. Chen Yan, you're the pretty one, you give it a try."

Chen Yan took a deep breath, then approached the shell. She knelt down, bringing her face close to its surface.

"Hello there, little one," she said softly. "We don't mean you any harm. We're just trying to help you. It's dangerous out here in the forest. Why don't you come with us? We can keep you safe."

For a moment, nothing happened. Then, ever so slightly, the shell shifted.

"It's working!" Huang Lei whispered excitedly.

Chen Yan shot him a glare, then turned back to the tortoise. "That's right, little one. You can trust us. We'll take good care of you."

The shell lifted a fraction higher, revealing the edge of a scaly leg.

Guo grinned. "Keep going, Chen Yan. You've almost got it."

Chen Yan reached out a hand, her fingers inches from the tortoise's shell. "Come on, little one. Just a bit more . . ."

Suddenly, the shell slammed back down, nearly crushing Chen Yan's fingers. She jerked back with a yelp.

"What happened?" Huang Lei asked.

Chen Yan shook her head, looking bewildered. "I don't know. It was working, and then . . ."

Guo's eyes narrowed. "It must have sensed your true intentions. These creatures are more perceptive than we gave them credit for."

Huang Lei kicked at the ground in frustration. "So, what now? We can't lift it, we can't trick it . . . are we just supposed to give up?"

Guo's face hardened. "No. We're not leaving empty-handed. If we can't take it alive, we'll have to . . ." He trailed off, but the implication was clear.

Chen Yan and Huang Lei exchanged uneasy glances.

"Are you sure about this, Guo?" Chen Yan asked quietly. "Killing such a rare creature . . . it feels wrong."

Guo's jaw clenched. "We don't have a choice. You know how things are for rogue cultivators like us. We need every advantage we can get."

Huang Lei nodded reluctantly. "He's right, Chen Yan. It's not pretty, but it's survival."

Chen Yan sighed, her shoulders slumping in defeat. "I suppose you're right. How should we do it? Isn't its defense basically impenetrable?"

As the trio discussed their grim plans, Kai's mind raced. He glanced at Liu Wei, who looked thoroughly confused and more than a little worried.

Time to make a decision, Kai thought. *These rogue cultivators are clearly desperate. If I reveal myself, they'll probably attack on sight. But I can't let them kill that tortoise, it could be a valuable ally . . . or make us rich!*

He narrowed his eyes, focusing on the System's ability to analyze opponents. Information flooded his mind as he analyzed the three cultivators.

Name: Chen Yan
Level: Qi Refining Stage 6 Strength: 38 Agility: 44 Endurance: 41

Name: Guo
Level: Qi Refining Stage 6 Strength: 42 Agility: 42 Endurance: 42

Name: Huang Lei
Level: Qi Refining Stage 6 Strength: 45 Agility: 35 Endurance: 45

All Qi Refining stage six, but with different stat distributions, Kai noted. *Chen Yan's built for speed, Guo more balanced, and Huang Lei's the tank of the group.*

He studied their attire, noting Chen Yan's light, flexible clothing, Guo's robes with various pouches (likely for tools or talismans), and Huang Lei's heavier, protective gear.

Their equipment matches their stats. This could be tricky if it comes to a fight.

He turned his attention to the tortoise, his eyes widened at the information that appeared.

Spirit Shell Tortoise (Infant)

Level: Qi Refining Stage 9
Strength: 77
Agility: 10
Endurance: 99
Special Ability: Impenetrable Shell
Note: Extremely rare beast with immense potential for growth

Holy crap, Kai thought. *No wonder they want it so badly. But why isn't it defending itself? Is it because it's too slow?*

He pondered the situation, weighing his options. *If I help the tortoise, I could potentially gain a powerful ally. Plus, taking out these rogue cultivators would fill up my respawn slots. It's risky, but the potential rewards are too good to pass up.*

Kai didn't feel particularly guilty about planning a sneak attack. The cultivators showed up as red dots on his map, which usually indicated hostile intent. *The life of a rogue cultivator is brutal,* he reasoned. *They'd probably attack me on sight and rob my corpse if they knew I was here.*

New Quest: Rescue the Spirit Shell Tortoise
Objective: Prevent the rogue cultivators from capturing the rare spirit beast
Reward: 600 XP, Increased reputation with Spirit Beasts, ???
Failure: Decreased reputation with the inhabitants of the Whispering Woods, potential loss of unique ally
Accept? Y/N

Kai blinked in surprise. *Well, that's convenient timing. At least the System agrees with my decision.*

Without hesitation, he mentally selected 'Y' to accept the quest. The blue box disappeared, replaced by a small quest tracker in the corner of his vision.

This confirms it. Saving the tortoise is definitely the right move. And that mystery reward looks promising.

He then began considering his options for a sneak attack. *I could try* creating a bow with Qi Condensation, but I haven't practiced enough to be sure of a one-shot kill at this distance. And I need to take at least one of them out immediately to have a chance.

After a moment's consideration, Kai settled on a plan. *Stealth assassin approach it is. Time to channel my inner rogue.*

Kai turned to Liu Wei, speaking in a whisper. "I'm going to engage them. When I give the signal, I want you to engage from the trees using your throwing knives. Aim to break their coordination. Got it?"

Liu Wei nodded hesitantly. "Understood, Master."

Kai turned his focus on his qi, condensing it into the shape of two sharp daggers. Then, with a deep breath, he activated his Swift Wind Step technique.

In the clearing, the trio were still discussing how to kill the tortoise.

"Maybe if we all attack at the same time at a targeted . . ." Guo was saying when a blur of movement caught Chen Yan's eye.

"Watch out!" she cried, but it was too late.

Kai materialized behind Guo, who seemed to be the leader of the group. Without hesitation, he plunged both daggers into the man's back, aiming for his heart.

Guo let out a strangled gurgle, blood bubbling from his mouth as he collapsed.

Cultivator Guo eliminated.
+100 XP

Kai stood over Guo's body, daggers dripping with blood. He kept his expression neutral despite the adrenaline coursing through his veins. "I'm the one who's going to end your little spirit beast-hunting expedition."

As he faced the remaining two cultivators, a part of Kai's mind was analyzing the XP reward. *Only 100 XP for killing a stage-six Qi Refining cultivator? I expected a little more, considering I got 300 XP for killing that stage-seven bandit leader.*

Right, I was three stages below that stage seven when I killed him. Now I'm at the same stage as this stage-six cultivator. It seems the System balances the XP based on my level relative to my enemies.

A grim realization settled in. *At this rate, I'd need to kill ten enemies at my level to advance to stage seven. That's . . . a lot of fighting ahead.*

"You bastard!" Chen Yan screamed, her hands already moving to form a martial arts stance.

Huang Lei dropped into a fighting stance, his fists glowing with earthen energy. "Who the hell are you?" he growled.

"I'm just someone who doesn't appreciate bullies picking on rare spirit beasts," Kai replied coolly, his qi-daggers at the ready. "Now, are we going to do this the easy way, or the hard way?"

Two stage-six cultivators. If I can take them both out, that's another 200 XP. But even with the reward from the quest, it's still not enough to level up!

CHAPTER EIGHTEEN

Chen Yan's lips curled into a sneer. "Oh, so you're one of those bleeding hearts who can't bear to see a poor little animal get hurt? Trust me, kid, in this world, it's kill or be killed."

If only you knew, I've probably killed more digital creatures than you've had hot meals, Kai thought, like *that* counted for something.

"I'm well aware of how the world works," Kai said. "But that tortoise is more valuable alive than dead. You're just too shortsighted to see it."

"If we can't have it then no one can," Huang Lei's said as his eyes narrowed. "But what do you know about it?"

Kai smirked. "More than you, apparently."

Without warning, Chen Yan lunged forward, her hands glowing with pale blue energy. Kai barely had time to dodge as she unleashed a flurry of strikes, each one trailing wisps of frost.

Ice-type skills? Kai rapidly countered with a Flame Palm Strike, the heat from his hand melting the frost on Chen Yan's fingers. She hissed in pain and jumped back.

Huang Lei seized the opportunity to charge in, his earth-infused fists swinging in wide arcs. Kai activated his Swift Wind Step, narrowly avoiding a punch that left a small crater in the ground where he'd been standing.

These guys aren't messing around, Kai thought. *Time to get creative.*

He focused his qi, condensing it into a long staff. Chen Yan and Huang Lei's eyes widened in surprise.

"What kind of technique is that?" Chen Yan demanded.

Kai smirked. "Wouldn't you like to know?"

He twirled the staff, using it to keep both opponents at bay. Huang Lei tried to close in, but Kai swung the staff low, sweeping the man's legs out from under him.

Chen Yan took advantage of the distraction to unleash another ice attack. Kai raised his staff to block, but the frost began to creep along its length.

Crap, didn't think that through, Kai realized. He quickly dissipated the staff, letting the ice shatter harmlessly on the ground.

"Interesting trick," Chen Yan said, her eyes narrow. "But parlor tricks won't save you."

She began weaving complex patterns in the air, frost trailing from her fingertips. The temperature around them plummeted.

She's charging up for a big attack, Kai thought. *Can't let her finish.*

He condensed his qi, rapidly shaping it into a series of small daggers. He then fanned out his arm, sending five qi-daggers flying towards Chen Yan in a wide spread. Her eyes widened in shock as the glowing projectiles flew towards her.

At the last second, Huang Lei leaped in front of his companion, a wall of earth rising to block the attack. Three of the qi-daggers embedded themselves into the impromptu shield before dissipating, while two flew past on either side.

Chen Yan ducked to avoid one of the stray daggers, while the other grazed her arm, leaving a thin, glowing cut.

"Nice try," Huang Lei growled. "But we've got each other's backs."

Teamwork, Kai thought as he gritted his teeth. *Always complicates things.*

He glanced at the spirit tortoise, still withdrawn into its shell. *Come on, little guy. A little help would be nice.*

Despite being grazed by the dagger, Chen Yan finished her technique, unleashing a wave of freezing energy that swept across the clearing. Kai activated his Iron Skin Technique, feeling the cold wash over him without penetrating.

Huang Lei, protected by his earth abilities, charged through the frost. His fist, now encased in stone, swung towards Kai's head.

Kai ducked under the blow, feeling the wind of its passage ruffle his hair. He countered with a Flame Palm Strike to Huang Lei's midsection, but the bigger man barely flinched.

Tough guy, Kai thought. *Need to find a weak spot.*

He backpedaled, trying to create some distance. Chen Yan pursued, ice daggers forming in her hands.

"You can't run forever," she taunted, flinging the daggers at Kai.

He deflected most with hastily condensed qi-shields, but one slipped through, leaving a shallow cut on his arm. Kai hissed in pain, feeling the cold seep into the wound.

This is getting dicey, he thought. *Time for some backup.*

"Now, Liu Wei!" Kai shouted.

From the bushes came a volley of throwing knives. They weren't particularly accurate, but they forced Chen Yan and Huang Lei to break off their attack, diving for cover.

"Another one?" Chen Yan snarled. "How many of you are there?"

Kai used the momentary distraction to close the distance to Chen Yan. His Flame Palm Strike caught her in the shoulder, and she cried out in pain as the heat seared through her clothes.

Huang Lei roared in anger, the ground trembling beneath their feet. Cracks spread across the clearing, forcing Kai to hop from one stable patch to another.

Terrain manipulation, Kai noted. *Gotta be careful not to lose my footing.*

He condensed his qi into a grappling hook, using it to swing to a nearby tree branch. From his new vantage point, he rained qi-arrows down on his opponents.

Chen Yan wove a dome of ice to shield herself and Huang Lei. The arrows shattered against it, but cracks began to form in the icy barrier.

"We can't keep this up forever," Chen Yan panted. "We need to end this quickly."

Huang Lei nodded. "I've got an idea. Cover me."

As Chen Yan reinforced their ice shield, Huang Lei placed his hands on the ground. The earth began to rumble ominously.

What's he up to? Kai wondered.

Suddenly, stone spikes erupted from the ground, shooting towards Kai's perch. He leaped away just in time, the branch he'd been standing on impaled by the rocky projections.

Kai landed in a roll, coming up with qi-daggers in hand. He flung them at Chen Yan, forcing her to dodge and breaking her concentration on the ice shield.

Huang Lei seized the opportunity to charge, his body now covered in a layer of living stone. Kai's eyes widened as the man barreled towards him like an unstoppable juggernaut.

Oh, crap, Kai thought. *That's gonna hurt.*

He tried to dodge, but Huang Lei anticipated the move, changing direction with surprising agility for someone covered in rock. His stone-encased fist caught Kai in the ribs, sending him flying across the clearing.

Kai hit the ground hard, the air driven from his lungs. His vision swam as he struggled to his feet.

That . . . that wasn't fun, he thought dizzily. *Note to self: don't let the big guy hit me again.*

Chen Yan pressed the advantage, sending a barrage of ice shards his way. Kai managed to condense a shield just in time, the frozen projectiles shattering against it.

"Liu Wei!" Kai called out. "A little help here!"

More throwing knives came flying from the bushes, forcing Chen Yan to break off her attack. One knife found its mark, embedding itself in her thigh.

Chen Yan cried out in pain and anger. "You little rat! I'll freeze you solid when I find you!"

Kai used the distraction to catch his breath, his mind racing. *Okay, think. What would I do in a game situation like this?*

He glanced around the clearing, taking in the terrain. The spirit tortoise was still withdrawn in its shell, seemingly oblivious to the battle raging around it. Trees surrounded them on all sides, their branches reaching overhead.

Making multiple qi-platforms will take too much qi. I can instead use the environment to my advantage.

He condensed his qi into a long rope, then flung it upwards, wrapping it around a sturdy branch. Using it like a vine, he swung towards Huang Lei, both feet extended.

The big man, still encased in his stone armor, didn't have time to dodge. Kai's kick caught him square in the chest, the momentum of the swing adding to the impact.

Huang Lei stumbled backwards, cracks appearing in his stone coating. He growled in frustration, trying to grab Kai, but the rope allowed him to swing out of reach.

Chen Yan, limping slightly from the knife in her leg, sent more ice attacks Kai's way. He used the rope to swing erratically, making himself a difficult target.

This is more like it, Kai thought. *Now I've got the mobility advantage.*

He released the rope at the apex of a swing, soaring over Chen Yan's head. As he passed, he unleashed a Flame Palm Strike downwards, catching her with a glancing blow on the shoulder.

Chen Yan screamed in pain and rage, frost spreading from her in all directions. The temperature in the clearing plummeted, ice crystals forming on the grass and trees.

Kai landed and immediately had to dodge as icicles began raining down from the branches overhead. One caught him on the arm, leaving a nasty gash.

Okay, maybe pissing her off wasn't the best idea, he thought, wincing at the pain.

Huang Lei, his stone armor now repaired, charged at Kai once more. This time, Kai was ready. He condensed his qi into a trip wire, stretching it between two trees.

The big man, focused on Kai, didn't see the trap until it was too late. He tripped, his momentum carrying him forward to crash face-first into a tree trunk.

The impact shattered Huang Lei's stone armor, leaving him dazed and vulnerable. Kai seized the opportunity, unleashing a flurry of Flame Palm Strikes on the man's exposed back.

Huang Lei roared in pain, trying to swat Kai away. But without his armor, the strikes were taking their toll.

Chen Yan, seeing her companion in trouble, redoubled her efforts. She formed a massive spear of ice, hurling it at Kai with all her might.

Kai saw it coming at the last second. He dove to the side, feeling the rush of frigid air as the spear passed inches from his face. It embedded itself in a tree behind him, the wood creaking ominously from the sudden cold.

Too close, Kai thought, his heart racing. *Need to end this soon.*

He glanced at Liu Wei's hiding spot, then back at his opponents. An idea began to form.

"Liu Wei!" he called out. "Remember that move we practiced?"

There was a moment of confusion, then understanding dawned in Liu Wei's eyes. He nodded, readying his remaining throwing knives.

Kai charged toward Chen Yan, zigzagging to avoid her ice attacks. Just as he neared her, he shouted, "Now!"

Liu Wei's knives came flying from the bushes. Chen Yan, focused on Kai, didn't see them coming. Three found their mark, embedding themselves in her back.

Chen Yan screamed in pain and surprise, her concentration breaking. The ice forming around her hands shattered.

Kai seized the moment, closing the distance using Swift Wind Step. His Flame Palm Strike caught her square in the chest, the heat searing through her clothes and skin.

Skill Leveled Up!
Swift Wind Step (Level 3)
Your Agility increases by 30% when activated

Chen Yan's eyes widened in shock and pain. She stumbled backwards, her breath coming in ragged gasps. Then, without a sound, she collapsed to the ground.

> Cultivator Chen Yan eliminated
> +100 XP

As Kai stood over Chen Yan's body, his chest heaving from exertion, he felt a sudden warmth on his wrist. Glancing down, he saw that all three prongs on his trident-like mark had turned red.

Three lives, he sighed with relief.

He then turned to face Huang Lei, who was staring at Chen Yan's fallen form in disbelief.

"Chen Yan?" Huang Lei whispered, his voice cracking. Then his face contorted in rage. "You . . . you killed her!"

Why is he so shocked? Kai wondered. *Isn't this what rogue cultivators do every day? Kill and rob others? Well, looks like I'm going to have to kill him even though it won't give me another life. In these stories, leaving an enemy alive always leads to revenge plots. I can't take that risk, not after the bandit incident.*

"I did," Kai replied. "And you're next."

"You think I'd just let you kill me?!" With a roar, Huang Lei slammed his fists into the ground. The earth trembled, and Kai watched in shock as Huang Lei's body began to change.

Rocks and soil swirled around the man, covering his skin. His muscles bulged, growing to inhuman proportions. When the transformation was complete, Huang Lei stood nearly twice his original size, his body a patchwork of stone and flesh.

> Warning: Enemy power surge detected
> Huang Lei's stats have temporarily increased to Qi Refining Stage 8
> Current stats:
> Strength: 63
> Agility: 40
> Endurance: 60

Oh, you've got to be kidding me, Kai thought, his eyes widening. *A rage-induced power-up? That's so cliché . . . and so dangerous.*

Huang Lei's eyes, now glowing with an unearthly light, fixed on Kai. "I'll crush you!" he roared, his voice distorted and gravelly.

Kai barely had time to think before Huang Lei was upon him. A massive fist swung towards him, and Kai knew that if it connected, it would likely take his head clean off.

He desperately condensed his qi into a shield, holding it up just as the blow landed. The impact sent shockwaves through Kai's body, and he felt the shield crack under the immense pressure.

This isn't good, Kai thought, gritting his teeth against the pain. *I can't take many hits like that.*

He tried to counterattack with a Flame Palm Strike at the rogue cultivator's chest, but against Huang Lei's stone-enhanced body, it barely left a scorch mark.

Huang Lei grinned savagely, grabbing Kai by the front of his shirt. "Burn this," he growled, before throwing Kai across the clearing.

Kai sailed through the air, unable to control his flight. He slammed into a tree trunk with bone-jarring force, stars exploding in his vision.

As he struggled to his feet, he saw Huang Lei charging towards him again, each footstep leaving small craters in the ground.

Shit, Kai thought, his mind racing, *I'm going to lose another life now.*

He tried to dodge, but his battered body was too slow. Huang Lei's fist, now the size of a boulder, came flying towards him.

In that moment, something unexpected happened. The spirit tortoise, which had remained inactive throughout the battle, suddenly appeared in front of Kai.

Kai, seizing the opportunity, grabbed the tortoise shell. He used it as a shield, feeling the impact reverberate through his arms as Huang Lei's fist connected.

But the shell held, not even a crack appearing on its surface.

Huang Lei's eyes widened in shock. "What? How—"

His moment of surprise was all Kai needed. With his free hand, he condensed his qi into a long, sharp spike. Before Huang Lei could react, Kai thrust the spike forward with all his strength.

The qi weapon found its mark, piercing Huang Lei's throat. The big man's eyes bulged, his mouth opening and closing soundlessly. His stone armor began to crumble, revealing the man beneath.

Huang Lei stumbled backward, clutching at his throat. Then, with a final, gurgling gasp, he collapsed to the ground.

Kai stood there, panting heavily, the spirit tortoise's shell still held in one hand. He stared at Huang Lei's fallen form, a mix of guilt and relief swirling within him.

Cultivator Huang Lei eliminated
+200 XP

I did it. I actually did it.

Quest Completed: Rescue the Spirit Shell Tortoise
Reward: 600 XP, increased reputation with Spirit Beasts
New Skill Unlocked: Spirit Beast Communication (Level 1)
Level Up!
You are now Qi Refining Stage 7

Quest Completed: Rescue the Spirit Shell Tortoise
Reward: 600 XP, increased reputation with Spirit Beasts
New Skill Unlocked: Spirit Beast Communication (Level 1)
Level Up!
You are now Qi Refining Stage 7

CHAPTER NINETEEN

Kai stood in the clearing, his chest heaving as he caught his breath. The bodies of the three cultivators lay scattered around him. He glanced at the spirit tortoise, still hidden safely in its shell.

Time to check my stats, Kai thought. He focused, calling up his status window.

Name: Kai Thorn
XP: 0/2,000   Level: Qi Refining Stage 7   Qi: 200/200   Strength: 50   Agility: 53   Endurance: 51   Intelligence: 28   Wisdom: 27
Skills: Qi Condensation (Level 3)   Basic Cultivation Technique (Level 3)   Unarmed Combat (Level 2)   Deception (Level 3)   Iron Skin Technique (Level 2)   Swift Wind Step (Level 3)   Flame Palm Strike (Level 3)   Mental Fortitude (Passive)   Spirit Beast Communication (Level 1)

Qi Concealment (Level 1)

Qi Detection (Level 1)

It took saving a rare tortoise and killing three cultivators at the same level just to break through, Kai sighed, running a hand through his hair.

He turned his attention to the spirit tortoise, which had yet to emerge from its shell. Kai cleared his throat and spoke, "Hey there. I'm Kai. Thanks for the help earlier."

To his surprise, the tortoise's head popped out of the shell, its eyes wide with wonder. "You . . . you can speak the beast tongue?" it asked, its voice slightly squeaky.

"Only the basics," Kai smiled, which was true since he had just acquired the skill. "I'm still learning."

The tortoise's eyes sparkled with excitement. "Oh, how wonderful! I am Zhi-Zhi, wise spirit of the shell and guardian of ancient knowledge."

"Nice to meet you, Zhi-Zhi," Kai said, bowing slightly. "Thank you again for your help. That could have ended badly if you didn't interfere when you did."

At that moment, Liu Wei dropped down from the trees, landing gracefully beside Kai. He looked between his master and the tortoise, confusion evident on his face. To him, Kai appeared to be talking normally but the beast was just making strange noises.

Kai noticed Liu Wei's bewilderment and realized his servant was being left out of the conversation. He turned back to the tortoise. "Say, Zhi-Zhi, would you mind speaking in the human tongue? My friend here doesn't understand beast language."

Zhi-Zhi's eyes narrowed slightly, as if offended by the implication that he might not be able to speak human language. But as the tortoise glanced at Liu Wei's confused expression, its features softened.

"Of course," Zhi-Zhi said, now in perfect human speech. "My apologies for the oversight, young cultivator. I am Zhi-Zhi, a spirit tortoise of great wisdom and power."

Claiming to have great wisdom and power somehow makes me doubt it, Kai thought with a wry smile.

Liu Wei's eyes widened in amazement. "It . . . it can actually talk!" he exclaimed, then quickly bowed. "Forgive me, noble spirit. I am Liu Wei, Master Kai's servant!"

"Great!" Kai said. "Now that we've introduced ourselves, I have to ask. Zhi-Zhi, why didn't you do anything earlier? Those cultivators were trying to capture you."

Zhi-Zhi's head retreated slightly into his shell, his eyes narrowing. "Young one, you must understand that we spirit beasts operate on a different level than mere mortals. Those low-level cultivators could never have harmed me. They would have grown bored and left eventually."

Interesting, Kai thought. *He's either incredibly powerful or incredibly naive. Maybe both.* "I see. Well, I'm glad we were able to resolve the situation quickly."

A spirit beast companion could be incredibly useful. It's like having a legendary pet in an MMO. But how do I convince it to join us?

"So, Zhi-Zhi," Kai said casually, "where are you headed? Do you need any protection on your journey?"

The tortoise's head emerged fully from its shell, and it puffed out its chest. "Protection? Ha! My shell is all the protection I need, young cultivator." Then, almost as an afterthought, it added, "Though, I am traveling in that direction." Zhi-Zhi pointed with its head toward the east.

Kai's eyes lit up. *That's the same direction as the treasure spot. Perfect.* "What a coincidence! We're headed that way, too. Maybe we could travel together?"

Zhi-Zhi seemed to consider this for a moment. "Well . . . I suppose it wouldn't hurt to have some company. Very well, young Kai. You may accompany me on my journey."

Kai grinned. *Quest companion acquired,* he thought triumphantly. He turned to Liu Wei, who was looking at him with wide eyes. "A . . . a spirit beast? Traveling with us?" He looked at the small tortoise with distrust. "Is that safe, Master?"

Kai clapped a hand on Liu Wei's shoulder. "Don't worry. Zhi-Zhi here is on our side. This is a great opportunity for us to learn more about spirit beasts."

Liu Wei nodded weakly, still looking unsure about the prospect of having a spirit beast join their party.

"All right," Kai said, clapping his hands together. "Let's get moving. We've got a lot of ground to cover."

They set off, with Zhi-Zhi leading the way. However, Kai quickly realized that their pace had slowed to an agonizing crawl. The spirit tortoise moved at a speed that made snails look like sprinters.

I thought with an agility of ten, it would at least move at a normal pace, Kai thought, frustration building. *At this rate, we'll reach the treasure spot sometime next century.*

After about fifteen minutes of painfully slow progress, Kai cleared his throat. "Uh, Zhi-Zhi? I don't mean to be rude, but . . . is there any way we could move a bit faster?"

Zhi-Zhi's head swiveled around, his eyes narrowing. "Faster? Young one, haste is the enemy of wisdom. We spirit tortoises move at the perfect speed for contemplation and observation of the world around us."

Kai bit back a sigh. *Great. We've got a philosopher tortoise.* "I understand, Zhi-Zhi. It's just that we're on a bit of a time constraint. Would you perhaps like a lift? To, uh, give you a better vantage point for observation?"

The tortoise looked offended for a moment, then seemed to consider the offer. "Well . . . I suppose a higher viewpoint could provide new insights. Very well, I shall accept your offer."

Kai nodded, relieved the tortoise had taken up his suggestion. He turned to Liu Wei. "Liu Wei, would you mind carrying Zhi-Zhi on your head? It'll give him the best view."

Liu Wei's eyes widened, and he looked at Kai as if to say, "Why me?" But being the loyal servant he was, he nodded. "Of course, Master."

With some awkward maneuvering, they managed to get Zhi-Zhi situated on top of Liu Wei's head. The young man wobbled slightly under the unexpected weight but quickly found his balance.

As they resumed their journey at a much more reasonable pace, Kai found himself pondering the spirit tortoise. *The System identified it as a baby, but Zhi-Zhi acts like he's ancient. Something doesn't add up.*

"Zhi-Zhi," Kai said, "if you don't mind me asking, how old are you?"

The tortoise puffed up with pride. "I have seen one hundred summers, young Kai. A mere blink in the lifespan of a spirit tortoise, but filled with wisdom beyond measure, I can assure you of that."

Kai's eyebrows shot up. *A hundred years old and still considered a baby? These spirit beasts are something else.* "That's impressive, Zhi-Zhi. What's the typical lifespan for a spirit tortoise?"

"Ah, young one," Zhi-Zhi said, his voice taking on a lecturing tone, "we spirit tortoises live for thousands of years naturally. Some say the oldest among us have seen the rise and fall of entire civilizations."

"Wow," Kai said, genuinely impressed. "So, you're still quite young by spirit tortoise standards?"

Zhi-Zhi's head retreated slightly into his shell. "Well, yes. But do not make the mistake of thinking that makes me any less knowledgeable! Age is but a number, and wisdom knows no bounds!"

Age is but a number? That kind of thinking would get you locked up back home, Kai suppressed a smirk.

As they walked, Zhi-Zhi began to tell them tales of his adventures and profound insights into the nature of the world. Liu Wei listened with rapt attention, clearly in awe of the spirit beast. Kai, however, found himself growing increasingly skeptical.

"And so," Zhi-Zhi was saying, "I told the great Phoenix of the Southern Mountains, 'My friend, true immortality lies not in rebirth, but in the eternal flame of wisdom!' And do you know what happened next?"

"What happened?" Liu Wei asked eagerly.

"The Phoenix bowed its head in recognition of my superior insight and granted me a single feather as a token of respect!" Zhi-Zhi declared proudly.

Kai raised an eyebrow. *That sounds . . . unlikely.* "Wow, Zhi-Zhi. That's quite a tale. Can we see the feather? A phoenix feather must be an incredible sight."

The tortoise's eyes widened slightly, and he seemed to fidget. "Oh, well . . . you see, young Kai, the feather is . . . it's a very delicate artifact. Exposure to the air of the mortal realm could damage its ethereal properties. I keep it safely tucked away in my . . . uh . . . spirit space! Yes, that's it. For safekeeping, you understand."

Uh-huh, Kai thought, his suspicions confirmed. *He's definitely making this up as he goes along.*

"Of course, how thoughtful of you to preserve such a rare treasure," Kai said, keeping his tone neutral. "Perhaps you could tell us more about this Phoenix? How did you come to meet such a legendary creature?"

Zhi-Zhi hesitated for a moment. "Well, you see, it was during my great pilgrimage to the . . . uh . . . the Sacred Peaks of Enlightenment! Yes, that's it. A treacherous journey that only the wisest and bravest of spirit beasts dare to undertake."

Kai nodded, playing along while mentally rolling his eyes. *This spirit beast might be a hundred years old, but he's got the imagination of a children's story writer. I wonder if any of his "wisdom" is actually true, or if it's all tall tales.*

"Master," Liu Wei whispered, his eyes shining with admiration, "we are so fortunate to have such a wise and experienced spirit beast with us!"

"We really are." Kai patted Liu Wei's shoulder. *Poor kid. He's buying every word of this.*

Kai decided to test the tortoise's knowledge a bit more directly to see if there was any truth in the tortoise's stories.

"Zhi-Zhi," he said, "I've been wondering about a cultivation technique I heard of. It's called the 'Celestial Phoenix Rebirth Method.' Have you heard of it?"

Kai had completely made up this technique on the spot, but the tortoise nodded.

"Ah, yes, the Celestial Phoenix Rebirth Method. A most potent and dangerous technique. It allows the cultivator to . . . uh . . . be reborn from their own ashes, growing stronger with each rebirth. But it comes at a great cost, you see. One must be prepared to sacrifice much."

He's just saying what anyone could guess from the name, Kai thought, suppressing a sigh. *Time to press for more specific details.*

"That sounds fascinating, Zhi-Zhi," Kai said, keeping his voice neutral. "Could you tell me more about the specific sacrifices required? I've heard conflicting information about the technique's details."

The tortoise's eyes darted around for a moment before he replied, "Well, you see, young cultivator, the Celestial Phoenix Rebirth Method requires the practitioner to sacrifice . . . their core! Yes, that's it. With each rebirth, one must destroy their cultivation core and rebuild it anew. It's a process of constant destruction and renewal, mirroring the cycle of the phoenix itself."

Kai nodded slowly, processing the information. *He's almost certainly making this up on the spot,* he thought. *The hesitation, the convenient explanations that match the technique's name . . . it all points to fabrication.*

And yet, a small part of Kai's mind couldn't help but wonder. *For all I know, there actually could be a Celestial Phoenix Rebirth Method out there somewhere, it sounds like a legit technique. And maybe it does work exactly like Zhi-Zhi described.*

"That sounds incredible, Master!" Liu Wei's eyes widened. "Have you thought about learning such a technique?"

"If it's a real technique, then why not? But remember, Liu Wei, not everything you hear about cultivation is true. It's important to verify information before acting on it."

The tortoise nodded vigorously. "Yes, yes, very wise, young human. Trust, but verify, as the ancient sages say."

Now it's quoting Ronald Reagan. Kai had to suppress a chuckle.

As they continued their journey, the tortoise's stories became more and more outlandish. He even began to claim he had the position of royal advisor to a kingdom of talking trees.

"Zhi-Zhi," Kai said during a pause in the tortoise's monologue, "all these adventures sound amazing. But I'm curious, what was your most recent experience before we met you?"

The tortoise fell silent for a moment, caught off guard by the question. "My . . . most recent experience?"

"Yes," Kai pressed gently. "What were you doing just before those cultivators tried to capture you?"

Zhi-Zhi's head retreated further into his shell. "Well, I . . . that is to say . . . I was engaged in deep meditation! Yes, contemplating the mysteries of the universe."

Kai nodded, keeping his expression neutral. "I see. And before that?"

"I . . . I was . . ." Zhi-Zhi stammered, then suddenly blurted out, "I was learning to swim, okay? My mother said I needed to practice!"

A heavy silence fell over the group. Liu Wei looked confused, glancing between Kai and the now thoroughly embarrassed tortoise on his head.

Kai sighed, a mix of amusement and sympathy washing over him. *Just as I thought. He's not some ancient, all-knowing spirit. He's just a kid trying to act grown up.*

As Kai was wondering whether to expose the poor tortoise or to continue humoring it, he suddenly noticed something on his map function. A massive red spot appeared, moving towards them at an incredible speed, almost as if it had teleported.

What the hell? Kai thought, his heart racing. *That can't be good.*

"Liu Wei, get ready—" Kai started to warn, but before he could finish, a rumbling sound erupted from beneath their feet.

In less than a second, thick tree roots burst from the ground, wrapping themselves tightly around Kai and Liu Wei's legs. They were bound in place, unable to move.

"What the—" Kai grunted, struggling against the roots. He looked up to see Zhi-Zhi, who had been thrown into the air from Liu Wei's head, retreating into his shell in panic.

Great, Kai thought, his mind racing to find a solution. *Just when I thought things were going smoothly. Whatever that red spot on the map was, it's definitely here now.*

He scanned the area frantically, trying to spot their attacker. The forest around them seemed to have come alive, trees creaking and leaves rustling as though they were greeting their emperor.

This is no ordinary ambush, Kai realized. *We're dealing with something way beyond our current level.*

CHAPTER TWENTY

Kai glanced at Liu Wei, who was frantically trying to free himself from the roots. The young man's face was pale with fear.

"Liu Wei, stay calm," Kai said, keeping his voice steady despite the panic rising in his chest. "We need to think this through."

Suddenly, a translucent blue screen appeared before Kai's eyes, displaying information about their attacker.

Danger! Powerful Entity Detected
Name: Ancient Spirit Tree
Realm: Peak Nascent Soul
Age: 10,000 years
Special Abilities: ???
Warning: Extreme caution advised. Entity far exceeds current power level.

Kai's face went pale as he read the information. *We're dead. We are so dead.*

He glanced up at the massive tree looming before them. Its trunk was as wide as a house, with bark that seemed to shift and move like living skin. Countless branches reached towards the sky, their leaves a mix of gold and emerald. An aura of ancient power radiated from every fiber of its being.

As Kai stared at their impending doom, he recalled the cryptic warning from that strange, rabbit-squirrel creature they'd encountered earlier.

"Beware the guardian of the hollow tree. Its bark is worse than its bite, but its bite is still pretty bad."

Could this be what that creature was warning us about? Kai wondered. *A Spirit Tree from the Nascent Soul Realm would certainly qualify as a formidable guardian, especially in the tutorial stages. If this is the guardian, we're in serious trouble. Its "bark"—that initial attack with the roots—was definitely bad enough. I don't even want to imagine what its "bite" might be.*

Okay, think. There has to be a way out of this. Kai's mind raced through potential escape routes. *Qi Condensation to create a blade and cut through the roots? No, a Nascent Soul Realm entity's defenses would be impenetrable at my level. Swift Wind Step to outrun it? Laughable, it probably controls this entire forest. I probably move at a snail's pace in its eyes. Maybe if I . . .*

With each idea, Kai's hope dwindled. The power gap was simply too vast. He sighed, shoulders slumping in defeat.

I'm going to die. As soon as I respawn, I need to use the brief window of surprise to create qi-platforms and escape into the sky. Please, please *tell me this thing can't fly. Trees can't fly, right?* He paused, remembering where he was. *It's a xianxia world. Of course it can probably fly. Why wouldn't a tree be able to fly here? I'm so screwed.*

Just as Kai was resigning himself to his fate, a familiar squeaky voice piped up.

"Mother! Mother, please don't hurt them!"

Kai's eyes widened as Zhi-Zhi's head popped out of his shell. The little tortoise was looking up at the massive tree with what could only be described as a pleading expression.

Mother? Did that little fibber just call that monstrosity "mother"? Kai's mind reeled. *Wait a second. Didn't Zhi-Zhi claim to be an envoy to a kingdom of trees? I thought he was making that up, but . . .*

The roots holding Kai and Liu Wei suddenly stopped tightening. A deep, melodious voice resonated through the clearing, seeming to come from everywhere and nowhere at once.

"Zhi-Zhi, my child. Are these humans bothering you?"

Zhi-Zhi shook his head. "No, Mother! I was just sharing some of my vast wisdom with them. They're my . . . my disciples! Yes, that's it. I've taken them under my tutelage."

The tree's branches swayed gently, and Kai could have sworn he heard a sigh rustle through its leaves. "Oh, Zhi-Zhi. Are you at it again?"

Zhi-Zhi's head retreated slightly into his shell, but he quickly popped back out. "Mother, you don't understand! This human, Kai, he helped when some bad humans wanted to capture me!"

The roots around Kai and Liu Wei's legs began to loosen. "Is this true, young human?" the tree asked, its voice softer now.

Kai nodded vigorously. "Yes, Ancient One. My companion and I found three rogue cultivators attempting to harm Zhi-Zhi. We . . . intervened."

Please let that be enough, Kai thought.

The roots retracted completely, freeing Kai and Liu Wei. The tree's voice took on an apologetic tone. "I see. I must thank you for protecting my son. Forgive my hasty actions."

"There's no need for thanks, Ancient One," Kai bowed deeply, his heart pounding in his chest. "We were simply doing what was right."

And by "right," I mean "trying to gain an advantage," Kai thought. *Let's just keep that part to ourselves, shall we? But if we hadn't made the choice to help Zhi-Zhi, we'd be dead right now. No amount of respawns would be enough to survive this.*

Liu Wei, who had been uncharacteristically quiet until now, suddenly blurted out, "But how can a tree be a tortoise's mother?"

Oh, for the love of . . . Liu Wei, you idiot! Kai nearly facepalmed. *Didn't anyone teach you not to question the family dynamics of nascent soul beings?* He shot a panicked glance at the enormous tree, half-expecting to be smote on the spot.

To his relief, a sound like gentle laughter rustled through the leaves. "An understandable question, young one. I am not Zhi-Zhi's birth mother, but I have raised him since he was nothing more than an egg. I found him abandoned in the forest and took him under my protection."

The tree's voice became a whisper. "His true parents . . . well, that is a tale for another time."

Kai felt the tension in his shoulders ease slightly. *Okay, crisis averted. Note to self: give Liu Wei some lessons on when to keep his mouth shut.*

Zhi-Zhi, apparently eager to bring the attention back to himself, began recounting the battle with the rogue cultivators. Kai listened with growing amazement as the little tortoise spun a tale that barely had any similarity to reality.

" . . . and then, with my impenetrable shell, I deflected the ice witch's attacks! Young Kai here provided adequate support, distracting the earth brute while I delivered the finishing blow with my secret technique!"

Kai managed to keep a neutral expression, but internally he was torn between amusement and exasperation. *Adequate support? I practically did all the work! But you know what? If it keeps us alive, Zhi-Zhi can take all the credit he wants.*

The tree's branches swayed gently, and Kai got the distinct impression it was used to Zhi-Zhi's embellishments. Nevertheless, it praised the little tortoise.

"How brave you were, my child! Truly, you are growing into a formidable spirit beast."

Zhi-Zhi preened under the praise, puffing out his little chest as much as his shell would allow.

The tree's attention then turned back to Kai. "Tell me, young cultivator, what brings you so far from human settlements? Humans do not usually come out all this way . . . they know better."

How much should I reveal? Kai hesitated for a moment, weighing his words carefully. *If I lie and it catches me, we're done for. But the truth might not be much safer . . .*

Taking a deep breath, he decided on honesty. "We were searching for a treasure, Ancient One. An old map showed something of value in this area."

The tree's aura grew serious, and Kai felt a subtle pressure bearing down on him. "A treasure, you say? Tell me, does anyone else know of this map? Have you spoken to others about your destination?"

Kai shook his head quickly. "No, I retrieved the map from a bandit's corpse. No one else knows we're here."

Please don't kill us for knowing your location. We'll leave right now and never come back. We'll swear a blood oath if that's what it takes.

To Kai's relief, the tree's aura relaxed once more. "I see. That is . . . fortunate."

Before Kai could figure out what the old tree meant by that statement, the ground before them began to shift. Small mounds of earth rose up, and from each one emerged a fruit. Kai counted five in total, each a different vibrant color.

The tree spoke again. "Humans, what you see before you are the true treasures of this forest. Once every century, I produce fruits imbued with elemental essence. Each has the power to increase one's affinity for an element."

Kai's eyes widened as System notifications began to pop up in his vision.

Item Discovered: Fruit of Blazing Flame
Effect: Permanently increases Fire affinity by 20%
Rarity: Legendary

Item Discovered: Fruit of Flowing Water
Effect: Permanently increases Water affinity by 20%
Rarity: Legendary

Item Discovered: Fruit of Unyielding Earth
Effect: Permanently increases Earth affinity by 20%
Rarity: Legendary

Item Discovered: Fruit of Howling Wind
Effect: Permanently increases Wind affinity by 20%
Rarity: Legendary

> Item Discovered: Fruit of Blessed Lightning
> Effect: Permanently increases Lightning affinity by 20%
> Rarity: Legendary

Holy crap. Those fruits are insane! A permanent 20% increase to elemental affinity? That's the kind of power-up you'd normally have to complete an entire story arc to get!

Kai struggled to keep his composure as his mind raced with the possibilities. *But why is the tree showing these to us? Is this a test? Or . . .*

CHAPTER TWENTY-ONE

Humans, for helping my son, I give you a choice. You can both select one fruit to consume."

Is this for real? Kai's eyes widened. *A power-up served on a silver platter?* He glanced at Liu Wei, who looked equally stunned.

Zhi-Zhi, the little tortoise, let out a squeak of surprise. "Mother! You're giving them fruits? But . . . but you only let me have one every ten years!"

The tree's leaves rustled in what sounded suspiciously like a sigh. "Zhi-Zhi, my child, these humans protected you. They deserve a little reward."

Zhi-Zhi retreated into his shell, grumbling something about "unfair treatment" and "ungrateful humans."

Looks like someone's a bit entitled, Kai thought, suppressing a smirk. *I guess even spirit beasts can be spoiled brats.*

Liu Wei looked at Kai, uncertainty clear in his eyes. "Master, what should we do?"

Kai paused, his mind racing. *Could this be a trap? No, that doesn't make sense. If the tree wanted to harm us, it could have done so already. Why resort to tricks against Qi Refining cultivators? We're less than ants to it.*

Kai glanced at his map function and noticed a significant change. The large red dot that had represented the Ancient Spirit Tree had now turned green, indicating it was now friendly. He let out a small sigh of relief and made his decision.

"Thank you for your generosity." Kai bowed to the ancient tree.

The tree's aura seemed to warm slightly. "Choose wisely, humans. Each fruit holds the power to enhance your elemental affinity. You may never get a chance like this again."

Kai nodded, already analyzing the options before him. *Okay, time to think this through. Which element should I choose?*

He closed his eyes, visualizing the different elemental paths of cultivation as if they were skill trees.

Fire Path:
- *Offensive power*
- *Destruction and purification*
- *Yang energy*

Water Path:
- *Flexibility and adaptability*
- *Healing and purification*
- *Yin energy*

Earth Path:
- *Defense and stability*
- *Strength and endurance*
- *Balance of Yin and Yang*

Wind Path:
- *Speed and agility*
- *Freedom and unpredictability*
- *Yang energy with Yin aspects*

Lightning Path:
- *Speed and destructive power*
- *Heavenly authority*
- *Pure Yang energy*

Kai opened his eyes. *As much as I'd love to be a jack of all trades, that's not realistic in this world. Specialization is key.*

He remembered the upcoming Azure Sky Sect recruitment. *They specialize in wind and lightning techniques. If I want to catch the eye of a powerful master, I should align my talents with their focus.*

Kai weighed the pros and cons of wind and lightning.

Wind, Pros:
- *Enhanced speed and agility*
- *Versatile in both offense and defense*
- *Useful for information gathering (sound transmission)*

Cons:
– Less raw destructive power
– Potentially less effective against certain elements

Lightning, Pros:
– Incredible speed and destructive force
– Associated with heavenly authority
– Potential for paralyzing effects
Cons:
– Less versatile than wind
– Higher risk of self-harm if not controlled properly

After careful consideration, Kai made his choice. *Lightning it is. It's got speed and power, plus it's the element of heavenly tribulation. In a xianxia world, that's got to mean something. There's always some deeper Dao philosophy at work.*

Kai turned to Liu Wei and gestured towards the fruits. "You should choose first."

Liu Wei's eyes widened in surprise. "Me? But Master, surely you should—"

Kai shook his head. "I insist. Choose whichever fruit calls to you."

Liu Wei hesitated for a moment, then nodded. He approached the fruits cautiously, his eyes darting between them. Finally, he reached out and picked up the Fruit of Howling Wind.

Kai nodded in approval. *Good choice. It'll complement his stealthy fighting style.*

Liu Wei stood there awkwardly, holding the fruit and looking unsure of what to do next.

Kai resisted the urge to roll his eyes. "Go ahead and eat it, Liu Wei."

"Oh! Right, of course." Liu Wei laughed nervously. He brought the large fruit to his mouth and took a big bite. His face contorted as he chewed, clearly struggling with the texture or taste.

It's like watching a kid eat vegetables for the first time, Kai thought, amused.

After what seemed like an eternity, Liu Wei finally managed to swallow the last bit of the fruit. As soon as he did, a soft green aura began to swirl around him. It grew in intensity, whipping his clothes and hair about as if he stood in the center of a miniature tornado. Then, as quickly as it had appeared, the aura faded, sinking into Liu Wei's skin.

Kai raised an eyebrow. "How do you feel?"

Liu Wei blinked, looking down at his hands. "I . . . I'm not sure. Maybe a bit lighter? It's hard to describe."

Kai nodded, then focused on Liu Wei's stats.

Liu Wei
Level: Qi Refining Stage 3 Qi: 50/50 Strength: 20 Agility: 24 Endurance: 20 Intelligence: 13 Wisdom: 10 Loyalty: 65/100 Elemental Affinities: Wind: 20%
Skills: Basic Qi Gathering technique Stealth (Level 2) Lockpicking (Level 2) Dagger Proficiency (Level 2)

It really worked! A straight 20% boost to wind affinity. That's a significant advantage. Now it's my turn.

Kai approached the remaining fruits and picked up the Fruit of Blessed Lightning. He glanced at Liu Wei, who was still examining himself for any visible changes.

Time to show how it's done, Kai thought. He focused his qi, using his Qi Condensation skill to form a small, sharp blade. With quick, precise movements, he sliced the fruit into manageable pieces.

Liu Wei watched, his cheeks reddening slightly in embarrassment. "Oh. That . . . that does seem easier."

Kai smirked and popped a slice of the fruit into his mouth. Unlike Liu Wei, he chewed and swallowed without difficulty, quickly finishing the entire fruit.

For a moment, nothing happened. Then, a brilliant blue-white aura exploded around Kai. Arcs of electricity danced across his skin, and the air filled with the sharp scent of ozone. Kai's eyes blazed with inner light, small sparks jumping between his pupils.

As the lightning aura faded, Kai felt a surge of power coursing through his veins. He quickly checked his stats.

Name: Kai Thorn
XP: 0/2,000

Level: Qi Refining Stage 7
Qi: 200/200
Strength: 50
Agility: 53
Endurance: 51
Intelligence: 28
Wisdom: 27
Elemental Affinities:
Lightning: 20%

Skills:
Qi Condensation (Level 3)
Basic Cultivation Technique (Level 3)
Unarmed Combat (Level 2)
Deception (Level 3)
Iron Skin Technique (Level 2)
Swift Wind Step (Level 3)
Flame Palm Strike (Level 3)
Mental Fortitude (Passive)
Spirit Beast Communication (Level 1)
Qi Concealment (Level 1)
Qi Detection (Level 1)

As Kai processed the changes, a new System notification appeared.

Lightning Affinity Increased to 20%
Effect: You will learn lightning-related skills 20% faster, and all lightning skills will be 20% more effective.

Perfect, Kai grinned. *This should give me an edge in cultivation and combat.* Suddenly, another notification appeared.

Quest: Rescue the Spirit Shell Tortoise
Status: Complete
Secret Reward Received!

Kai's eyes widened in surprise. *Wait, what? The fruit was the secret reward?*

He furrowed his brow, a disturbing thought occurring to him. *If the System expected me to be rewarded by the tree, then . . . doesn't that mean the System can think? Is it sapient?*

A chill ran down Kai's spine as he considered the implications. He'd always assumed the System was just a set of rules and algorithms, but this suggested something more.

Hey, System, Kai thought deliberately, *are you . . . alive?*

He waited, heart pounding, but no response came. The System remained as silent and impassive as ever.

Come on, say something, Kai mentally urged. *If you're sapient, now would be a great time to let me know.*

Still nothing.

Kai frowned, a mix of disappointment and relief washing over him. *Maybe I'm reading too much into this. It could just be a preprogrammed response based on likely outcomes.*

But a nagging doubt remained in the back of his mind. The System's apparent foresight was uncanny, and he couldn't shake the feeling that there was more to it than met the eye.

I'll have to keep a closer eye on these System messages, Kai decided. *There might be more to this "game" than I realized.*

"The ability to condense qi . . . that's an interesting skill," the Ancient Spirit Tree said, drawing Kai's attention back to the real world. "Where did you learn to do something like that?"

Kai knew lying to a Nascent Soul Realm being would be futile and potentially fatal. He opted for a version of the truth. "I don't know where I got this mark from, but whenever I channel qi through it," he said, showing the trident mark on his wrist, "I can condense qi into various forms."

The tree's aura shifted, and Kai felt a probing sensation on his wrist. Even though he wasn't pleased by the rude action, he suppressed his discomfort, not wanting to offend the powerful being.

After a moment, the tree spoke again. "Curious. I sense nothing unique about the mark itself. You must have a strong background, young cultivator."

Kai shrugged, letting the tree draw its own conclusions. *Better to let it think I'm from some mysterious powerful sect than try to explain the whole "transported from another world" thing.*

As the tree's attention lingered on him, Kai began to feel uncomfortable. He turned to Liu Wei. "We should get going. We've imposed on the honored spirit's hospitality long enough."

He bowed deeply to the Ancient Spirit Tree. "Thank you again for your generosity."

Before they could leave, however, Zhi-Zhi spoke up. "Mother, can I go with them? Please?"

The tree's aura flickered with concern. "My child, the outside world is dangerous. You are safe here."

"But Mother," Zhi-Zhi argued, his voice taking on a wheedling tone, "I can't stay protected here forever! How am I supposed to become a great and wise spirit beast if I never leave the forest?"

The tree's branches swayed, as if caught in an unseen wind. It was silent for a long moment before finally sighing. "Very well, my son. But you must be careful."

With another rustle of leaves, a single golden leaf floated down from the tree's branches. "Take this, Zhi-Zhi. It is a life-saving treasure that will protect you once against any danger at the Nascent Soul Realm or below."

Zhi-Zhi's eyes lit up with excitement. He reached out to take the leaf, but the tree's voice stopped him.

"And do try not to lose it this time," the tree added, a hint of exasperation in its tone. "Unlike the Profound Wisdom Pearl you misplaced while 'meditating' by the river."

Zhi-Zhi's head retreated slightly into his shell. "That wasn't my fault! A fish jumped out of the water and startled me!"

Kai and Liu Wei exchanged glances, both suppressing smiles.

Zhi-Zhi quickly recovered from his embarrassment. He carefully took the golden leaf, examining it with wide eyes. Then, to Kai and Liu Wei's shock, he opened his mouth and swallowed it whole.

"Zhi-Zhi!" Kai exclaimed. "What are you doing?"

The little tortoise looked up at him, confusion evident in his eyes. "What? Oh! You don't know about my storage space, do you? I can store things inside my body. It's safer this way. I won't lose it!"

Kai nodded slowly, filing away this information for later. *A living storage system. Even though I have my own inventory, that could still be incredibly useful.*

The Ancient Spirit Tree's voice rang out one last time. "Young cultivator, please take care of my son. He can be a . . . handful."

"I understand," Kai said, bowing once more. "I'll do my best to keep him safe."

With that, the three of them set off, leaving the ancient tree behind. As they walked, Kai let out a long breath, feeling the tension leave his body.

Man, being in the presence of a Nascent Soul Realm being is intense. It's like being a level one character standing next to a raid boss.

As they made their way through the forest, a notification popped up.

New Quest Acquired: Tame the Spirit Beast
Objective: Gain Zhi-Zhi's trust and loyalty

Reward: ???

Let's hope the System actually gives out the reward this time, instead of piggybacking on someone else's generosity. I'd rather not have to rely on convenient coincidences every time I complete a quest.

CHAPTER TWENTY-TWO

Liu Wei made his way through the forest, his eyes fixed on the back of his master. As they walked, Liu Wei's mind wandered to the events that had brought him to this point. *How quickly life can change. Just a few days ago, I was nothing more than a lowly bandit, trapped in a life I despised.*

The memory of that day still sent chills down his spine. He had watched from his hiding spot as Kai, then a stranger to him, confronted the bandit leader. He had really thought that Kai would defeat the bandit leader in their duel, but when he saw the leader's blade slice through Kai's neck, his heart had nearly stopped.

I thought all hope was lost then. I believed I'd be stuck as a bandit forever.

A heavy sigh escaped his lips as he remembered his failed escape attempts. Each time, he had been caught and beaten, the bandits threatening to harm his family if he tried again. The thought of his village, of his family, made his chest tighten with longing.

I wonder if they're okay. It's been so long . . . I hope the bandit leader kept his word and left them alone.

No use dwelling on the past, Liu Wei shook his head, trying to dispel the gloomy thoughts. *My life is so much better now.*

His gaze returned to Kai, and a small smile tugged at his lips. Despite being Kai's servant, Liu Wei felt their relationship was something more. Yes, his master could be cold and distant at times, but he had also taken the time to train Liu Wei, helping him improve his qi-sensing skills and combat abilities.

Even though we're both at the Qi Refining Realm, I wouldn't mind being his disciple. In fact, I'd love it. There's something special about Master Kai, beyond just being a cultivation prodigy. It's like he has this aura . . . as if he's the hero of his own story.

His musings were interrupted by an excited squeak from the tortoise sitting on his head.

"Hey, hey!" Zhi-Zhi called out. "You two should really become my disciples! If you do, I guarantee you'll both become immortals one day!"

Liu Wei couldn't help but smile. When they first met the hundred-year-old tortoise, he had thought Zhi-Zhi was wise beyond his years. Now, after spending time with him, Liu Wei realized the tortoise was still very much a child at heart.

"Oh, really?" Liu Wei asked, humoring the little beast. "And how exactly would you make us immortals, Zhi-Zhi?"

The tortoise puffed up his chest proudly. "Well, first I'd teach you all about the profound mysteries of the universe! Then we'd meditate for a thousand years under a waterfall!"

"A thousand years?" Liu Wei laughed. "That's quite a long time, Zhi-Zhi. What would we eat?"

"Eat?" Zhi-Zhi looked confused for a moment before his eyes lit up. "Oh, right! Humans need to eat. Well, we'd . . . we'd eat spirit fruits! Yes, that's it! Spirit fruits that grow only once every hundred years!"

As they bantered back and forth, Liu Wei kept glancing at Kai. His master's behavior had been puzzling him lately. Kai would often stare off into space, his face cycling through various expressions—excitement, annoyance, disappointment—for no apparent reason.

What could he be doing? Liu Wei wondered. *Does he have some special technique that lets him see the future? Or maybe he can sense things far beyond our range? It would explain why we've barely been attacked by beasts on this journey.*

Suddenly, Kai turned and fixed Liu Wei with an intense blue-eyed stare. Liu Wei felt his breath catch, startled by the sudden attention. But then Kai smiled, and Liu Wei felt himself relax.

"Liu Wei," Kai said, "how would you like to get some battle experience?"

Liu Wei blinked in confusion. He couldn't sense any beasts nearby, and a quick glance at Zhi-Zhi showed the tortoise looked equally perplexed.

Is Master Kai suggesting we spar right here in the forest? Liu Wei thought, alarmed.

"Master," Liu Wei began hesitantly, "isn't it dangerous to fight here? We could be ambushed by—"

Kai's laughter cut him off. "No, no. Nothing like that. Come, follow me."

Relieved but still curious, Liu Wei followed as Kai led them to a small clearing. A small lake stretched before them, its surface like a mirror reflecting the sky above. Liu Wei scanned the area but saw nothing out of the ordinary.

"There," Kai said, pointing towards the water's edge.

Liu Wei squinted, following his master's finger. At first, he saw nothing, but then . . . movement. A small, crab-like creature scuttled along the shore, its shell glistening with moisture.

"It's a spirit beast," Kai explained. "Qi Refining stage three. A perfect opponent for you, Liu Wei."

Liu Wei felt his mouth go dry as Kai and Zhi-Zhi turned to look at him expectantly. He swallowed hard and nodded awkwardly. "I . . . I understand, Master."

Taking a deep breath, Liu Wei started to walk directly towards the crab-like beast. He had only taken a few steps when he felt Kai's hand on his shoulder.

"What are you doing?" Kai asked, his voice tinged with amusement.

Confused, Liu Wei replied, "I'm . . . going to fight it?"

Kai shook his head, a small smile playing on his lips. "This isn't a duel, Liu Wei. You can ambush it."

Liu Wei felt his face grow hot with embarrassment. *Of course! How could I be so stupid?* He remembered similar situations with the bandits, how they'd always been baffled by his direct approach.

"I'm sorry, Master," Liu Wei mumbled. "I'll do better."

Pushing aside his embarrassment, Liu Wei focused on concealing his qi signature. He crept towards the spirit beast, his footsteps light and careful on the soft earth.

The crab-like creature remained oblivious to his approach, busy scavenging along the lakeshore. When Liu Wei was just a few paces away, he pounced.

His fist, infused with qi, slammed into the beast's shell. There was a satisfying crack, and the creature let out a high-pitched shriek of pain and surprise.

But the battle was far from over. The spirit beast whirled around, its pincers snapping viciously at Liu Wei's legs. He jumped back, narrowly avoiding the sharp claws.

"Watch its movements!" Kai called out. "Predict where it will strike next!"

Liu Wei nodded, his eyes never leaving the enraged beast. It scuttled sideways, trying to flank him. Remembering Kai's advice, Liu Wei anticipated its next move and sidestepped just as the creature lunged.

"Good!" Kai shouted. "Now counterattack while it's off-balance!"

Liu Wei didn't hesitate. He drove his heel down onto the beast's exposed back, channeling his qi for extra impact. The creature's shell cracked further, and it let out another pained cry.

"Ooh, ooh!" Zhi-Zhi bounced excitedly. "Now do a backflip and land on its head!"

Without thinking, Liu Wei attempted the acrobatic move. But as he twisted in the air, he realized his mistake. The spirit beast's pincer clamped onto his ankle, sending a jolt of pain through his leg.

Liu Wei crashed to the ground, wincing. The crab-like creature advanced, its remaining pincer raised menacingly.

"Ignore the tortoise!" Kai's voice cut through Liu Wei's panic. "Focus on your strengths. You're agile, use that!"

Gritting his teeth against the pain, Liu Wei rolled to his feet. He circled the beast, staying light on his toes despite his injured ankle. The creature turned to keep him in sight, but its movements were slower now, hampered by its damaged shell.

Liu Wei saw his opportunity. He feinted left, then darted right as the beast committed to its attack. In one fluid motion, he brought his fist down on the crack in its shell, channeling every bit of qi he could muster.

The spirit beast's shell finally gave way with a sickening crunch. It let out one final, weak chirp before collapsing.

Panting heavily, Liu Wei stood over his fallen opponent. His body ached, and his ankle throbbed, but a sense of accomplishment washed over him.

He turned to see Kai approaching, a smile on his face. "Well done, Liu Wei. You made that look easy."

Liu Wei felt his chest swell with pride at his master's words. "Thank you, Master. I couldn't have done it without your guidance."

Zhi-Zhi suddenly bounced into view. "Hey, don't forget about me! I helped, too! My advice was super important!"

Liu Wei awkwardly rubbed the back of his head, forcing a smile. "Ah, yes . . . thank you, too, Zhi-Zhi. Your, uh, input was very . . . interesting."

If by "help" you mean nearly getting me killed, Liu Wei thought to himself. *I'm pretty sure if I had followed all of Zhi-Zhi's advice, I'd be crab food by now.*

"Every bit of experience helps, Zhi-Zhi," Kai chuckled, patting the enthusiastic tortoise's shell. Glancing at the fallen spirit beast, Kai asked, "So, what are you going to do now?"

Confused, Liu Wei looked back at the creature. "I . . . I'm not sure what you mean, Master?"

Kai raised an eyebrow. "You're just going to leave the corpse there?"

Liu Wei's eyes widened. "Oh! Of course not, I'll collect it right away!" He hurried back to the fallen beast, his face burning with embarrassment once again.

As Liu Wei carefully gathered up the spirit beast's remains, he couldn't help but reflect on the battle. Despite the pain in his ankle, he felt . . . alive. It was so different from his time with the bandits, where violence had only ever brought him shame and regret.

Is this what it means to be a true cultivator? To face challenges head-on and grow stronger from them?

He glanced at Kai, who was now in conversation with Zhi-Zhi. His master's casual confidence, the way he seemed to know exactly what to do in any situation—it was inspiring.

I want to be like that someday. Strong, confident, always in control.

As he finished collecting the spirit beast's remains, Liu Wei made a silent vow to himself. He would work harder, train more diligently, and do whatever it took to make Kai proud. Maybe then, he could become a disciple rather than just a servant.

With the crab-like creature in his possession, Liu Wei rejoined Kai and Zhi-Zhi. The little tortoise was bouncing around excitedly, recounting Liu Wei's battle with his usual, dramatic embellishments.

"And then he went whoosh! And the crabby went splat!" Zhi-Zhi exclaimed, his eyes wide with excitement.

Kai chuckled, patting the tortoise's shell. "I'm not sure that's exactly how it happened, Zhi-Zhi, but Liu Wei did do well."

Liu Wei felt a warmth spread through his chest at Kai's words. It was a simple compliment, but coming from his master, the man who spared his life, it meant the world.

"Thank you, Master," Liu Wei said, bowing slightly. "I still have much to learn, though."

Kai nodded, a thoughtful expression on his face. "That's true for all of us, Liu Wei. The path of cultivation is endless. But you've made good progress. I think it's time we took your training to the next level."

"Really, Master?" Liu Wei's eyes widened with excitement.

"Yes," Kai confirmed. "Using qi-enhanced punches and kicks isn't going to cut it anymore. I'll teach you some proper qi techniques."

Liu Wei could barely contain his enthusiasm. "Thank you, Master! I'll work hard to learn them." Then a thought occurred to him. "Master, will I be able to read the scrolls we took from the bandits? I've always wanted to learn them, but the bandits, they never let me . . ."

At the mention of the scrolls, a flicker of embarrassment crossed Kai's face. It was gone so quickly that Liu Wei almost thought he had imagined it. His master quickly composed himself, shaking his head.

"No, not the scrolls," Kai said, his voice steady. "I'll just teach the techniques to you directly. It'll be more efficient that way."

Master Kai is going to teach me personally, Liu Wei thought, his heart swelling with emotion. *He's investing time in my growth, just like a true master would with his disciple. Maybe . . . maybe I'm not just a servant to him after all.*

CHAPTER TWENTY-THREE

As Kai, Liu Wei, and Zhi-Zhi reached the top of the final hill, the Misty Waterfall Village came into view. The architecture, a unique blend of fantasy and historical elements, no longer shocked Kai as it had weeks ago. Now, it felt almost . . . familiar.

"Home sweet home," Kai murmured, a small smile tugging at his lips.

Liu Wei, with Zhi-Zhi sat comfortably on his head, stepped up beside him. "It's good to be back, Master Kai."

Zhi-Zhi looked down at the village, his tiny eyes narrowing. "This is where you're from? I thought you'd be from one of the big cities."

Kai chuckled. "Surprised? Us village boys are no less than city folk."

If only that were true in this world, Kai thought. *Back on Earth, maybe. But here? A Foundation Establishment cultivator could rule a place like this. In a big city, they'd be lucky to sweep the streets.*

"It's quite . . . quaint," Zhi-Zhi said, clearly trying to be diplomatic.

Liu Wei patted the tortoise's shell. "It may not be grand, but it's peaceful. After my time with the bandits, I've learned to appreciate that."

As they made their way down the hill, Kai found himself smiling at the memory of Liu Wei's battle with the crab-like spirit beast. The young man had shown real potential.

A System notification popped up.

Liu Wei's Loyalty: 80/100

The poor kid's been through a lot. A little positive attention, and he's practically eating out of my hand. In any other situation, I'd feel bad about manipulating him like this, but in this world . . . I need all the allies I can get. As long as he doesn't betray me, he can join me in reaching the peak.

"Master," Liu Wei spoke up, interrupting Kai's thoughts. "Do you think the village elders will be upset we were gone so long?"

Kai shook his head. "I doubt it. We were only gone about a week. That's pretty fast for a round trip to the Whispering Woods."

As they entered the village, Kai noticed something . . . off. The usual bustle was subdued. People moved with an air of . . . was that nervousness?

What's going on here? Kai wondered. *It's like everyone's on their best behavior. Could it be . . .*

His thoughts were interrupted by the sight of Zhang Wei hurrying towards them. The old man's eyes widened as he noticed Zhi-Zhi.

"Kai, my boy! You're back!" Zhang Wei exclaimed, before his gaze fixed on the tortoise. "But . . . what is a spirit beast doing here?"

Before Kai could respond, Zhi-Zhi puffed up his tiny chest and spoke in what he clearly thought was an impressive voice. "I am their master."

Zhang Wei's jaw dropped. He looked from Zhi-Zhi to Kai, then back again. Seeing no one contradict the tortoise, he bowed deeply. "Forgive me, honored spirit beast. I didn't realize—"

Kai couldn't hold back his laughter. "Stand up, Elder Zhang. There's no need for that. We helped Zhi-Zhi out of a tight spot, and now he's traveling with us. That's all."

Zhi-Zhi deflated a bit. "I didn't need help," he muttered. "No one can break my shell."

Ignoring the pouting tortoise, Kai turned back to Zhang Wei. "Now, what's got everyone so worked up? The village feels . . . tense."

Zhang Wei's eyes lit up. "Ah, yes! I'm so glad you made it back in time. The Outer Elder from the Azure Sky Sect arrived a few hours ago. Tomorrow, he'll be testing the youth of the village for cultivation potential!"

"That's great news," Kai replied. "But I assume Liu Wei and I don't need to be tested?"

Zhang Wei nodded. "Correct. You've both already entered the Qi Refining Realm. But . . ." He lowered his voice. "I've arranged for you to meet the Outer Elder tonight. At my house. For dinner."

"Tonight?" Kai blinked. "Elder Zhang, I appreciate the thought, but we've been traveling for days. We're tired, dirty—"

"Nonsense!" Zhang Wei waved off Kai's concerns. "This is a once-in-a-lifetime opportunity! You need to make a good first impression if you want to go far. Now, listen carefully. There are some things you need to know about proper etiquette . . ."

For the next several minutes, Zhang Wei rattled off a list of do's and don'ts that made Kai's head spin.

"Always address him as 'Honored Elder.' Never speak unless spoken to. Keep your eyes lowered, but not so low that it seems disrespectful. If he offers you a cup of tea, accept it with both hands. Sip it slowly, but not too slowly. If he asks you a question, answer truthfully, but don't volunteer information . . ."

Jesus Christ, Kai thought. *I grew up in America. What do I know about all this bowing and scraping?*

But Kai knew the stakes. One wrong move, one perceived slight, and he could kiss his cultivation dreams goodbye. Or worse, get slapped into paste by an offended Outer Elder.

" . . . and whatever you do, don't mention the Crimson Phoenix Sect. The Azure Sky Sect has a blood feud with them going back three thousand years. Got all that?" Zhang Wei finally finished, looking expectantly at Kai.

If it wasn't for cultivation boosting my memory, I wouldn't have a prayer remembering all this, Kai thought. But outwardly, he just nodded. "I understand, Elder Zhang. Thank you for the guidance."

Zhang Wei beamed. "Excellent! Now, go get cleaned up. I need to prepare for dinner. Oh, and Kai?"

"Yes, Elder?"

"I'm proud of you, boy. You've come a long way in a short time. I know you'll make a good impression tonight."

As Zhang Wei hurried off, Kai felt a warmth in his chest that had nothing to do with qi cultivation. He pushed the feeling aside, focusing on the task at hand.

"Liu Wei," he said, turning to his companion. "Get some rest. We've got a big night ahead of us."

Liu Wei bowed. "Yes, Master Kai. And . . . thank you. For everything."

As Liu Wei headed off to his own hut, Kai was left alone with Zhi-Zhi. The little tortoise looked from Kai to the simple mud-brick structure that served as Kai's home.

Zhi-Zhi sighed dramatically. "You really are a village boy, aren't you?"

Kai just shook his head, smiling. "Come on, oh wise and ancient one. Let's get you settled in."

Inside the hut, Kai quickly set about cleaning himself up. As he splashed water on his face from a wooden basin, he caught sight of his reflection. The face that looked back at him was leaner, harder than it had been just a few weeks ago.

I've changed. This world is changing me.

"So," Zhi-Zhi's voice piped up from where he was exploring the small space. "This is how mortals live? It's so . . . primitive."

Kai dried his face with a rough cloth. "Not all mortals. Just us simple village folk."

"Hmph," Zhi-Zhi snorted. "I still can't believe you're not from a big city. You seem too . . . I don't know. Worldly?"

"There's a lot you don't know about me," Kai laughed.

More than you could possibly imagine, he added silently.

As Kai changed into his cleanest set of robes—which, admittedly, weren't that clean—he found his mind wandering to the upcoming dinner. Meeting an Outer Elder of the Azure Sky Sect . . . it was a big deal. Possibly a game-changer.

I need to play this smart. Make a good impression.

"Hey," Zhi-Zhi called out, interrupting Kai's musings. "What am I supposed to do while you're at this fancy dinner?"

Kai turned to the tortoise, considering. "You know, that's a good question. I don't think bringing a spirit beast to dinner would be appropriate. Even if you are our 'master.'"

Zhi-Zhi puffed up indignantly. "I am a noble spirit beast! Descended from the great Dragon Turtle! I should be the guest of honor at any dinner!"

"Uh-huh," Kai said, unconvinced. "And how many great and noble spirit beasts do you know who live in mud huts and eat porridge?"

Zhi-Zhi deflated. "Well . . . when you put it that way . . ."

"Tell you what," Kai said, kneeling down to the tortoise's level. "Why don't you stay here and meditate? Work on your cultivation. I'm sure a wise and powerful being like yourself has many profound insights to contemplate."

Zhi-Zhi's eyes lit up. "You're right! I shall enter deep meditation and unravel the mysteries of the universe!"

That should keep him occupied, Kai thought with amusement. *And out of trouble.*

As the sun began to set, Kai made his way to Zhang Wei's home. The old man's dwelling was larger than most in the village, befitting his status as an elder, but it was still modest by any real standard.

Liu Wei was already there, looking nervous but clean in a set of borrowed robes. Zhang Wei ushered them inside, fussing over their appearance.

"Remember," the old man hissed as he straightened Kai's collar. "Address him as 'Honored Elder.' Keep your eyes lowered, but not too low. And for heaven's sake, don't mention—"

"The Crimson Phoenix Sect," Kai finished for him. "I remember, Elder Zhang. Don't worry."

Zhang Wei nodded, but he still looked worried. "Good, good. Now, let me go check on the food. You two wait here."

As Zhang Wei bustled off to the kitchen, Kai turned to Liu Wei. The young man was fidgeting with the sleeves of his robe.

"Nervous?" Kai asked.

Liu Wei nodded. "I've never met anyone important before. Well, except you, Master Kai."

Kai raised an eyebrow. "I'm not that important, Liu Wei."

"You are to me," Liu Wei said quietly. "You saved me from the bandits. Gave me a chance at a real life. At cultivation."

Kai felt that warmth in his chest again. "Just follow my lead," he said aloud. "And remember what Elder Zhang told us. We'll be fine."

Before Liu Wei could respond, there was a commotion outside. The sound of raised voices, shuffling feet. Then, a presence. It was like the air itself grew heavier, charged with an invisible energy.

Qi, Kai realized. *I'm sensing his qi.*

The door swung open, and a figure stepped through. He was tall, imposing, dressed in blue and white robes. His face was ageless, neither young nor old, with eyes that held the wisdom of centuries.

This, Kai knew without being told, was the Outer Elder of the Azure Sky Sect.

CHAPTER TWENTY-FOUR

Zhang Wei hurried forward, bowing deeply. "Honored Elder Feng, these are the young cultivators I was telling you about, Kai Thorn and Liu Wei."

Kai and Liu Wei bowed low, careful to keep their eyes respectfully lowered as Zhang Wei had instructed.

Elder Feng's gaze swept over them, lingering on Kai. "Rise, young ones. Let me look at you properly."

As Kai straightened, he felt the weight of the Elder's qi pressing against him. It was potent, far beyond anything he'd sensed from any other cultivator. But compared to the overwhelming presence of Zhi-Zhi's mother, the Ancient Spirit Tree . . .

This is nothing, Kai thought, suppressing a smile. *But then again, if an Outer Elder was at the Nascent Soul Realm, Azure Sky Sect would probably be the number one sect in the whole kingdom, not just one of the greater sects in the region.*

And as if triggered by Kai's thoughts . . .

> Name: Feng Yuliang
> Title: Outer Elder of Azure Sky Sect
> Cultivation: Pseudo Core Formation Realm
> Your Level is too low to observe the character's stats.

Pseudo Core Formation? That's a transition stage between Foundation Establishment and true Core Formation. Interesting. If an Outer Elder is at this level, the main elders are probably at Nascent Soul. And the Sect Master . . . who knows?

Kai suppressed a smirk as he recalled some of the more ridiculous realm names he'd encountered in xianxia novels. *Origin Realm? Ascendant Realm?*

Heavenly Dao? Creators really just make up whatever sounds cool after a certain point.

Kai's musings on cultivation realms were interrupted as Elder Feng's eyes widened fractionally. "Young Kai, Zhang Wei told me you were progressing rapidly through the Qi Refining stages, but I didn't expect this. You're already at the seventh stage?"

Kai bowed his head slightly. "This junior has been fortunate in his cultivation, thanks to Elder Zhang's guidance."

Elder Feng waved off Kai's humble response. "No need for false modesty. Even starting later than most, you're already surpassing many Outer Disciples. Well done."

Zhang Wei beamed with pride as though it was him who was praised.

Elder Feng's gaze sharpened as it fell on Liu Wei. "And you . . . I hear you used to be a bandit."

Liu Wei's face flushed with shame. "I . . . I was forced into it, Honored Elder. I never wanted—"

Elder Feng raised a hand, silencing him. "Your heart will be tested in the trials. If the Azure Sky Sect finds any trace of demonic cultivator tendencies, you will not be allowed to enter. Understand?"

Liu Wei nodded, eyes downcast. "Yes, Honored Elder."

Kai felt a pang of sympathy for Liu Wei. *Poor guy. He's too soft-hearted to have any demonic tendencies. It's me they should be worried about.*

"Dinner's ready, let's eat!" Zhang Wei announced.

As they moved to the dining area, Kai's thoughts turned inward. *I hope they don't realize just how selfish I really am. Let's hope their tests aren't too thorough.*

The group settled around the low table, kneeling on cushions as servants brought out dishes of steamed fish, fragrant rice, and various vegetable dishes. The meal began in silence, broken only by the clink of chopsticks against bowls.

Elder Feng took a sip of tea, then turned to Zhang Wei. "Old friend, your cooking is as delightful as ever. You should have joined the Azure Sky Sect's kitchen instead of attempting Foundation Establishment."

Zhang Wei chuckled, but Kai noticed the slight tightening around his eyes. "You flatter me, Honored Elder. I'm just glad I can still be of some use to the sect, even in my . . . diminished state."

Kai observed the interaction closely. *Despite calling Zhang Wei "old friend," there's a clear power dynamic here. Zhang Wei is practically kowtowing with every word.*

"Nonsense," Elder Feng said, waving his hand. "Your eye for talent is as sharp as ever. These two boys are proof of that."

Liu Wei, who had been quiet until now, hesitantly spoke up. "Honored Elder, may I ask . . . what are the trials like? For entering the sect?"

"Worried about your past, are you?" Elder Feng's eyes narrowed slightly. "The trials test more than just cultivation level. They probe the very essence of a cultivator's spirit. Those with impure hearts or evil intentions will be rejected, no matter their talent."

Liu Wei swallowed hard and nodded, returning his attention to his bowl.

Kai decided to steer the conversation in a different direction. "Elder Feng, I'm curious about the Azure Sky Sect's specialties. I've heard your wind and lightning techniques are unparalleled."

The elder's eyes lit up. "Ah, a young man with good taste! Indeed, our Thundercloud Palm and Gale Step techniques are renowned throughout the cultivation world. But tell me, young Kai, what element calls to you?"

"Lightning," Kai replied without hesitation. "I find its raw power and speed fascinating."

Elder Feng nodded approvingly. "A fine choice. Lightning cultivation is challenging but rewarding. Perhaps, if you join our sect, I could give you some pointers."

The meal continued, with Elder Feng telling them tales of the Azure Sky Sect's glorious history. Kai listened attentively, filing away every piece of information for future use. *Knowledge is power, especially in a world like this.*

As the final dishes were cleared away, Elder Feng set down his teacup and fixed Kai with an intense gaze. "Young Kai, I will be honest, you've caught my eye. I rarely take personal disciples, but I see great potential in you. How would you like to become my disciple, here and now?"

I knew this was coming, Kai thought. *If I were in his position, I'd do the same. Snatch up the promising recruit before anyone else gets the chance.*

He glanced at Zhang Wei and saw the old man's smile falter. The look in his eyes clearly said, *Politely refuse.*

Kai bowed deeply. "Honored Elder, I'm deeply grateful for your offer, but . . . I'm not ready to make such a momentous decision yet. I'd like to complete the trials and enter the Azure Sky Sect properly before considering such an honor."

Elder Feng laughed, a sound that didn't quite reach his eyes. "My boy, if I take you as my disciple right now, you won't need to compete in any trials. You'll become an Azure Sky Sect disciple immediately."

Kai's smile stiffened slightly. *This elder is persistent. He knows I'm making excuses, but he won't back down.*

"Thank you again, Honored Elder," Kai said carefully. "But I still feel I need time to think about it. This is a life-changing decision, after all."

The warmth drained from Elder Feng's face. "You misunderstand, young Kai. I decide who joins the sect. If you're not interested in my generous offer, perhaps the Azure Sky Sect has no need of you at all."

Zhang Wei's eyes widened in alarm. "Honored Elder, please. The boy means no disrespect. He's simply overwhelmed by your generosity."

Kai's eyes narrowed. *He's trying to intimidate me. But he won't actually harm me. His reputation as a righteous cultivator is too important, and if word got back to the sect that he killed a prodigy for rejecting his offer, he'd lose his role. And it's not like he'd be able to stop word from getting back, Zhang Wei would make sure the sect heard about it.*

Just to be sure, Kai glanced at his map. The green dot representing Elder Feng remained unchanged. *Still not hostile. Time to push back a little.*

Kai smiled, the expression not quite reaching his eyes. "Actually, Honored Elder, during our recent trip to the Whispering Woods, the Crimson Phoenix Sect expressed interest in recruiting me. If the Azure Sky Sect isn't interested, perhaps I should consider their offer instead."

Zhang Wei's face went from pale to ashen. Kai could almost hear the old man's voice in his head, *I told you not to mention them!*

Elder Feng's face turned serious, his aura flaring. The pressure of his Pseudo Core Formation cultivation bore down on Kai like a physical weight, making it difficult to breathe.

CHAPTER TWENTY-FIVE

Y ou dare," Feng growled, his voice low and dangerous. "You dare mention those crimson demons in my presence?"

Maybe I pushed a little too hard there, but I can't back down now, Kai thought, fighting to keep his breathing steady. *This is definitely a dialogue tree with major consequences. I need to choose my words carefully. Too aggressive, and I'll trigger a combat event. Too submissive, and I'll lose reputation points with the Azure Sky Sect.*

"I only wished to be transparent about my options," Kai managed to say, his voice strained but still steady. "They seemed quite eager to recruit new talent. I thought it's important to consider all opportunities. Surely a sect as great as Azure Sky isn't threatened by a little competition?"

For a moment, it seemed as though Outer Elder Feng might actually strike Kai. The air crackled with qi, and both Zhang Wei and Liu Wei looked ready to intervene, futile as it might be.

But then Feng threw back his head and laughed. The oppressive aura vanished as quickly as it had appeared.

"You've got spirit, I'll give you that," Feng said, wiping a tear from his eye. "Not many would dare to speak to me like that, let alone mention those red-robed bastards."

He fixed Kai with an appraising look. "Very well. You want to prove yourself in the trials? So be it. But know this, I'll be watching your performance very closely. Impress me, and my offer still stands. Disappoint me . . ." His eyes hardened. "Well, let's just say you'd be better off with a second-rate righteous sect like those Crimson Phoenix bastards."

"Thank you for your understanding, Outer Elder." Kai bowed. "I won't let you down."

As he straightened, Kai caught Zhang Wei's eye. The old man looked both relieved and exasperated.

Sorry, old man, Kai thought. *But I'm not about to let anyone railroad me into a decision, no matter how powerful they are.*

"Now then," Feng said, his tone lighter as he settled back onto his cushion. "Tell me more about this encounter with the Crimson Phoenix Sect. What exactly did they say to you?"

Kai's mind raced. He had never actually met anyone from the Crimson Phoenix Sect. This was a dangerous game he was playing, but he couldn't back down now. He'd have to fabricate a story, and fast.

Keep it vague, he told himself. *Don't give too many details that could be disproven.*

"It was during our journey to the Whispering Woods," Kai began, keeping his voice steady. "We encountered a group of cultivators wearing crimson robes. At first, we thought they might be bandits or rogue cultivators, but their demeanor was . . . different."

Feng leaned forward, his eyes intense. "Different how?"

"They weren't like rogue cultivators, they were disciplined, organized. Their leader approached us directly. He said they were scouting for new talent in the region."

Kai paused, gauging Feng's reaction. The Outer Elder's face remained impassive, but there was a tightness around his eyes that suggested barely contained anger.

"Go on."

"They spoke of opportunities their sect could offer—advanced cultivation techniques, access to rare resources. It was . . . intriguing, I'll admit."

Liu Wei shifted uncomfortably beside Kai, clearly confused by this fabricated story. Kai shot him a warning glance, silently urging him to stay quiet.

"And what did you tell them?" Feng asked, his tone dangerously soft.

Kai allowed a small smile. "I told them I was flattered by their interest, but that I had other plans. Specifically, that I was hoping to join the Azure Sky Sect."

Feng's eyebrows rose slightly. "Oh? And how did they react to that?"

"They seemed . . . disappointed," Kai said, choosing his words carefully. "They made some disparaging remarks about Azure Sky's traditions, implying that I'd be wasting my potential."

A low growl escaped Feng's throat, but he quickly composed himself. "I see. And you weren't swayed by their . . . persuasive arguments?"

Kai shook his head firmly. "No, Outer Elder. I've heard stories of the Azure Sky Sect from Elder Zhang, he had already convinced me to join the sect. The

Crimson Phoenix Sect might be a powerful rival, but I trust Elder Zhang's judgement. I just hope the trust isn't misplaced."

He was laying it on thick, and he knew it. But from the pleased glint in Feng's eye, it seemed to be working.

"Well said, young Kai," Feng nodded approvingly. "Those devils were trying to lead you astray. You were right to listen to old Zhang. Perhaps I was too hasty in my judgment earlier."

As Kai began to relax, thinking he had successfully navigated this dangerous conversation, Feng suddenly leaned forward, his eyes boring into Kai's.

"Tell me, did they mention any specific plans? Locations they were interested in?"

Kai's heart raced. This was the most dangerous part of his deception. He needed to provide something that sounded valuable without being too specific. His mind quickly cycled through common tropes from xianxia stories he'd read back on Earth.

Secret realm opening? Heavenly tribulation? Ancient inheritance? Come on, there's got to be something generic enough to be believable . . .

"They were careful not to reveal too much," Kai said, feigning thoughtfulness. "But . . . I do remember overhearing something about a 'Celestial Alignment' happening soon. They seemed quite focused on preparing for it, though I'm not sure of the details."

Kai held his breath, hoping he'd struck the right balance. In most xianxia stories, celestial events were prime opportunities for breakthroughs or accessing hidden realms. If the Azure Sky Sect and Crimson Phoenix Sect were truly rivals, it wasn't far-fetched that they'd both be interested in such an event.

Feng's eyes widened fractionally, a flash of recognition crossing his face before he schooled his features back into neutrality.

"I see," he said, his voice thoughtful. "That is . . . interesting information. Thank you for sharing it."

As Feng turned to engage Zhang Wei in conversation, Kai felt a subtle shift in his consciousness. A System notification appeared before him.

Skill Leveled Up!
You have successfully deceived a high-level cultivator.
Your ability to craft believable lies and maintain composure under pressure has improved.
Deception has reached Level 4!

Kai suppressed a smile. *Well, that's certainly useful. Though I'll need to be careful not to rely on it too much. In this world, getting caught in a lie could be fatal.*

The rest of the evening passed in a blur of polite conversation and veiled probing questions. Kai carefully navigated the social minefield, revealing just enough information to satisfy Outer Elder Feng's curiosity without giving away too much.

As the night wore on, Feng finally stood. "Well, this has been an . . . interesting evening. I look forward to seeing how you perform in the trials, young Kai. Don't disappoint me."

With that, Elder Feng strode towards the door, pausing only to nod at Zhang Wei. "Thank you for your hospitality, old friend. We'll speak again soon."

As the door closed behind the Outer Elder, the tension in the room finally broke. Zhang Wei collapsed into his chair, wiping sweat from his brow.

"By the heavens, boy," he gasped, staring at Kai with a mix of awe and horror. "What were you thinking, mentioning the Crimson Phoenix Sect? I told you specifically not to bring them up!"

Kai allowed himself a small smile. "I'm sorry for worrying you, Elder Zhang. But it worked out in the end, didn't it?"

Liu Wei shook his head in disbelief. "Master Kai, that was . . . I've never seen anyone stand up to a powerful cultivator like that before."

"Don't praise him!" Zhang Wei snapped. "That kind of recklessness could have gotten us all killed!"

Kai raised his hands in the air. "I understand your concern, Elder Zhang. But I had a feeling Elder Feng wouldn't actually harm us. He's too smart for that."

Zhang Wei sighed. "You're playing with fire, Kai. The rivalry between the Azure Sky Sect and the Crimson Phoenix Sect goes back centuries. It's not something to be used as a bargaining chip."

"I know," Kai said, his expression turning serious. "But I couldn't let him strong-arm me into becoming his disciple. Something about that offer felt . . . off."

Zhang Wei nodded slowly. "You're not wrong. Feng has always been ambitious. Taking a prodigy like you as his personal disciple would have raised his status in the sect considerably whilst also limiting your development . . ."

He didn't need to finish the thought. Kai understood all too well. *Politics. It's always politics, no matter what world you're in.*

"What do we do now?" Liu Wei asked.

Kai stood, stretching muscles that had been tense throughout the confrontation. "Now? We prepare for the trials. Once we arrive at the Azure Sky Sect, an Outer Elder like Feng Yuliang wouldn't mean much."

Zhang Wei nodded approvingly. "Well said. But Kai . . ." his expression grew stern, "no more reckless gambles. The cultivation world is not a game. One wrong move could cost you everything."

If only you knew, Kai thought, suppressing a smile. *But you're right. I need to be more careful.*

"I understand, Elder Zhang," he said aloud. "Thank you for your guidance. And . . . I'm sorry for causing you so much stress tonight."

The old man waved off the apology. "What's done is done. Get some rest, both of you. Oh, and remember to attend the Talent Ceremony tomorrow!"

CHAPTER TWENTY-SIX

The morning sun peeked over the horizon, casting a golden glow across the Misty Waterfall Village. Kai stood at the edge of the town square, watching as villagers began to gather for the Talent Ceremony.

Liu Wei shifted beside him, his eyes darting nervously among the crowd. "It feels strange not to be participating, Master. Do you think the other villagers will resent us for already being cultivators?"

Kai shook his head, his gaze steady as he scanned the crowd. "I doubt it, Liu Wei. Most of them are probably too focused on their own chances to worry about us."

Not that it matters what they think anyway. In this world, strength is what counts. As long as they can't harm us, their opinions are irrelevant.

Sat on top of Liu Wei's head, Zhi-Zhi puffed out his tiny chest. "Besides, they should be honored to witness my presence at such an event!"

Kai suppressed a smile. *This little guy's ego is something else.*

"Let's focus on observing the ceremony," Kai said, his voice low. "We might spot potential allies or rivals among the candidates."

Liu Wei nodded, his posture relaxing slightly. "You're right, Master."

As more villagers filed into the square, Kai noticed Elder Zhang bustling about, directing people and ensuring everything was in order. The old man's face was a mixture of excitement and worry.

He's probably concerned about how I'll behave after last night's . . . eventful dinner, Kai thought.

Near the center of the square, a simple wooden chair had been set up on a raised platform. Next to it stood a small table with a velvet cloth draped over it.

"Look," Liu Wei whispered, pointing. "That must be where the Outer Elder will sit."

Kai nodded. "And I bet that cloth is covering some sort of testing crystal."

As if on cue, a hush fell over the crowd. Outer Elder Feng strode into the square, his blue and white robes billowing slightly in the morning breeze. Trailing behind Feng was a frail-looking old man Kai vaguely recognized as the village leader.

I almost forgot that guy existed. Elder Zhang does all the real work around here.

The village leader cleared his throat and addressed the crowd in a wavering voice. "Esteemed villagers, welcome to this year's Talent Ceremony! We are honored to have Outer Elder Feng of the Azure Sky Sect with us today. He will test our youth for cultivation potential using the sacred Spirit Essence Crystal."

A murmur of excitement rippled through the gathering. Kai watched as parents hugged their children, whispering words of encouragement.

In every xianxia novel I've read, this is always a big moment, Kai thought. *The start of the protagonist's journey. I'd better keep my eyes open.*

Elder Feng took his seat on the wooden chair, his piercing gaze sweeping over the assembled villagers. When his eyes met Kai's, there was a flicker of . . . something but it was gone too quickly to tell.

"Let us begin," Feng announced, his voice carrying easily across the square. He reached for the velvet cloth and pulled it away, revealing a palm-sized crystal that seemed to glow with an inner light.

Elder Zhang stepped forward, unrolling a scroll. "We will proceed in alphabetical order. When your name is called, please step forward and place your hand on the crystal."

The first name was called, and a nervous-looking boy of about fifteen stumbled forward. He placed a trembling hand on the crystal, and . . . nothing happened. The crystal remained dark.

Feng's face remained impassive. "Next," he called out.

And so it went. One by one, the village youth approached the crystal. Most produced no reaction at all. A few caused the crystal to flicker weakly, drawing gasps from the crowd.

Liu Wei leaned in close to Kai. "Master, how bright does the crystal need to get for someone to be accepted?"

Kai kept his eyes on the proceedings as he answered. "I'm not too sure but from what I can see, it needs to glow steadily for at least a few seconds. A weak flicker isn't enough."

Zhi-Zhi snorted. "If I touched that crystal, it would probably explode from my immense spiritual power!"

Kai and Liu Wei exchanged amused glances but said nothing.

As the ceremony continued, Kai found his mind wandering. *I wonder if this is how the System chose me back on Earth. Some cosmic crystal deciding I had the right "stats" to be isekai'd?*

His thoughts were interrupted by a collective gasp from the crowd. Kai's attention snapped back to the platform, where a young girl stood with her hand on the crystal. It was glowing steadily, brighter than it had for anyone else so far.

Elder Feng leaned forward, his eyes narrowing slightly. "Interesting," he murmured. "You have some potential, child. Not enough for the Azure Sky Sect, but perhaps one of the smaller sects would take you on."

The girl's face fell slightly, but her family erupted in cheers. Kai could understand their excitement. Even the chance to join a minor sect was a big deal in a village like this.

As the girl stepped down, Elder Zhang called out the next name. "Shen Yu, please step forward."

A young man detached himself from the crowd. Kai estimated him to be around sixteen, with a lean build and sharp features. What caught Kai's attention, however, was the boy's eyes. They were calm, almost unnaturally so for someone about to face a life-changing test.

I don't know much about this one, Kai realized. *He's always kept to himself. Could he be . . .*

As Shen Yu approached the crystal, the crowd fell silent. Even Liu Wei and Zhi-Zhi stopped their whispered commentary, caught up in the tension of the moment.

Shen Yu placed his hand on the crystal without hesitation. For a moment, nothing happened. Then, slowly, a faint glow began to emanate from the stone. It grew steadily brighter, until it surpassed any glow before it.

Outer Elder Feng nodded, a small smile playing at the corners of his mouth. "Well done, Shen Yu. You have earned the right to attempt our trials."

The crowd cheered again, but Kai barely heard them. His eyes were fixed on Shen Yu's face, watching for any reaction.

There was none.

No shock. No joy. No relief. Shen Yu's expression remained as calm and unreadable as it had been before the test.

That's not normal, Kai thought, his mind racing. *A village boy with the chance to enter an immortal sect should be ecstatic, or at least surprised. Unless . . .*

"Master Kai?" Liu Wei's voice broke through his thoughts. "Is something wrong?"

Kai shook his head slightly. "No, nothing's wrong. Just . . . thinking."

As Shen Yu melted back into the crowd, Kai's mind whirled with possibilities. *Could he be a hidden protagonist? A reincarnator? A regressor? In xianxia novels, there's always someone with a secret past or future knowledge.*

He ran through the possibilities:

Reincarnator: Someone reborn into this world with memories of their past life.

Regressor: Someone who's lived through these events before and come back in time to change things. They'd know exactly what to expect, which could explain Shen Yu's lack of reaction.

Hidden Protagonist: Someone with a secret background or special ability, waiting for the right moment to reveal themselves.

Or, Kai reminded himself, *he could just be an unusually calm teenager. Not everything has to follow story logic.*

Still, Kai made a mental note to keep an eye on Shen Yu. In a world of cultivation and immortal sects, it paid to be cautious.

Elder Feng's voice cut through Kai's thoughts. "We will depart for the Azure Sky Sect in three days. Those who have been selected should prepare themselves. When we arrive at the sect, that is when the real trial begins."

As he said this last part, Feng's eyes locked onto Kai. There was a clear message in that gaze: You'd better be ready.

Then, almost as an afterthought, Feng's gaze shifted slightly. His eyes widened as he noticed Zhi-Zhi perched on top of Liu Wei's head.

Crap, Kai thought. *He seems interested in our little "master" here.*

As the crowd began to disperse, chattering excitedly about the results of the ceremony, Kai felt a hand on his shoulder. He turned to see Elder Zhang, looking both relieved and apprehensive.

"Kai, my boy," Zhang said in a low voice. "A word, if you please."

Kai nodded. "Of course, Elder Zhang. Liu Wei, why don't you take Zhi-Zhi back to my hut? I'll meet you there later."

Liu Wei bowed slightly. "Yes, Master."

As Liu Wei walked away, Zhi-Zhi's voice could be heard complaining. "But I wanted to show that Outer Elder my true power! He would have begged me to join his sect!"

Kai followed Elder Zhang to a quiet corner of the square. The old man's face was creased with worry.

"Kai," Zhang began, "I hope you understand the opportunity before you. The Azure Sky Sect is one of the most prestigious in the region. If you impress them during the trials . . ."

Kai held up a hand. "I understand, Elder Zhang. I won't let you down."

Zhang's expression softened. "I know you won't, my boy. It's just . . . after last night's dinner, I worry that you might . . . ruffle some feathers."

Kai couldn't help but smile. "You mean you're worried I'll mouth off to the wrong person and get myself killed?"

Zhang winced. "Well, I wouldn't put it quite so bluntly, but . . . yes."

"Don't worry," Kai said, his voice taking on a serious tone. "I know how to play the game. I'll be on my best behavior."

As long as no one tries to take advantage of me, he added silently.

Zhang studied Kai's face for a moment, then nodded. "Very well. I trust you, Kai. Just remember, one wrong move can be fatal."

"I'll remember," Kai promised. *Trust me, old man, I've read enough xianxia to know how cutthroat this world can be.*

As Elder Zhang walked away, Kai's gaze drifted back to where Shen Yu stood, still as calm and unruffled as before. The boy's parents were hugging him, tears of joy streaming down their faces, but Shen Yu's expression remained neutral.

There's definitely more to that kid than meets the eye, Kai thought. *I'll need to keep a close watch on him during the trials.*

With that thought, Kai turned and began making his way back to his hut. He had a lot to prepare for in the next three days.

As Kai walked through the village, he couldn't help but notice the change in atmosphere. Everywhere he looked, people were talking excitedly about the Talent Ceremony and Shen Yu's success.

"Did you see how the crystal lit up for him?"

"I always knew that Shen boy was special!"

"Do you think he'll become a great cultivator?"

Kai tuned out the chatter, his mind focused on the tasks ahead. *I need to make sure I'm fully prepared for these trials. Who knows what kind of tests the Azure Sky Sect will throw at us?*

As he approached his hut, he heard raised voices from inside.

Kai sighed. *What are those two arguing about now?*

He pushed open the door to find Liu Wei and Zhi-Zhi in the middle of a heated debate.

"I'm telling you, I could have made that crystal explode with my power!" Zhi-Zhi was saying, his tiny face scrunched up in indignation.

Liu Wei rolled his eyes. "And I'm telling you, Master Zhi-Zhi, that's not how the test works. It's not about raw power, it's about potential and affinity."

"Hmph!" Zhi-Zhi turned his back on Liu Wei. "What do you know about it, anyway? You're just a former bandit!"

Liu Wei's face flushed with anger, but before he could retort, Kai cleared his throat loudly.

Both Liu Wei and Zhi-Zhi turned to look at him, their argument forgotten for the moment.

"Master Kai!" Liu Wei said, bowing slightly. "How did your talk with Elder Zhang go?"

Kai moved into the hut, closing the door behind him. "It went fine. He's just worried about how we'll behave at the Azure Sky Sect."

Zhi-Zhi puffed up his chest. "He needn't worry about me! I'll show those sect elders what true nobility looks like!"

Kai and Liu Wei exchanged glances, both trying not to laugh.

"I'm sure you will, Zhi-Zhi," Kai said, keeping his voice neutral. "But for now, we need to focus on preparing for the journey and the trials ahead."

Liu Wei nodded eagerly. "What should we do first, Master Kai?"

If this were a game, now would be the time to grind for experience and upgrade our equipment. Kai thought as he sat down on a simple wooden stool. *But apart from that Roach Carapace Fragment, I don't have any other materials that could make a worthwhile item.*

"Well, it's too late to attempt another breakthrough now," Kai said aloud. "Instead, we need to make sure we have a few techniques up our sleeves. It's time I teach you some techniques!"

CHAPTER TWENTY-SEVEN

Kai sat cross-legged in the fields outside his little hut. Opposite him, Liu Wei mirrored his position, his expression a mix of eagerness and nervousness. To Kai's right, Zhi-Zhi sat on a smooth stone.

"All right, Liu Wei," Kai began. "We're going to start with the Swift Wind Step technique."

"I've been looking forward to learning this for years, Master!" Liu Wei exclaimed.

Kai smiled, pleased by Liu Wei's enthusiasm. "Well, thanks to that fruit you ate in the Whispering Woods, which boosted your wind affinity by 20%, you're in an excellent position to learn it quickly."

"I'm ready to begin but Master," Liu Wei said, his brow furrowing in confusion, "why focus on this technique specifically? Wouldn't it be better to work on overall qi cultivation with the Azure Sky Sect trials so close?"

"Good question. In a perfect world, we'd have time to round out all aspects of your cultivation. But we don't have that luxury. The trials are just around the corner, and we need to play to your strengths." Kai paused, letting his words sink in. "Your main advantage is your speed and agility. The Swift Wind Step will enhance those natural talents. In a trial situation, being able to move quickly and unpredictably could make all the difference."

It's basic gaming strategy. Buff your strongest stats first, especially when you're on a time crunch.

Liu Wei's eyes lit up with understanding. "I see! So, we're focusing on what I'm already good at, rather than trying to improve my weaknesses."

"Exactly," Kai nodded approvingly. "In the long run, we'll work on all aspects of your cultivation. But for now, we need to make you as formidable as possible in your areas of strength."

Zhi-Zhi, who had been uncharacteristically quiet until now, suddenly spoke up. "Ah, yes! As the ancient saying goes: 'A fish that swims faster than the current need not worry about the direction of the river.'"

Kai and Liu Wei exchanged puzzled glances.

"Um, Zhi-Zhi," Kai began gently, "I'm not sure that saying really applies here. Or . . . exists at all."

The tortoise puffed up indignantly. "Of course it does! It's a very old and wise saying. You humans simply haven't lived long enough to hear it."

Right, because you're such an ancient and wise being at the ripe old age of . . . what, a hundred? Kai thought, suppressing a smirk. Instead, he reached out and patted Zhi-Zhi's shell. "Of course, Zhi-Zhi. Thank you for sharing your wisdom with us."

Looking pleased with himself, the tortoise settled back onto his stone.

Turning his attention back to Liu Wei, Kai took a moment to gather his thoughts. When he'd used the Skill Scroll for Swift Wind Step, the scroll had disintegrated, its knowledge absorbed directly into his mind. He understood the technique on a fundamental level but translating that understanding into teachable instructions was proving to be a challenge.

It's like trying to explain how to ride a bike. You know how to do it, but putting it into words is trickier than you'd expect.

"Okay," Kai began, "the key to the Swift Wind Step is in the name itself. You're not just moving quickly, you're becoming one with the wind. Start by visualizing your qi as a gentle breeze flowing through your body."

Liu Wei closed his eyes, his face scrunching up in concentration.

"Don't force it," Kai advised. "Let the qi flow naturally, like a stream finding its path. Now, focus on your feet. Imagine the wind gathering there, coiling like a spring."

Liu Wei nodded, his eyes still closed.

"When you're ready to move, release that coiled energy. Let it propel you forward, but don't fight against it. Move with the flow of the wind."

Kai watched as Liu Wei's face twisted in confusion. *Maybe I'm being too abstract,* he thought. *Time for a more practical demonstration.*

"Here, let me show you," Kai said, standing up. He took a few steps back, giving himself some room. "Watch closely."

Kai closed his eyes, taking a deep breath. He felt his qi stirring, responding to his will. In his mind's eye, he saw it swirling around his feet, building up like a miniature cyclone. Then, with a sudden burst of energy, he released it.

To Liu Wei and Zhi-Zhi, it looked as if Kai had simply vanished. A heartbeat later, he reappeared several meters away, leaves and dust swirling in his wake.

"Wow!" Liu Wei exclaimed, his eyes wide with amazement. "That was incredible, Master!"

Even Zhi-Zhi looked impressed, though he quickly hid it behind a mask of indifference. "Hmph. I suppose that's somewhat impressive. For a human."

Kai walked back to his starting position, a slight smile on his face. "That's the basic idea. Now you try, Liu Wei. Remember, visualize the wind, gather it at your feet, then release."

Liu Wei nodded eagerly, getting to his feet. He closed his eyes, his face a mask of intense concentration. After a few moments, he opened his eyes and tried to move.

Instead of the graceful dash Kai had demonstrated, Liu Wei stumbled forward awkwardly, nearly falling flat on his face.

"That's . . . not quite right," Kai said, trying to keep the amusement out of his voice.

Liu Wei's face fell. "I don't understand. What am I doing wrong?"

Before Kai could respond, Zhi-Zhi spoke up. "Ah, young human, you're thinking about it all wrong! You need to be more . . . more . . ." The tortoise paused, clearly struggling to come up with something profound. "More wind-like! Yes, that's it. Be the wind!"

Liu Wei's confusion only seemed to deepen. "Be . . . the wind? How do I do that?"

Zhi-Zhi nodded sagely. "It's simple! Just . . . um . . . blow around? No, wait, that's not right. Swoosh! Yes, you need to swoosh!"

Kai couldn't help but chuckle at the tortoise's well-meaning but utterly useless advice. "I think what our wise friend is trying to say," he interjected, shooting an amused glance at Zhi-Zhi, "is that you need to relax more. You're too tense."

He stood up, walking over to Liu Wei. "Here, let me try to explain it differently. Forget about the wind for a moment. Focus on your body. Feel the energy flowing through you."

Liu Wei nodded, closing his eyes again.

"Now, imagine that energy gathering in your core," Kai continued, his voice calm and steady. "When you're ready to move, let that energy flow down to your feet, then push off with it. Don't try to control every aspect of the movement. Let your body flow with the energy."

Liu Wei's brow furrowed in concentration. He took a deep breath, held it for a moment, then exhaled slowly. Suddenly, he moved.

It wasn't as smooth or as fast as Kai's demonstration, but it was a definite improvement. Liu Wei managed to dash forward several steps before stumbling to a stop.

"That's it!" Kai exclaimed, genuinely pleased. "That's the basic idea. You just need to refine it now."

Liu Wei's face lit up with a mixture of pride and excitement. "I did it! I mean, it wasn't perfect, but I felt it! The energy, the movement . . . it was amazing!"

Zhi-Zhi huffed from his perch on the stone. "Well, I suppose it wasn't terrible. For a beginner."

Kai smiled at the tortoise's backhanded compliment. "High praise from our esteemed spirit beast friend."

Turning back to Liu Wei, Kai's expression grew more serious. "Now comes the hard part. You need to practice this over and over until it becomes second nature. The goal is to be able to use the Swift Wind Step without even thinking about it."

Liu Wei nodded eagerly. "I understand, Master Kai. I won't let you down!"

For the next hour, Liu Wei practiced the technique relentlessly. Each attempt brought small improvements, but also new challenges. Sometimes he would move too quickly and lose his balance. Other times, he wouldn't gather enough energy and would barely move at all.

Kai watched closely, offering advice and encouragement. "Remember, it's not just about speed. It's about control. Feel the flow of energy and move with it, not against it."

As Liu Wei continued to practice, Zhi-Zhi couldn't resist adding his own commentary. "Bah! What good is all this running around anyway? True strength lies in standing your ground!"

"Oh?" Kai raised an eyebrow at the tortoise. "And I suppose you'd just hide in your shell if an enemy attacked?"

"Hide?" Zhi-Zhi puffed up. "I never hide! I strategically defend myself with my impenetrable armor!"

Kai chuckled, reaching out to pat the tortoise's shell again. "Of course you do. But remember, Zhi-Zhi, not all of us are blessed with such formidable defenses. We fragile humans sometimes need to rely on speed and agility."

The tortoise seemed to consider this for a moment before nodding sagely. "Ah, yes. I suppose you poor, shell-less creatures must make do with what you have. Carry on with your running practice, then."

As Liu Wei continued his attempts, Kai found his mind wandering. *It's strange*, he thought. *In all the games I've played, learning skills was instantaneous. Click a button, spend some points, and bam! New ability unlocked. But here, even with my gamer-like abilities, learning a skill instantaneously is one thing, but you still got to put in the practice.*

He watched as Liu Wei made another attempt, this time managing to dash several meters before losing control and tumbling to the ground. The young man got up, brushing dirt from his clothes, a look of determination on his face.

He's got potential. More than I initially gave him credit for. With the right training, he could become a formidable cultivator.

A notification popped up in Kai's vision.

Liu Wei's Loyalty: 85/100

As Liu Wei prepared for another attempt, Kai called out, "Wait a moment, Liu Wei. Let's take a short break. You don't want to exhaust your qi reserves completely."

Liu Wei nodded, wiping sweat from his brow as he walked back to where Kai and Zhi-Zhi were sitting. He plopped down on the grass, breathing heavily.

"How am I doing, Master Kai?" he asked, a mix of hope and anxiety in his voice.

Kai considered his answer carefully. *In a game, I'd have exact stats to reference. Here, I have to rely on observation and intuition.* "You're making good progress," he said finally. "Your control is improving with each attempt. The key now is to make the movement more fluid, more natural."

Liu Wei nodded eagerly. "I think I understand. It's like . . . like when I used to scout for the bandits. I had to move quickly and quietly, without thinking about each individual step."

"That's a good analogy, Liu Wei. This technique isn't so different from that. The main difference is that you're using qi to enhance your natural abilities."

Just as Kai finished talking, he noticed a message pop up.

New Title Acquired: Novice Instructor

Description: Your efforts in teaching others have been recognized.

You now have a 5% increased chance of successfully imparting knowledge when instructing others in skills or techniques you know.

New System Feature Unlocked: Teaching XP

You can now earn XP from teaching. XP will be gained when a student successfully learns or improves in a skill you're teaching.

Kai's eyebrows rose slightly, but he managed to keep his expression neutral. *Another title, and a new System feature? This could be a game-changer.*

He quickly glanced at his existing title.

Village Protector

Description: You have proven yourself as a defender of Misty Waterfall Village.

+10% to all stats when fighting to protect the village or its inhabitants.

Interesting, Kai thought. *This new title is more specialized, but it could be incredibly valuable in the long run. Especially if I end up taking on more disciples in the future. And earning XP from teaching? That's a whole new avenue for progression.*

He pushed the thought aside, focusing on the task at hand. "All right, Liu Wei. Now that you've got the basic movement down, let's work on incorporating it into combat situations."

Liu Wei's eyes lit up with excitement. "Like how you used it against those rogue cultivators? That was incredible, Master. One moment you were there, the next you were behind them."

Kai nodded, pleased by Liu Wei's enthusiasm and recollection. "Exactly. The true power of the Swift Wind Step comes from how you use it in battle. It's not just about moving fast, it's about moving smart."

"I remember," Liu Wei said. "You used it to dodge attacks that seemed impossible to avoid, and to strike from unexpected angles. It was like you were everywhere at once."

"Those are exactly the kind of applications we'll be working on," Kai nodded. "The technique can be used both offensively and defensively."

"So, how do we practice these combat applications, Master?" Liu Wei asked eagerly.

"Let's set up a little test," Kai grinned. "I want you to try and tag me using the Swift Wind Step. Don't hold back, I can handle it."

"Tag you?" Liu Wei's eyes widened. "But Master, you're so much more skilled with the technique than I am."

"That's the point," Kai explained. "In a real battle, your opponents won't go easy on you. This will help you learn to use the technique under pressure. Remember how I used it against the rogue cultivators. Try to apply those same principles."

Liu Wei took a deep breath. "I understand. I'll do my best."

CHAPTER TWENTY-EIGHT

Before we start," Kai said, his expression turning serious, "I'm going to suppress my qi to stage three Qi Refining. It'll make things fairer and give you a fighting chance."

Kai closed his eyes, focusing inward at the qi flowing through his meridians. Slowly, he began to restrict the flow, dampening his energy until it matched that of a stage-three Qi Refining cultivator.

This should level the playing field a bit, Kai thought. *It'll make things more challenging for me, too, which is perfect for training.*

Opening his eyes, Kai noticed Liu Wei watching him with anticipation.

"Now, let's begin," Kai said with a slight smirk.

Without warning, he activated his Swift Wind Step. Even with his qi suppressed, the world around him blurred as he moved with impressive speed, leaving a swirl of dust in his wake. He reappeared behind Liu Wei, tapping him lightly on the shoulder.

"Too slow."

Before Liu Wei could react, Kai was gone again, moving to a new position. He watched as his student frantically scanned the area, trying to locate him.

He needs to feel the qi, not rely on his eyes, Kai thought.

From his vantage point, Kai observed Liu Wei closing his eyes, presumably sensing the flow of energy around him. *Good, he's starting to get it.*

Suddenly, Liu Wei's eyes snapped open, and he gathered qi in his feet, propelling himself forward. Kai watched, impressed, as his student moved faster than ever before, the world blurring around him.

"Not bad," Kai said. "But you're still thinking too linearly. The Swift Wind Step isn't just about moving fast in a straight line."

Liu Wei nodded, catching his breath. "I understand. I need to be more . . . unpredictable?"

"Exactly," Kai confirmed. "Now, let's try again. This time, focus on changing directions mid-step."

As they continued to practice, Zhi-Zhi watched from his rock, his expression a mixture of boredom and poorly concealed jealousy. "Hmph," he muttered, "I could move that fast too if I wanted to. I just choose not to."

Overhearing the tortoise's grumbling, Kai called out, "Feel free to join us, Zhi-Zhi. I'm sure Liu Wei would benefit from trying to dodge your . . . um . . . lightning-fast attacks."

The tortoise's eyes widened in alarm. "Ah, no, that's quite all right. I wouldn't want to . . . er . . . overwhelm you with my superior combat techniques."

"Of course," Kai said, trying not to laugh. "I'm sure you'd be great at this if you weren't so focused on 'standing your ground.' It must be tough being so strategically immobile."

"It's not immobility!" Zhi-Zhi puffed up. "It's . . . it's tactical positioning! Something you flighty humans wouldn't understand!"

"Right, tactical positioning," Kai nodded, winking at Liu Wei. "Well, if you change your mind about showing us your 'lightning-fast' moves, just let us know."

Zhi-Zhi retreated partway into his shell, muttering something about "disrespectful youngsters who don't appreciate the finer points of combat strategy."

Kai shook his head at the tortoise's antics as he turned his attention back to Liu Wei, the young man was improving rapidly. His movements were becoming smoother, more fluid. *He's got real potential,* Kai thought approvingly.

After about an hour of practice, Liu Wei was panting heavily, sweat beading on his forehead. Despite his fatigue, there was a gleam of excitement in his eyes.

"This is amazing, Master Kai," he said between breaths. "I've never moved like this before. It's like . . . like I'm becoming one with the wind itself."

Kai nodded, pleased with his student's progress. "That's exactly the feeling you should have. The Swift Wind Step isn't just a technique, it's a way of harmonizing with the natural world around you."

As Liu Wei took a moment to rest, Kai considered his next move. *In a game, this would be the point where I'd increase the difficulty. But I need to be careful not to push him too hard too fast.*

"All right, Liu Wei," Kai announced. "You're doing well, but let's make things a bit more challenging."

Liu Wei straightened up, his fatigue seemingly forgotten in the face of a new challenge. "I'm ready, Master. What did you have in mind?"

Kai grinned. "This time, I'm going to fight back. Nothing too serious, just some light sparring. Your goal is still to tag me, but now you'll have to dodge my attacks as well."

"Now this sounds interesting!" Zhi-Zhi perked up. "Finally, some real action!"

Kai raised an eyebrow at the tortoise. "Oh? And here I thought you didn't approve of all this 'running around.'"

Zhi-Zhi huffed, trying to maintain his dignified air. "Well, I suppose there might be some small value in learning to dodge. Not that I need to, of course, with my impenetrable shell."

For someone who claims to be above it all, he sure is invested in our training, Kai thought, amused. "Well then, Zhi-Zhi, why don't you be our referee? Make sure we're following the rules."

"Yes, yes, I suppose I could do that. Someone needs to keep you humans in line, after all."

As Zhi-Zhi settled into his new role, Kai turned back to Liu Wei. "Remember, the goal is still to tag me. But now you'll need to be aware of my movements as well. Ready?"

Liu Wei nodded, settling into a ready stance. "Ready, Master."

"Then begin!"

Kai activated his Swift Wind Step, disappearing in a blur of motion. Liu Wei, anticipating this, immediately moved as well. The field became a whirlwind of activity as master and student dashed back and forth.

To an outside observer, it would have looked like a strange dance. Kai would appear in one spot, arm outstretched to tag Liu Wei, only for the younger man to vanish just in time. Liu Wei, in turn, would materialize behind Kai, fingers grasping at empty air as Kai slipped away.

"Keep your movements unpredictable," Kai called out as he dodged another of Liu Wei's attempts. "Don't fall into a pattern!"

Liu Wei gritted his teeth, focusing intently. He gathered qi in his feet, preparing to dash forward, but at the last moment changed direction, spinning to his left instead.

The sudden change caught Kai off guard. For a brief moment, his eyes widened in surprise. *Clever,* he thought approvingly. *He's learning fast.*

But even as Liu Wei's fingers brushed the fabric of his robe, Kai was already moving, twisting away in a graceful arc.

"Close," Kai said with a grin. "But not quite close enough."

Liu Wei didn't respond, already gathering qi for his next attempt. His face was a mask of concentration, eyes darting back and forth as he tried to predict Kai's next move.

From his position on the rock, Zhi-Zhi was practically bouncing with excitement. "Oh! He almost had you there, Kai! Come on, Liu Wei, show him what you've got!"

Zhi-Zhi sure is getting into it, Kai thought, amused by the tortoise's enthusiasm.

As the sparring continued, Kai noticed Liu Wei's movements becoming smoother, more instinctive. *He's starting to get it,* Kai realized. *The Swift Wind Step isn't just a technique to be used consciously. At its highest level, it becomes an extension of the cultivator's will.*

Deciding to test Liu Wei's progress, Kai suddenly changed tactics. Instead of dodging, he went on the offensive, his hand darting out in a mock strike towards Liu Wei's chest.

Liu Wei's eyes widened in surprise, but his body reacted instinctively. Qi surged through his legs, and he blurred backwards, narrowly avoiding Kai's touch.

"Good!" Kai called out encouragingly. "That's exactly what I was looking for. You're starting to internalize the technique."

Liu Wei's face lit up at the praise, but he didn't let it distract him. Immediately, he launched into another series of rapid movements, trying to catch Kai off guard.

As they continued to spar, Kai felt a familiar sensation. It was subtle at first, a slight tingling in his extremities. But as he executed another Swift Wind Step, narrowly avoiding Liu Wei's outstretched hand, the feeling intensified.

Is this . . .? Kai thought, excitement building. *Yes, I think it is!*

Sure enough, a moment later, a notification appeared in his vision.

Skill Leveled Up!
Swift Wind Step has reached Level 4!
Your Agility increases by 40% when activated
You have gained 50 XP!

Kai couldn't help but smirk. *This is why it's better to have a training partner,* he thought. *The pressure of real combat, even simulated, pushes you to improve faster than solo practice ever could.*

"All right, Liu Wei, let's take a break. You've earned it."

Liu Wei, panting heavily, nodded gratefully. He stumbled over to where Zhi-Zhi was sat, collapsing onto the grass beside the rock.

"That was . . . intense," Liu Wei gasped between breaths.

Zhi-Zhi nodded sagely. "Indeed, indeed. You humans and your running around. I must admit, it was . . . somewhat impressive. For beings without shells, of course."

Kai joined them, settling down on the grass. He felt a sense of satisfaction as he looked at Liu Wei. The young man was exhausted, but there was a new light in his eyes, a confidence that hadn't been there before.

He's growing, Kai thought approvingly. *Not just in skill, but in spirit. This is what it means to be a teacher.*

As if in response to his thoughts, another notification appeared.

Teaching XP Gained: 50 XP

Kai nodded to himself, pleased. *Not bad for a day's work. Liu Wei is improving rapidly, and I'm gaining XP from teaching. It's a win-win situation.*

"You did well today, Liu Wei," Kai said aloud. "You're grasping the essence of the Swift Wind Step faster than I expected."

Liu Wei's face lit up at the praise. "Thank you, Master. It's . . . it's incredible."

Zhi-Zhi huffed. "Yes, yes, very impressive. But let's not forget the importance of a strong defense. Perhaps tomorrow we could focus on something more . . . stationary?"

Kai chuckled. "Don't worry, Zhi-Zhi. We'll get to defensive techniques soon enough. But for now, Liu Wei needs to focus on mastering this skill."

As the sun began to set, they decided to call it a day. Liu Wei bowed deeply to Kai. "Thank you for the lesson, Master. I'll continue to practice on my own."

"Good," Kai nodded. "Remember, consistent practice is key. Even a little bit each day will yield results over time."

Just like grinding skills in an RPG, Kai thought. *Small, consistent gains add up to big improvements.*

As Liu Wei headed back to his own quarters, Zhi-Zhi waddled over to Kai. "I suppose you did an adequate job teaching the boy," the tortoise said grudgingly.

Kai grinned. "Why, Zhi-Zhi, was that almost a compliment?"

The tortoise huffed. "Don't let it go to your head. I've seen better teachers in my time. Of course, they were all tortoises . . ."

"Of course they were," Kai said, trying not to laugh. "Come on, let's head back. I think we've both earned some rest."

As they made their way back to Kai's hut, he found himself reflecting on the day's training. *In games, training montages are usually just cutscenes or time-skips. But, the process itself is valuable. There's so much to learn from the act of teaching.*

Once inside, Kai settled onto his bed, crossing his legs in a meditative pose. Zhi-Zhi retreated into his shell in the corner of the room, pretending to meditate but quickly falling asleep. For such a small creature, his snores were surprisingly loud.

All right, Kai thought, *time to check out this crafting menu.*

He focused his mind, and a translucent window appeared before him.

Crafting Menu
Available Materials:
Roach Carapace Fragment (Rare) x1
Recipes:
None available
Craft an item:
[ ] + [ ] = ???

Just as I thought, Kai sighed. *The Roach Carapace Fragment is a rare material, but by itself it's useless for crafting. And even though I have enough spirit stones from the bandits to probably buy some basic materials, the Misty Waterfall Village doesn't exactly have a thriving market for cultivation resources.*

Closing the crafting menu, Kai reached into his inventory and pulled out a spirit stone. It was about the size of a small pebble, glowing with a soft, blue light. As he held it in his palm, he could feel the qi pulsing within it, like a tiny heartbeat.

I've been using XP to level up so far because I'm always in the middle of action. But now that I have some downtime, let's see if these spirit stones are as useful as they claim to be in all those novels.

Kai closed his eyes, recalling the Basic Qi Gathering technique Zhang Wei had taught him. He focused on his dantian, the energy center in his lower abdomen, and began to circulate his qi.

Breathe in, drawing qi from the spirit stone. Breathe out, guiding it through the meridians, then circle it into the dantian.

As Kai cycled his breath and qi, he could feel the spirit stone in his hand growing cooler. The qi within it was slowly being drawn into his body, refining and strengthening his own energy.

Time seemed to stretch as Kai focused on the technique. He lost track of how long he sat there, absorbing the qi from the spirit stone. Finally, when he could no longer sense any energy within the stone, he opened his eyes.

The once-glowing spirit stone was now dull and lifeless in his palm, its energy completely depleted. As Kai set it aside, he noticed a notification.

Skill Leveled Up!
Basic Qi Gathering technique has reached Level 2!

> You can now gather qi 2x faster.
> You have gained 50 XP!

Kai smiled, pleased with the progress. He quickly checked his stats.

> Name: Kai Thorn
>
> XP: 155/2,000
> Level: Qi Refining Stage 7
> Qi: 200/200

My qi is back to full, and I gained five XP from absorbing the spirit stone. But that's it. Kai frowned, doing some quick mental math. *At this rate, I'd need almost 350 spirit stones to break through to level eight. That's . . . not great.*

Kai shook his head, putting the thought aside. *The Basic Qi Gathering technique is just that, basic. Once I enter the sect, I'll gain access to better techniques. The conversion rate from those should be much higher and more worthwhile.*

He looked at the dull spirit stone, turning it over in his hand. *There's no point in grinding to level up this basic technique when I'll be replacing it soon. Better to save my resources for when they'll have a bigger impact.*

Stretching out on his bed, Kai let his mind wander to the next day's training plans. *Tomorrow, I'll work on my Iron Skin Technique,* he thought with a wry smile. *The only way to level up Iron Skin is to become a punching bag. It's not going to be comfortable, but no pain, no gain, right?*

In the corner, Zhi-Zhi let out a particularly loud snore, briefly interrupting Kai's thoughts.

At least someone's getting a good night's sleep, Kai thought, amused. *I wonder if spirit beasts dream. And if they do, what does a baby tortoise dream about?*

Shaking his head at the thought, Kai closed his eyes, allowing himself to fall asleep.

CHAPTER TWENTY-NINE

The next morning, Kai woke feeling refreshed. He sat up and glanced over at Zhi-Zhi's corner.

The little tortoise was already awake, he was perfectly positioned so his shell gleamed in the early morning light, giving him a dignified and wise look.

I bet he's been awake for hours, trying to get that "wise old master" effect just right, Kai thought, amused. *Did he practice different poses? Test out various angles to catch the light? I can almost picture him shuffling back and forth, muttering about optimal feng shui for maximum sagacity.*

"Good morning, Zhi-Zhi," Kai said, smiling. "Ready for some training?"

"A true cultivator is always ready to impart wisdom, young Kai," the tortoise replied. "I suppose I can spare some time to oversee your training."

"I'm honored by your generosity," Kai said, keeping his face straight with effort. "Shall we head outside?"

As they made their way to the training field, Kai spotted Liu Wei already there, practicing the Swift Wind Step. The young man was dashing back and forth across the field, his movements growing smoother with each repetition.

"Excellent work, Liu Wei!" Kai called out as they approached. "Your control is improving rapidly."

Liu Wei stopped, bowing deeply to Kai. "Thank you, Master. I've been practicing since dawn."

Kai nodded. "Keep at it for now. I'm going to work on a different skill this morning."

As Liu Wei resumed his practice, Kai turned to Zhi-Zhi. "All right, my friend. Today, we're going to work on defensive techniques. Specifically, my Iron Skin Technique."

Zhi-Zhi's eyes lit up. "Ah, now that's a proper technique! None of this dashing about nonsense. A strong defense is the foundation of true power!"

Says the creature with a built-in shield, Kai thought wryly. But he nodded in agreement. "Exactly. And who better to learn from than a master of defense like yourself?"

The tortoise preened at the compliment. "Well, I suppose I could share some of my vast knowledge. What exactly does this 'Iron Skill Technique' entail?"

Kai explained the basics of the skill: how it allowed him to reinforce his body with qi, increasing his durability and resistance to damage. "The tricky part," he concluded, "is that to increase my skill, I need to actually take hits while the skill is active."

Zhi-Zhi nodded. "Ah, yes. The time-honored tradition of learning through pain. Very wise."

Easy for you to say, Kai thought. *You're not the one who's about to get beaten up.*

"So," Kai said, clapping his hands together. "I'm going to activate the skill, and then I need you to . . . well, attack me."

The tortoise blinked. "Are you certain, young Kai? My power is not to be underestimated."

"Absolutely," Kai nodded. "I'm counting on your strength for this. As a peak Qi Refining cultivator, your attacks will be perfect for pushing my Iron Skin to its limits."

Zhi-Zhi puffed up with pride. "Finally, you recognize my true power! Prepare yourself, young Kai. You're about to experience the might of a superior cultivator!"

This is going to hurt, Kai thought, steeling himself. *But pain is just another form of experience points in this world.*

"I'm ready when you are, Zhi-Zhi." Kai announced, his skin taking on a subtle metallic sheen.

The tortoise's eyes gleamed with anticipation. Without warning, he charged forward with surprising speed for his stubby legs. His head connected with Kai's shin with a resounding *thwack.*

"Gah!" Kai gasped, stumbling back. Even through his Iron Skin, the force of the blow was impressive. *Yep, definitely going to feel that tomorrow.*

"Ha!" Zhi-Zhi exclaimed, looking smug. "How's that for a wake-up call?"

Kai grinned through the pain. "Excellent start. Keep it coming!"

For the next hour, Zhi-Zhi unleashed a barrage of physical attacks. His lack of agility didn't matter since Kai was deliberately standing still, acting as a willing punching bag. Each impact pushed Kai's Iron Skin Technique to its limit, the constant stress forcing it to adapt and grow stronger.

"Adamantine Shell Slam!" Zhi-Zhi cried out, withdrawing into his shell. It began to glow with a soft, golden light before he shot forward like a cannonball, slamming into Kai's midsection.

"Oof!" Kai wheezed, doubling over. His Iron Skin flickered but held. *This is exactly what I needed. High-level impacts to really test the technique's limits.*

As they continued, Kai could feel his Iron Skin growing more resilient. The impacts, while still jarring, were becoming easier to withstand.

Finally, Zhi-Zhi stepped back, looking slightly winded but immensely satisfied. "Ready for the grand finale, young Kai? I'll show you a true qi technique!"

Kai nodded, bracing himself. *This is where the real test begins.*

Zhi-Zhi's shell began to glow brightly, the air around him crackled as he gathered his qi. "Celestial Tortoise's Roar!"

A visible wave of qi, far more potent than Kai had anticipated, erupted from Zhi-Zhi's mouth. It slammed into Kai with devastating force, completely overwhelming his Iron Skin Technique.

Kai felt the protective layer shatter like glass, the remaining energy crashing into his now unprotected body. The impact lifted him off his feet, sending him flying backward several meters before he crashed to the ground with a painful thud.

"Urgh . . ." Kai groaned, struggling to catch his breath. Every part of his body ached, and he could already feel bruises forming.

Zhi-Zhi's eyes widened in shock. He quickly waddled over to Kai, his earlier bravado replaced by genuine concern. "Kai! Are you all right? I . . . I didn't mean to . . . that is . . . oh, dear. I may have . . . slightly miscalculated the power required for a human of your . . . fragile constitution."

Despite the pain, Kai couldn't help but chuckle at Zhi-Zhi's flustered state. He held up a hand, waving off the apology. "It's okay, Zhi-Zhi. This is exactly what I needed."

Zhi-Zhi blinked in confusion. "You . . . needed to be blasted across the field?"

Kai smiled but before he could respond, his attention was caught by a notification that had appeared.

> Iron Skin Technique has reached Level 4!
> Durability increases by 40% when activated
> New ability unlocked: Iron Rebound
> Damage absorbed has a 5% chance to be reflected at the attacker

"Wait, what?" Kai muttered, momentarily forgetting his pain. "Iron Rebound?"

This is new, he thought, his mind racing. *The scroll never mentioned anything about reflecting damage. Is this some kind of hidden ability?*

Zhi-Zhi, still looking concerned, tilted his head. "What is it, Kai? Are you all right?"

Kai nodded absently, his thoughts elsewhere. "Yeah, I'm fine. Just . . . surprised."

Could it be that all skills have secret abilities that aren't known? Kai wondered. *Or is this something unique to my situation?*

He thought back to the games he used to play, how sometimes skills would evolve or unlock new abilities as they leveled up. But this felt different. The Iron Skin scroll had been quite detailed in its description, and there had been no hint of this reflective ability.

Or maybe, Kai mused, a new idea forming, *the system is giving me new abilities based on how I use the skills. I've been using Iron Skin as a punching bag, taking hit after hit. Could that have influenced its evolution?*

If this was true, it meant that Kai had even more control over his growth than he'd initially thought. By using skills in specific ways, he might be able to shape their development.

"Kai?" Zhi-Zhi's voice broke through his thoughts. "Are you sure you're all right? Perhaps I really did overdo it with that last attack."

Kai shook his head, focusing back on the present. He gave Zhi-Zhi a reassuring smile. "No, you did exactly what I needed, Zhi-Zhi. In fact, you helped me discover something incredibly valuable."

The tortoise puffed up slightly, curiosity overriding his concern. "Oh? And what might that be?"

Kai patted Zhi-Zhi's shell. "Let's just say that sometimes, pushing past your limits can lead to unexpected breakthroughs. Thank you for your help, my friend."

As they made their way back to the hut, Kai was limping slightly but had a satisfied smile on his face. *If this is true for Iron Skin, what about my other skills? What hidden potential might they have?*

He knew one thing for certain. He had a lot more experimenting to do.

CHAPTER THIRTY

A few days had passed since the Talent Ceremony, and Kai, Liu Wei, and Zhi-Zhi made their way through the busy crowd as they headed towards the village entrance.

Just a few more steps, and we're off to the Azure Sky Sect, Kai thought. *Time to see if all that grinding was enough.*

He glanced at the tiny spirit beast sitting on Liu Wei's head. Zhi-Zhi had his chest puffed out, looking for all the world like a proud emperor surveying his domain.

"Zhi-Zhi," Kai said, breaking the silence, "are you absolutely sure you want to come with us to the Azure Sky Sect? It's more of a place for human cultivators, I'm not sure how they treat spirit beasts there."

The tortoise turned his head, fixing Kai with a haughty stare. "Of course I'm sure! You two clearly need my guidance and protection. Consider yourselves lucky I've decided to grace you with my presence."

Liu Wei chuckled nervously. "We're certainly grateful, Master Zhi-Zhi. Though I hope we won't need too much protection at a righteous sect."

"Ha!" Zhi-Zhi scoffed. "You clearly don't know much about cultivator politics, my naive disciple. Even 'righteous' sects can be cutthroat."

Kai nodded, his expression turning serious. "Zhi-Zhi's right, Liu Wei. We need to be on our guard, especially . . ." He trailed off, remembering Elder Feng's keen interest in their spirit beast companion.

"Especially what, Master?" Liu Wei asked, his brow furrowing with concern.

Kai shook his head. "Nothing specific. Just . . . keep your wits about you, both of you. And Zhi-Zhi, try not to draw too much attention, okay?"

The spirit beast huffed. "As if I could help being extraordinary! But fine, I'll try to dim my radiance . . . a little."

As they walked, Kai's thoughts drifted to the new skill he'd unlocked. *Iron Rebound. 5% chance to reflect damage . . . not bad for a passive ability. But why couldn't I unlock anything new from Swift Wind Step or Flame Palm Strike?*

He'd spent hours over the past few days pushing those skills to their limits, hoping to trigger some hidden technique or evolution. But no matter how he varied his qi flow or adjusted his movements, nothing new had manifested.

Maybe there's a cooldown on skill evolution? Or perhaps Iron Skin was just a special case. I'll have to keep experimenting.

Liu Wei's voice broke through Kai's musings. "Master, do you think . . . do you think we'll make it into the sect?"

Kai turned to his companion, noting the anxiety on Liu Wei's face. The former bandit had made remarkable progress in his cultivation, but his confidence still lagged behind his abilities.

"We've got a good chance," Kai replied. "You've worked hard, Liu Wei. Your Wind affinity is strong, and you've got skills that many pampered young masters lack. Just stay focused during the trials and trust in your abilities."

Liu Wei nodded, some of the tension leaving his shoulders. "Thank you, Master. I just . . . I can't help but worry. This is such a big opportunity, and after everything that happened with the bandits . . ."

"Hey," Kai said, placing a hand on Liu Wei's shoulder. "The past is the past. You're not that person anymore. Actually, you were never that kind of person. The Azure Sky Sect will see that."

At least, I hope they will, Kai added silently. *If not, we might need to find a backup plan.*

As they approached the village entrance, Kai spotted Elder Zhang Wei deep in conversation with Outer Elder Feng. The two older cultivators stood apart from a small crowd of villagers, their expressions serious.

Kai's gaze swept the gathering, quickly locating Shen Yu. The mysterious youth stood silently by Elder Feng's side, his face an expressionless mask. Unlike the other villagers, who buzzed with excitement and nervous energy, Shen Yu seemed utterly unaffected by the momentous occasion.

Still playing it cool, huh? Kai mused, studying the boy. *Either he's got nerves of steel or . . .*

His train of thought was interrupted as Elder Zhang spotted their approach. The old man's face lit up with a mixture of pride and concern.

"Ah, there you are!" Zhang called out, waving them over. "Come, come. Elder Feng was just asking about you."

As they drew closer, Kai noticed Elder Feng's gaze fixate on Zhi-Zhi. The Outer Elder's eyes narrowed slightly, a calculating look visible for just a moment before his expression smoothed into a benign smile. "Are you prepared for your journey?"

Kai bowed. "Yes, Elder Feng. We're ready to depart."

Elder Feng's eyes turned to Zhi-Zhi, a hint of curiosity in his gaze. "And who might this little one belong to? I don't believe I've seen such an . . . interesting spirit beast before."

Before Kai could answer, Zhi-Zhi bristled. "I am the great Zhi-Zhi! And I belong to no one, thank you very much. I'm not some common pet to be owned and paraded about! I am my own master!"

A hush fell over the villagers. Even Liu Wei seemed to hold his breath, waiting to see how the Outer Elder would react to the spirit beast's bluntness—or as some would call it, rudeness.

Elder Feng's eyes widened slightly before a smile spread across his face. It wasn't a kind smile, though. There was something predatory lurking beneath the surface.

Crap, Kai thought. *All he is thinking now is that Zhi-Zhi is up for grabs. This could be trouble.*

"My apologies, noble spirit beast," Feng said, his tone smooth as silk. "I meant no offense. It's rare to encounter one such as yourself, especially in a small village like this."

Kai stepped forward, hoping to redirect the conversation. "Zhi-Zhi has been a great help to us, Elder Feng. He is our friend, and his wisdom has been invaluable in our cultivation journey."

"I'm sure it has," Feng murmured, his gaze still locked on the tiny tortoise.

Elder Zhang cleared his throat, breaking the tension. "Well then, shall we proceed with the farewells? I'm sure you're eager to be on your way."

The next few minutes passed in a blur of tearful goodbyes and well-wishes from the villagers. Kai found himself surrounded by people he'd barely spoken to during his time in the village, all suddenly eager to claim a connection to the promising young cultivator.

Kai turned to Elder Zhang. The old man's eyes were misty, though he tried to hide it behind a gruff exterior.

"Elder Zhang," Kai said, bowing deeply. "I can't thank you enough for everything you've taught me."

Zhang waved off the thanks, though Kai could see he was pleased. "Bah, you did all the hard work yourself, boy. I just pointed you in the right direction. Now, remember what I taught you about sect politics. Keep your head down, work hard, and don't draw too much attention to yourself."

"I'll do my best, Elder Zhang. And don't worry about the village. I'm sure they'll be fine without us."

At this, Kai turned to Elder Feng, his expression carefully neutral. "Although, I must admit I am a bit concerned, Elder Feng. The village was recently attacked by bandits, and now that we're leaving . . ."

He let the implication hang in the air, watching Feng's reaction closely.

The Outer Elder waved a hand dismissively. "You needn't worry. Should any of you successfully enter the Azure Sky Sect, the village will naturally fall under our protection."

Elder Zhang nodded in agreement. "It's true. When I was still a disciple of the sect, Misty Waterfall Village enjoyed the full protection of Azure Sky. It was only after I . . . left that they had to fend for themselves."

It makes sense that the sect's protection is conditional on having an active disciple.

As Kai finished saying goodbye to Chen Lao, he heard the patter of small feet running towards him. He turned to find Mei Li, her eyes already wet with tears.

"You promised you wouldn't leave so soon!" she blurted out, her lower lip trembling. "You said you'd teach me more stuff!"

Kai knelt to her level. "I know, Mei Li. I'm sorry. But remember what we talked about? Sometimes we have to go on journeys to help protect the people we care about."

"But I don't want you to go," she sniffled, wiping her nose with her sleeve. "Who's going to show me cool moves?"

"Hey, come on now," Kai said gently, reaching out to wipe a tear from her cheek. "I'll come back to visit. And you know what? I bet by the time I return, you'll have practiced so hard that you'll be able to show me some cool moves instead."

Mei Li's eyes brightened slightly at this idea. "Really? You think I could?"

"Of course! And you know what else?" Kai leaned in as if sharing a secret. "When you're older, maybe you can join a sect, too. Then we could both be immortal cultivators."

"Promise?" Mei Li asked, her face lighting up. "Promise you'll help me join a sect when I'm bigger?"

"If that's what you want when you're older, I promise I'll do everything I can to help," Kai smiled. "But for now, you need to focus on growing up strong and smart, okay?"

Mei Li stood up straighter, trying to look serious despite her tearstained face. "I will! I'll practice every day! And when I'm big, I'll join your sect and we can go on adventures together!"

"That sounds like a plan," Kai chuckled, ruffling her hair.

Mei Li threw her arms around his neck, hugging him tight. "Don't forget about us, okay?" she whispered.

"Never," Kai promised, hugging her back. "How could I forget my favorite student?"

When they separated, Mei Li reached into her pocket and pulled out a slightly crumpled paper flower. "I made this for you," she said shyly. "So you won't forget your promise."

Kai accepted the gift carefully, treating it like a precious treasure. "Thank you, Mei Li. I'll keep it safe, I promise."

As he stood to leave, Mei Li called out one last time. "Kai! I'm going to get super strong, just wait and see!"

"I know you will, Mei Li. I know you will."

I never knew what I was missing, not having siblings. But now I think I understand what it's like to have a little sister.

As Mei Li stepped back, joining her father and the other villagers, Kai's gaze was drawn once more to Shen Yu. The boy stood stoically as his family wept and clung to him, his expression never wavering. It was as if their tears and pleas simply didn't register.

Kai stepped closer, curiosity getting the better of him. As he approached, Shen Yu's eyes met his. The boy held Kai's gaze steadily, showing no hint of intimidation or deference.

That's . . . not normal, Kai thought, his eyes narrowing slightly. *I'm at Qi Refining stage seven, he should be able to sense my cultivation. Even if he can't see my exact level, he should feel a natural pressure weighing down on him. So why isn't he reacting at all?*

As if in response to his thoughts, a message flashed before Kai's eyes.

Name: Shen Yu
Level: Mortal

Kai blinked in surprise. *Either he really is just a talented kid, or he has a way to hide himself from the System . . .*

His thoughts were interrupted by Elder Feng's voice. "Attention, everyone! It's time for us to depart."

The Outer Elder raised his hand, a look of concentration passing over his face. With a flash of light, a small object appeared in his palm. As the light faded, Kai saw that it was a miniature ark, no larger than a child's toy boat.

Right on cue, Kai thought, suppressing a smirk. *The magical transport item. Typical recruiter gear in every xianxia story I've read.*

Elder Feng smiled at the gathered crowd. "This is a simple transportation artifact. Now, young cultivators, please step forward."

As Kai, Liu Wei, and Shen Yu moved towards the ark, Zhi-Zhi looked down from his vantage point on Liu Wei's head.

"That tiny thing is supposed to carry us?" the spirit beast scoffed. "I've seen more impressive vessels in puddles!"

Elder Feng's smile tightened slightly. "I assure you, noble spirit beast, this ark is more than capable of transporting us safely and swiftly to the Azure Sky Sect."

Zhi-Zhi huffed but said nothing more, settling back into his favorite spot.

Elder Feng made a subtle gesture with his hand. Suddenly, the miniature boat began to grow, rapidly expanding before their eyes.

A gasp rose from the villagers as the tiny ark swelled to the size of a small ship, easily large enough to accommodate their group. Even Liu Wei's eyes widened in awe.

"It . . . it grew!" one villager exclaimed.

"Immortal magic!" another whispered.

Kai maintained his neutral expression, entirely unsurprised by the display. *Standard size-changing artifact. Probably mass produced by the sect's artificers for these recruitment trips.*

As they prepared to board, Kai took one last look at the village that had been his home for the past month. Some of the faces he knew well, others only in passing, but all had been part of his introduction to this world.

It's strange. In games, you never think twice about leaving the starting village. But now . . .

He pushed the thought aside. There was no time for sentimentality. The Azure Sky Sect was waiting, and with it, new challenges and opportunities.

This is it.

CHAPTER THIRTY-ONE

The moment Kai's foot touched the deck of the ark, he felt a subtle shift in the ambient qi. It was as if the air around them had been brought to life. He glanced at Liu Wei, wondering if his companion had noticed the change. Judging by the wide-eyed look on Liu Wei's face, he had.

"Impressive, isn't it?" Elder Feng said, a hint of pride in his voice. "This ark is infused with wind- and water-attributed spirit stones. It can cover vast distances in a fraction of the time it would take to travel on foot."

Zhi-Zhi, still sitting on Liu Wei's head, snorted. "I've seen faster. Why, in my younger days, I once rode a bolt of lightning across half the continent!"

Kai suppressed a smile. *I really need to get the full story behind Zhi-Zhi sometime. His backstory keeps getting more and more ridiculous.*

As Shen Yu boarded the ark, Kai watched him closely. The boy's movements were smooth and graceful, betraying a level of body control that seemed at odds with his apparent lack of cultivation.

Another anomaly, Kai thought. *His stats say he's just a normal mortal, but he moves like a trained martial artist. What's your deal, Shen Yu?*

Once everyone was aboard, Elder Feng made a series of complex hand gestures. The ark shuddered slightly, then began to rise into the air.

Liu Wei gasped, clutching the railing. "We're . . . we're flying!"

"Of course we are," Zhi-Zhi said, rolling his eyes. "Did you expect us to sail through the trees?"

Kai placed a hand on Liu Wei's shoulder. "It's okay, Liu Wei. This is perfectly normal for cultivators. Just think of it as . . . an extremely smooth carriage ride."

As the ark ascended above the treetops, Kai took a moment to survey their surroundings. The village looked tiny from this height, a cluster of buildings nestled in a sea of green. In the distance, he could make out the faint outline of mountains, their peaks shrouded in mist.

So that's where we're headed. The Azure Sky Sect is probably located on one of those peaks. It looks close but is actually far away, classic xianxia style.

Elder Feng's voice broke through Kai's thoughts. "Young cultivators, our journey will take several hours. I suggest you use this time wisely. For those of you who have already begun your cultivation journey, quiet meditation would be appropriate."

The Outer Elder's gaze settled on Shen Yu. "As for you, young man, I believe it's time you learned the basics of qi sensing and gathering. Come, sit with me."

Kai watched with interest as Shen Yu moved to sit cross-legged in front of Elder Feng. The boy's face remained impassive, but Kai thought he detected a flicker of . . . something in his eyes. Anticipation? Or was it recognition?

This should be interesting, Kai thought. *Let's see how an expert teaches the basics . . . and how our mysterious friend here reacts.*

Elder Feng smiled at Shen Yu. "Now then, young one. Before we begin gathering qi, you must first learn to sense it. Your body can already feel qi, but your mind needs to recognize and interpret those sensations."

Shen Yu nodded. There was no hint of the nervousness or excitement one might expect from a complete novice.

"Close your eyes," Elder Feng instructed. "Take a deep breath and try to feel the world around you. Don't focus on what you can hear or smell. Instead, try to sense the energy that flows through all things."

Shen Yu obeyed, his eyelids sliding shut as he took a deep breath. His posture was perfect, Kai noticed, as if he'd sat in meditation a thousand times before.

"Good," Elder Feng continued. "Now, I'm going to release a small amount of qi. Try to feel it with your mind, not your body."

Kai watched as Elder Feng extended his hand, palm facing Shen Yu. A faint, barely visible shimmer appeared in the air between them.

"Do you feel anything?" Elder Feng asked.

"Yes," Shen Yu said simply. "I can sense it clearly."

Elder Feng's eyebrows rose slightly. "Oh? That's . . . quite impressive for a first attempt. Can you describe what you're sensing?"

"It's like a gentle current," Shen Yu replied, his eyes still closed. "Warm and flowing, but intangible. It reminds me of sunlight on water."

That's an oddly poetic description for someone who's supposedly never sensed qi before, Kai thought.

Elder Feng seemed equally surprised but quickly composed himself. "Well done, Shen Yu. You have a natural talent for this. Now that you can sense qi, we can move on to gathering it."

The elder's voice took on a more instructional tone. "Qi Gathering is the foundation of all cultivation. First, I want you to focus on your breathing and imagine a warm light at the center of your body, behind your navel. This is your dantian, the core of your qi."

Shen Yu nodded, his breathing steady and rhythmic.

"As you breathe in," Elder Feng continued, "imagine you're drawing in the qi you can now sense from the world around you. It enters through your nose, flows down to your dantian, and makes that light grow. As you breathe out, let that energy circulate through your body."

As Kai watched, he saw a faint shimmer begin to form around Shen Yu almost immediately. It was subtle, but to Kai's trained senses, it was unmistakable.

That's . . . not normal, Kai thought, his mind racing. *Even a prodigy shouldn't be able to gather qi this quickly on their first try.*

Elder Feng's eyes widened, a look of astonishment crossing his face. "Shen Yu, this is . . . remarkable. You're already beginning to circulate qi. Can you feel it?"

"Yes," Shen Yu replied calmly. "It's moving in a circular path, just as you described. From the dantian, up the spine, over the head, down the front, and back to the core."

Elder Feng seemed at a loss for words for a moment. "That's . . . that's correct. The microcosmic orbit. But how did you . . .?"

Shen Yu opened his eyes, his gaze meeting Elder Feng's. "It just felt natural," he said, his voice neither boastful nor apologetic.

Natural? There's nothing natural about this. Either Shen Yu is the biggest cultivation prodigy I've ever seen, or . . .

A message flashed before Kai's eyes.

Shen Yu

Level: Qi Refining Stage 1
Qi: 10/10
Strength: 15
Agility: 15
Endurance: 15
Skills: Basic Qi Circulation

Or he really isn't what he seems, but whatever he is, Shen Yu just became the most interesting person on this boat.

Suddenly, Shen Yu's eyes darted across the horizon, his usual calm demeanor was tinged with a hint of tension.

"We should be careful," he said quietly.

Kai raised an eyebrow. "Oh? Why's that?"

Instead of answering, Shen Yu just shook his head slightly.

Kai frowned. Something about Shen Yu's warning set off alarm bells in his mind. He decided to check his map. His eyes widened as he noticed three large red spots appear on the map, moving rapidly towards their position.

What the hell? Kai thought. *Those can't be good.*

Before he could voice his concerns, the boat violently rocked. Something large whooshed past, barely missing them.

"What was that?" Liu Wei cried out, stumbling to keep his balance.

The boat rocked again as another shape flew by. And then a third time.

Kai gripped the railing, his mind racing. *Three fast-moving objects. Big enough to shake the boat. Just what kind of beasts are we up against?*

As if in answer to his thoughts, three massive winged creatures burst into view. They circled the ark, their powerful wings creating gusts of wind that buffeted the small vessel.

Kai's eyes widened as he took in their appearance. Each beast was easily the size of a small house, with wings spanning at least thirty feet. Their bodies were covered in scales that shimmered in the sunlight. One drake was a deep blue. Another was a vibrant green. The last one, larger than the others, had rich purple scales.

Great, Kai thought. *Dragon wannabes.*

A quick glance at his status window confirmed his fears.

Thunderwing Drake
Level: Foundation Establishment (Peak)
HP: 4,000/4,000

"Liu Wei, Zhi-Zhi, stay low," Kai said. "These aren't your average birds."

Liu Wei nodded, his face pale. "Y-Yes, Master Kai."

Zhi-Zhi, however, puffed out his tiny chest. "Ha! As if I would cower before such lowly beasts," the spirit tortoise declared as he waddled over to a corner of the boat and plopped down. "I shall allow you youngsters the chance to prove yourselves. Consider this a valuable learning experience!"

With that, Zhi-Zhi retreated into his shell, leaving only his eyes peeking out.

I'm not surprised in the least. Kai shook his head with a smile at the tortoise's antics.

Elder Feng stood at the bow of the ark, his face grim as he surveyed the circling drakes. Kai approached him.

"Elder Feng," Kai said, keeping his voice low. "What are our options here?"

The Outer Elder's expression was tense. "This is . . . unfortunate. While I am at the Pseudo Core Formation Realm, which would typically be enough to handle three peak Foundation Establishment creatures, an aerial battle changes things significantly."

Right. Humans aren't exactly built for midair combat. And he's outnumbered three to one.

"What about the ark?" Kai asked. "What are its defensive capabilities?"

Elder Feng shook his head. "I'm afraid this vessel was designed for travel, not combat. It has no significant defensive measures."

Damn. But I guess that makes sense. Sects probably wouldn't waste resources on defenses for a simple recruitment trip. Talk about bad luck.

CHAPTER THIRTY-TWO

S tay on the boat," Elder Feng commanded as he drew his sword and leapt into the air. The blade glowed with qi, allowing him to stand on it as if it were a flying platform.

There it is! The classic "flying sword." Kai's eyes widened. *I wonder how long it'll take me to learn it.*

As the elder met the three Thunderwing Drakes in the air, the beasts began to circle him. Elder Feng made sure to keep his back to the boat, not letting them get around him.

When the first drake dove at him, mouth open wide, Elder Feng didn't even flinch. He raised his hand, and a powerful gust of wind slammed into the drake, sending it tumbling backward.

The other two drakes attacked from opposite sides, trying to catch Elder Feng between them. Lightning crackled around their mouths, building up for a devastating attack. But Elder Feng was ready.

He spun in the air, his robes flapping wildly. As the drakes unleashed their lightning strikes, Elder Feng's hands shot out, fingers splayed. Two brilliant bolts of lightning erupted from his palms, meeting the drakes' attacks midair.

The beasts shrieked in pain, their scales smoking. They backed away, regrouping.

Nice crowd control, Kai thought, watching closely. *He's not just defending, he's controlling the battlefield.*

Elder Feng pressed his advantage, he thrust his palm towards the green drake, unleashing a concentrated blast of wind that slammed into its chest, sending it tumbling backward.

The purple drake retaliated, its jaws crackling with electricity as it lunged for Elder Feng's leg. The elder pivoted midair, narrowly avoiding the bite. In the same motion, he brought his elbow down on the drake's neck, channeling a bolt of lightning through the strike. The beast convulsed, smoke rising from its scales.

It's like watching a wizard duel, Kai thought.

The blue drake circled around, trying to flank Elder Feng. It inhaled deeply as it began to gather lightning qi. Elder Feng noticed just in time. He raised both hands, forming a swirling vortex of wind between them. As the drake released a stream of lightning, Elder Feng's wind barrier caught the attack, dispersing it harmlessly into the air.

Without missing a beat, Elder Feng clasped his hands together. The air around him began to ripple and distort. Suddenly, he threw his arms wide, and a shockwave of pure qi erupted in all directions. The drakes shrieked as the invisible force battered their bodies, sending them reeling.

Elder Feng has area-of-effect attacks to handle multiple enemies, and he's using the sky as his arena. Smart.

The green drake, recovering fastest, dove at Elder Feng with its claws extended. The elder met the attack head-on, his fist crackling with lightning as it collided with the drake's talons. There was a blinding flash and a thunderous boom.

When Kai's vision cleared, he saw the drake's front leg hanging limply, its scales blackened and cracked.

The purple drake's tail whipped towards the elder, only for him to catch it barehanded, using the beast's momentum to swing it into its blue companion. The drakes crashed into each other with a sickening crunch.

He's making it look easy. If it was me fighting, I wouldn't last more than a few seconds against even one of these drakes, Kai thought, a chill running down his spine. *The gap between Qi Refining and Foundation Establishment is big but the gap between the stages of Foundation Establishment seem even bigger. A Pseudo Core Formation cultivator really is on another level.*

One of the drakes, frustrated, tried to dive past Elder Feng towards the boat. The elder's eyes widened. He abandoned his offensive, racing to intercept the drake.

"Wind Wall!" Elder Feng shouted, throwing both hands forward. A massive barrier of swirling air appeared between the drake and the boat.

The drake slammed into the wind wall, roaring in anger. But Elder Feng's quick defense left him vulnerable. The other two drakes seized the opportunity, one biting into his shoulder while the other raked its claws across his back.

Elder Feng grunted in pain but didn't falter. He maintained the wind wall, protecting the boat even as blood soaked his robes.

Damn, Kai thought, his fists clenched. *He could've dodged that if he wasn't worried about us.*

As the battle raged on, the elder struggled to fend off all three drakes while still protecting the boat, his movements were slower, his attacks less powerful, his actions more cautious.

He needs help, Kai thought desperately. *But what can we do? At our level, we'd just get in the way . . .*

"The elder is making a mistake," Shen Yu's voice cut through his thoughts.

Kai's ears perked up at this. He moved closer to Shen Yu. "What do you mean?"

Shen Yu turned to look at Kai, his eyes unreadable. For a moment, Kai thought the boy might not answer. Then, to his surprise, Shen Yu spoke.

"The Thunderwing Drakes have a weakness to sound. High-pitched noises disorient them."

"And how exactly do you know that?"

Shen Yu shook his head. "That's beside the point. We need to help the elder before he gets himself killed trying to protect us."

He's deflecting, Kai thought. *But he's also right. We need to do something.*

Making a split-second decision, Kai focused on his hand, channeling his qi, he began to shape the energy.

Let's see . . . circular shape, thin material for better resonance . . . Kai's brow furrowed in concentration as he molded the qi. Slowly, a translucent gong took shape in his hand.

Shen Yu nodded approvingly. "I was just going to suggest you do that."

Liu Wei, who had been watching wide-eyed, finally found his voice. "Master, what are you doing?"

Before Kai could answer, Zhi-Zhi's muffled voice came from within his shell. "Isn't it obvious? He's creating a sonic weapon to exploit the drake's auditory vulnerability! I was going to suggest it myself, but I wanted to see if any of you would figure it out."

Kai suppressed a smirk. *Nice save, "Master" Zhi-Zhi. Pretend you knew all along.*

With the gong formed, Kai quickly shaped another qi construct—this time, a simple hammer. He knew he had to work fast; maintaining multiple qi constructs was taxing, and he could only hold them for a few seconds at most.

Usually, that's fine for battle. Quick trip wires or barriers to catch opponents off guard. But this needs to pack punch after punch.

Without wasting another moment, Kai brought the hammer down on the gong. A clear, resonant tone rang out, surprisingly loud for its size. The effect on the Thunderwing Drakes was immediate and dramatic.

The blue-scaled beast was the closest, it recoiled violently at the sound. Its wings buckled, causing it to drop several feet in the air. It thrashed its head from side to side, eyes unfocused and disoriented.

The drake with green-tinged scales let out a high-pitched screech. Its flight pattern became erratic, spiraling awkwardly as it tried to escape the sound.

The larger drake with purple markings seemed the least affected. Still, it shook its massive head, momentarily stunned.

Elder Feng was also startled by the unexpected sound but he recovered quickly. His eyes narrowed, recognizing the opportunity Kai had created.

With a burst of speed, Elder Feng shot towards the blue drake, the most vulnerable target. Wind and lightning crackled around his outstretched hand. He struck the drake's exposed underbelly, just behind its left foreleg where the scales were thinnest.

The impact was devastating. Lightning arced through the drake's body, and a sickening crack echoed as ribs shattered under the force of the blow. The blue drake's eyes rolled back, and it let out an agonized roar.

Smoke rising from its scales, the injured drake desperately flapped its wings as it fled from battle.

The green and purple drakes, however, shook off their disorientation quickly. Their eyes, now glowing with rage, fixed on Elder Feng. With ear-splitting shrieks, they charged at him simultaneously.

It worked better than I expected, Kai thought. *But those two recovered fast. And now they look pissed. I need to give the elder another opening.*

As the gong dissipated, he immediately began forming another one. While he worked, he heard Shen Yu speak up again.

"I've never seen anyone form qi constructs as easily as you do," the boy commented, a hint of genuine interest in his voice.

Kai couldn't help but laugh. "Well, being a mortal, I'd be surprised if you had."

A moment later, Kai finished shaping the second gong but that was when he noticed something odd. Shen Yu had moved. The boy was now standing on the opposite side of the boat, as far from Kai as he could get without being obvious about it.

What's he up to? Kai wondered. But there was no time to dwell on it. The qi constructs would collapse soon, and he needed to act.

Once again, Kai brought the hammer down on the gong. The sound rang out, even louder than before. This time, the effect on the Thunderwing Drakes was even more pronounced.

The green drake, already wounded from Elder Feng's earlier attacks, reacted violently. Its wings seized up, muscles spasming uncontrollably. Unable to maintain its flight, the massive beast began to plummet. It let out a terrified shriek as it fell, its body twisting and turning in a futile attempt to regain control. It quickly plummeted from the sky, its massive body crashing into the forest below.

The purple drake, however, had a very different reaction. Its eyes began to glow an angry red, and its movements became erratic. Sparks of electricity danced across its scales as its qi went haywire.

Kai's eyes widened in realization. *Oh, crap. It's gone into rage mode.*

Does everyone in this world have a berserk button or something? he thought, remembering his encounter with the rogue cultivator. *Note to self: Kill enemies before they get a chance to power up.*

Before anyone could react, the enraged drake let out an ear-splitting roar and dove . . . straight at the boat.

Time seemed to slow down as Kai assessed the situation. Liu Wei was standing closest to the incoming beast. Shen Yu, unsurprisingly, was the farthest away. Zhi-Zhi was still hiding in his shell.

That sneaky bastard, Kai thought, a mixture of admiration and annoyance coloring his thoughts. *He could have warned us.*

At the speed the drake was moving, it would reach them long before Elder Feng could turn around and intercept it. In its berserk state, the beast would likely kill Liu Wei before anyone could stop it.

Shit, Kai thought, his mind racing. *There goes a respawn.*

Without hesitation, he activated his Swift Wind Step skill. In a burst of speed, he appeared in front of Liu Wei, shoving him backward just as the drake reached them.

"Master, no!" Liu Wei cried out, his eyes wide with horror.

Kai looked up to see the drake's glowing red eyes and rows of razor-sharp teeth looming over him.

Come on, Iron Rebound, Kai prayed. *Now would be a really good time to—*

Pain exploded through his body as the drake's jaws clamped down. There was no magical reflection of damage, no last-second save. Just razor-sharp teeth tearing through flesh and bone.

The electricity from the bite set every nerve ending on fire. Kai felt his ribs crack like twigs, puncturing lungs and rupturing organs. The drake shook its head violently, and Kai's world became a blur of agony and vertigo.

So much for protagonist luck, Kai thought bitterly as darkness began to creep in at the edges of his vision. *Guess I'll just have to respawn.*

As he fell, Kai saw Elder Feng appear behind the beast. The elder shoved his hand right through the drake's back. His fingers came out the other side, sparking with lightning. The drake began convulsing, its jaws loosening just enough for Kai to fall.

Kai hit the deck of the boat hard. He could hear Liu Wei screaming "Master!" and Zhi-Zhi's shell clattering as the spirit tortoise finally emerged.

As the darkness closed in, the last thing Kai heard was Shen Yu whispering, "Let's see if that was also an 'illusion.'"

CHAPTER THIRTY-THREE

From within the safety of his shell, Zhi-Zhi peeked out at the chaotic scene unfolding before him. His eyes widened as he watched Kai conjure a translucent gong out of pure qi. The young human's ability to manipulate energy into solid constructs never ceased to amaze the spirit tortoise.

How does he do that? Zhi-Zhi wondered. *I've never seen anyone shape qi so easily, not even Mother could do that.*

As impressive as Kai's skill was, it paled in comparison to the terror inspired by the three massive Thunderwing Drakes circling above. Just the aura emanating from the Foundation Establishment beasts made Zhi-Zhi's shell quiver. If not for the life-saving treasure his mother had given him, he never would have dared to venture so far from the safety of the forest.

Being a spirit beast is terrifying, Zhi-Zhi lamented. *Humans want to hunt or tame us, while other beasts want to devour us to increase their power. Why can't the world just be peaceful? It would be so nice to relax all day without worrying about being eaten or captured.*

But almost as quickly as the thought formed, he shook his head.

No, peaceful is boring. I don't like boring. That's why I left home with Kai in the first place. I wanted fun and adventure! His inner voice took on a slightly whiny tone. *I just wish fun didn't always come with so much danger.*

As Kai brought the qi-hammer down on the gong, a resonant tone rang out across the sky. The effect on the Thunderwing Drakes was immediate and dramatic. The beasts recoiled, their wings faltering as the sound disoriented them.

Amazing! Such a simple trick, yet so effective against Foundation Establishment creatures. I wonder if he'd teach me how to do that, Zhi-Zhi mused. Then he caught himself. *But wait, I can't just ask him outright. I have an image to maintain. If they realize I'm not the wise, all-knowing spirit beast I pretend to be, they'll never accept me as their master!*

Zhi-Zhi's mind raced through various scenarios, trying to come up with the perfect plan. Finally, he settled on an idea that seemed foolproof.

I've got it! I'll tell Kai I want to observe his technique and offer feedback. That way, he'll have to show me how it's done and explain the process. Then I can pretend to correct him, maintaining my wise facade while secretly learning the skill!

Zhi-Zhi congratulated himself on his cunning plan, already imagining all the amazing things he could create with qi constructs.

I could make a comfy pillow to nap on, or a little parasol for shade, maybe even—

His daydreaming was cut short by a blur of motion. Kai vanished from where he'd been standing, reappearing in front of Liu Wei just as the terrifying purple drake dove towards the boat. In a split second, Kai shoved the former bandit out of harm's way.

Zhi-Zhi's eyes went wide with horror as the drake's massive jaws clamped down on Kai's body. Blood sprayed across the deck as the beast's teeth tore through flesh and bone.

"No!" Zhi-Zhi cried out, his head emerging fully from his shell for the first time since the battle began. He watched helplessly as Kai's limp form fell to the deck with a sickening thud.

Time seemed to stand still. The world around Zhi-Zhi faded away as memories of his past flooded his mind.

He remembered his early days, alone and afraid. He had never known his true parents, left to fend for himself in a hostile world. It was the ancient spirit tree who had taken pity on him, raising him as her own. But even under her protection, Zhi-Zhi had always felt isolated. The other spirit beasts kept their distance, too afraid of angering his powerful foster mother to risk befriending him.

And humans . . . Zhi-Zhi shuddered at the memories. Every encounter with cultivators had ended the same way. They either tried to hunt him for his valuable spirit beast core or attempted to subjugate him as a tamed companion.

A single tear rolled down Zhi-Zhi's scaly cheek as he gazed at Kai's broken body.

Why? he thought bitterly. *Why did it have to be him?*

Unlike the others, Kai had been different. He had saved Zhi-Zhi from those rogue cultivators, even though he had no obligation to do so. He had invited Zhi-Zhi to travel with them, treating him as an equal rather than a prize to be won. And most remarkably, Kai hadn't been intimidated by Zhi-Zhi's foster mother. He had accepted the spirit tortoise for who he was, flaws and all.

He was my friend, Zhi-Zhi realized. *My first real friend.*

"Don't worry, little one," Elder Feng's voice cut through Zhi-Zhi's grief. "I'll take good care of you now."

"Care for me?" Zhi-Zhi's normally high-pitched voice came out as a low growl. His eyes narrowed as he glared at the elder. "I don't need anyone to take care of me! Kai wasn't my caretaker, he was my friend!"

Elder Feng's brow furrowed. "I understand you're upset, but—"

"You understand nothing!" Zhi-Zhi snapped. His tiny body began to glow with a fierce golden light. "Kai was the first person to treat me like an equal, like a true companion. And now he's gone because *you* couldn't protect us!"

The spirit tortoise's gaze burned with an intensity that made even the Pseudo Core Formation cultivator take a step back. A golden leaf—the life-saving treasure gifted to him by his foster mother—appeared in Zhi-Zhi's clawed hand.

This is all my fault, Zhi-Zhi thought, his anger giving way to crushing guilt. *I should have used the leaf immediately. I shouldn't have hid in my shell like a coward.*

"Listen here," Zhi-Zhi said, his voice quavering. "I am Zhi-Zhi, son of the Ancient Spirit Tree. I've lived for a hundred years, and I've never felt as useless as I do right now."

The golden leaf in Zhi-Zhi's hand began to pulse with energy, but it was erratic, matching the spirit beast's emotions. Elder Feng's eyes widened as he sensed the immense, unstable power contained within the small talisman.

"Young spirit beast," Elder Feng said, his voice now tinged with concern, "please, calm yourself. This power—"

"Calm?" Zhi-Zhi scoffed, tears welling in his eyes. "How can I be calm? I could have saved him! I had this the whole time, and I did nothing!" He raised the golden leaf, his claws trembling. "One touch of this, and even a Pseudo Core Formation cultivator like you wouldn't stand a chance against my mother's Nascent Soul attack. But I was too scared to use it when it mattered!"

Zhi-Zhi's fierce expression crumbled, replaced by one of anguish and self-loathing. "I hid in my shell while Kai fought. I watched as that drake attacked him, and I did nothing. What kind of friend am I?"

His grip on the golden leaf tightened, but not with the intent to use it. Instead, it was as if he was clinging to it for comfort. "I'm no mighty spirit beast. I'm just a coward who pretends to be wise. Kai deserved a better friend than me."

"I should have been braver. I should have fought alongside him. Maybe then . . ." The leaf's golden glow began to fade as Zhi-Zhi's voice trailed off, unable to finish the thought.

The tortoise looked up at Elder Feng, his eyes filled with a mixture of defiance and despair.

"So, don't tell me you'll take care of me," Zhi-Zhi said softly. "I don't deserve it. I couldn't even take care of my friend when he needed me most."

CHAPTER THRITY-FOUR

Kai opened his eyes to find himself suspended in an endless void. The familiar nothingness surrounded him, just as it had the last time he died. He couldn't feel his body or see any part of himself. It was as if he had become one with the emptiness.

Well, this is familiar. At least I know what to expect this time.

A glowing message materialized before him, its light the only thing visible in the vast darkness:

Congratulations!
You have completed the Trident.
Unlocking new ability!
Name: Reset
Description: Reset allows you to respawn back in time.
Each prong grants 3 seconds of rewind. As the mark evolves, rewind time may increase.

Reset? That's . . . incredibly powerful. And convenient.

One of his main concerns had been explaining away his "deaths" to increasingly powerful cultivators. The "illusion" excuse might work on mortals and low-level practitioners, but someone like Elder Feng would be far more skeptical.

Looks like I've just unlocked the ultimate "Get Out of Awkward Death Free" card. No more explaining to suspicious elders why my "death illusion" felt so real. Sorry, creepy cultivation uncles, this protagonist's not getting kidnapped for your secret experiments anytime soon!

Initiating Reset in 3 . . . 2 . . . 1 . . .

The void began to melt away, reality bleeding back into existence. Kai found himself observing the scene on the boat, but from an out-of-body perspective. He saw his own corpse sprawled on the deck, blood pooling beneath it.

Elder Feng stood over the body, his expression unreadable. "How unfortunate," the cultivator murmured. He turned to Zhi-Zhi, who had finally emerged from his shell. "Don't worry, little one. I'll take good care of you now."

Zhi-Zhi bristled, his tiny form shaking with anger. "Care for me? I don't need anyone to take care of me! Kai wasn't my caretaker, he was my friend!"

Kai's non-existent eyes narrowed. *My body's not even cold, and the elder is already trying to claim Zhi-Zhi. But at least the little guy is loyal.*

His gaze shifted to Shen Yu. The boy was frowning at Kai's corpse, a look of confusion and . . . disappointment? It was as if he had expected Kai to spring back to life at any moment.

What do you know, Shen Yu?

Before he could ponder further, the scene began to rewind. It was like watching a video in reverse, everything moving backwards at high speed. The rewinding slowed, then stopped completely. Kai found himself looking at a frozen tableau of the boat, mere seconds before his death.

He saw himself, hands outstretched, in the process of crafting a second qi-gong. Shen Yu was frozen mid-step, clearly in the act of distancing himself from the impending danger.

Sneaky bastard, Kai thought. *He knew what was coming, but how? Has he experienced this before? If so, was I there in the previous timeline? Or is he actually a reincarnator with some kind of precognitive ability? Hell, for all I know, he could have his own System.*

Kai shook the thoughts out of his non-existent head as he focused on the plan. Time had rewound to just after he had used the first sound attack on the drakes. He had time to save Liu Wei and himself.

---

3 . . . 2 . . . 1 . . .

Kai felt a pulling sensation, as if his consciousness was being sucked into his body. The world blurred, then snapped back into focus. He was back in his body, hands still forming the qi-gong.

Without missing a beat, Kai called out, "Liu Wei! Come here, quickly!"

Liu Wei's head snapped towards him, eyes wide with confusion. "Master?"

Kai kept his focus on the forming gong. "Move with me," he instructed, stepping sideways towards the far end of the boat.

Liu Wei hurried to keep pace, stumbling slightly as he moved. "What's happening?"

"Just stay close," Kai muttered, his eyes never leaving the qi construct in his hands. They shuffled across the deck, the half-formed gong floating between Kai's palms.

As they reached the far side of the boat, they found themselves standing next to Shen Yu, who regarded them with a mixture of surprise and suspicion.

Sorry, not-so-mysterious boy. We're all going to survive this time.

"Zhi-Zhi," Kai called out. "I need you to let Liu Wei use your shell as a shield."

The tiny tortoise puffed up. "Excuse me? I am not some common piece of armor to be passed around!"

Kai fixed him with a stern look. "Zhi-Zhi, please. It could save his life."

Grumbling, Zhi-Zhi relented. "Fine, fine. But only because you asked so nicely." He hopped into Liu Wei's outstretched hands.

Liu Wei held the shell-covered spirit beast like a small shield. It wasn't much, barely the size of a dinner plate, but Kai knew it could deflect a critical blow if needed.

Now for the encore, Kai thought, focusing on the qi-gong he had just created. With a sharp movement, he struck it.

The clear, resonant tone rang out even louder than before. The effect on the Thunderwing Drakes was immediate and dramatic.

The green drake, already wounded from Elder Feng's earlier attacks, reacted violently. Its wings seized up, muscles spasming uncontrollably. Unable to maintain flight, the massive beast began to plummet. It let out a terrified shriek as it fell, its body twisting and turning in a futile attempt to regain control. Within seconds, it had disappeared from view, crashing into the forest below.

The purple drake, however, had a very different reaction. Its eyes began to glow an angry red, and its movements became erratic. Sparks of electricity danced across its scales as its qi went haywire.

Here we go again, Kai thought, bracing himself. *Berserk mode activated.*

The enraged drake let out an ear-splitting roar and dove straight for the boat. But this time, Kai was ready. He, Liu Wei, and Shen Yu were positioned as far from the drake's trajectory as possible.

Elder Feng, noticing the beast's charge, abandoned his offensive stance and raced to intercept it. Lightning crackled around his hands as he positioned himself between the drake and the boat.

The drake's jaws snapped shut mere inches from the boat's railing. In the same instant, Elder Feng's lightning fist punched clean through the beast's chest. The drake's roar turned into a gurgle as electricity coursed through its body.

With a final, violent spasm, the Thunderwing Drake went limp. Its massive form crashed onto the deck of the boat, causing the entire vessel to rock precariously.

For a moment, everyone stood frozen, the sudden silence almost deafening after the chaos of battle. Then Elder Feng turned to face them, his robes singed and torn but a triumphant smile on his face.

"Well done, young Kai," he said, nodding approvingly. "That was quick thinking with the sound attack. And I see you made sure to protect your companions as well. Very commendable."

"Thank you, Elder Feng," Kai bowed slightly. "I'm just glad we all made it through safely."

Yeah, all of us except me the first time around, Kai thought bitterly. *And you didn't seem too broken up about that, did you?*

Outwardly, he maintained his polite demeanor. "Your combat skills are truly impressive, Elder. We would have been lost without your protection."

Elder Feng waved off the compliment, though Kai noticed the pleased glint in his eyes. "It was nothing. Protecting promising young cultivators is part of my duty as an Outer Elder."

Sure it is, Kai thought. *Along with snatching up rare spirit beasts when the opportunity presents itself.*

Liu Wei, still clutching Zhi-Zhi like a shield, stepped forward. "That . . . that was incredible, Elder Feng! And Master Kai, your quick thinking saved us all!"

Zhi-Zhi squirmed in Liu Wei's grasp. "Yes, yes, everyone's very impressed. Now would you mind putting me down? I am not a handbag!"

Liu Wei quickly set the spirit beast down, looking sheepish. "Sorry, Master Zhi-Zhi. And thank you for protecting me."

Zhi-Zhi puffed up his tiny chest. "Well, of course. Someone has to look after you youngsters.

As the others continued their conversation, a blue screen appeared before Kai.

Thunderwing Drake eliminated
Total XP Earned: 8,000 Your Share: 2,000 XP
Qi Condensation has reached Level 4!
You have gained 50 XP

Huh, party XP distribution, Kai mused, eyeing the numbers. *Just like in an MMO. I guess the System considers Elder Feng part of our "party" for this fight.*

His gaze drifted to the Outer Elder, who was busy talking to Shen Yu.

He doesn't have a leveling system like mine. All that extra XP, just going to waste. You know, System, if you're feeling generous, you could always redistribute that unclaimed XP my way. No need to let it disappear into the void.

Unfortunately, System remained stubbornly silent on the matter. Kai sighed. *Worth a shot, I suppose. Still, 2,000 XP isn't bad for a single encounter. Especially one where I technically died. Wait . . . 2,000 XP? That's enough to—*

His thoughts were cut short as a sudden surge of energy coursed through his body. The qi in his dantian began to churn and expand, breaking through an invisible barrier. Kai felt his meridians widening to accommodate the increased flow of energy.

A soft golden glow emanated from his skin, lasting only a few seconds but impossible to miss. When it faded, Kai could feel the difference—his qi was denser, more potent, and he had a greater reservoir to draw from.

Level Up! You are now Qi Refining Stage 8!

The sudden breakthrough didn't go unnoticed. Elder Feng's eyebrows shot up in surprise, his gaze sharpening as he studied Kai intently. Liu Wei's mouth fell open in shock, while Zhi-Zhi stopped mid-rant, his tiny eyes widening at Kai.

Even Shen Yu, usually so impassive, couldn't hide his astonishment. The boy's eyes narrowed, a calculating look replacing his initial surprise.

"Young Kai," Elder Feng said slowly, "did you just . . . advance a stage in your cultivation?"

Kai smiled awkwardly, acutely aware of all the attention focused on him. "Ah, yes," he replied, trying to sound casual. "I was close to breaking through anyway. The intensity of the battle must have given me that final push I needed."

Close to breaking through from zero to 2,000 XP in an instant, sure, Kai thought wryly. *But they don't need to know that.*

"Most impressive. It's rare to see someone advance so quickly, especially right after such an intense battle. You truly are full of surprises, young Kai."

Liu Wei looked at Kai with awe. "That's amazing, Master! To think you could break through again so quickly!"

Zhi-Zhi, not to be outdone, puffed up. "Well, of course he did! He's my disciple, after all. I knew he had it in him all along!"

Kai suppressed a chuckle at the spirit beast's claim. *Sure you did, Zhi-Zhi. Sure you did.*

As the others continued to express their amazement, Kai's eyes drifted to his right wrist. The familiar trident mark was there, but something had changed. Where before there had been three vibrant red prongs, now one had turned a deep, inky black.

Interesting, Kai thought, relief washing over him. *So, it only used up one prong. That's much better than I expected.*

He flexed his wrist slightly, studying the mark. *I was worried Reset might use all three prongs at once. That would've made it a last-resort ability at best. But this . . . this I can work with.*

Anyway, let's see what my stats are like now.

Name: Kai Thorn

XP: 50/4,000
Level: Qi Refining Stage 8
Qi: 250/250
Strength: 60
Agility: 63
Endurance: 62
Intelligence: 30
Wisdom: 29

Titles:
Novice Instructor
Elemental Affinities:
Lightning: 20%

Skills:
Qi Condensation (Level 4)
Basic Cultivation Technique (Level 3)
Unarmed Combat (Level 2)
Deception (Level 4)
Iron Skin Technique (Level 3)
Swift Wind Step (Level 4)
Flame Palm Strike (Level 3)
Mental Fortitude (Passive)
Spirit Beast Communication (Level 1)
Qi Concealment (Level 1)
Qi Detection (Level 1)
Iron Rebound (Level 1)

4,000 XP? That's . . . a lot. I can't exactly expect to kill my way to the next breakthrough. Not unless I want to become the sect's resident psychopath.

But if things in the sect are anything like the novels I've read . . . Well, I'll probably face plenty of trials there. And if I'm lucky, there might be quests that let me level up faster. Or maybe my growth is going to slow to a snail's pace now . . . no, make that a tortoise's pace.

With that thought his gaze drifted to Zhi-Zhi, who was currently perched on Liu Wei's head, giving him advice on what to do when face to face with a dragon.

"Now listen closely, my naive disciple. When confronted by a dragon, the first thing you must do is compliment its scales. Dragons are vain creatures, you see. A well-placed compliment can mean the difference between being eaten and being . . . well, only slightly singed."

Liu Wei's brow furrowed in confusion. "Um, Zhi-Zhi? Where did this talk of dragons come from? I thought we were discussing the Azure Sky Sect trials . . ."

Zhi-Zhi waved a tiny claw dismissively. "Trials, dragons, it's all the same in the grand scheme of things! Now, as I was saying, after the compliment . . ."

"After?" Liu Wei asked, still bewildered but deciding to humor the spirit beast.

"Why, you run, of course!" Zhi-Zhi declared. "Run as fast as your legs can carry you. Unless you're me, in which case you stand your ground and challenge the dragon to a battle of wits. I once outsmarted a whole family of celestial dragons, you know. They still speak of it in the heavenly realms to this day!"

Liu Wei nodded slowly, clearly unsure how to respond to this unexpected tangent. "I . . . see. Thank you for the advice. I'll keep it in mind if I ever encounter a dragon."

Kai shook his head, a small smile playing on his lips as he listened to the tortoise continue to ramble.

Who knows? Maybe someday that random bit of dragon advice will come in handy. In this world, anything seems possible.

CHAPTER THIRTY-FIVE

As the flying boat glided through the air, Kai stood at the bow, his eyes fixed on the horizon. The wind whipped through his hair, carrying the scent of mountain air and something else, something mystical. In the distance, a magnificent structure began to take shape, growing larger with each passing moment.

So this is the Azure Sky Sect, it's everything I imagined it to be.

The sect sprawled across a series of mountain peaks, connected by impossibly thin bridges that seemed to defy gravity. Pagodas with curved roofs of deep blue tiles reached towards the sky, their eaves adorned with carvings of blue and white dragons. Waterfalls cascaded down the mountainsides, their mist creating rainbows in the sunlight. At the highest peak stood a grand palace, its golden roof gleaming like a beacon.

It really does seem like something out of a fantasy novel.

"Impressive, isn't it?" Elder Feng's voice broke through Kai's thoughts.

Kai nodded, not taking his eyes off the sight before him. "It's . . . magnificent."

Liu Wei stumbled to the railing, his eyes wide. "I've never seen anything like it! Master, is this what all sects look like?"

Kai chuckled. "I wouldn't know, Liu Wei. This is my first time seeing one, too."

Though I've seen plenty in games and anime, he added silently. *But nothing quite compares to the real thing.*

Zhi-Zhi, perched on Liu Wei's head, puffed out his chest. "Bah! You should have seen the Celestial Tortoise Palace in the Heavenly Realms. Now *that* was impressive. This is . . . adequate, I suppose."

Kai raised an eyebrow at the spirit beast. "Oh? And when exactly did you visit this Celestial Tortoise Palace?"

Zhi-Zhi's eyes darted back and forth. "Well, you see . . . it was . . . a very long time ago. Yes, that's it! So long ago that the details are a bit fuzzy. But trust me, it was magnificent!"

As they drew closer, Kai noticed formations etched into the mountains. *Defensive arrays,* he realized. *Probably designed to keep out intruders and contain the sect's qi.*

The boat began its descent, aiming for a large plateau near the base of the central mountain. As they approached, Kai's eyes widened at the sight before him. The plateau was teeming with people—a sea of faces and colorful robes as far as he could see.

"Ah, there are the other Outer Elders with their recruits," Elder Feng said, a note of tension in his voice. "We're . . . a bit late."

Late to an important event with this many people? That's never good in these kinds of stories, Kai thought.

As their boat touched down on the edge of the plateau, Kai did a quick headcount. There had to be at least a few hundred potential recruits, if not more, each accompanied by their respective Outer Elders. The chatter of the crowd washed over them, a mix of excited whispers and nervous murmurs.

From within the crowd, several voices rose above the rest, directed at Elder Feng:

"Well, well, look who finally decided to join us!"

"If you were any more late, Feng, we might have started without you!"

Elder Feng straightened his robes, putting on a dignified air as he stepped off the boat. "My apologies for the delay, fellow Elders. We encountered some . . . unexpected challenges on our journey."

A bald elder with a thick black beard and black eyes scoffed. "Challenges? What kind of challenges could possibly delay an Outer Elder of the Azure Sky Sect?"

Elder Feng's expression tightened slightly. "We were attacked by a group of Thunderwing Drakes."

"Thunderwing Drakes?" another elder, a woman with gray hair, asked incredulously. "And all your recruits survived?"

Elder Feng nodded, a hint of pride creeping into his voice. "Indeed. Thanks in no small part to the quick thinking of one of my recruits."

Here we go, Kai thought, bracing himself for the attention he knew was coming.

As if on cue, the other Outer Elders began boasting about their own recruits.

"Well, that's certainly impressive," said the bald elder. "But let me introduce you to Xu Na." He gestured to a girl with long black hair and pale skin. "She's already reached the third stage of Qi Refining, and she's only fifteen!"

Third stage at fifteen? Not bad. But not exactly earth-shattering either.

The gray-haired woman stepped forward. "And this is Zhao Jian," she said, pointing to a muscular young man. "He may be a mortal, but he's already mastered three different martial arts styles. I expect great things from him once he begins cultivating."

Martial arts prodigy, huh? Classic trope. Wonder how he'll stack up once qi gets involved.

As the introductions continued, Kai noticed a pattern. Most of the recruits were either mortals or in the early stages of Qi Refining. The highest he heard mentioned was a boy named Wu Feng, who had reached the fifth stage.

Interesting, Kai thought. *I'm already ahead of the curve. But this can't be all of it, for a sect as big as the Azure Sky Sect, there should be some geniuses. Where are the arrogant young masters?*

Finally, Elder Feng cleared his throat. "Allow me to introduce my own recruits. This is Liu Wei, he's at the third stage of Qi Refining."

Liu Wei bowed nervously, his face flushed with embarrassment at the sudden attention.

"And this," Elder Feng continued, a hint of smugness in his voice, "is Kai Thorn. He's the one who devised the strategy that saved us from the Thunderwing Drakes. Kai has already reached the eighth stage of Qi Refining."

A shocked silence fell over the gathered elders and recruits. Kai could feel dozens of eyes boring into him, filled with disbelief, suspicion, and in some cases, fear.

"Eighth stage?" the bald elder sputtered. "That's . . . that's impossible! How could a mere mortal reach such a level without joining a sect?"

The gray-haired woman narrowed her eyes. "Did you perhaps acquire some sort of treasure, young man? A cultivation manual or a rare herb, perhaps?"

"No, Elder," Kai replied. "I simply . . . practiced a lot."

Great answer, he chided himself. *Very convincing. They'll definitely believe that.*

The other recruits were whispering among themselves now, casting furtive glances in Kai's direction. He could see the uncertainty and worry in their eyes.

They're probably wondering how they can compete with someone like me, Kai realized. *I need to be careful. Making enemies before the trials even begin would be a bad move.*

Elder Feng cleared his throat, continuing his introductions. "And lastly, this is Shen Yu." He gestured to the calm-faced boy. "A remarkable talent who broke through to Qi Refining on his first attempt."

The other Outer Elders' eyebrows shot up in surprise.

"On his first attempt?" the bald elder asked. "That's quite . . . unusual."

The gray-haired woman peered at Shen Yu closely. "Indeed. Almost as unusual as reaching the eighth stage of Qi Refining without a sect." Her gaze flicked between Shen Yu and Kai, suspicion evident in her eyes.

Shen Yu merely bowed politely, his face betraying no emotion. "I was fortunate to receive good guidance," he said simply.

Just then, another Outer Elder, a portly man with a jovial face, spoke up. "Well, Feng, you've certainly brought an interesting group this year." His eyes twinkled mischievously. "But tell me, have you picked up another spirit beast?"

Elder Feng's smile tightened almost imperceptibly. "Ah, you must be referring to—"

"Another spirit beast?" Zhi-Zhi's voice rang out. "I'll have you know, I am no mere beast! I am Zhi-Zhi, the great and powerful spirit tortoise of the Celestial—"

"The spirit beast is with the boy," Elder Feng interrupted hastily, gesturing towards Kai.

Kai nodded, trying to keep a straight face. "Yes, Zhi-Zhi is . . . my companion."

The portly elder chuckled. "A spirited little thing, isn't he? And quite rare, too, if I'm not mistaken."

Zhi-Zhi puffed up with pride. "Of course I'm rare! I'm one of a kind, I'll have you know!"

Kai could see the other Outer Elders eyeing Zhi-Zhi. He already felt the start of a headache coming on. *Looks like Elder Feng isn't the only one interested in "acquiring."*

The gray-haired woman's gaze lingered on Zhi-Zhi for a moment before returning to Kai. "First, an eighth-stage Qi Refining cultivator, and now a rare spirit beast. You've certainly found some . . . interesting recruits this time, Feng."

Elder Feng's smile remained fixed in place, but Kai could sense a hint of tension in his voice as he replied, "Indeed. The Misty Waterfall Village proved to be quite the source of talent this year."

As the introductions continued, Kai noticed several of the Outer Elders casting envious glances at Elder Feng. Their eyes darted between Kai, Shen Yu, and Zhi-Zhi, a mix of jealousy and calculation in their gazes.

The portly elder chuckled, elbowing Elder Feng playfully. "Well, well, Feng. Looks like you might be up for the big reward this year, eh? The Sect Leader will be impressed with this batch."

Of course there's a reward system, Kai thought. *It's the perfect way to motivate Outer Elders to scout for talent. And let's be honest, it explains why Elder Feng was so keen on protecting us. To him, we're basically valuable merchandise.*

Elder Feng tried to look modest, but Kai could see the gleam of satisfaction in his eyes. "Now, now," he said, "let's not get ahead of ourselves. The trials haven't even begun yet."

The bald elder shook his head, a sly grin on his face. "I wouldn't count your spirit stones just yet, Feng. I've heard that Elder Zhou managed to recruit the young masters from the Sun and Moon clans this year."

A ripple of excitement passed through the crowd at this news.

Ah, there it is, Kai thought, suppressing a smirk. *I was wondering when the young master archetypes would show up.*

As if summoned by the mention of their names, the crowd suddenly parted. A tall elder strode through the gap, flanked by two young men. Even at a glance, Kai could tell these were the "young master" types he'd read about in countless stories.

The first young man swaggered forward, his head held high and a cocky grin on his face. His robes were made of the finest silk, embroidered with golden suns. He scanned the crowd with an air of superiority, as if daring anyone to meet his gaze.

Great, Kai thought. *The brash, hot-headed type. Bet he's got a short temper to match that ego.*

The second young man moved with a more measured grace. His robes, adorned with silver crescent moons, were just as fine as his companion's. But where the first young man's eyes blazed with barely contained arrogance, this one's gaze was cool and calculating.

And there's the calm, cunning one, Kai noted. *Probably thinks he's three steps ahead of everyone else.*

Elder Zhou stepped forward, his voice booming across the plateau. "Ah, Elder Feng, you've finally arrived. Let me introduce you to my recruits: Young Master Sun Jun of the Sun Clan, and Young Master Lu Chen of the Moon Clan. Both these boys have reached the eighth stage of Qi Refining!"

The elder paused, clearly expecting gasps of amazement or murmurs of awe. Instead, he was met with an awkward silence. The crowd shifted uncomfortably, glancing between the new arrivals and Kai.

Sun Jun's cocky grin faltered slightly. "What's wrong with you people?" he demanded. "Didn't you hear? We're at the eighth stage of Qi Refining!"

Lu Chen remained silent, but his eyes narrowed as he scanned the crowd, sensing that something was off.

The gray-haired woman cleared her throat. "Ah, yes. Most impressive, young masters. However, it seems you're not the only ones to reach such a level. Elder Feng's recruit, Kai Thorn, he too has reached the eighth stage of Qi Refining."

Sun Jun's jaw dropped. "What?! That's impossible! He looks like some nobody from a backwater village, how can he be at the same level as us?"

Before Kai could respond, Zhi-Zhi's voice rang out. "Nobody? Backwater village? How dare you insult my disciple, you arrogant pup!"

Oh, no, Kai thought, inwardly facepalming. *Zhi-Zhi, please don't . . .*

But the spirit tortoise was just getting started. "Let me tell you something, you silk-robed peacock! My disciple, Kai, is a once-in-a-millennium talent! He's mastered techniques that would make your ancestors weep with envy!"

Kai tried to keep his face neutral, but he could feel a headache coming on. *Zhi-Zhi, we talked about this. You're not my master, and I definitely haven't mastered any enviably ancient techniques.*

Zhi-Zhi, oblivious to Kai's internal distress, continued his tirade. "Why, in my younger days, I trained countless prodigies who went on to become immortals! And let me tell you, none of them showed half the potential of my dear disciple, Kai!"

Sun Jun's face turned an interesting shade of purple. "You . . . you dare? Do you know who I am?"

"A loudmouthed braggart with more pride than sense, that's who you are!" Zhi-Zhi retorted.

Lu Chen's calm facade cracked slightly, a flicker of amusement crossing his face before he quickly suppressed it. "How . . . interesting," he said, his voice tight. "And how did this village boy manage such a feat?"

"Hard work and determination, Young Master Lu. Nothing more." Kai smiled as he stepped forward, trying to salvage the situation. He gently patted Zhi-Zhi's shell. "And perhaps a bit of . . . enthusiastic encouragement from my spirited companion here."

Sun Jun's face turned red with anger. "Hard work? Don't make me laugh! You must have cheated somehow. There's no way a commoner could match us!"

Lu Chen placed a hand on Sun Jun's shoulder, restraining him. "Calm yourself, brother," he said softly. But Kai could see the calculation in Lu Chen's eyes as he studied him. "We'll have plenty of time to . . . test . . . this village prodigy during the trials."

Elder Zhou looked like he had swallowed something sour. His eyes darted between Kai and his prized recruits, clearly recalculating his chances for that reward.

"Yes, well," Elder Zhou said, forcing a smile. "The more talented recruits, the better for Azure Sky Sect. Wouldn't you agree, Feng?"

Elder Feng nodded, but Kai could see the smugness in his eyes. "Indeed, Zhou. May the best recruits win."

As the crowd began to disperse, Kai caught Liu Wei's worried glance. "Master Kai," Liu Wei whispered, "I think you might have made some powerful enemies."

Kai sighed, watching as Sun Jun shot him a venomous glare while Lu Chen whispered something to Elder Zhou. "Yeah," he said. "Somehow, I'm not surprised. Welcome to the Azure Sky Sect, I guess."

He glanced at Shen Yu, wondering how the mysterious boy was reacting to all this. To his surprise, Shen Yu caught his eye and gave him the slightest of nods, a ghost of a smile playing at the corners of his mouth.

Great, Kai thought sarcastically. *The calm, mysterious one finds this amusing. That's never a good sign. Well, at least things are starting to feel more like a proper xianxia story. Arrogant young masters, check. Deadly rivalries before the trials even begin, check. Now all we need is a hidden big bad and maybe a love interest or two, and we'll have the full set.*

"Now, now, my dear disciple," Zhi-Zhi said, misinterpreting Kai's expression, "there's no need to worry. With my guidance and your talent, we'll have this sect eating out of our hands in no time! Why, I remember when I advised the Jade Emperor himself on matters of cultivation. It all started when . . ."

CHAPTER THIRTY-SIX

Before Zhi-Zhi could finish his story, a hush fell over the crowd. The air seemed to grow heavy, charged with qi that made the hairs on the back of Kai's neck stand up.

This pressure . . . Kai thought, instinctively tensing. *It's similar to what I felt from Zhi-Zhi's mother, but not quite as overwhelming.*

Zhi-Zhi, who had been mid-boast, suddenly went quiet. His tiny eyes widened, and he quickly retreated into his shell, peeking out cautiously.

A figure appeared at the top of the grand staircase leading up to the central palace. Even from this distance, Kai could feel the immense power radiating from the newcomer. The Outer Elders immediately bowed their heads in respect.

"Greetings, Nascent Soul Elder Tao."

The Nascent Soul elder descended the stairs with graceful steps, each movement seeming to bend the very air around him. As he drew closer, Kai could make out his features—a face that looked no older than thirty, but no doubt the elder had lived for centuries.

"Elder Feng," the Nascent Soul cultivator spoke, "I trust your journey was . . . eventful?"

Elder Feng bowed deeper. "Yes, Elder Tao. We encountered some difficulties, but thanks to the resourcefulness of my recruits, we overcame them."

Elder Tao's gaze swept over the gathered recruits, lingering for a moment on Kai. A slight furrow appeared in his brow, so quick Kai almost missed it.

Did he sense something about me? Kai wondered, trying to keep his expression neutral. *Or am I just being paranoid?*

Before Kai could ponder further, more figures appeared at the top of the staircase. Other Inner Elders, each radiating an aura of power that made the Outer Elders seem like children in comparison.

A translucent blue screen materialized before his eyes as he looked at the first elder.

> Elder Tao
> Level: Early Nascent Soul Realm
> Age: 940 years

Early Nascent Soul, huh?

Kai quickly scanned the other Inner Elders, noting that most of them registered as mid to late Nascent Soul cultivators. The memory of the colossal tree spirit, with its Peak Nascent Soul status, flashed through his mind.

The power scaling in this world is still insane. But at least I have some frame of reference now. While these guys are powerhouses, they're still a step below the ancient tree spirit.

As the Inner Elders took their places, a new pressure filled the air. It was unlike anything Kai had felt before—a presence so vast and overwhelming that it seemed to distort reality itself.

Oh, boy, Kai thought, his heart racing. *I think I know who this is.*

Zhi-Zhi, who had been unusually quiet, suddenly popped his head out of his shell. "Oh, my," he whispered. "It's been a long time since I felt power like this. Not since I arm-wrestled the Jade Emperor himself. Though, of course, his was much more impressive."

Kai resisted the urge to facepalm. *Even now, Zhi-Zhi? Really?*

A figure appeared at the top of the stairs, shrouded in mist that seemed to defy the laws of nature. As the mist parted, it revealed a black-haired man, or perhaps something beyond a mere man. He appeared neither young nor old, his sharp features perfect and timeless. His black eyes, when they opened, seemed to contain entire universes.

The Outer Elders fell to their knees. Even the Inner Elders bowed deeply. Kai felt an irresistible urge to prostrate himself before this being, but he managed to resist, settling for a deep bow instead.

"Greetings, Sect Master," the elders called out.

Sect Master, Kai repeated in his mind, trying to process what he was seeing. *A being whose cultivation surpasses even the Nascent Soul Realm. Just how powerful is he?*

> Unknown Entity Level: ???
> Unable to identify.
> Entity's level exceeds your perception ability by a significant margin.

Not surprising, Kai thought, remembering his encounter with the forest critter. *But let's check something else . . .*

When he opened his map, he was surprised to see the Sect Master's position was clearly marked. There was an impossibly large green dot, but a dot nonetheless.

Well, that's interesting. The forest critter didn't show up on the map at all, but the Sect Master does. So, he's incredibly powerful, definitely beyond Nascent Soul, but not quite at the level of that strange creature.

As Kai turned his focus back to the elders before him, he caught a glimpse of Shen Yu out of the corner of his eye. The usually impassive boy's eyes had widened slightly, a flash of . . . something passing across his face. Recognition? Fear? Anger? It was gone as quickly as it had appeared.

Does Shen Yu know something about the Sect Master? Or is he just as overwhelmed as the rest of us?

The Sect Master's gaze swept over the crowd, seeming to pierce through each person it fell upon. When it reached Kai, he felt as if his very soul was being examined. It took every ounce of his willpower not to flinch away.

Finally, the Sect Master spoke, his voice somehow both a whisper and a thunderclap. "Thank you all for attending the Azure Sky Sect trials."

This is it, Kai thought, his mind already racing with possibilities. *The start of my cultivation journey in this world. Well, the official start, anyway.*

He glanced around at the other recruits, noting their reactions. Some looked eager, others terrified. Liu Wei was fidgeting nervously beside him, while Shen Yu maintained his usual impassive expression.

The Sect Master raised a hand, and silence fell instantly. "Before we begin," he said, his voice carrying effortlessly across the plateau, "I would like to remind you all of the purpose of these trials."

Kai listened intently, not wanting to miss a single word. *In games, the quest-giver's speech often contains crucial information. I doubt this will be any different.*

"The Azure Sky Sect seeks not just talent, but potential," the Sect Master continued. "We look for those who can grow, adapt, and overcome challenges. These trials will test not only your current abilities but your capacity to learn and evolve. And remember to pay attention to your surroundings. The sect has hidden aids and hints throughout the trial grounds. Those with keen observation skills may find their path . . . easier."

Hidden aids and hints? Kai thought excitedly. *That's practically screaming "secret quests" and "bonus objectives." I'll definitely need to keep my eyes open for those.*

The Sect Master's gaze swept over the crowd once more. "Remember, while competition is natural, these trials are not meant to pit you against each other. Your true opponent is yourself—your limits, your fears, your doubts."

Zhi-Zhi nodded sagely, as if he had been the one to come up with this wisdom.

Classic motivational speech, Kai thought. *But in a world of cultivators and qi, I wonder how literally I should take that "your true opponent is yourself" bit.*

"Now," the Sect Master said, a hint of a smile playing at the corners of his mouth, "let us begin with the first trial."

CHAPTER THIRTY-SEVEN

The first trial you will face is known as the Trial of Endurance," the Sect Master continued, "You will be transported to a mini-realm, a pocket of space created and controlled by our sect. Within this realm, each of you will face a series of challenges."

An excited whisper rippled through the crowd. Kai caught fragments of conversation around him.

"A pocket realm?"

"I've heard stories, but never thought I'd see one!"

"How do they even create something like that?"

I wonder if it's like the instance dungeons in MMOs, Kai mused.

"For those unfamiliar with the concept," the Sect Master explained, noticing the confusion on some faces, "a pocket realm is a small, self-contained space separate from our world. It allows us to create controlled environments for training and trials."

Liu Wei's eyes widened. He leaned closer to Kai and whispered, "Master, is such a thing really possible?"

Kai nodded, keeping his eyes on the Sect Master. "With qi, many things are possible."

The Sect Master's voice grew stern. "Listen carefully, for this is crucial. You have one hour to complete the trial. Those who finish early will rank higher than those who finish later. Anyone who fails to complete the trial within the hour will be expelled from the sect."

A gasp rippled through the crowd. Kai could see the panic setting in on many faces. *One hour time limit with expulsion as the penalty. Classic high-stakes scenario.*

"One hour? I'll finish it in half that time!" Sun Jun scoffed.

His companion, Lu Chen, remained silent but his eyes narrowed in concentration.

Kai glanced at Shen Yu, curious about his reaction. The calm-faced boy showed no change in expression, as if the news didn't faze him at all.

Either he's incredibly confident, or he's mastered the art of the poker face, Kai thought. *But with his mysterious background, I'm going with incredibly confident.*

The Sect Master raised a hand, calling for silence. "There's more you should know. The difficulty of the challenges will depend on your cultivation level. For those who have yet to begin cultivating, the trials will be adjusted to a level a mortal can withstand."

Kai frowned at this news. *Well, there goes my advantage. I was hoping my higher cultivation level would give me an edge.*

Liu Wei let out a sigh of relief. "That's good news for me, right, Master Kai?"

Kai nodded, but his mind was racing. *If the challenges scale with cultivation level, then raw power might not be enough. This could be more about problem-solving and adaptability.*

Zhi-Zhi, who had been uncharacteristically quiet, suddenly piped up. "Ha! Scaling difficulty? That's nothing new. Why, I once participated in a heavenly tournament where the challenges adapted to our very thoughts! Of course, I won easily, but—"

"Shh," Kai hushed the spirit tortoise gently. "Let's focus on what's happening now, okay?"

The Sect Master's gaze swept over the crowd once more. "Are you ready to begin?"

Before anyone could respond, he clapped his hands. A blinding light enveloped the recruits, and Kai felt a sudden pulling sensation.

Here we go, he thought, bracing himself. *Time to put all that gaming experience to use.*

In an instant, the recruits vanished, leaving only the Sect Master and the elders on the plateau.

The Sect Master turned to face the elders, his expression unreadable. His gaze swept over them one by one, finally settling on the Outer Elders.

"You will receive your rewards after the trial."

The Outer Elders straightened, their eyes lighting up with anticipation. Elder Feng, in particular, seemed to be holding his breath.

With a casual gesture, the Sect Master reached into his storage ring and produced a small, glowing red pill.

The Outer Elders' eyes widened in recognition. Elder Zhou let out an audible gasp.

"C-Core Formation Pill!" he stammered, unable to contain his shock.

The Sect Master smiled, a rare expression that made him look almost human. "Indeed. If one of your recruits reaches the top of the leaderboard, the Outer Elder who brought them in will be awarded this pill."

The reaction was immediate. Elder Feng's eyes gleamed with barely contained greed. Elder Zhou straightened his back, a determined look crossing his face. Even the usually composed Elder Li couldn't help but stare at the pill with longing.

"Sect Master," Elder Zhou ventured, his voice filled with hope, "the young masters I recruited, Sun Jun and Lu Chen, they're both at the eighth stage of Qi Refining. Surely they have a good chance of claiming the top spot?"

The Sect Master's smile faded, replaced by a look of mild disappointment. "Is that supposed to impress me, Elder Zhou?"

Elder Zhou faltered, taken aback by the Sect Master's response. "But . . . but Sect Master, they're only sixteen! To reach such a level at their age—"

The Sect Master held up a hand, cutting off Elder Zhou's protests. "You misunderstand, Elder Zhou. While their cultivation is indeed noteworthy for their age, it is not as impressive as you seem to think."

He paused, letting his words sink in before continuing. "Those born into powerful clans like the Sun and Moon have advantages from birth. Access to high-quality resources, expert guidance, and optimal cultivation environments. Many such 'prodigies' struggle to break through to Core Formation, their potential stunted by early advantages that become crutches. Their current level is expected, not exceptional."

The other elders nodded in agreement, some looking relieved that their own recruits weren't being dismissed outright.

Elder Tao stepped forward. "Sect Master, if I may ask . . . do you intend to take a disciple this time?"

The question hung in the air. The Sect Master was known for his discerning eye and high standards. It had been five years since he last accepted a personal disciple.

The Sect Master paused, considering the question. "If any of the participants show talent comparable to Wang Lin, then yes, I see no reason why I shouldn't nurture them myself."

At the mention of Wang Lin, the Sect Master's prized disciple, a ripple of excitement passed through the gathered elders. Wang Lin was a legend in the sect, known for his unparalleled talent and rapid advancement. The twenty-year-old was only half a step away from breaking into the Nascent Soul Realm!

Elder Feng, emboldened by the Sect Master's words, spoke up. "Sect Master, if I may, what about my recruit, Kai Thorn? He's also at the eighth stage of Qi Refining, but he comes from a simple village with no clan backing."

The Sect Master's eyes narrowed slightly, a flicker of interest passing across his face. "Yes, that boy . . . Kai. He is indeed interesting."

Elder Zhou, still smarting from the dismissal of his prized recruits, couldn't help but interject. "But Sect Master, what if the boy simply found some hidden resources or a powerful treasure? That could explain his rapid advancement without clan support."

The Sect Master let out a laugh, the sound echoing across the plateau. "Elder Zhou, at my level of cultivation, do you think such things would escape my notice?"

He shook his head, amusement clear in his voice. "I can sense when cultivators have used external resources to bolster their progress. That boy, Kai, has definitely not used any. In fact, I would be surprised if he's ever even used a simple healing pellet. His qi is remarkably pure."

Elder Zhou's face fell, but the Sect Master wasn't finished.

"Even if he did use some sort of treasure, the fact that it could hide its effects from my senses would make it, and by extension him, all the more remarkable."

The elders murmured among themselves, casting curious glances at Elder Feng, who was trying, and failing, to hide his smug expression.

The Sect Master turned to Elder Tao, his expression serious. "Send someone to investigate this Kai Thorn. I want to know everything about him—his background, his training, any unusual encounters he may have had. Something tells me this boy will surprise us all."

The Inner Elder bowed deeply. "It will be done, Sect Master."

The Sect Master then raised his hands, conjuring streams of water, his fingers blurred as he formed complex patterns in the air, coalescing the water into hundreds of screens. Each watery display flickered to life, showing a different recruit navigating the challenges of the pocket realm.

As the Sect Master's gaze fell on a particular screen, a small smile played at the corners of his mouth.

This year's trials, he thought, *might be more interesting than I anticipated.*

CHAPTER THIRTY-EIGHT

The blinding light faded, and Kai found himself standing in complete darkness. He blinked, trying to adjust his eyes, but it was no use. The darkness was absolute.

I'm surprised I'm not falling through the air or anything. Small mercies, I guess.

He took a deep breath, calming his nerves. *Okay, think. What would a cultivator do in this situation?*

The answer came to him quickly. Channeling qi to enhance vision was a common trope in cultivation novels. Kai focused, drawing qi to his eyes. It took a few attempts, but eventually, he felt a warm sensation in his eyes, and a faint blue glow illuminated the area immediately around him.

Not bad for a first try, Kai thought, pleased with himself. *But man, this is a crude method. There's got to be a proper technique for night vision somewhere in this world.*

With his qi-enhanced vision, Kai could make out that he was standing in some sort of tunnel. The walls were rough stone, and the ceiling was low enough that he could touch it if he stretched his arm.

All right, let's see what we're working with here. Kai opened his map, hoping it would give him some clue about where to go. To his disappointment, the map showed only a small area around him, with the rest shrouded in fog.

Limited visibility, huh? Typical dungeon mechanics. Kai sighed. *Well, let's try qi sensing then.*

Kai closed his eyes, extending his senses outward. He felt . . . nothing. No enemies, no traps, no other cultivators. Just empty tunnel stretching out in both directions.

That's . . . concerning, Kai thought. *Either there's nothing here, or whatever is here is beyond my ability to sense. Neither option is particularly comforting.*

Just then, a message appeared before his eyes.

> Quest: Complete the Trial of Endurance
> Objective: Reach the end of the tunnel and exit the pocket realm
> Time Limit: 1 hour
> Reward: Based on ranking upon completion
> Failure: Expulsion from Azure Sky Sect

Nothing unexpected.

Kai glanced down the dark tunnel stretching out before him. *I've got a feeling this is going to be one of those "endless" tunnels. You know, the kind where no matter how far you run, you never seem to get anywhere.*

He took a deep breath. *Well, standing here isn't going to get me anywhere. Time to start running.*

With that thought, Kai began to jog down the tunnel. He kept his senses alert, eyes darting from side to side as he moved.

No point in conserving energy if I've only got an hour. Better to move quickly and deal with obstacles as they come.

As he ran, Kai's mind raced through possible scenarios.

In games, these kinds of trials usually have a few standard elements. Physical obstacles, maybe some puzzles, probably a boss fight at the end. But this is the cultivation world, so who knows what kind of crazy qi-based challenges they might throw at us.

After several minutes of running, Kai hadn't encountered any obstacles or changes in the tunnel.

This is . . . suspiciously uneventful. Either I'm incredibly lucky, or they're lulling us into a false sense of security.

Just as the thought crossed his mind, the tunnel ahead split into seven paths. Kai skidded to a halt, eyeing the branching passages warily.

And there it is. Classic maze scenario. It's not a proper dungeon without getting lost at least once.

Kai closed his eyes, trying to sense any differences between them. Nothing.

All right, let's think about this logically. The Sect Master mentioned hidden aids and hints. There's got to be something here to guide us . . .

Kai began examining the area more closely. He looked at the floor, the walls, even the ceiling. At first, nothing stood out. But then, as he was about to give up and just pick a tunnel at random, he noticed something.

Near the entrance of each tunnel, there was a small, almost imperceptible symbol etched into the stone. Kai had to channel more qi to his eyes to see them clearly.

Now we're getting somewhere. But what do these symbols mean?

He studied each symbol carefully. They seemed to be stylized representations of natural elements—fire, water, earth, wind, lightning, light, and darkness.

Elemental affinities, Kai realized. *Each tunnel probably corresponds to a different element. But which one is the right path?*

Kai thought back to his status window. His strongest elemental affinity was lightning, at 20%.

It can't be that simple, can it? Kai wondered. *Just pick the tunnel that matches your element?*

He shook his head. *No, that's too obvious. It's got to be a trick. Usually, the obvious choice is rarely the right one.*

Kai thought harder, trying to recall everything he knew about cultivation novels and game dungeons.

Wait a minute, he thought. *In a lot of stories, cultivators have to face their weaknesses to grow stronger. What if . . .* Kai's gaze lingered on the darkness symbol. Something about it made him uneasy. *Is that discomfort a sign I should avoid it, or a challenge I need to overcome?*

He shook his head, realizing he might be overthinking things. *Maybe there's more than one correct choice. The strongest affinity might be easiest but longest, while the weakest could be hardest but shortest. And this is a race, after all. But then again, I could be overthinking this . . .*

After a moment's hesitation, Kai pulled out a small knife from his storage ring and carefully carved a mark into the wall near the entrance.

Just in case I need to backtrack. Always leave yourself an escape route.

Taking a deep breath, Kai stepped towards the tunnel marked with the darkness symbol. *Time to face my fears, I guess.*

As soon as he entered, the darkness engulfed him completely. Even his qi-enhanced vision couldn't penetrate the inky blackness. He closed his eyes, focusing on his other senses. The stone beneath his feet felt rough, and a cool breeze whispered past his ears.

This darkness is intense, Kai thought. *It's like being in one of those pitch-black cave levels in a game. I half expect to run into some kind of monster any second now.*

He opened his eyes and looked at his map, relieved to see at least a small area around him illuminated. *Not much, but better than nothing.*

Kai extended his qi sense, probing for any nearby threats. So far, the tunnel seemed empty.

I could try to create some light with qi. But that might drain my reserves too quickly. Better to save my strength in case I need to fight.

As he walked, Kai kept one hand on the rough stone wall to his right, using it to guide his path. The coolness of the stone under his fingers provided a small comfort in the oppressive darkness.

At least I know I'm still moving forward. Though for all I know, this tunnel could be curving around in circles.

Kai paused for a moment, focusing on his qi sense. He extended his awareness outward, probing for any sign of danger or other presences. But just like before, he sensed nothing but empty tunnel stretching out before and behind him.

This is starting to feel like one of those psychological horror games, Kai thought with a wry smile. *The kind where the real enemy is your own mind as you wander through endless dark corridors.*

He shook his head, dispelling the thought. *No. Focus, Kai. This is a test, not a game. There has to be some purpose to all this darkness.*

As he continued forward, Kai tried to piece together the logic behind this trial.

Okay, let's think about this systematically, he reasoned. *The Sect Master called this the Trial of Endurance. So far, the only thing I'm enduring is this darkness. Is that the point? To see how long we can handle being deprived of sight?*

It made a certain kind of sense. In the world of cultivation, adaptability was key. Being able to function without relying on one of your primary senses could be a valuable skill.

Or maybe, Kai thought, *this is about overcoming fear. Plenty of people are afraid of the dark, after all. Testing our mental fortitude in the face of the unknown.*

He chuckled softly to himself. *If that's the case, all those late nights gaming in the dark are finally paying off.*

Suddenly, Kai's foot struck something solid. He stumbled slightly, catching himself against the wall.

What the—?

Crouching down, Kai felt along the ground with his hands. His fingers brushed against something smooth and cylindrical.

Is this . . . a step?

Kai's heart rate picked up as he explored further. Yes, it was definitely a step. And beyond it, he could feel more steps leading upward.

Stairs, Kai realized. *I've reached some kind of staircase.*

A mixture of excitement and wariness filled him. On one hand, this was the first change he'd encountered since entering the darkness tunnel. It had to mean he was making progress. On the other hand, in games, stairs usually meant you were about to face a new challenge or enter a boss room.

Well, standing here isn't going to get me anywhere, Kai thought. *Time to see what's waiting for me up there.*

Taking a deep breath, Kai placed his right foot on the first step.

Instantly, an overwhelming pressure slammed down on him. It felt like the very air had turned to lead, pressing down on his body from all directions. Kai's eyes widened in shock and he instinctively stepped back.

As soon as his foot left the step, the pressure vanished.

What . . . what was that? Kai wondered, his heart pounding. *It felt like standing in front of one of those super-powerful cultivators. Like that Nascent Soul elder, but even stronger.*

Cautiously, Kai reached out with his foot again, lightly touching the first step. The pressure returned immediately, though not as intensely as before. It was as if the staircase was reacting to his presence, exerting force in proportion to how much weight he put on it.

I see, Kai thought, a grim smile spreading across his face. *So that's the game we're playing.*

This had to be a true trial of endurance. To overcome the increasing pressure and reach the top of the stairs. But how many steps were there? And how intense would the pressure become?

One way to find out, I guess.

Before attempting the stairs again, Kai decided to take stock of his resources. He pulled up his status window to review his stats and skills.

Name: Kai Thorn

XP: 50/4,000
Level: Qi Refining Stage 8
Qi: 250/250
Strength: 60
Agility: 63
Endurance: 62
Intelligence: 30
Wisdom: 29

Titles:
Novice Instructor
Elemental Affinities:
Lightning: 20%

Skills:
Qi Condensation (Level 4)
Basic Cultivation Technique (Level 3)
Unarmed Combat (Level 2)

Deception (Level 4)
Iron Skin Technique (Level 3)
Swift Wind Step (Level 4)
Flame Palm Strike (Level 3)
Mental Fortitude (Passive)
Spirit Beast Communication (Level 1)
Qi Concealment (Level 1)
Qi Detection (Level 1)
Iron Rebound (Level 1)

Let's see . . . My strength, agility, and endurance are all in the low sixties. Not bad, but will it be enough? And what about my mental stats? This feels like it's testing more than just physical ability.

Iron Skin might help resist the physical pressure. And Mental Fortitude could be crucial for staying focused and determined. This is going to test both body and mind. But the test is tailored towards my cultivation realm so I should be able to do this.

Kai took a deep breath, steeling himself for the challenge ahead. He knew he couldn't stand here forever—the one-hour time limit was ticking away.

All right, no more stalling. Time to face this head-on.

CHAPTER THIRTY-NINE

Let's do this."

Kai placed his right foot on the first step, bracing for the pressure. It slammed into him immediately, but this time he was prepared. He gritted his teeth and pushed through, lifting his other foot to the second step.

Okay, this is just like those high-gravity training rooms in anime, Kai thought, gritting his teeth as the pressure doubled. *I have to push through it.*

He focused on his Iron Skin Technique, willing his body to become more resilient. A faint metallic sheen covered his skin as the skill activated, the pressure was still immense, but it no longer felt like his bones were about to snap.

Good to know my skills work here. Now, let's see what else I can use.

He closed his eyes, focusing on his Swift Wind Step skill. As he activated it, he felt a sudden lightness in his limbs. When he opened his eyes again, he found himself moving more smoothly, almost gliding to the next step.

"Now we're talking," Kai grinned, picking up the pace.

But the staircase wasn't done with him yet. As he climbed higher, the pressure intensified, threatening to overwhelm him once more. Kai gritted his teeth, feeling the strain in every muscle.

Come on, focus. You've got this.

Despite the mounting pressure, Kai's mind remained clear, his thoughts sharp and focused. He silently thanked his passive Mental Fortitude skill for keeping his head in the game.

"One step at a time," Kai reminded himself, pushing onward. "Just like grinding levels in a game."

He settled into a rhythm, using Swift Wind Step to move more efficiently as he climbed. The steps blurred beneath him as he ascended, his breaths coming in controlled gasps.

By the fortieth step, Kai was drenched in sweat. His muscles screamed in protest with each movement. He paused, leaning against the wall for support.

"This . . . isn't . . . so bad," Kai muttered between breaths, trying to convince himself.

But even as the words left his mouth, he looked up, squinting into the darkness above, but there was still no end in sight.

"Okay," he admitted to the empty air. "Maybe I spoke too soon."

Just then, he heard a voice echoing from somewhere above.

"Having trouble already? Pathetic."

Kai's head snapped up, trying to locate the source of the voice. "Who's there?" he called out.

A mocking laugh was his only answer.

Frowning, Kai quickly pulled up his map interface, but it showed only empty space around his lone marker.

Weird. No one else here, at least according to this.

Kai glanced back up into the darkness. *Either this is part of the test, or there's another unfathomable being trolling me.*

He pushed himself off the wall, determined to continue. As he climbed, the voice continued to taunt him.

"You'll never make it to the top," it sneered. "Why don't you just give up now?"

Kai gritted his teeth, refusing to respond. *This has to be part of the test,* he reasoned. *They're trying to break me mentally.*

The voice grew more insistent as Kai climbed higher. It hurled insults, mocked his efforts, and tried to plant seeds of doubt in his mind.

"You're not good enough," it hissed. "You don't belong here. You're just a fraud pretending to be a cultivator."

That last barb hit a little too close to home. Kai faltered, nearly missing a step.

No, he thought fiercely. *I might not be from this world, but I've earned my place here. I won't let some disembodied voice tell me otherwise.*

Kai pressed on but as he climbed, he noticed something strange. The pressure seemed to fluctuate slightly with each step. Sometimes it would increase dramatically, other times it would ease up just a bit.

There's a pattern here, Kai realized. *If I can figure it out, maybe I can use it to my advantage.*

He began to pay closer attention to the changes in pressure. After a few more steps, he started to see the pattern.

It's like a rhythm, Kai thought excitedly. *Three steps of increasing pressure, then one step where it eases up slightly.*

Armed with this knowledge, Kai adjusted his climbing strategy. He would push hard through the three high-pressure steps, then use the brief respite on the fourth to catch his breath and prepare for the next cycle.

This new approach made the climb more manageable, but it was still grueling work. Kai's muscles burned with exertion, and his qi reserves were starting to run low.

I need to conserve energy, he realized. *Who knows what's waiting for me at the top?*

Kai began to ration his qi usage more carefully. He only activated his skills when absolutely necessary, relying more on his physical strength and endurance.

As he climbed higher, the taunting voice grew more desperate in its attempts to discourage him.

"You're going to fail," it snarled. "Just like you've failed at everything else in your life."

Kai couldn't help but laugh at that. "Nice try," he called out to the darkness. "But you'll have to do better than that."

The voice fell silent for a moment, seemingly taken aback by Kai's response.

That's right, Kai thought with a smirk. *You can't break me that easily.*

He continued his ascent, feeling a renewed sense of confidence. The pressure was still intense, but Kai had found his rhythm. He moved steadily upward, one step at a time.

As he climbed, Kai's thoughts drifted to the others who must be taking this trial. *I wonder how Liu Wei is doing. And Shen Yu . . . I bet this is a cakewalk for him.*

The thought of his fellow recruits spurred Kai on. He didn't want to fall behind, especially not to that arrogant Sun Jun.

After what felt like hours, but was probably only about a few minutes, Kai noticed a change. The oppressive darkness seemed to be lightening slightly. He could just barely make out the outline of the steps ahead of him.

I must be getting close to the top, Kai thought with excitement.

But as the light grew stronger, so did the pressure. Each step now felt like he was trying to move through solid rock. Kai's progress slowed to a crawl.

"Come on," he grunted, forcing himself to take another step. "Just . . . a little . . . farther."

The taunting voice had gone quiet, replaced by the sound of Kai's heavy breathing and the pounding of his heart.

Finally, after what seemed like an eternity, Kai saw it—a faint glimmer of light ahead. The top of the staircase was within reach.

With a final burst of effort, Kai dragged himself up the last few steps. When his foot met level ground, the oppressive pressure vanished so abruptly that he almost fell forward. He stumbled, catching himself at the last moment.

"I . . . I made it?" Kai whispered, hardly daring to believe it.

He stood still for a moment, catching his breath and letting his eyes adjust. The darkness here was different, not quite as absolute as it had been on the staircase. Kai could make out vague shapes and outlines.

As his vision cleared, Kai's eyes widened. Before him, sitting on what appeared to be a throne, was a figure. But as the figure slowly stood and faced him, Kai realized with a start that it wasn't a person or a beast. It was literally just a black silhouette, featureless and somehow more terrifying for its lack of details.

What in the world . . . ? Kai thought, his mind racing to process what he was seeing.

Before Kai could think anything further, the figure appeared before him with startling speed, its right hand reaching toward Kai's face.

Oh, shit!

CHAPTER FORTY

In a split second, Kai activated Swift Wind Step, darting to the left. The black silhouette's fingers grazed his cheek as he moved, sending a chill down his spine.

Kai stumbled, breathing heavily as he put some distance between himself and the strange entity.

That was too close. What is this thing?

As if in answer to his question, a translucent blue screen materialized before his eyes.

Shadow Construct
Level: Qi Refining Stage 8 Qi: 250/250 Special Ability: Pressure Manipulation

Qi Refining stage eight? It's at the same level as me. Kai's eyes narrowed as he processed the information. *But I'm exhausted from climbing those stairs. This isn't good.*

The Shadow Construct turned to face him. Kai tensed, ready for another attack.

He didn't have to wait long. The faceless being lunged forward, its arm stretching impossibly as it reached for Kai once more.

Kai ducked under the elongated limb, feeling the air whoosh above his head. He sprang back up, throwing a quick jab at the construct's midsection.

His fist connected, but it felt like punching a dense fog. The construct's form rippled at the impact, but quickly solidified again.

Physical attacks aren't very effective, Kai realized. *Time to switch tactics.*

He focused his qi, channeling it into his palm. "Flame Palm Strike!"

A burst of fire erupted from Kai's hand as he thrust it forward. The flames streaked towards the Shadow Construct, illuminating the dark chamber with an orange glow.

For a moment, Kai thought he'd succeeded. But at the last second, the construct's form wavered and shifted, allowing the flames to pass harmlessly through where its center had been a moment before.

The fire attack struck the far wall, leaving a scorched mark but doing no damage to the shadow being.

Well, at least fire seems to affect it, Kai thought, a glimmer of hope rising. *But it's too agile for it to land cleanly.*

The construct's form solidified again, its featureless head tilting as if studying Kai. Then, without warning, the construct attacked again. This time, instead of reaching for him, it seemed to . . . expand. The air around Kai suddenly felt heavy, as if gravity had increased tenfold.

Kai's knees buckled under the intense pressure. It felt like he was back on the staircase, fighting against that oppressive force. He gritted his teeth, fighting to stay upright.

This must be its Pressure Manipulation ability, he realized. *But how do I counter it?*

The strange being moved closer, its form looming over Kai. With each step it took, the pressure intensified. Kai felt like his bones might snap at any moment. In desperation, he activated Iron Skin.

A faint metallic sheen covered his body, providing some relief from the crushing force. But it wasn't enough. The construct was still advancing, and Kai knew he couldn't withstand this pressure much longer.

Think, Kai, think! he urged himself. *There's got to be a way out of this.*

As the construct reached for him again, an idea struck Kai. It was risky, but it just might work.

He deactivated Iron Skin, allowing the full force of the pressure to hit him. Pain erupted through his body, but he forced himself to focus.

Come on, just a little closer, he thought, watching the black hand approach.

At the last possible moment, Kai activated Swift Wind Step again. He shot forward, passing through the being's incorporeal form.

As he emerged on the other side, Kai felt the pressure lessen dramatically. He spun around, facing the construct again.

Just as I thought. Its Pressure Manipulation has a limited range. If I can stay mobile, I might have a chance.

The black figure turned, seeming almost confused by Kai's maneuver. It reached out again, but Kai was ready this time.

He darted to the side, then forward, then back, using Swift Wind Step to stay just out of its reach. Each time he moved, he felt the pressure intensify, then lessen as he escaped its range.

But Kai knew he couldn't keep this up forever. His qi reserves were already low from the staircase climb, and each use of Swift Wind Step drained them further.

I need to end this quickly, he realized. *But how?*

As he dodged another of the construct's attacks, Kai's mind raced through possible strategies.

There's got to be a way to use my skills together. Something to give me an edge against this thing.

Then it hit him. *Wait a minute. This thing is made of . . . shadows, right? What if I could trap it somehow?*

"All right, you shadowy nuisance," Kai muttered. "Let's see how you handle this."

He focused on his Qi Condensation skill, pulling his qi into a visible form. In his hands, a shimmering net of blue qi began to take shape.

The Shadow Construct lunged at him again, its form stretching impossibly. Kai grinned. "Perfect timing."

He threw the qi-net forward, expanding it as it flew. The construct, mid-attack, couldn't dodge. The net enveloped the shadowy being, its energy crackling as it made contact.

The construct writhed within the net, its form distorting as it tried to escape.

I've only got a few seconds before this thing dissipates, Kai thought.

With his right hand, Kai began channeling qi for his Flame Palm Strike. The shadow being was still struggling against the net, its movements growing more frantic as if it sensed the danger.

"Sorry, pal," Kai said. "But I'm ending this now."

Just as he felt his qi net beginning to weaken, Kai thrust his flame-wreathed palm forward. "Flame Palm Strike!"

The fiery attack connected with the trapped construct. For a split second, nothing happened. Then, with a sound like a thunderclap, the shadow being exploded into wisps of darkness.

The force of the explosion sent Kai stumbling backward. He caught himself, breathing heavily as he watched the last traces of the shadow being dissipate into the air.

Did that . . . did that actually work? Kai thought, hardly daring to believe it.

He stood there for a moment, waiting to see if the Shadow Construct would reform. But the chamber remained empty and silent.

A grin spread across Kai's face. "Huh. I guess sometimes the crazy plans do work out."

He wiped the sweat from his brow, feeling the drain on his qi reserves. That combination attack had taken a lot out of him, but it had paid off.

As the adrenaline of the fight began to wear off, Kai felt the full extent of his exhaustion. He'd pushed himself to the limit with that last attack.

"I really hope that was the end of the trial," he muttered. "Because I don't think I have another fight in me right now."

As if in answer to his words, Kai heard a loud clap. The dark chamber shimmered and then dissolved around him.

Suddenly, Kai found himself back on the plateau where the trial had begun.

He blinked, disoriented by the sudden change. As his vision cleared, he saw all the elders seated on thrones, their eyes fixed on him. The Sect Master sat in the center, a slight nod of approval on his otherwise impassive face.

"Congratulations," the Sect Master's voice rang out. "You have completed the trial in fifteen minutes, securing the second-fastest time."

Kai's eyes widened in surprise. *Fifteen minutes? That's it?* His perception of time in the trial realm had been completely distorted. What felt like hours of grueling challenge had apparently lasted only a quarter of an hour.

As the implications of the Sect Master's words sank in, Kai's eyes narrowed. *Second fastest? Then who . . .*

He turned, scanning the plateau. His gaze landed on a familiar figure standing off to the side, face as blank and unreadable as ever.

Shen Yu.

Why am I not surprised? Kai thought, a wry smile tugging at the corner of his mouth.

Kai's eyes scanned the area, searching for a familiar tiny figure who should be waiting for him. A frown appeared on his face when he couldn't spot Zhi-Zhi anywhere.

"Excuse me, Sect Master," Kai called out, bowing. "May I ask where my friend is? The spirit tortoise who was with me earlier?"

The Sect Master turned to Kai, a hint of amusement in his eyes. "Ah, you speak of the small but spirited creature. He is currently undertaking the trial, just as you did."

Kai's eyes widened in surprise. "Zhi-Zhi is in the trial? I . . . I didn't realize he would be participating as a disciple candidate."

"Indeed," the Sect Master nodded. "All beings who wish to join the Azure Sky Sect must prove their worth, regardless of their nature or origin."

I can't believe I didn't consider this, I had thought the sect didn't take in spiritual beasts as disciples, Kai thought, shaking his head. *I just assumed Zhi-Zhi would tag along if I passed. I didn't expect the sect to test him separately.*

As Kai pondered this new information, he noticed a commotion near the edge of the plateau. More recruits were appearing, looking dazed and exhausted. The air was filled with excited chatter as they compared their experiences.

The Sect Master turned to address the new arrivals. "Ah, it seems more of our aspirants have completed the trial. Well done, all of you."

As the Sect Master began explaining the results to the other recruits, Kai took the opportunity to catch his breath and assess his condition.

He felt drained, both physically and in terms of qi. The climb up the endless staircase and the fight with the Shadow Construct had pushed him to his limits.

I need to be careful, Kai thought. *If there are more trials coming, I can't afford to be this depleted.*

He glanced around, noting the reactions of the other recruits. Many looked shocked to learn that Kai and Shen Yu had completed the trial so quickly. Some, like Sun Jun, wore expressions of barely concealed anger and jealousy.

Great, Kai thought sarcastically. *I'm sure this won't cause any problems later.*

As more recruits continued to appear, Kai noticed Liu Wei stumbling onto the plateau. The former bandit looked exhausted but relieved.

Kai made his way over to his follower. "Liu Wei," he called out. "Are you all right?"

Liu Wei's face lit up at the sight of Kai. "Master Kai! I did it! I actually completed the trial!"

Kai smiled, genuinely pleased to see Liu Wei had succeeded. "Well done. I knew you had it in you. How did you find it?"

Liu Wei's brow furrowed in confusion. "The wind tunnel was challenging, but I managed to overcome the wind spirit at the end rather quickly."

Just then, Elder Feng approached them, a scroll in his hand. "Ah, Liu Wei. Well done on completing the first trial. Your time was . . . forty-five minutes."

Liu Wei's jaw dropped. "Forty-five minutes? But that's impossible! It couldn't have been more than five or ten minutes!"

Kai's eyes narrowed as he processed this information, a theory beginning to form.

"Liu Wei," Kai asked, "you said you chose the wind route, right?"

Liu Wei nodded, still looking bewildered. "Yes, it seemed the most suitable for me, given my wind affinity."

Interesting, Kai thought. *My speculation might be correct after all.*

"I think I understand what's happening here," Kai said aloud. "The trial ground must have some sort of time distortion effect. If you chose an element that suited you, like wind in your case, it felt like it went by quickly. But in reality, it took longer."

Liu Wei's eyes widened in understanding. "And for those who chose an element that was difficult for them . . ."

"Exactly," Kai nodded. "It would have felt like it took a long time but actually finished quicker."

Kai thought back to his own experience in the darkness tunnel. It had felt like an eternity, but he'd finished in just fifteen minutes.

"That's . . . that's ingenious," Liu Wei said, awe in his voice. "It forces you to face your weaknesses, but rewards you for doing so."

Kai smiled, impressed by Liu Wei's quick grasp of the concept. "Precisely. It's a clever way to test not just our abilities, but our willingness to challenge ourselves."

Liu Wei suddenly looked around, his brow furrowing.

"Master," he said, "where's Zhi-Zhi? I haven't seen him since we started the trial."

Kai's expression grew serious. "The Sect Master told me he's still in the trial. Apparently, Zhi-Zhi is being tested as a disciple candidate, too."

Liu Wei's eyes widened in surprise. "Really? I didn't know spirit beasts could become disciples. But wait . . ." His face filled with concern as he glanced at the sky, noting the position of the sun. "The time limit is almost up, isn't it?"

Kai nodded, a knot of worry forming in his stomach. "Yeah, it is. I'm getting worried. Zhi-Zhi talks a big game, but I've never actually seen him in a real test like this."

They both turned their attention to the spot where recruits had been materializing, willing their small friend to appear. The seconds ticked by, feeling like hours.

Liu Wei fidgeted nervously. "Do you think he'll make it, Master? What happens if he doesn't complete the trial in time?"

Kai's jaw tightened. "I don't know. The Sect Master said those who don't complete the trial in time will be expelled. I'm not sure if that applies to spirit beasts too, but . . ."

He left the sentence hanging, not wanting to voice his fears. The thought of continuing without Zhi-Zhi, as annoying as the little tortoise could be sometimes, left a hollow feeling in Kai's chest.

"Come on, Zhi-Zhi," Kai muttered under his breath. "Where are you?"

Suddenly, just as the last second of the trial approached, there was a small pop of displaced air. A tiny figure materialized on the plateau, its shell tightly closed.

"Zhi-Zhi!"

CHAPTER FORTY-ONE

Slowly, a small head peeked out from the shell. Zhi-Zhi's eyes were wide, and Kai could see a tremor in the tortoise's tiny limbs.

"Are you okay?" Kai asked. "What happened in there?"

Liu Wei crouched down, his eyes scanning the spirit tortoise for any signs of injury. "You had us worried, little friend."

At the sound of their voices, Zhi-Zhi seemed to remember himself. He puffed out his chest, his usual air of bravado returning. "Ah, my dear disciples! Worry not, for I have triumphed over the Earth Trial with ease!"

Kai raised an eyebrow. "The Earth Trial? What was that like?"

Zhi-Zhi waved a tiny claw dismissively. "Oh, it was nothing for a being of my caliber."

Kai raised an eyebrow. "You cut it pretty close there, Zhi-Zhi. We were worried you might not make it in time."

Zhi-Zhi's expression faltered for a moment before he harrumphed. "Time? Bah! Such arbitrary limits are beneath beings of true power and wisdom. In my day, we understood that greatness cannot be rushed!"

Liu Wei tried to hide a smile. "But Zhi-Zhi, didn't you once tell us about how you won a race against the Jade Emperor himself?"

The spirit tortoise's eyes darted back and forth. "Well, yes, but . . . that was different! This trial was clearly biased against those of us with shells. Do you know how hard it is to climb stairs when you're a tortoise?"

Despite his bravado, Kai could see that Zhi-Zhi was embarrassed about finishing last. The tortoise's tiny claws fidgeted nervously.

"Hey," Kai said gently, "what matters is that you made it. You passed the trial, just like us."

Zhi-Zhi's expression softened slightly. "Well, of course I did. I couldn't very well let my disciples show me up, could I?"

Despite his boastful words, Kai noticed that Zhi-Zhi's eyes still held a hint of fear. Liu Wei seemed to notice too, exchanging a concerned glance with Kai.

"I faced an earth golem of tremendous size!" Zhi-Zhi began his usual ramble. "But of course, its attacks were futile against my impenetrable defense. Not a single blow could penetrate my shell!"

As Zhi-Zhi spoke, Kai's mind painted a very different picture. He imagined the tiny tortoise, hidden within his shell, trembling in terror as a massive golem relentlessly pounded away.

But wait, Kai thought, a frown forming on his face. *If Zhi-Zhi was defending the whole time, how did he actually defeat the golem?*

Liu Wei, seemingly having the same thought, gently asked, "That's amazing, Zhi-Zhi! But . . . how did you actually beat the golem if you were in your shell the whole time?"

Zhi-Zhi's boastful expression faltered for a moment. "Well, you see . . . that's . . . that's a secret technique passed down through generations of celestial tortoises! Yes, that's it! I can't reveal such sacred knowledge to just anyone, you understand."

Before Kai could ask the tortoise any more questions, the Sect Master's voice boomed across the plateau.

"Attention, all recruits!" he called out. "Congratulations to those who have successfully completed the Trial of Endurance."

His gaze swept over the assembled crowd, his expression growing somber. "To those who did not complete the trial within the time limit, I'm afraid your journey with us ends here. We thank you for your effort and wish you the best in your future endeavors."

Kai watched as several crestfallen recruits were led away by sect members. He felt a slight pang of sympathy for them, but he knew this was the nature of such trials.

It's harsh, he thought, *but I guess that's how these sects maintain their standards.*

The remaining participants looked up as the Sect Master's gaze swept over them. "You have proven yourselves worthy of consideration for our sect. However, this was merely the first of three trials you must face."

A murmur of excitement and nervousness rippled through the crowd. Kai's ears perked up. *Just like I expected, three trials but I wonder what the others will be like.*

The Sect Master continued, "Before we proceed, let us acknowledge the top performers in this trial. In first place, completing the trial in twelve minutes, we have Shen Yu."

All eyes turned to Shen Yu, who bowed slightly, his face still devoid of any emotion.

"In second place," the Sect Master went on, "with a time of fifteen minutes, we have Kai Thorn."

Kai felt dozens of eyes turn to him. He straightened his posture, trying not to show how exhausted he still felt. He noticed Sun Jun glaring at him from across the plateau.

Suddenly, a blue window appeared in Kai's vision.

Congratulations!
You have completed the Trial of Endurance
You have achieved second place in the Trial of Endurance
You have been awarded a new skill!
Name: Rock Hard (Passive)
Description: physical toughness, making your body more resistant to damage and strain, increases your Durability by 5 points
You have gained 50 XP!

Kai blinked in surprise. *A new skill? This could be useful. Extra durability might help me survive whatever they throw at us next.*

"And in third place, with a time of eighteen minutes, we have Young Master Sun Jun of the Sun Clan."

Sun Jun's chest puffed out with pride, but Kai could see the frustration in his eyes. Being third clearly wasn't good enough for the young master.

As the Sect Master continued reading out the rankings, Kai felt a presence beside him. He turned to see Shen Yu standing there, his calm gaze fixed on the Sect Master.

"Congratulations on your victory," Kai said, keeping his voice low.

Shen Yu glanced at him, the barest hint of surprise flickering in his eyes. "Thank you," he replied, his voice barely above a whisper. "You performed admirably as well."

Kai nodded, studying Shen Yu's face for any clue about what he might be thinking. "I'm curious," he ventured, "what kind of challenge did you face in your trial?"

For a moment, Shen Yu was silent. Then, so quietly Kai almost missed it, he said, "Shadows. Many shadows."

Before Kai could ask for clarification, the Sect Master's voice rose again. "The second trial will begin tomorrow at dawn. Use this time to rest and recover. You will need all your strength for what is to come."

With that, the elders began to rise from their thrones. Outer Elder Feng approached Kai and Liu Wei, a proud smile on his face.

"Well done, both of you," he said. "Especially you, Kai. Second place is a remarkable achievement for a new recruit."

Kai bowed slightly. "Thank you, Elder Feng. I couldn't have done it without your guidance."

Yeah, right, Kai thought. *You're just happy because my success means you're closer to whatever prize they're offering the elders. Probably some pill to help you break through to Core Formation.*

Elder Feng glanced down at Zhi-Zhi. "And you, little one. You may have finished last, but completing the trial is an accomplishment in itself, especially for a spirit beast your size."

Zhi-Zhi puffed up his chest. "Last? Bah! I simply chose to savor the experience, unlike these impatient youngsters. In my day, we understood that true mastery takes time!"

Kai and Liu Wei exchanged amused glances, while Elder Feng chuckled.

"Of course, of course," the elder said diplomatically. "Now, come along. Let me show you to your quarters. You've all earned a good rest, regardless of how long it took you to finish."

As they followed Elder Feng, Kai gently patted Zhi-Zhi's shell. "You did well, Zhi-Zhi," he whispered. "No need to make excuses."

Zhi-Zhi huffed but leaned into Kai's touch, a mix of embarrassment and gratitude in his tiny eyes.

As they followed Elder Feng, Kai's mind was racing. *Shadows. Many shadows,* he repeated Shen Yu's words in his head. *What does that mean? Did he face multiple constructs? Or something else entirely?*

Their group made their way across the plateau, heading towards a series of buildings nestled against the mountainside. As they walked, Kai overheard snippets of conversation from the other recruits.

" . . . never felt anything like it . . ."

" . . . thought I was going to die for sure . . ."

" . . . how did that village boy beat us?"

Kai smirked at the last comment. *If they only knew.*

Liu Wei fell into step beside him. "Master," he whispered, "do you think the next trial will be as difficult?"

Kai considered for a moment. "Probably more so," he replied honestly. "They'll want to push us to our limits. I think they'll test different things to see what we're really capable of."

Liu Wei's face paled slightly. "I . . . I'm not sure I'm ready for that."

Kai placed a reassuring hand on his shoulder. "You made it through this trial, didn't you? You're stronger than you give yourself credit for, Liu Wei."

The former bandit's eyes widened at the praise. "You really think so?"

"I know so," Kai said with a smile. "Just keep focused and trust in your abilities. You'll do fine."

Liu Wei nodded, standing a little straighter. "Thank you, Master. I won't let you down."

CHAPTER FORTY-TWO

As they approached the buildings, Elder Feng turned to address them. "These will be your quarters for the duration of the trials," he explained. "You'll find everything you need inside. Food will be provided in the common area, and there are meditation rooms available for those who wish to use them."

He pointed to a large building at the center of the complex. "That is where you'll gather for announcements and to receive instructions for the next trial. Make sure you're there tomorrow at dawn."

Kai nodded, taking in the layout of the area. *Good to know. I should familiarize myself with this place, just in case.*

"Now," Elder Feng continued, "get some rest. You've all earned it." With that, he departed, leaving the recruits to settle into their new accommodations.

Kai turned to Liu Wei. "Let's check out our rooms and then grab some food. I don't know about you, but I'm starving after that trial."

Liu Wei nodded eagerly. "Yes, Master Kai. I feel like I could eat an entire spirit beast!" He paused, glancing nervously at Zhi-Zhi. "Uh, no offense intended, of course."

Zhi-Zhi huffed. "As if a mere mortal like you could ever hope to consume a majestic being such as myself. Why, I once feasted on an entire mountain of spirit herbs, and it barely satisfied my godly appetite!"

Kai chuckled, shaking his head. "I'm sure you did, Zhi-Zhi. Come on, let's go."

As they made their way to their assigned quarters, Kai's mind was already working on strategies for the next trial.

I need to regain my qi as quickly as possible. Some food and meditation should help. I should also try to gather more information about what the other recruits faced in their trials. Knowledge is power, after all.

They reached a row of small, individual buildings. Each had a simple wooden door with a number carved into it. Kai found the one matching the jade token he'd been given earlier and pushed it open.

The room inside was sparse but comfortable. A bed, a small table with two chairs, and a cushioned mat for meditation. A window looked out over the misty mountains surrounding the sect.

"Not bad," Kai murmured, setting his pack down. "Definitely beats the little hut."

Liu Wei's voice called from next door. "Master, these rooms are amazing! I've never stayed anywhere so nice!"

Kai smiled at his follower's enthusiasm. "Enjoy it while you can, Liu Wei. I have a feeling we won't be spending much time here once the trials really get going."

Suddenly, Zhi-Zhi's voice piped up from down the row. "Hey! Why is my door so small? Don't they know who I am?"

Curious, Kai stepped out and looked. Sure enough, between his and Liu Wei's rooms was a much smaller door, perfectly sized for the spirit tortoise.

Kai walked over and peered inside. The room was a miniature version of his own, complete with tiny furniture. "Well, look at that," he chuckled. "They gave you your own place, Zhi-Zhi."

Zhi-Zhi puffed up with pride. "Of course they did! It's about time my greatness was recognized. Though I must say, this is rather quaint compared to my chambers in the Celestial Tortoise Palace."

Kai rolled his eyes but couldn't help smiling. "I'm sure it is. But hey, at least you don't have to share with us 'mere mortals' anymore."

"Indeed!" Zhi-Zhi agreed, scuttling into his new home. "Now I can meditate in peace without your constant snoring interrupting my profound thoughts."

"I don't snore," Kai protested weakly, then shook his head.

After freshening up and changing into clean robes provided in the room, the three made their way to the common area.

The common area was a large, high-ceilinged hall with cloud patterns carved into the wooden beams above. Long tables of polished oak stretched in neat rows, already half-filled with chattering recruits. Along the far wall, a serving area bustled with activity as workers ladled out steaming dishes from large woks and cauldrons.

The aroma of sizzling meats, fragrant herbs, and sweet pastries filled the air, causing Kai's stomach to audibly growl. Liu Wei's eyes widened at the sight of so much food.

"I've never seen so many dishes in one place," he whispered in awe.

As they approached the serving area, Kai picked up a wooden tray and began selecting dishes. He spooned some rice onto his plate, then added a helping of stir-fried vegetables with tender strips of pork. A bowl of mushroom soup came next, followed by a small plate of delicate dumplings.

Zhi-Zhi looked down at Kai's selections. "Hmph! This is what passes for a feast in the mortal realm?" he sniffed. "Why, in the Celestial Tortoise Palace, we dined on ambrosia and nectar that would make your taste buds explode with joy!"

Kai rolled his eyes, adding a sweet bun to his tray. "Well, we'll have to make do with mortal food for now, Zhi-Zhi. Try not to be too disappointed." He picked up a small saucer and filled it with a variety of vegetable pieces for the spirit tortoise.

As Kai scanned the room, looking for a place to sit, he spotted Sun Jun and Lu Chen sitting at a table near the center of the room, surrounded by a group of admiring recruits. Sun Jun was gesturing dramatically, no doubt bragging about his performance during the trial.

Typical arrogant young master, Kai thought with a smirk. *Always has to be the center of attention.*

He and Liu Wei found an empty table near the edge of the room. As they sat down, Kai noticed Shen Yu entering the common area. The mysterious youth filled his plate quietly and then, to Kai's surprise, began walking in their direction.

"Mind if I join you?" Shen Yu asked, his voice as calm and emotionless as ever.

Kai raised an eyebrow but nodded. "Be our guest."

As Shen Yu sat down, Liu Wei's eyes widened. "Um, congratulations on gaining first place in the trial."

Shen Yu inclined his head slightly. "Thank you. You did well to complete it as well."

An awkward silence fell over the table as they began to eat. Kai studied Shen Yu out of the corner of his eye, trying to glean any information he could from the other youth's behavior.

He's a hard one to read. No wasted movements, no unnecessary words. Is it all an act, or is this really who he is?

Suddenly, a translucent blue screen flickered into existence before Kai's eyes.

Name: Shen Yu
Level: ???   Cultivation: ???

The window flickered erratically, as if struggling to maintain a stable reading. For a brief moment, Kai caught a glimpse of numbers far beyond what should be possible for a new recruit, but they vanished before he could process them fully.

What the hell? Kai thought, his mind racing. *Is System glitching out, or is there something seriously weird going on with this guy?*

After a few seconds of unstable flickering, the status window finally settled.

Name: Shen Yu

Cultivation: Qi Refining Stage 4
Qi: 75/75
Strength: 25
Agility: 28
Endurance: 26

Kai's eyes widened in disbelief. *Qi Refining stage four? Already? But he only started training a few days ago. How is that even possible?*

A part of Kai's mind, the part still stuck in gamer logic, wondered if Shen Yu had somehow found a way to gain XP and level up rapidly. But he quickly dismissed the thought. *This isn't a game, Kai. People don't just level up here, only I level up . . . right? It's more likely he has already cultivated before.*

Deciding to test the waters, Kai plastered on a friendly smile and spoke up. "Hey, Shen Yu, congrats on reaching stage four already. That's really impressive."

Liu Wei's chopsticks clattered to the table. "Stage four? But . . . but how?"

Zhi-Zhi, not to be outdone, puffed out his chest. "Hmph! Of course he reached stage four. I knew it all along. Why, in my day, reaching stage four in a matter of days was considered slow progress!"

Shen Yu's eyes widened almost imperceptibly at Kai's words. He nodded, a hint of wariness in his expression. "Thank you."

Kai leaned forward, his curiosity piqued. "If you don't mind me asking, how did you break through so quickly? Any tips for the rest of us?"

Shen Yu made a gesture that almost looked like a shrug, his face returning to its usual blank mask. He didn't reply, instead focusing on his food.

Okay, he doesn't want to talk about it, Kai thought. *Time to change tactics.*

"Say, Shen Yu," Kai began, trying to sound casual, "there's something that's been nagging at me. When we talked earlier about the trial, you mentioned shadows. Did you pick the Darkness Element?"

Shen Yu stopped eating and looked up at Kai, his dark eyes unreadable. After a moment, he set down his chopsticks and spoke.

"I did choose the Darkness Element," Shen Yu said, his voice low. "If you want to finish the trial quickly, you need to face your fears. The Darkness Element doesn't necessarily mean you're afraid of the dark. It will pick something from your fears and have you face it."

Kai nodded, processing this information. "I see. So, what exactly did you face? When you said shadows, I thought—"

"It's not the shadow you are thinking of," Shen Yu interrupted, his tone final. He didn't elaborate further.

Interesting. He's willing to share some information, but he's clearly holding back. What kind of shadows could be so terrible that he won't even talk about them?

Aloud, Kai said, "I think I understand what the trials were testing now. It was about facing our weaknesses, right? Pushing us out of our comfort zones to see how we'd adapt."

Shen Yu regarded Kai for a moment, his expression thoughtful. "Your assumption is close," he said finally, "but it isn't accurate."

Kai's eyebrows rose. "Oh? How do you know if it isn't right?"

Shen Yu didn't reply, instead returning his attention to his meal.

He clearly knows more about these trials than he's letting on, Kai realized. *But how? And why is he sharing anything at all?*

Deciding to press his luck, Kai leaned in closer. "Say, Shen Yu, since you seem to know a lot about these trials . . . any idea what's coming next?"

Shen Yu paused, his chopsticks halfway to his mouth. He stared blankly at Kai for a long moment, as if weighing his options. Finally, he set his chopsticks down and spoke a single phrase, "The Enlightenment Stone."

Liu Wei, who had been listening intently, couldn't contain his curiosity. "The Enlightenment Stone? What's that?"

Shen Yu sighed, as if resigning himself to explaining. "Everyone will be given a stone. The stone will find a technique that you have the most affinity for. You will then be expected to comprehend it."

"What if you've already learned the technique it chooses?" Kai asked.

"The stone can tell from your qi which techniques you have used," Shen Yu replied.

Kai's eyes narrowed as he caught the specific wording. *Used, not known. Interesting distinction. Could that mean . . .*

Before Kai could pursue that line of thought, Liu Wei spoke up again. "But what about people who haven't cultivated before? How will they be tested?"

Shen Yu's expression softened slightly. "They will be given a different test. They'll be sent to a special meditation chamber, not the basic one here. It's a place designed to help a mortal become a cultivator. They will be timed and ranked according to who breaks through to the first stage of Qi Refining the fastest."

A place that can help mortals become cultivators? Kai thought, intrigued. *I wonder how that works. Some kind of qi-rich environment, maybe?*

As Kai pondered this new information, Shen Yu suddenly spoke again, his voice low and intense.

"I can tell from your performance that you want to be the Sect Master's disciple."

Kai hesitated for a moment before nodding. It was true, after all. Being chosen as the Sect Master's disciple would give him a significant advantage in this world.

Shen Yu leaned in close, his voice dropping to a whisper. "A word of warning. I'd recommend you pick someone else."

With that cryptic statement, Shen Yu stood and walked away, leaving a stunned silence in his wake.

Kai's eyes narrowed as he watched Shen Yu's retreating form. *What was that about? Was he threatening me? Or . . . warning me?*

Liu Wei leaned in, his voice hushed. "Master, what do you think he meant by that?"

Kai shook his head, his mind racing. "I'm not sure, Liu Wei. But I intend to find out."

Zhi-Zhi, who had been uncharacteristically quiet during the exchange, suddenly piped up. "Bah! Don't listen to that upstart youngster. In my day, we didn't need warnings or stones or fancy trials. We became disciples through sheer force of will and the strength of our shells!"

Despite the tension of the moment, Kai couldn't help but smile at the little tortoise's bravado. "Is that so, Zhi-Zhi? And how many disciples did you take on in your illustrious career?"

Zhi-Zhi puffed up his chest. "Why, I'll have you know that I . . . that is to say . . . well, a true master doesn't need disciples! We're too busy with important celestial matters to bother with teaching!"

Liu Wei chuckled, some of the tension leaving his shoulders. "Of course, Zhi-Zhi. We wouldn't want to distract you from your important duties, which is why we had to reject your offer of taking us as your disciples."

As the conversation lightened, Kai's mind continued to work, analyzing every detail of his interaction with Shen Yu.

There's definitely more to him than meets the eye. Those flickering stats, his rapid advancement, his knowledge of the trials . . . and now this warning about the Sect Master. What's his angle?

Kai glanced around the common area, noting the other recruits still chatting and eating.

I need more information, Kai decided. *About Shen Yu, about these trials, about the Sect Master . . . about everything.*

"Liu Wei," Kai said, turning to his follower. "After we finish eating, I want you to mingle with the other recruits. See what you can find out about their experiences in the trial. Anything unusual, any patterns in the challenges they faced. Anything they know about the sect. And anything they know about the number one prospect. Can you do that?"

"Of course, Master. I'll be discreet."

CHAPTER FORTY-THREE

As dawn broke over the Azure Sky Sect, Kai stood on the plateau alongside hundreds of other hopeful disciples. The cool mountain air nipped at his skin, but he barely noticed, his mind focused on the challenge ahead. The elders sat on their thrones, their faces impassive as they surveyed the crowd.

Kai's eyes scanned the participants, picking out familiar faces. Liu Wei stood nearby, nervousness evident in his fidgeting hands. Zhi-Zhi perched on a rock, trying to look dignified despite his tiny size. Sun Jun and his cronies clustered together, shooting glares at anyone who dared look their way. And Shen Yu . . . Kai frowned. The enigmatic youth stood apart from the others, his face as unreadable as ever.

As Kai waited for the trial to begin, his mind wandered to the information Liu Wei had gathered the previous evening.

"Master Kai," Liu Wei had reported, his voice low and excited. "I talked to as many people as I could. A few of them had heard about the Enlightenment Stone from family or friends in the sect. It seems Shen Yu was telling the truth about that part."

Kai had nodded, unsurprised. "And what about the Sect Master?"

Liu Wei's face had fallen slightly. "Not much, I'm afraid. Everyone agrees he's one of the strongest cultivators in the Eastern Region, but beyond that . . ." He shrugged helplessly.

"And Shen Yu?"

"That's the strange thing, Master. No one seems to know anything about him. But they're all curious about Misty Waterfall Village now, since both of you are from there."

Shen Yu knew about the Enlightenment Stone. He has inside knowledge of the sect. But no one knows anything about him which suggests either his contacts are much higher level, or he doesn't have any because he himself is the source . . .

His thoughts were interrupted as one of the elders stood, raising a hand for silence. The chatter among the participants died down immediately.

The Sect Master rose from his throne, his presence commanding instant attention. His voice, though not raised, carried clearly across the plateau.

"Young cultivators," he began, "you stand now at the threshold of your second trial, the Trial of Comprehension."

Kai listened intently as the Sect Master explained the trial. It was similar to what Shen Yu had described.

"Each of you will receive an Enlightenment Stone," the Sect Master continued. "When you channel your qi into it, the stone will implant a technique into your mind, one that aligns with your innate talents and cultivation path."

He paused, his gaze sweeping over the crowd. "You will have twenty-four hours to comprehend this technique to the first level and demonstrate it successfully. Those who fail will be eliminated from consideration as disciples."

A murmur rippled through the crowd at this. Kai's eyes narrowed. *Twenty-four hours. That's a tight deadline for most cultivators at this level. I wonder how many will make it.*

The Sect Master raised his hand, and silence fell once more. "As for those who are still mortal . . ."

He gestured to a group off to the side, comprising about a third of the recruits. "You will be led to a special meditation chamber by Elder Feng. There, you will attempt your breakthrough to the first stage of Qi Refining."

Kai watched as the group of mortals was led away, a mix of nervousness and excitement on their faces. *That's a pretty big group,* he thought. *I wonder how many will actually succeed in becoming cultivators.*

As the group of non-cultivators was led away, Kai caught Liu Wei's eye. His follower looked relieved to have already begun his cultivation journey.

The remaining participants spread out across the plateau at the Sect Master's instruction, giving each other space to work. Kai found a spot near the edge, where he could observe the others without being too conspicuous.

With a wave of his sleeve, the Sect Master sent small, unremarkable-looking stones flying through the air. Each participant caught one, Kai included.

"Channel your qi into the stone," the Sect Master instructed. "The technique will be implanted in your mind. Remember, you have twenty-four hours. Begin!"

Kai held the stone in his palm, feeling its smooth surface. He took a deep breath, centering himself, then began to channel his qi.

Immediately, a familiar blue screen appeared before his eyes.

New Technique Available: Lightning Step
Would you like to learn this technique?
Yes/No

Huh, convenient, Kai thought with a smirk. *It's like accepting a free quest reward.* He mentally selected "Yes."

The stone in his hand began to glow, and suddenly, information flooded into Kai's mind. Images, sensations, and instructions all poured in at once, threatening to overwhelm him. But Kai's gaming-honed mind quickly began to sort and categorize the information.

New Skill Acquired: Lightning Step (Level 1)
Description: A movement technique that allows the user to move at incredible speeds, leaving behind a trail of lightning.
At higher levels, can be used for short-range teleportation.

Kai opened his eyes, blinking as he processed the new information. *Okay, so I've "learned" it, but can I actually do it?*

He looked around, noticing that other participants were still deep in concentration, their faces scrunched up as they absorbed the information from their stones. He knew he had an advantage, his System had allowed him to learn the technique instantly, but that didn't mean he could perform it perfectly right away.

Time to break this down, Kai thought, settling into a meditative pose. *Let's treat this like analyzing a new game mechanic.*

He closed his eyes, focusing on the technique in his mind. *Okay, Lightning Step. It's about speed and electricity, while Swift Wind Step was about agility and air currents. The qi flow is similar, but the energy conversion is different.*

Kai visualized the technique step by step:

Gather qi in the dantian.

Circulate the qi through the body, focusing on the legs and feet.

Convert the qi into lightning energy.

Channel the lightning energy into rapid movement.

Control the direction and stop safely.

Seems simple enough in theory. But execution is always trickier than tutorial levels make it seem. At least I have some experience with Swift Wind Step to draw from.

After about ten minutes of meditation and mental practice, Kai decided to attempt the technique. He stood up, noticing that most of the other participants were still deep in concentration. The elders' eyes seemed to narrow, focusing on him with interest.

Kai took a deep breath, centering himself. *Here goes nothing. Let's see if I can speedrun this trial.*

He gathered his qi, feeling it swirl in his dantian. Then, he began to circulate it through his body, concentrating on his legs and feet. As the energy flowed, Kai tried to envision it transforming into lightning, crackling and sparking within him.

This feels different from Swift Wind Step. More intense, harder to control.

With a burst of effort, Kai attempted to launch himself forward using the Lightning Step. For a split second, he felt a surge of speed, electricity crackling around him. But then, just as quickly, he lost control. The energy dispersed, and Kai stumbled, barely keeping himself from falling flat on his face.

Well, that was anticlimactic, Kai thought, straightening up. *Lightning is harder to control than it looks in anime.*

He noticed Shen Yu's eyes on him, narrowed in concentration. The mysterious youth closed his eyes again, seemingly redoubling his efforts.

Kai was about to attempt the technique again when a sudden gust of wind caught his attention. He turned to see Shen Yu performing a series of smooth, flowing movements.

Shen Yu's hands traced graceful arcs through the air, leaving faint trails of silvery qi. As he moved, the wind around him began to pick up, swirling faster and faster. Small leaves and bits of grass were lifted off the ground, caught in the growing vortex.

Then, with a sharp gesture, Shen Yu thrust his palm forward. The swirling wind condensed into a visible blade of air, about as long as a sword. It shot forward with incredible speed, slicing cleanly through a nearby rock before dissipating.

"Wind Slicer Technique," Shen Yu announced calmly, his voice carrying across the plateau.

The Sect Master nodded approvingly. "Excellent work, Shen Yu. You've completed the trial first, in just under eleven minutes. Truly impressive."

Kai couldn't help but feel a twinge of suspicion. *That's . . . convenient timing*, he thought. *It's almost as if he was waiting for me to get close before finishing. Did he already know the technique?*

The ease with which Shen Yu had performed the Wind Slicer Technique seemed at odds with the struggle Kai had witnessed on the faces of other participants. It was as if Shen Yu had simply been going through the motions, waiting for the right moment to reveal his mastery.

Closing his eyes, Kai focused once more on the Lightning Step technique. This time, he paid extra attention to the control aspect. *It's not just about generating the lightning,* he realized. *It's about directing it, making it an extension of my will. With Swift Wind Step, I flowed with the currents. Here, I need to be the current.*

With this new understanding, Kai attempted the technique again. He gathered his qi, circulated it through his body, and transformed it into crackling lightning energy. But this time, instead of trying to move immediately, he held the energy for a moment, feeling its ebb and flow.

Then, with a burst of concentration, Kai released the energy. The world blurred around him as he shot forward, leaving a trail of sparks in his wake. For a brief, exhilarating moment, Kai felt like he was flying.

He came to a stop several meters away, his heart racing but a grin spreading across his face. *Now that's more like it! Even faster than Swift Wind Step, but trickier to control.*

"Well done," the Sect Master's voice rang out. "Kai Thorn, you've completed the trial second, with a time of twelve minutes."

Kai bowed respectfully, trying to hide his satisfaction. *Second place isn't bad. Especially considering the competition.*

CHAPTER FORTY-FOUR

With his own trial complete, Kai took the opportunity to observe how the others were faring. He first looked for Liu Wei.

His follower was standing with his eyes closed, a look of intense concentration on his face. Occasionally, a gentle breeze would ruffle his clothes, but he seemed to be struggling to maintain it.

Looks like he got a wind technique. Makes sense, given his affinity. But he's having trouble controlling it. Hopefully he can pull through before the time limit.

Next, Kai's gaze fell on Zhi-Zhi. To his surprise, the tiny tortoise seemed to be making good progress. A faint green glow surrounded Zhi-Zhi's shell, and as Kai watched, small vines began to sprout from the ground around him.

A wood-based technique? Kai raised an eyebrow. *Interesting choice for a tortoise. But he seems to have a knack for it. Maybe it's got something to do with his "mother"?*

Lu Chen caught Kai's attention next. The young noble was moving through a series of fluid motions, water droplets forming in the air around him. His face was the picture of peace, almost as if he were dancing rather than practicing a martial technique.

Water element, huh? He seems pretty comfortable with it, Kai observed. *Must be a good match for his temperament. I wouldn't be surprised if he finishes near the top.*

Finally, Kai's eyes landed on Sun Jun. The arrogant young master's face was contorted in frustration as he attempted to perform what looked like a fire-based technique. Flames would flicker to life around his hands, only to sputter out moments later.

Struggling with control. All that raw power, but he can't seem to direct it properly. Still, with his resources and training, he'll probably figure it out eventually.

As the hours passed, more and more participants completed their trials.

Some managed to perform their techniques with varying degrees of success, while others struggled until the very end.

As the third hour approached, Lu Chen stood, his arms flowing like water itself. As he completed his final gesture, an orb of water formed between his palms. With a gentle push, the orb expanded into a swirling shield of liquid, rotating rapidly around Lu Chen's body. Droplets flew off, each seeming to dance in the air before returning to the shield.

The elders nodded approvingly at this display of the "Whirlpool Shield Technique."

"Excellent control, Lu Chen," one elder commented. "A fine defensive technique, executed with precision."

Lu Chen bowed, the water shield dissipating into a fine mist around him. He had finished third, just behind Kai.

Sun Jun, on the other hand, struggled for nearly five hours before he let out a loud *kiai* and thrust his palm forward. A burst of intense flame erupted from his hand, forming a fiery fist that shot forward several meters before exploding in a shower of sparks. The heat was so intense that those nearby could feel it on their skin.

"Impressive power, Young Master Sun," an elder remarked. "Though perhaps work on refining your control in the future."

Sun Jun nodded, trying to hide his heavy breathing. Despite the delay, he'd still managed to secure fourth place in the rankings.

And Zhi-Zhi, much to everyone's surprise, showed remarkable aptitude with his wood technique. The tiny tortoise managed to grow a small tree in just over five hours, securing fifth place.

"Ha! Did you see that?" Zhi-Zhi boasted to the other participants. "This is but a fraction of my true power!"

Kai couldn't help but smile at the tortoise's antics.

After nearly seven hours of intense concentration, Liu Wei finally grasped the essence of his wind technique. His face, covered in sweat, broke into a wide smile as he prepared to demonstrate for the elders.

Taking a deep breath, Liu Wei spread his arms wide. He began to slowly spin. As he turned, wisps of wind started to swirl around him, picking up loose leaves and dust.

Gradually, Liu Wei's spin quickened, and the wind responded in kind. A visible funnel of air formed around him, stretching from the ground to just above his head. The whirlwind wasn't large, maybe a meter in diameter, but it was unmistakably real.

Inside the vortex, Liu Wei's clothes and hair whipped about wildly. Despite his obvious exhaustion, his eyes shone with pride and joy.

"Windshield Vortex," Liu Wei announced, his voice slightly muffled by the rushing air.

He held the technique for a full minute before letting it dissipate. As the wind died down, Liu Wei stumbled slightly, clearly drained from the effort.

One of the elders nodded approvingly. "A solid foundation, Liu Wei. With practice, this technique could provide excellent defense against projectiles and even some physical attacks."

Liu Wei bowed deeply, his chest heaving as he caught his breath. "Thank you, honored elder. I will continue to refine it."

Kai, watching from nearby, felt a surge of pride for his follower. *Not bad at all, Liu Wei,* he thought. *You've come a long way from being a simple bandit.*

As the twenty-four-hour mark arrived, the Sect Master raised his hand, calling for attention. "The trial is complete," he announced. "Those who have not yet mastered their techniques, I'm afraid your journey with us ends here."

A wave of his hand, and the Enlightenment Stones flew back to him, glowing faintly with residual qi. Then, with another gesture, a shimmering screen of water appeared in the air before him.

"Behold," the Sect Master said, "the results of the selection so far."

The water rippled, and names began to appear, ranked from top to bottom. Kai's eyes quickly scanned the list.

1. Shen Yu
2. Kai Thorn
3. Lu Chen
4. Sun Jun
5. Liu Wei
6. Zhi-Zhi

Not bad at all. Kai nodded to himself, satisfied with the results. *We've all made it through. But Shen Yu . . . he's going to be tough to beat.*

As the participants began to disperse, discussing their results and new techniques, Kai felt a presence beside him. He turned to see Shen Yu standing there, his dark eyes unreadable.

"Congratulations," Shen Yu said, his voice low. "Your comprehension speed was . . . impressive."

Kai nodded, studying the other youth's face. "Thanks. But clearly it isn't as fast as yours."

For a moment, they stood in silence, each taking the measure of the other. Then Shen Yu spoke again, his voice barely above a whisper. "That might not be the case."

Before Kai could respond, Shen Yu turned and walked away.

What did he mean by that? Kai wondered. *Is he confirming that he already knew the technique beforehand, I'm almost certain he is either a regressor or reincarnator, I just don't know which one . . .*

As Kai mulled over the enigma that was Shen Yu, Liu Wei approached, his face beaming with pride.

"Master Kai!" he exclaimed. "I did it! I actually managed to complete the technique!"

Kai smiled, genuinely happy for his follower. "Well done, Liu Wei. I knew you had it in you."

Liu Wei's smile faltered slightly. "But . . . it was nothing compared to you."

Kai placed a hand on Liu Wei's shoulder. "Hey, don't worry about that. What matters is that you passed. Many others didn't make it this far. You should be proud."

Liu Wei's smile returned, brighter than before. "You're right, Master. Thank you."

As Liu Wei chatted excitedly about his new wind technique, they were interrupted by a familiar voice.

"Ah, my faithful disciples! Bask in the glory of your master's achievement!" Zhi-Zhi waddled up to them, his tiny chest puffed out. "From last place to sixth place! Sixth, I tell you! A most auspicious number, wouldn't you agree?"

Kai couldn't help but smile at the tortoise's enthusiasm. "Indeed, Zhi-Zhi. You did very well. That wood technique of yours was quite impressive."

Zhi-Zhi preened at the praise. "Of course it was! In my younger days, I once grew an entire forest with a single thought! This paltry sapling was but child's play for one of my immense talents!"

Liu Wei chuckled. "Of course, great Zhi-Zhi. We're honored to be in the presence of such a master of wood techniques."

As the group continued their lighthearted banter, the Sect Master's voice suddenly rang out across the plateau, silencing all conversations.

"Disciples," he said, "you have done well to come this far. But your journey is not yet complete. Tomorrow, you will face your greatest challenge yet: the Trial of the Heart."

The Trial of the Heart. Kai had been expecting this.

It's not just about power or technique. It's about character.

His mind flashed back to Elder Feng's warning to Liu Wei, trying to scare the former bandit about this very trial. The Azure Sky Sect was known for its righteousness, its dedication to justice and protecting the weak. This trial wasn't about combat or comprehension, it was about moral fiber.

They want to know if we're worthy of their teachings, if we align with their values. This could be tricky.

He glanced at Liu Wei, who looked nervous but determined, clearly remembering Elder Feng's words. Zhi-Zhi, on the other hand, was already boasting about his "immense spiritual fortitude." Kai couldn't help but smirk at the tortoise's unwavering confidence.

At least I've had time to prepare for this, Kai reassured himself. *I might not be the paragon of virtue they're looking for, but I'm not a villain either. I just need to show them that sometimes, the ends can justify the means—if the cause is right.*

As Kai looked around at the other disciples, he assessed their potential reactions to this trial. Sun Jun, for all his arrogance, came from a respected family known for their contributions to the sect. Lu Chen had a reputation for kindness and generosity. And Shen Yu . . . well, Shen Yu remained an enigma.

I wonder how many others here are putting on a front. How many of us don't fit the mold of the perfect, righteous cultivator? The real question is, how will the sect judge us?

As the disciples began to disperse, heading back to their quarters to rest and prepare for the coming challenge, Kai's mind was already working on strategies. This wasn't a game he could easily min-max or find exploits for. This was about presenting the core of who he was as a person in the best light possible.

I need to be smart about this. Show them that sometimes true righteousness requires making tough choices. After all, in this world, pure idealism can be a luxury not everyone can afford.

CHAPTER FORTY-FIVE

The sun rose over the Azure Sky Sect, casting a warm glow on the trial quarters. This secluded area, separated from the main sect, housed the participants as they prepared for their final challenge.

Kai stood at the window of his small room, gazing out at the misty mountains surrounding them.

I had thought the village was the tutorial area, but boy was I wrong. Being stuck here is like I'm unable to access the main game until I clear these trials.

He turned back to his room, eyeing the meditation mat in the corner. The elders had stressed the importance of mental preparation for the upcoming Trial of the Heart. Most participants were spending their time in deep reflection or meditation.

But sitting still was never my strong suit, Kai thought with a smirk. *Time to see what the others are up to.*

As he stepped into the hallway, Kai nearly collided with Liu Wei, who was pacing back and forth, muttering to himself.

"Whoa there," Kai said, steadying his follower. "What's got you so worked up?"

"Master Kai!" Liu Wei said with wide eyes. "I . . . I can't stop thinking about what Elder Feng said. About the Trial of the Heart. What if they look into my past and see, you know," he lowered his voice, "my time as a bandit?"

Poor guy's really spiraling, Kai thought. *Time for some tough love.*

"Liu Wei," Kai said firmly, "look at me."

Liu Wei raised his eyes, meeting Kai's steady gaze.

"You are not defined by your past," Kai said. "You're defined by your choices now. You chose to leave that life behind. You chose to follow a better path. That's what matters."

"But—"

"No buts," Kai interrupted. "The Azure Sky Sect doesn't want perfect people. They want people who can recognize their mistakes and strive to be better. That's you, Liu Wei."

Liu Wei's eyes widened. "You really think so, Master?"

Kai nodded. "I know so. Or else I wouldn't keep telling you this. Now, take a deep breath and remember why you're here."

He's come so far. I can't let him falter now.

"Thank you, Master," Liu Wei said softly. "I . . . I think I feel better now."

"That's the spirit," Kai said with a grin. "Now, how about we grab some breakfast? Can't face a trial on an empty stomach."

As they made their way to the common area, Kai's mind was already working on strategies. *The Trial of the Heart. It's not just about power or skill. They want to know our character. But how do you measure something like that? There has to be a system, a set of criteria they're using . . .*

His thoughts were interrupted by a familiar voice.

"Behold, my loyal disciples! Your master has achieved perfect enlightenment through rigorous meditation!"

Zhi-Zhi waddled towards them, his tiny chest puffed out with pride. The spirit tortoise had somehow acquired a miniature set of monk's robes, complete with a small wooden prayer bead necklace.

Kai raised an eyebrow. "Enlightenment, huh? That was fast."

"Of course it was!" Zhi-Zhi declared. "For one of my immense spiritual fortitude, such trivial matters as moral quandaries are child's play!"

"That's, uh, very impressive, great Zhi-Zhi," Liu Wei chuckled. "Any tips for the rest of us?"

Zhi-Zhi's eyes gleamed. "Ah, you wish to learn from my boundless wisdom! Very well, I shall impart upon you the secret to passing this trial." He paused dramatically. "Simply be as magnificent as me!"

Kai rolled his eyes. "Thanks for the advice, oh wise one. I'm sure we'll all keep that in mind."

As they entered the common area, Kai noticed several other participants already gathered there. Some sat in quiet contemplation over their meals, while others engaged in hushed conversations.

Sun Jun and his group occupied a table near the center, their voices carrying across the room.

" . . . and then I told the elder, 'With all due respect, sir, but I believe my interpretation of the Righteous Fist technique is far superior,'" Sun Jun boasted, earning nods of approval from his cronies.

Kai shook his head as he grabbed a tray. *Typical. Even now, he can't help showing off. But maybe that confidence will serve him well in the trial . . .*

They found a quiet table near the edge of the room. As Kai began to eat, he noticed Shen Yu sitting alone in the corner, his eyes closed in meditation even as he mechanically lifted food to his mouth.

Liu Wei followed Kai's gaze. "Master, do you think Shen Yu will have trouble with the Trial of the Heart? He seems so . . . cold."

Kai shrugged. "Hard to say. Just because someone doesn't wear their heart on their sleeve doesn't mean they lack one. He could surprise us all."

As they finished their meal, Lu Chen approached their table.

"Good morning, Kai, Liu Wei," he said with a slight bow. "I hope your preparations for the trial are going well?"

Kai nodded, studying Lu Chen's carefully neutral expression. "Well enough. And yours?"

Lu Chen smiled, but it didn't quite reach his eyes. "Oh, I believe I'm adequately prepared. The Chen family has a long history with the Azure Sky Sect, after all. We know what's expected."

Ah, there it is, Kai thought. *A subtle reminder of his connections.*

Aloud, Kai said, "I'm sure you'll do fine. May the best cultivators succeed."

Lu Chen's smile tightened almost imperceptibly. "Indeed. Well, good luck to you both." He bowed again and walked away.

Liu Wei let out a breath he'd been holding. "Master, do you think he was trying to intimidate us?"

Kai chuckled. "In his own polite way, yes, but don't let it get to you. Remember, this trial isn't about family connections or past glory. It's about who we are now, in this moment."

They spent the rest of the morning in the common area, observing the other participants and discussing strategies in low voices. Kai couldn't help but analyze everyone's behavior, looking for clues about the upcoming trial.

" . . . but what if they ask about that time I . . ."

" . . . my father says the key is to project confidence, no matter what . . ."

" . . . I heard they use some kind of truth-revealing artifact . . ."

It's like trying to solve a puzzle without all the pieces, he mused. *But every bit of information helps. Who knows what could give us an edge?*

Zhi-Zhi, who had been uncharacteristically quiet, suddenly yawned. "Well, my faithful disciples, it seems the time has come for me to engage in some deep, spiritual meditation. Do not disturb me unless the heavens themselves are falling!"

With that, the spirit tortoise retreated into his shell, which began to let out soft snoring sounds moments later.

Kai chuckled, shaking his head. "At least someone's not stressed about the trial."

As Kai turned to talk with Liu Wei, he suddenly felt a strange sensation wash over him. It felt like a wave of static, briefly distorting his perception. He blinked, shaking his head to clear it.

"Master, are you all right?"

Kai held up a hand, trying to focus. "I'm fine, just felt a bit . . . odd for a moment there."

What was that? Kai wondered. *Some kind of qi fluctuation?*

Out of habit, Kai tried to pull up his status window to check if anything had changed. But to his shock and growing alarm, nothing happened. He tried again, concentrating harder this time. Still nothing.

This isn't right, Kai thought, a cold feeling settling in his stomach. *The System has never failed before. It's always been there, even when I'm asleep or unconscious. But now . . . it's gone.*

"Master?" Liu Wei's worried voice broke through Kai's rising panic. "You look pale. Should we go see one of the medical cultivators?"

Kai forced himself to take a deep breath, his mind racing. *Okay, don't panic. Think this through logically. I still have access to qi. I can still feel my cultivation base. So it's not like I've lost everything. But without the System . . .*

"I'm okay, Liu Wei," Kai said, trying to keep his voice steady. "Just . . . thinking about the trial."

Liu Wei nodded sympathetically, but Kai could see the confusion in his eyes.

I can't tell him, Kai realized. *He wouldn't understand, and I can't risk anyone finding out about the System . . . or its absence.*

As they continued their conversation, Kai's mind was working overtime. *Is this part of the trial? Some kind of illusion or test? Or has something gone seriously wrong?*

He glanced around the room, studying the other participants more closely now. Everyone seemed normal, going about their business as usual. No one else appeared to be experiencing anything strange.

Okay, think. If this is an illusion, what's the objective? To see through it? To resist it? Or is the illusion itself just a setting for the real trial? Will they now test my heart?

Just as Kai was about to suggest they return to their rooms to regroup and think, a commotion erupted from the direction of the main entrance. The sound of splintering wood echoed through the hallways, followed by gasps and cries of alarm.

"What in the name of the Celestial Tortoise Palace is going on?" Zhi-Zhi exclaimed, popping his head out of his shell.

Kai and Liu Wei exchanged worried glances before hurrying towards the source of the disturbance, with Zhi-Zhi scuttling along behind them.

"Wait for me, you impertinent disciples!" the spirit tortoise huffed. "A master should always lead the charge!"

As they rounded the corner, they were met with a shocking sight. The massive doors that sealed off the trial quarters had been smashed open. Standing in the wreckage were three figures, their auras releasing power that far exceeded anything Kai had felt from the other participants.

Foundation Establishment cultivators!

CHAPTER FORTY-SIX

The three intruders wore the distinctive outer disciple robes of the Azure Sky Sect, white fabric with silver cloud patterns. The leader, a tall man with a sharp nose and narrowed eyes, stepped forward. His companions flanked him, a stocky woman with close-cropped hair and a thin youth with a scar across his left cheek.

For a moment, Kai's hand twitched, instinctively trying to bring up his status window. But nothing appeared. The familiar blue screens that had become second nature to him were absent.

This feels wrong. I've gotten so used to seeing stats pop up for everyone. Without my System . . .

The tall man's voice boomed across the room, silencing the confused murmurs of the disciples. "Listen up, you pathetic worms! When you enter the Azure Sky Sect, you'll need protection. We're here to offer our . . . services."

"Protection?" one of the braver participants spoke up. "From what?"

"From us, of course. The sect can be a dangerous place for newcomers. Accidents happen all the time. But with our . . . generous offer, you'll be safe," the woman beside the leader sneered. "Consider it an investment in your future."

Kai's eyes narrowed as he watched from the sidelines.

This scenario, it's like something straight out of a cultivation novel, he thought. *The bullies arrive to extort the new disciples, setting the stage for the protagonist to swoop in and save the day. Is this what the trial is testing? Our willingness to stand up against injustice? But then again this could be real, it is a cultivation world, after all.*

Liu Wei shifted nervously beside him. "Master," he whispered, "what should we do?"

Before I do anything, I need to confirm if this is really part of the trial. If it's just a test, being righteous is the smart play. But if it's real . . . I'd rather not get involved in unnecessary drama.

"For now, we wait and watch," Kai murmured back to Liu Wei. "Let's see how this plays out."

Zhi-Zhi puffed up his chest. "Hmph! In my day, we didn't need protection from anyone! Why, I once faced down an entire army of spirit beasts with nothing but my impenetrable shell and my razor-sharp wit!"

Kai raised an eyebrow at the spirit tortoise. "Is that so? And how did that work out for you?"

Zhi-Zhi deflated slightly. "Well . . . I may have spent most of that battle hiding in my shell. But it was a strategic retreat!"

Kai's eyes widened slightly at Zhi-Zhi's response, he did not expect the tortoise to actually admit that.

As the Foundation Establishment cultivators began moving through the crowd, demanding "protection fees" from the terrified participants, Kai observed their behavior closely.

The thin man approached a trembling young woman. "You there! Hand over your spirit stones if you know what's good for you!"

The woman fumbled with her pouch, nearly dropping it in her haste. "P-Please, I'm from a small clan, I don't have much . . ."

The stocky woman sneered at a group of young men huddled together. "What's the matter, boys? Too scared to stand up for yourselves? Pathetic!"

One of the men, his face pale with fear, stepped forward. "We . . . we don't want any trouble. How much do you want?"

Something's off here. Why aren't they paying any attention to me? In every story I've read, the protagonist always gets singled out in situations like this. Kai glanced at Liu Wei and Zhi-Zhi, who were watching the scene with a mix of fear and indignation. *And why aren't they targeting my companions? That would be the easiest way to provoke me.*

"This is outrageous!" Liu Wei whispered. "Someone should stand up to these bullies!"

Zhi-Zhi nodded. "If I were in my true form, I'd show these upstarts the meaning of real power!"

Kai patted the spirit tortoise's shell absently, his mind still working through the puzzle. "I'm sure you would, Zhi-Zhi. But let's watch for now."

As the Foundation Establishment cultivators continued their intimidation tactics, more inconsistencies began to pile up in Kai's mind.

If this were real, wouldn't the sect elders have noticed by now? This has to be part of the trial. But I can't let on that I know. I need to act as if this is real . . . while still making the "right" choice.

Suddenly, the atmosphere in the room shifted as Sun Jun stepped forward, his face flushed with anger. "How dare you treat us this way! Do you know who I am? I am Sun Jun of the Sun Clan!"

The tall leader turned slowly, a cruel smile spreading across his face. "Oh? And you think your family name means anything to us?"

Lu Chen moved to stand beside his friend, his voice cold and calm. "You're making a grave mistake. Our families have deep connections within the sect. This behavior will not go unpunished."

The stocky woman laughed. "Big words from such little boys. Why don't you show us what you can do?"

This doesn't make sense. Foundation Establishment cultivators shouldn't be picking fights with young masters who have powerful backing. Unless . . .

Before Kai could complete the thought, the leader moved with blinding speed. His hand shot out, striking Sun Jun squarely in the chest. The young master's eyes widened in shock as he was sent flying across the room, crashing into the far wall with a sickening thud.

"Sun Jun!" Lu Chen cried out, his usual composure cracking. He turned to face the attackers, his hands glowing with qi as he prepared a technique.

But the thin man was already moving. With a flick of his wrist, he sent a wave of invisible force that slammed into Lu Chen. The young cultivator managed to land on his feet, but he skidded backward, his face pale with the effort of remaining upright.

Gasps of horror echoed through the room. Liu Wei grabbed Kai's arm, his voice trembling. "Master, we have to do something!"

Zhi-Zhi had retreated partially into his shell, only his eyes visible as he peeked out. "Perhaps . . . perhaps a strategic withdrawal is in order? To plan our counterattack, of course!"

This can't be real. Those young masters have connections that far outstrip mere Foundation Establishment cultivators. No one would dare treat them like this, unless it's all an illusion or they were courting death.

The concept of "courting death" was deeply ingrained in cultivation society. Only fools or the truly powerful would dare to offend scions of major clans so blatantly. These Foundation Establishment cultivators were either suicidal or . . .

It has to be an illusion, Kai concluded. *In a real xianxia world, those cultivators would be asking for swift and brutal retribution from the Sun and Moon clans. No one with a functioning brain would risk that unless they had the backing of an immortal powerhouse.*

Kai glanced at Liu Wei and Zhi-Zhi, noting their reactions. *And despite their comments, these "bullies" aren't paying us any attention. If this were real, they'd have noticed us by now. But it looks like they're not putting Liu Wei or Zhi-Zhi in danger because it's obvious I'd defend my friends. This is about seeing if I'll stand up for someone I don't like when they're being treated unjustly.*

Normally, I wouldn't lift a finger to help Sun Jun, Kai thought. *But since this isn't real and it's just a test, I can play the hero without any real consequences. And they can't tell that I know it's an illusion, so they won't think I'm faking it.*

The tall leader advanced on the fallen Sun Jun, who was struggling to rise. Qi began to swirl around the man's fist, coalescing into a swirling vortex of energy.

"Let's see how tough you are now, young master," he sneered, raising his fist.

Time to make my move, Kai thought, his body tensing.

In a flash, Kai activated his Swift Wind Step technique. The world blurred around him as he crossed the distance in an instant, materializing between Sun Jun and the attacker.

"That's enough," Kai said, his voice steady despite the pounding of his heart. He poured his qi into a barrier, forming a shield of energy just as the Foundation Establishment cultivator's attack landed.

The impact was tremendous. Kai felt his barrier shatter almost instantly, the force of the blow sending him staggering backward. He managed to stay on his feet, but his arms trembled with the effort of absorbing the shock.

Damn, that hurt more than I expected, Kai thought, gritting his teeth. *Even if it's an illusion, they're not pulling any punches.*

As he slowly straightened up, facing the shocked expressions of the "bullies" and the other participants, a new thought occurred to Kai.

Wait a minute. Why isn't the trial over yet? I made the "right" choice, didn't I? Do they expect me to actually fight these guys to the death?

The leader's eyes narrowed as he regarded Kai. "Well, well. Looks like we have a hero in our midst. You've got guts, kid. But do you have the strength to back it up?"

This is getting complicated. How far do I need to take this to pass the trial?

Kai could feel the eyes of everyone in the room on him, waiting to see what he would do next. Liu Wei and Zhi-Zhi were calling out to him.

"Master Kai, be careful!"

"Show them the power of my disciple, Kai! Er . . . I mean, the power I've bestowed upon you!"

Sun Jun, still on the ground behind Kai, looked up with a mixture of surprise and grudging respect. "Why . . . why are you helping me?"

Kai didn't turn around, keeping his eyes fixed on the three attackers. "Because it's the right thing to do," he said, loud enough for everyone to hear. *And because it's probably what the trial expects of me,* he added silently.

The stocky woman cracked her knuckles, a predatory grin spreading across her face. "Ooh, I like this one. He's got spirit. Let's see how long it lasts!"

As the three Foundation Establishment cultivators began to advance, Kai fell into a defensive stance.

If this is still part of the trial, I need to show courage and determination, even in the face of overwhelming odds. But if it's real . . . well, I'm in serious trouble.

CHAPTER FORTY-SEVEN

The leader of the Foundation Establishment cultivators stepped forward, his eyes narrowing as he surveyed the scene. He turned to his two companions.

"Zhou Ling, Yang Ming, stand back," he commanded. "I'll handle this myself."

The stocky woman, Zhou Ling, frowned but nodded. "Fine, Deng Long. Just don't take too long. We have other disciples to . . . educate."

"Hah! These little ones aren't even worth our time." The thin man did an exaggerated bow, a mocking grin on his face. "We'll leave them to you, Brother Deng." With that, he took several steps back, crossing his arms as he prepared to enjoy the show.

Kai's eyes narrowed as he focused on Deng Long. Without the System, he couldn't get a clear read on the power difference between them. Still, he'd read enough cultivation novels to know that even an early Foundation Establishment cultivator could easily take on multiple Qi Refining disciples.

Guess it's time to see if that holds true here, Kai thought, a wry smile tugging at his lips.

Suddenly, Liu Wei stepped up beside him, his hands gripping two plain-looking daggers. "Master," he whispered, "how can I help?"

Kai glanced at his follower. *He's only at Qi Refining stage three. Against a Foundation Establishment cultivator, he doesn't stand a chance.*

"Stay back, Liu Wei," Kai murmured. "This fight is out of your league."

Deng Long cracked his knuckles. "You know what? Forget about fancy qi techniques. I'm going to beat that smile off your face the old-fashioned way."

Good, he's underestimating me, Kai thought. *That's the only chance I have. And no, not a chance to win, just a chance to survive. I'd be an idiot to think I could actually beat him.*

In a blur of motion, Deng Long vanished from sight. Kai's eyes widened as a fist materialized inches from his face. He activated Swift Wind Step, barely managing to dodge backwards. Even the aftereffect of the missed blow was enough to send Kai skidding back several feet.

Liu Wei, seeing his master in danger, also activated Swift Wind Step. He appeared behind Deng Long, slashing with his daggers towards his neck. But the Foundation Establishment cultivator simply twisted, avoiding the attack without even looking.

"Brave," Deng Long sneered, "but foolish." He backhanded Liu Wei, sending him tumbling across the room.

As Kai steadied himself, his mind raced. *This guy is way too OP. There's no way I can beat him at this stage. I need a strategy, fast.*

Taking a deep breath, Kai forced himself to calm down and think rationally. *Okay, game plan: fight evasively, keep my distance, and don't get hit. One solid blow and it's lights out.*

His eyes fell on Zhi-Zhi, who was peeking out from behind a table. *In anime, teamwork is always looked upon favorably in these kinds of trials. Even in a xianxia world, surely righteous sects care about that sort of thing.*

"Zhi-Zhi!" Kai called out. "I need you to be my shield!"

The spirit tortoise, who was now somehow cowering behind a pillar, poked his head out of his shell. "What? No way! I don't like being used as a meat shield!" But as Zhi-Zhi saw the look in Kai's eyes, his expression softened. "Oh, all right. But only because you're my favorite disciple!"

Zhi-Zhi retreated into his shell, which then shot towards Kai like a cannonball. Kai caught it with his left hand and moved it around, testing how heavy it felt.

Let's see just how impenetrable this shield really is.

Deng Long shook his head, turning back to Kai with an amused expression. "You're a slippery one, aren't you? But hiding behind a turtle shell won't save you."

"Tortoise!" came Zhi-Zhi's muffled voice from inside the shell.

Ignoring the spirit beast's protest, Kai called out to Sun Jun and Lu Chen. "Hey, you two! How about some support? Unless you want to face this guy alone?"

Sun Jun, who had managed to get to his feet, brushed dirt from his robes with a scowl. "Support? I'm usually the one being supported. But . . . since you helped me, I suppose I can make an exception this time."

Lu Chen simply nodded and took up position on Kai's other side. The three of them faced Deng Long, looking like they were in some kind of anime showdown.

Seeing this, Zhou Ling stepped forward and began manipulating qi. The ground beneath them started to shake.

"Don't think you can use numbers against—" she began, but was cut off as Deng Long's fist slammed into her back, sending her crashing to the floor.

"What did I tell you about getting involved?" Deng Long growled, standing over her.

Zhou Ling groaned weakly. "Sorry, boss. Won't happen again."

Deng Long turned back to Kai, Sun Jun, and Lu Chen, a predatory grin spreading across his face. "I can take all three of you brats with one hand tied behind my back." His gaze fell on Zhi-Zhi's shell in Kai's hand. "And when I'm done, I think I'll make some turtle soup."

"I told you, I'm a tortoise!" Zhi-Zhi's voice rang out from within the shell.

Deng Long laughed. "Tortoise soup it is, then!"

With that, he dashed forward, his fist aimed directly at Kai's face. Kai raised Zhi-Zhi's shell just in time, deflecting the blow. The impact sent shockwaves through Kai's arm, but the shell held firm.

Deng Long's eyes widened in surprise. He had clearly expected the shell to shatter on impact.

Now's our chance! Kai thought.

In that moment of surprise, Kai, Sun Jun, and Lu Chen launched a coordinated counterattack.

A qi-dagger materialized in Kai's right hand, stabbing towards Deng Long's head. Sun Jun's fist, wreathed in flames, aimed for the Foundation Establishment cultivator's right side. From the left, Lu Chen sent a spike of water qi hurtling towards their opponent.

For a split second, Deng Long's eyes widened. Then a smirk played across his lips as lightning qi crackled over his skin. In the blink of an eye, he vanished, leaving the three attacks to collide harmlessly where he had been standing.

"Where did he—" Lu Chen started to say, but was cut off as Deng Long reappeared behind him. A lightning-enhanced kick sent the young cultivator flying across the room. He slammed into the wall and crumpled to the ground.

One blow was enough to knock him out cold.

Damn, he's fast! Kai thought, his mind racing. *We need to stick together or he'll pick us off one by one.*

But before Kai could warn Sun Jun, Deng Long had already appeared behind the hot-headed young master. Sun Jun spun around, his fists blazing with fire qi as he roared a challenge.

What an idiot! Kai thought, watching in horror. *You can't outpower a Foundation Establishment cultivator!*

The clash was over in an instant. Sun Jun's flaming fists met Deng Long's lightning-charged punch, and the young master went flying. He hit the ground hard, his body twitching as sparks of electricity danced over his skin.

Deng Long landed lightly on his feet, turning to face Kai with a predatory grin. "Looks like it's just you and me now, kid. Ready to get on your knees and beg for mercy?"

Kai's mind was working overtime. *Why isn't this trial over yet? We showed courage, teamwork . . . what else do they want? Unless . . . unless this isn't a trial at all.*

A cold feeling settled in Kai's stomach as he considered the possibility that this might be real. He pushed the thought aside, focusing on the immediate threat.

Deng Long burst forward, his fist crackling with lightning as it hurtled towards Kai. Kai brought up Zhi-Zhi's shell, bracing for impact. The punch connected with a thunderous boom. The shell once again held firm, but the force of the blow sent Kai flying across the room.

He managed to land on his feet, but the impact had knocked the wind out of him. *This shell is amazing, but I can't take too many hits like that.*

Before Kai could catch his breath, Deng Long appeared at his left side. Kai started to raise the shell to defend, but Deng Long vanished again, reappearing on Kai's right.

Crap! I can't get the shield there in time!

In desperation, Kai activated Iron Skin. A metallic sheen spread over his body just as Deng Long's lightning-enhanced fist connected.

What happened next surprised everyone, Kai most of all.

Instead of Kai being sent flying, it was Deng Long who was suddenly airborne, as if he'd been hit by an uppercut to the jaw. He sailed through the air, a look of utter shock on his face.

Kai blinked, then a grin spread across his face as he realized what had happened. *No way! Did Iron Rebound actually activate? That 5% chance actually came through!*

Not wasting the opportunity, Kai quickly conjured a qi-dagger and hurled it at Deng Long, aiming for his neck. But even caught off guard, the Foundation Establishment cultivator's reflexes were impressive. He twisted in midair, his fist striking the side of the qi-dagger and deflecting it.

Deng Long landed on his feet, a look of anger and grudging respect on his face. He touched his jaw, then spat a mouthful of blood onto the floor.

"Impressive," he growled, wiping his mouth with his sleeve. "A Qi Refining cultivator actually made me bleed." His eyes narrowed dangerously. "But now . . . now you're going to die, boy."

Kai barely had time to register the threat before Deng Long was upon him.

A hand closed around his throat, lifting him off the ground. Kai found himself staring into Deng Long's cold eyes, his feet dangling uselessly in the air.

This . . . this can't be how it ends, Kai thought, his mind racing even as he struggled to breathe. *There has to be a way out of this. Think!*

Zhi-Zhi's shell clattered to the ground as Kai's grip loosened. The spirit tortoise emerged, his eyes wide with fear and determination.

"Unhand my disciple, you brute!" Zhi-Zhi cried out. He began to gather qi, preparing to unleash his most powerful technique. "Behold the might of the Celestial Tortoise! Heavenly Shell Cannon!"

A blast of golden energy shot from Zhi-Zhi's mouth, hurtling towards Deng Long. But the Foundation Establishment cultivator simply lashed out with his foot, catching Zhi-Zhi mid-attack. The spirit tortoise went flying across the room, his shell bouncing off the walls.

Deng Long turned his attention back to Kai, his grip tightening. "You're no hero, boy," he snarled. "Just another corpse."

With a cruel smile, Deng Long began to squeeze. As Kai struggled to breathe, his vision starting to darken at the edges, a part of his mind remained calm and analytical as the Mental Fortitude skill took effect.

If this is real, I'm about to die. If it's a trial, it's gone way too far. Either way, I need to do something drastic.

Suddenly, a blur of motion caught Kai's fading vision. Liu Wei appeared behind Deng Long and with a scream, he plunged his dagger into Deng Long's back.

The blade barely pierced Deng Long's qi-reinforced skin, but the unexpected attack made him loosen his grip on Kai's throat and turn his head. "You little—"

Kai gasped for air, his mind clearing just enough to seize the opportunity. With the last of his strength, he focused his qi into his right hand. A small, dense ball of qi began to form, growing more compact and intense with each passing second.

Deng Long, distracted by Liu Wei, didn't notice the gathering energy until it was too late. He turned back to Kai just as the qi ball was completed.

Kai didn't hesitate. With all the force he could muster, he slammed the condensed ball of qi directly into Deng Long's face.

The explosion was deafening. A blinding flash of light filled the room, accompanied by a shockwave that sent everyone still conscious staggering backwards.

When the light faded and the dust settled, Kai found himself on the ground, coughing and gasping. His entire body ached, and his right hand felt like it was on fire.

Blinking to clear his vision, Kai looked up to see Deng Long stumbling backwards, his hands covering his face.

When Deng Long lowered his hands, a big, round bruise covered the middle of his face. His nose looked broken, blood dripping from it. The skin around the bruise was red and puffy.

"You . . . you little bastards!" he yelled. His voice sounded funny because of his hurt nose. "I'll kill you both!"

Kai tried to move, to defend himself, but his body wouldn't respond. He'd put everything he had into that last attack, and now he had nothing left.

So this is it, Kai thought, a strange calm settling over him. *Either I pass this trial, or I respawn.*

Suddenly, Deng Long vanished from sight. Kai's eyes widened but before he could react, he felt a presence behind him.

A strong hand gripped his head.

Oh, shi—

There was a sharp crack.

And everything went dark.

CHAPTER FORTY-EIGHT

Kai's eyes snapped open, his heart racing. Instead of the void he'd usually appear in after his "death," he found himself back in the common area of the trial quarters. He blinked, taking in the scene around him.

Zhi-Zhi was curled up in his shell, seemingly asleep. Liu Wei stood frozen beside Kai, eyes closed as if in a trance. Glancing around the room, Kai realized all the other participants were in similar states—motionless, eyes shut, suspended in time.

A wave of relief washed over Kai. *So it really was just a trial,* he thought, letting out a breath he didn't realize he'd been holding.

Before he could attempt to wake up Liu Wei, movement caught his eye. Kai tensed, turning sharply only to relax as he saw the Sect Master materializing in the room.

The Sect Master's eyes crinkled with a smile. "Congratulations, you two," he announced. "You both completed the Trial of Heart at exactly the same time, five minutes."

Kai's brow furrowed in confusion. *You two?* His gaze swept the room, landing on Shen Yu, who was regarding him with an unreadable expression.

Of course, Kai thought. *Why was I even surprised? He likely already knew that it wasn't real and decided to play the hero, just like me.*

A flicker of worry passed through Kai as he remembered the disappearance of his system during the trial. Subtly, he attempted to bring up his status screen. To his relief, it flickered into view.

Name: Kai Thorn
XP: 100/4,000

Level: Qi Refining Stage 8
Qi: 250/250
Strength: 60
Agility: 63
Durability: 67
Intelligence: 30
Wisdom: 29

Titles:
Novice Instructor
Elemental Affinities:
Lightning: 20%

Skills:
Qi Condensation (Level 4)
Basic Cultivation Technique (Level 3)
Unarmed Combat (Level 2)
Deception (Level 4)
Iron Skin Technique (Level 3)
Swift Wind Step (Level 4)
Flame Palm Strike (Level 3)
Mental Fortitude (Passive)
Spirit Beast Communication (Level 1)
Qi Concealment (Level 1)
Qi Detection (Level 1)
Iron Rebound (Level 1)
Rock Hard (Passive)
Lightning Step (Level 1)

The trial was likely created by the Sect Master or some immortal treasure. For it to hide the system from my senses . . . that's concerning. Clearly, the system isn't as overpowered in this world as in other novels. Immortals seem to have some degree of protection against it.

Putting on his best "confused newcomer" face, Kai looked at the Sect Master. "Excuse me, Sect Master, but . . . what exactly happened? It all felt so real."

"What you experienced was the Trial of Heart," the Sect Master explained. "We were testing your core values, your true nature when faced with difficult choices."

He gestured to Kai and Shen Yu. "You both chose to sacrifice yourselves for others, even those you had no particular attachment to. This shows that, at your core, you possess righteous values."

Yeah, right, Kai thought, suppressing a snort. *If I'd thought it was real, I would've been more than happy to watch Sun Jun get taken down a peg or two. No way I'd waste a respawn on that guy. And I bet Shen Yu feels the same.*

But out loud, he simply said, "The illusion was incredibly lifelike. How did you create such a convincing scenario?"

The Sect Master's smile widened as he produced a small white crystal from his robes. At its center, Kai could see what looked like a miniature golden eye. "This," the Sect Master explained, "is one of our sect's treasures, the Eye of Veiled Truth. It's an Immortal-Rank artifact capable of weaving incredibly realistic illusions."

From the corner of his eye, Kai noticed Shen Yu's eyes widen almost imperceptibly. *Interesting. Looks like our resident mystery man recognizes that little bauble.*

"It seems unusual to use such a powerful artifact for disciple selection," Kai ventured, probing for more information.

The Sect Master's expression grew serious. "Many sects have been betrayed by disciples they thought they could trust. This allows us to see beyond cultivators' masks and into their true hearts." He then shook his head. "Besides, in times of peace, the poor thing doesn't get much use otherwise."

As if on cue, Zhi-Zhi's head popped out of his shell, eyes wide with terror. "Great heavens!" the spirit tortoise cried out. "How am I still alive? I saw death itself!"

Kai placed a hand on Zhi-Zhi's shell. "It's okay," he said. "It was just the trial. None of it was real."

Zhi-Zhi shook his head vigorously. "But . . . but I saw them die! Even my mother's sacred life-preserving leaf didn't work! I . . . I felt my own essence fade away . . ."

Kai's eyebrows shot up in surprise. *For Zhi-Zhi to "die" in the illusion, he must have exposed himself instead of just hiding . . . or the opponents he faced were capable of breaking through his shell.*

Before he could respond, Liu Wei's eyes snapped open. The former bandit's hand flew to his throat as he gasped for air. "Master!" he cried out. "My family . . . died! They all died!"

Kai patted Liu Wei's shoulder. "It's all right," he said, fighting back a sigh. "It wasn't real."

"You four have completed the trial in remarkable time," the Sect Master cut in. "While the others continue their tests, you may return to your quarters to rest and reflect."

He paused, his gaze moving between them. "Tomorrow morning, we will announce the results for all participants. Those who have succeeded will be allocated their positions within the sect."

"Thank you, Sect Master," Kai gave a bow and then guided Liu Wei and Zhi-Zhi towards the door.

As they left, he noticed Shen Yu heading towards his own quarters, the youth's face once again an unreadable mask.

Kai settled Liu Wei and Zhi-Zhi in his room, taking a deep breath to center himself. *Time to play counselor,* he thought. *Let's see what these two really went through.*

"All right," Kai said gently, "I know that was intense. But we're safe now, and it's over. Let's talk through what happened. It might help to share our experiences."

Zhi-Zhi, still trembling slightly, poked his head out of his shell. "You . . . you really want to know what I saw?" he asked, his voice uncharacteristically small.

Kai nodded encouragingly. "Of course. Why don't you go first, Zhi-Zhi?"

The spirit tortoise took a shaky breath, then began to speak. "It . . . it was terrifying! I found myself back at the Celestial Tortoise Palace. But it wasn't the peaceful paradise I remembered. It was under attack!"

Zhi-Zhi's eyes grew wide as he continued. "Demon beasts were every-where, their dark qi corrupting the very air. And my family . . . they were fighting for their lives."

His voice quivered. "They called out to me, begging me to use my legend-ary wisdom to save them. But I . . . I didn't know what to do!"

Zhi-Zhi looked down, ashamed. "I wanted to run, to hide in my shell where it was safe. But I knew if I did, everyone would die. So I . . . I forced myself to stay."

He took a deep breath. "I'm not wise or powerful. Not really. But I real-ized I could still help. I used my shell to shield the younger tortoises. It wasn't much, but it was something."

Zhi-Zhi's eyes met Kai's. "In the end, there were too many demons. They . . . they broke through our defenses. I saw the others fall, one by one. And then . . . then they came for me."

His voice dropped to a whisper. "I felt my shell crack . . ."

Kai listened intently, surprised by Zhi-Zhi's honesty, this was not a part of the tortoise he often saw.

"Zhi-Zhi," Kai said softly, "you . . . you did well."

Zhi-Zhi sniffled, then puffed up slightly. "Well, of course! The great Zhi-Zhi always rises to the occasion . . . even if it's scary."

Kai turned to Liu Wei, who had been listening silently, his face pale. "What about you, Liu Wei? What did you experience?"

Liu Wei swallowed hard, then: "Master, it . . . it was like reliving my worst nightmare. But this time, it was different."

He took a shaky breath. "I was back in my village, with my family. We were poor, struggling to survive. Then the bandits came."

Liu Wei's hands clenched into fists. "Their leader, he . . . he gave me the same choice as all those years ago. Join them, become a bandit, and my family would be spared. Refuse, and we'd all die."

His voice cracked. "I saw my little sister, Liu Ling. She's only eight, always smiling despite how hard things were after my father passed away. And my mother, she always worked day and night to keep us fed."

Liu Wei looked up at Kai, his eyes full of pain. "In the real past, I . . . I joined them. To save my family. But this time, in the trial, I refused."

Kai's eyes widened in surprise. *He chose to die? Even thinking it was real?*

Liu Wei continued, his voice barely a whisper. "They . . . they killed my mother first. She told me she was proud of me, even as she died."

Tears streamed down Liu Wei's face. "Then they turned to Liu Ling. She was so brave, Master. She didn't cry. She just hugged me and said it would be okay."

He shuddered. "When it was my turn, I felt . . . at peace. I'd chosen to die rather than become a monster. The bandit leader, he looked . . . confused. Angry. He asked me one last time if I'd join them."

Liu Wei's voice grew stronger. "I spat in his face. Told him I'd rather die a thousand deaths than become like him. That's when . . . that's when he cut me down."

"Liu Wei," Kai said, "what you did . . . that took incredible courage. You faced your greatest fear and made an unimaginably difficult choice. You're exactly what this sect needs."

And exactly what I need in a follower. Someone who'll put principles above self-preservation could be incredibly useful . . . if those principles align with my goals.

"It's thanks to your guidance, Master," Liu Wei nodded.

Kai smiled, but inwardly he felt a twinge of . . . something. Guilt?

"We've all grown stronger together," he said. "Now, let's have some rest. We'll find out how we did tomorrow."

Kai lay on his bed that night, staring at the ceiling as his thoughts turned to tomorrow.

Okay, let's break this down. Quest objective: Become the Sect Master's disciple. What are the win conditions?

He began to mentally list the factors that might influence the decision:

Performance in the trials. *Check. I aced those.*

Potential for growth. *With my System? Definitely check.*

Character and values. *Well, I faked that pretty well in the last trial.*

Unique abilities or backgrounds. *Isekai protagonist, so I think I have that covered.*

But then there's Shen Yu. He beat me in the trials. And there's definitely more to him than meets the eye. He could be serious competition.

Kai's thoughts drifted to Shen Yu's warning about the Sect Master. *Should I play it safe and aim for another elder as a master?* He pondered for a moment, then shook his head. *No, the benefits of being the Sect Master's disciple are too good to pass up. Besides, Shen Yu's motives are unclear. He's already proven he doesn't care if I live or die.*

His eyes fell on the trident mark on his wrist. *Worst case scenario, I always have my trump card. If things go south, I can respawn.*

Kai's thoughts then turned to the small crystal the Sect Master had shown them. *That artifact . . . it could see through my System, or at least interfere with it. I need to be careful. If they find out I'm from another world . . .*

He shook his head, refocusing. *No use worrying about what-ifs. I've done what I can. Now it's time to see if it pays off.*

With that thought, Kai closed his eyes, willing himself to sleep. Tomorrow, he would find out if he did enough to catch the Sect Master's eye.

CHAPTER FORTY-NINE

The next morning, Kai stood amongst the remaining participants on the grand plateau. His eyes scanned the crowd, noting the significant reduction in numbers. Where hundreds had stood just a few days before, now only about a hundred remained.

There was a nervous energy in the air as the students—well, disciples—whispered and fidgeted, waiting to hear their fate. Kai's eyes darted to the row of elders, who sat like a panel of college admissions officers. Their faces gave nothing away.

A scowl from across the plateau caught Kai's attention. Sun Jun, the arrogant young master, was glaring daggers at him. Kai suppressed a smirk.

Looks like someone heard about the results of the Trial of Heart.

Liu Wei, who was standing beside Kai, leaned over. "Master," he whispered, "have you noticed? There are so few of us left."

Before Kai could respond, Zhi-Zhi's head popped out from Liu Wei's robes. "Of course there are fewer participants, you simpleton!" the spirit tortoise declared. "Only the cream of the crop remains! The truly elite! Like myself, of course."

Kai shook his head. "You're both right, in a way," he said. "The sect must have kicked out those who failed yesterday's Trial of Heart as soon as they woke up."

Liu Wei's brow furrowed. "But why? Couldn't they still be useful to the sect?"

"Think about it," Kai explained, slipping into his instructor role. "The Trial of Heart tested our moral character and trustworthiness. There's no place in a powerful sect for people they can't trust."

Zhi-Zhi nodded. "Exactly! Just as I was about to say. The Azure Sky Sect can't afford to harbor potential traitors or troublemakers."

"So, what happens now?" Liu Wei asked, his voice barely above a whisper.

Kai's eyes scanned the plateau, taking in the nervous faces of the other participants. "Now, we wait to see where we'll be placed. Everyone here will enter the sect, but our performance will determine whether we end up in the Outer Sect, Inner Sect, or as Core Disciples."

Liu Wei's eyes widened. "Core Disciples?"

A ghost of a smile played on Kai's lips. "It's possible for anyone who's impressed the right people. And if someone's truly exceptional, they might even become the Sect Master's disciple, a Legacy Disciple."

Zhi-Zhi puffed out his tiny chest. "Well, I think we all know who's going to be chosen as the Legacy Disciple. After all, with my guidance—"

The spirit tortoise's boast was cut short as a hush fell over the crowd. All eyes turned to the sky, where a figure was descending from the heavens.

Showtime, Kai thought as the Sect Master gracefully touched down on the central throne.

Elder Tao, the Nascent Soul cultivator Kai had met earlier, rose from his seat. His voice, amplified by qi, rang out across the plateau. "Congratulations to all who stand before us today. You have successfully completed the trials and may now call yourselves official disciples of the Azure Sky Sect."

A ripple of excitement passed through the crowd, but Kai remained still, his eyes fixed on Elder Tao.

With a wave of his hand, Elder Tao conjured a screen of water in the air. "Here are the final results of the trial."

Kai's eyes quickly scanned the list.

Shen Yu
Kai Thorn
Zhi-Zhi
Liu Wei
Lu Chen
Sun Jun

Second place, just like I expected. Not bad, but not quite the protagonist's spot either. Still, having my whole group in the top spots is pretty impressive.

As if echoing his thoughts, Liu Wei let out a gasp. "Master Kai! We're all at the top of the list!"

Zhi-Zhi preened. "Of course we are! With my guidance, how could we be anywhere else?"

Kai allowed himself a small smile. "We did well," he said quietly. "But don't let it go to your head. The real challenge begins once we enter the sect."

As he spoke, a notification popped up in Kai's vision.

> Quest Complete: Join a Cultivation Sect
> Description: You have successfully passed the recruitment trials and joined the Azure Sky Sect
> Reward: Sect Membership, 1,000 XP, 3 Random Cultivation Resources
> Would you like to accept your cultivation resources now?

Not now, Kai thought, dismissing the prompt. *I'll check those out when I'm alone. No need to draw unnecessary attention here.*

Elder Tao's voice cut through Kai's thoughts. "Those ranked outside the top thirty will join the Outer Sect," he announced, gesturing to one of the Outer Elders. "Please follow Elder Bao. He will guide you to the Outer Sect territory and explain your duties."

Kai watched as over half of the remaining participants were led away, their faces a mix of disappointment and relief.

At least they made it into the sect, he thought. *For many, that's a life-changing opportunity in itself.*

Once the new Outer Disciples had left, Elder Tao continued. "The rest of you have earned the title of Inner Disciple," he paused, his gaze sweeping over the remaining participants. "However, some of you may be fortunate enough to be chosen as a disciple by an Inner Elder, elevating you to the status of Core Disciple."

A murmur of excitement rippled through the crowd. Kai's eyes narrowed slightly as he noticed Elder Tao's gaze lingering on him and a few others at the top of the list.

"And if fate truly smiles upon you," Elder Tao added, his voice dropping to a near whisper that somehow still carried across the plateau, "the Sect Master himself may choose to take a disciple."

The murmur grew to a fever pitch. Kai could practically feel the hunger radiating from those around him.

Keep calm, Kai reminded himself. *This is just like the climax of a recruitment arc in a game. Stay focused on the goal.*

Elder Tao raised a hand for silence. "Remember, that you have the right to decline if an elder chooses you as a disciple."

This announcement was met with confused whispers. Kai overheard one participant mutter to another, "Why would anyone do that?"

Why indeed? Kai thought. *Unless they had a very specific plan . . . or knew something that others didn't.*

His gaze drifted to Shen Yu, who stood apart from the others, his face an unreadable mask.

Elder Tao gestured, and five figures rose from their thrones. "Allow me to introduce our Inner Elders," he said. "Each a powerhouse at the Nascent Soul realm."

Kai studied each elder as they were introduced:

Elder Yu, a bulky man with a wild beard and hands that looked like they could arm-wrestle a mountain and win. Kai made a mental note: don't shake his hand.

Elder Lian, a young-looking woman with blue hair and eyes that seemed to hold the depths of the ocean.

Elder Xiao appeared next, so tiny that Kai almost missed her. But he knew that the petite brunette had more qi in her pinky than the participants combined.

The fourth Nascent Soul cultivator was Elder Jiang, a tall man whose face was as impassive as a statue.

And finally, Elder Wu, rotund and jolly-looking. He reminded Kai of the friendly guy who always worked the deli counter at his local supermarket back on Earth. The kind of person who'd slip you an extra slice of cheese with a wink.

Five Nascent Soul cultivators, Kai thought. *Any one of them could probably reshape a mountain with a thought.*

The selection process began. Elder Yu stepped forward first, his voice a rumble like distant thunder. "Sun Jun of the Sun Clan," he called out. "Would you like to take me as your master?"

Sun Jun strode forward, his head held high. "I would be honored, Elder Yu," he said, bowing deeply.

No surprise there, Kai thought. *The brash, arrogant young master type always seems to get picked early in these stories.*

Next was Elder Lian, her voice was nothing like the previous elder's, it was light and melodious, just like a spring breeze. "Lu Chen of the Moon Clan," she announced. "Will you accept me as your master?"

"The honor is mine, Master," Lu Chen bowed.

They're pairing the disciples with elders that match their temperaments, and I assume their elemental affinities, Kai realized. *It's a smart move. The right mentor can magnify a disciple's strengths and shore up their weaknesses.*

His analysis was interrupted when Elder Jiang spoke. "Liu Wei," he called out.

Kai felt Liu Wei stiffen beside him. "M-Me?" the former bandit stammered.

"Yes, you," Elder Jiang said, a hint of impatience in his tone. "I see potential in you, boy. Will you accept my guidance?"

Liu Wei looked at Kai, his eyes wide with a mix of excitement and fear. Kai gave him a subtle nod.

This is a great opportunity for him. And having a connection to one of the Inner Elders could be useful for me down the line. Especially if the sect is split into factions like they tend to be in novels.

"I . . . I accept, Elder Jiang," Liu Wei said, bowing deeply. "Thank you for this honor."

As Liu Wei took his place beside his new master, Kai's mind raced. *Three down, two to go. And neither Shen Yu, Zhi-Zhi, nor I have been chosen yet. What game are they playing?*

He scanned the faces of the remaining elders, looking for any hint of their intentions. But their expressions remained impassive, giving nothing away.

This isn't like the novels, Kai thought. *There's no arguing or competing over disciples. It's too orderly, too . . . choreographed. They must have decided all this beforehand.*

The thought was both reassuring and unsettling. On one hand, it meant the sect was well-organized and efficient. On the other, it suggested a level of behind-the-scenes maneuvering that Kai would need to be wary of.

Zhi-Zhi, who had been uncharacteristically quiet, suddenly piped up. "Ahem! I believe the esteemed elders have overlooked a prime candidate for discipleship. Namely, me!"

The spirit tortoise puffed out his chest, clearly expecting the elders to fall over themselves to claim him. Instead, they continued their selections, seemingly oblivious to Zhi-Zhi's existence.

"But . . . but . . ." Zhi-Zhi sputtered, his tiny eyes wide with disbelief. "Don't they realize what they're missing? The wisdom I could impart? The secrets of the universe I could reveal?"

Kai patted Zhi-Zhi's shell gently. "Maybe they're saving the best for last," he said, trying to keep the amusement out of his voice.

Or maybe they're not interested in a spirit beast who talks big but hides in his shell at the first sign of danger, he thought. *Though, I have to admit, Zhi-Zhi's "wisdom" can be unexpectedly useful . . . when he's not making things up. And who wouldn't want a rare spirit beast as a disciple?*

As the selection continued, Kai noticed that neither he nor Shen Yu had been chosen. *Interesting. Are they saving us for something special? Or is this a test of some kind?*

He glanced at Shen Yu, trying to gauge the other boy's reaction. As usual, Shen Yu's face was an unreadable mask. But for a split second, Kai thought he saw a flicker of . . . possible satisfaction in Shen Yu's eyes.

What is your goal? Kai wondered.

Before he could ponder further, a hush fell over the plateau. Kai looked up to see the Sect Master rising from his throne. The entire plateau fell silent, all eyes fixed on the most powerful cultivator present.

The Sect Master's gaze swept over the disciples, seeming to pierce through flesh and bone to examine their very souls.

"It seems," the Sect Master said, his voice somehow both a whisper and a thunderclap, "that we have some . . . interesting candidates remaining."

This is it, Kai thought, his heart rate picking up despite his efforts to stay calm. *The moment of truth. Time to see if I've done enough to catch the big fish.*

The Sect Master's eyes moved from Kai to Shen Yu, then to the still-fuming Zhi-Zhi. His expression was unreadable, but Kai thought he detected a glimmer of amusement.

"Shen Yu," the Sect Master said, his gaze settling back on Shen Yu. "Step forward."

CHAPTER FIFTY

The plateau fell silent as Shen Yu stepped forward. All eyes were on the young man as he stood before the Sect Master.

"Shen Yu," The Sect Master said. "Not only have you come first in all the trials, but when you began this trial a few days ago, you were only at the first stage of Qi Refining. Yet now you're already at the fifth stage."

A gasp rippled through the crowd. Even Kai's eyes widened slightly at this revelation.

Fifth stage already? He was only fourth stage two days ago. At this rate, he'll surpass me within a week. A wry smile tugged at the corners of Kai's mouth. *I wonder if this is actually Shen Yu's story, and I'm just a side character.*

The thought was both amusing and unsettling.

"To be able to accomplish this while coming from a simple village . . ." the Sect Master continued. "Elder Feng was not wrong. Your affinity for cultivation is second to none, not only in this trial but perhaps in the entire younger generation."

Liu Wei, who was once again standing beside Kai, whispered, "Younger generation?"

Kai leaned over slightly, keeping his eyes on the Sect Master. "In the cultivation world, the 'younger generation' usually refers to cultivators under a hundred years old," he explained quietly. "Age works differently for cultivators. Some can live for centuries or even millennia."

"Shh," Zhi-Zhi hissed. "Pay attention! This is important!"

Kai glanced at Elder Feng, the man was beaming with pride, no doubt already counting the rewards he'd receive for bringing in such a promising recruit.

With so many of his recruits in the top ten, I wouldn't be surprised if he got more than just a Core Formation pill.

The Sect Master's next words sent a ripple of excitement through the crowd. "Shen Yu, would you like to take me as your master?"

To everyone's surprise—including Kai's—Shen Yu smiled. It was a small, almost imperceptible curve of his lips, but on his usually stoic face, it was as noticeable as a shout.

Shen Yu bowed lightly. "It would be my honor, Sect Master. Thank you for this opportunity."

The elders smiled, nodding in approval. But Kai's eyes narrowed, his mind working furiously.

Wasn't Shen Yu the one warning me not to pick the Sect Master as my master? Kai thought, suspicion creeping into his mind. *Yet here he is, doing exactly that. So he really was trying to sabotage me all along . . .*

Kai shook his head slightly, pushing the thought aside. *It doesn't matter. I'd already decided not to listen to him anyway.*

As Shen Yu took his place beside the Sect Master, Kai couldn't help but feel a mix of admiration and wariness. The other boy's cultivation speed was truly phenomenal, even by the standards of this world. It was both exciting and terrifying to think about what Shen Yu might become in the future.

The crowd's reaction was just as exaggerated as Kai expected from a xianxia. Eyes widened, jaws dropped, and a few even stumbled back a step.

"Did you see that? The Sect Master himself chose that village boy!"

"The Sect Master said he went from first stage to fifth in just days but is that even possible?"

"My older brother said the Sect Master has only taken one disciple in over five centuries. But a village boy! This . . . this is huge!"

Just then, Elder Feng's laugh cut through the chatter. "I told you all, didn't I? The Misty Waterfall Village was a goldmine of talent this year!"

Some of the other Outer Elders grumbled, shooting envious glances at Feng. One of them spoke up. "Don't get too cocky, Feng. We'll see how they perform in the Sect Tournament."

Elder Feng's grin only widened. "Oh? You think your recruits can defeat a disciple of the Sect Master, Zhang?"

Before the other elder could respond, the Sect Master raised a hand for silence. The plateau immediately fell quiet, all eyes turning back to the most powerful cultivator present.

Kai held his breath as the Sect Master's gaze swept over the remaining participants and stopped on him.

"Kai Thorn," the Sect Master began, "had it not been for Shen Yu's exceptional performance, you would have been our number one talent. And make no mistake, you would have deserved that title. Your talent is the kind seen only once in a hundred years."

As the Sect Master spoke, a translucent blue screen materialized before Kai's eyes.

Congratulations!
You have gained the title "Once in a Hundred Years Talent"!
Description: Despite not gaining first place or having the fastest cultivation speed, you are still a talent rarely seen.
Effects:
Increases XP gained from absorbing qi by 2x
Increases your maximum Qi by 50 points

Kai blinked, forcing himself to ignore the notification for now. *I'll check that out later,* he thought. *Right now, I need to focus on what's happening.*

The Sect Master continued, his eyes never leaving Kai's face. "Kai Thorn, would you like to take me as your master?"

A collective gasp rose from the crowd. Kai could feel the weight of hundreds of eyes upon him, a mixture of shock, envy, and disbelief radiating from the other disciples.

Sun Jun looked as if he'd been slapped. His face turned an interesting shade of purple as he sputtered incoherently. Kai was surprised no blood was coughed up in the process.

Lu Chen maintained his usual calm demeanor, but Kai noticed a tightness around his eyes that betrayed his surprise and perhaps a hint of jealousy.

From the corner of his eye, Kai spotted Liu Wei. His former student was beaming with pride, clearly thrilled that his master had actually done it.

Zhi-Zhi puffed out his tiny chest. "Of course!" he declared loudly. "It's all thanks to my guidance. I knew my disciple would be recognized for his greatness!"

You didn't do anything, you little shell-dweller. But I suppose I should be grateful for small mercies. At least you're not causing trouble right now.

But what truly surprised Kai was the reaction of the Inner Elders. They were looking at each other with wide eyes and raised eyebrows, clearly caught off guard by this turn of events.

Even Shen Yu, standing beside the Sect Master, showed a flicker of surprise. His eyes widened slightly before his face returned to its usual impassive mask.

"It would be my honor, Sect Master," Kai fought to keep the smile off his face as he bowed. "Thank you for this opportunity."

As Kai straightened from his bow, another system notification appeared.

> Congratulations!
> You have become a disciple of the Sect Master and gained the title "Legacy Disciple"!
> Effects:
> Allows you to level up sect techniques twice as fast
> Grants 5 stat points that can be added to any physical attribute

Kai filed away this information for later as he moved to stand on the other side of the Sect Master, opposite Shen Yu. As he took his place, he saw disciples nudging each other, pointing at Kai and Shen Yu.

"Two disciples in one day?"

"Who is that Kai guy anyway? I've never heard of him before. He's not from any of the great clans."

"Did you see how fast he cultivated? He must have some kind of secret technique!"

Kai kept his expression neutral, but inwardly, he was grinning. *If they only knew,* he thought. *My "secret technique" is being an isekai protagonist with a System. But I think I'll keep that to myself.*

He glanced at Shen Yu, trying to gauge the other boy's reaction. Shen Yu's face was as impassive as ever, but there was a glint in his eyes that Kai couldn't quite decipher. Was it approval? Challenge? Or something else entirely?

I'll have to keep an eye on him, Kai decided. *Being fellow disciples might make us allies, but it could just as easily make us rivals. And in this world, rivals tend to end up killing each other . . .*

The Inner Elders were still muttering among themselves, clearly caught off guard by this unexpected turn of events. Whilst it seems they expected Shen Yu to be picked by the Sect Master, Kai's selection was a surprise even to them.

Kai caught snippets of their conversation:

"Two Legacy Disciples at once . . . I wonder how Young Master Wang Lin will feel about this."

"The other sects will be in an uproar when they hear about this."

"We'll need to increase security. These two will be prime targets for rival sects now."

I've read all about how Legacy Disciples are targeted. I think I'd rather stay in the safety of the sect until I'm OP. Going out for some excitement just isn't worth the risk. Kai nodded to himself.

Kai's gaze fell on Elder Feng, who looked as if he might burst with pride. He was practically bouncing on his toes, a wide grin splitting his face. The other Outer Elders were shooting him looks that ranged from grudging respect to outright envy.

"Well done, Feng," one of them grumbled. "You've certainly outdone yourself this time."

Elder Feng's grin, if possible, grew even wider. "What can I say? I have an eye for talent!"

More like you got lucky, Kai thought. *But I suppose luck is a talent in this world.*

As the commotion began to die down, Kai noticed the Sect Master's gaze shifting once more. This time, it landed on Zhi-Zhi, who was still perched on top of Liu Wei's head.

"Now," the Sect Master said, his voice carrying a hint of curiosity, "what are we going to do with you?"

"Ah, I see you've finally recognized my greatness as well!" Zhi-Zhi declared. "I suppose you'll be wanting to make me a disciple too, eh? Well, I'll have to think about it. After all, I can't just accept anyone as my master, you know!"

Shocked gasps ran through the crowd at the tiny tortoise's words. Even Kai had to fight to keep his expression neutral.

Zhi-Zhi, you idiot. This is the Sect Master you're talking to!

CHAPTER FIFTY-ONE

The Sect Master shook his head, a faint smile on his face. "You are all the same," he muttered, loud enough for the nearby disciples to hear.

Zhi-Zhi puffed out his chest. "What do you mean by that? I'll have you know I'm one of a kind!"

Before the Sect Master could respond, a thunderous voice boomed across the plateau. "Luo Qiang!"

Everyone's heads snapped up. A massive shadow loomed over them, growing larger by the second. With an earth-shaking impact, something enormous landed on the plateau. The ground trembled violently, causing many disciples to stumble and fall.

Kai, however, managed to keep his balance. His eyes widened as he took in the sight before him.

An enormous tortoise stood before them, easily the size of a small hill. But this was no ordinary tortoise. It had curved horns that sprouted from its head and the azure scales that covered its shell looked more draconic than reptilian.

A blue box popped up in Kai's vision.

Name: ???
Species: Dragonback Tortoise
Stats: ???
You are not of a sufficient level to see this being's stats.

Another being that is so powerful the System can't even show me its stats.

Kai glanced around, taking in the reactions of those around him. The Elders seemed surprised, but not alarmed. There was no hint of fear or preparation for battle in their postures.

Okay, so we're not under attack. They know this . . . creature. Is it the spiritual beast protector that sects tend to have?

This tortoise . . . it's definitely beyond the Nascent Soul level. But not quite at the Sect Master's level. There must be a realm between them. I really need to learn more about these cultivation stages soon. My knowledge of this world's power structure is only based on the novels, it's too limited.

The massive tortoise's gaze swept over the crowd, its eyes narrowing as it spoke again. "Luo Qiang, you said there was a youngling here."

As if on cue, its gaze settled on Zhi-Zhi, who was perched on a large stone. For the first time since Kai had met him, Zhi-Zhi seemed to lose his bravado. The spirit tortoise let out a sound that was somewhere between a squeak and a whimper before retreating into his shell.

"Oh ho," the huge tortoise chuckled. "A shy one, are we?"

The Dragonback Tortoise lumbered forward, each step causing a tremor that rippled through the ground. It lowered its massive head, bringing one enormous eye to the level of Zhi-Zhi's shell. It then tapped the shell with the tip of its horn.

"Come now, little one. No need to be afraid. I don't bite . . . much."

"Cang Long," the Sect Master called out. "Be careful. You might accidentally squash him."

Cang Long snorted. "Please, Luo Qiang. I've been handling delicate things since before you were born. Why, I once balanced an entire mountain on my back just to win a bet with the Mountain Spirit!"

Sun Jun, standing nearby, muttered under his breath, "Another one that just likes to spout nonsense."

Cang Long's head swiveled towards Sun Jun, eyes narrowing. "Did you say something, young human?"

Sun Jun's face went pale, then rapidly reddened. His eyes widened, and for a moment, it looked like he might burst into tears. "N-No, great one," he stammered. "I was just . . . admiring your magnificent shell!"

Cang Long preened at the compliment, his earlier suspicion forgotten. "Ah, yes. It is quite spectacular, isn't it? Did you know that each scale holds the essence of a star?"

As Cang Long launched into a tale how even a dying star wasn't able to penetrate its shell, Elder Tao stepped forward. "For those who don't know, this is Cang Long, the legendary beast of the Azure Sky Sect. He has been our protector for thousands of years."

"A guardian beast?" one disciple whispered.

"I thought those were just legends," another replied.

So, I was right, it really is the sect's guardian beast. That's . . . actually pretty cool. No wonder I couldn't see its stats. But why a tortoise with dragon features? I would've expected a full-fledged dragon to be the guardian of the Azure Sky Sect. Are dragons rare in this world or something?

Cang Long, who had finished with his tale, turned his attention back to Zhi-Zhi, who still hadn't emerged from his shell.

The great beast snorted, a gust of wind erupting from its nostrils. "It really is just a baby," it rumbled. "But a Spirit Tortoise . . . I haven't seen one of those in over a millennium."

Seeing that Zhi-Zhi was still hiding within its shell, Cang Long flared its nostrils in annoyance.

"Come out, little one," Cang Long commanded. "Where's your confidence? A Spirit Tortoise should stand tall and proud, not cower in its shell!"

Slowly, trembling, Zhi-Zhi poked his head out. "I . . . I'm not cowering," he said, his voice barely above a whisper. "I'm just . . . conserving energy. Yes, that's it!"

Cang Long let out a booming laugh. "Ha! So you do have some spirit. But you need to work on your delivery. Watch and learn."

The massive tortoise reared up on his hind legs, his voice echoing across the plateau. "I am Cang Long, Guardian of the Azure Sky Sect! My shell has weathered a thousand storms, my claws have carved valleys, and my roar has toppled mountains!"

He looked down at Zhi-Zhi expectantly. "Now you try."

Zhi-Zhi cleared his throat, trying to puff himself up. "I am Zhi-Zhi, a . . . baby spirit tortoise . . . uh . . . my shell has . . . weathered a light drizzle, my claws have . . . scratched an itch, and my voice has . . . mildly annoyed people?"

Cang Long shook his massive head. "We've got a lot of work to do."

Kai couldn't help but shake his head in disbelief. *I've never seen Zhi-Zhi like this before. Usually, he has all the confidence of the world and you can't get him to stop talking. Who knew all it would take to shut him up was a dragon-turtle the size of a hill?*

The Sect Master stepped forward. "Cang Long," he said, "perhaps you'd be willing to take young Zhi-Zhi as a disciple?"

Cang Long's eyes narrowed as he considered the proposal. "Hmm," he rumbled. "The youngling's personality needs a lot of work. But . . ." He paused, his gaze softening slightly. "He is a Spirit Tortoise. I suppose I could make an exception and take him in. After all, who better to teach him than the greatest tortoise cultivator in history?"

He turned back to Zhi-Zhi. "Well? Address me as 'Master,' youngling."

Zhi-Zhi's eyes bulged. "M-Master," he squeaked.

Cang Long nodded, satisfied. "Good, good. Now, let me tell you about the time I raced a phoenix and won . . ."

As Cang Long launched into what promised to be a long-winded tale of his own greatness, Kai couldn't help but smile.

Well, what do you know, he thought. *Looks like Zhi-Zhi found the perfect master after all. They're practically two peas in a pod.*

But this is good, having a connection to the sect's protector could be incredibly useful in the future.

The Sect Master clapped his hands sharply, the sound cutting through Cang Long's boasting and drawing everyone's attention back to him.

"Now that that's settled," the Sect Master said, "I believe we've kept you all here long enough. You are dismissed to your new quarters. Remember, I expect great things from each and every one of you."

He then turned to Kai and Shen Yu. "You two, wait here. Elder Feng will show you to your quarters shortly. We'll meet again soon to discuss your training."

Before either of them could respond, the Sect Master simply . . . vanished. There was no dramatic gesture, no flash of light. One moment he was there, and the next he wasn't.

Now that's what I call a dramatic exit, Kai thought, impressed despite himself. *I wonder how long it takes to learn that trick.*

As the crowd began to disperse, Kai noticed Liu Wei following his new master, Elder Jiang. The former bandit caught Kai's eye and gave him a small wave and a nervous smile before hurrying after his new master.

Kai's gaze then drifted to where Zhi-Zhi sat on a nearby rock. The tiny spirit tortoise wore an expression of pure torture as Cang Long continued his endless boasting.

Finally, Kai thought with a smirk, *Zhi-Zhi's getting a taste of his own medicine.*

CHAPTER FIFTY-TWO

As Kai and Shen Yu stood waiting for Elder Feng to arrive, an awkward silence hung in the air. Kai glanced at his fellow disciple, wondering if he should say something to break the tension.

Maybe I should try to get to know him better. We're going to be spending a lot of time together as the Sect Master's disciples.

But as he opened his mouth to speak, Kai hesitated. *On second thought, Shen Yu doesn't seem like the chatty type. Better to stay quiet for now and observe.*

So Kai remained silent, studying Shen Yu out of the corner of his eye. The other boy stood perfectly still, his face impassive. If the wait bothered him at all, he showed no sign of it.

I still can't get a read on this guy, Kai thought with a mix of frustration and grudging respect. *It's like he's an NPC with no idle animations.*

Before Kai could ponder further, Elder Feng appeared, slightly out of breath.

"Sorry for keeping you waiting," the elder said, bowing deeply.

Kai's eyebrows rose slightly at the bow. *Well, this is new. Usually we're the ones bowing to him.*

"Congratulations on becoming Legacy Disciples," Elder Feng continued, beaming at them. "I knew you were talented, but I never dreamed the Sect Master himself would take you as disciples!"

Kai studied the elder's face, noting the flush in his cheeks and the excited gleam in his eyes. *Looks like someone's been celebrating. I bet he got quite the reward for recruiting two Legacy Disciples.*

"Okay, young masters," Elder Feng said, clapping his hands together. "Let's get you to your new quarters."

Kai's eyes widened slightly at being called "young master." *Wow, talk about a complete 180. A few days ago, he was trying to intimidate me, and now he's bootlicking. How does he not feel embarrassed?*

But then Kai shook his head slightly. *This is just how things work in this world, I guess. Be nice to the strong, bully the weak. I'd better get used to it.*

Elder Feng reached into his storage ring and pulled out a longsword. This sword was much larger than the one he'd used to fly on during the battle against the Thunderwing Drakes.

"Hop on, young masters," Elder Feng said, jumping onto the sword himself. "It'll be faster this way."

Kai carefully stepped onto the sword behind Elder Feng, with Shen Yu taking up position at the rear. As they lifted off into the air, Elder Feng explained their surroundings.

"The trial area is separate from the main sect," he said. "We don't want to bring in anyone who might end up failing, you see."

Kai nodded, trying to focus on Elder Feng's words while also maintaining his balance on the flying sword. He noticed that Shen Yu seemed to have no trouble at all staying steady.

Of course he doesn't. I bet he's done this a hundred times in his past life, or whatever his background really is.

As they got close to the main entrance of the Azure Sky Sect, Kai's mouth almost fell open. A huge gate towered in front of them. It was made of smooth blue-gray stone. On the face of the gate was a giant azure dragon, carved so carefully that it almost looked alive.

The dragon's long body wound around the entire gate, its tail curling at the bottom and its head resting at the very top. Its claws gripped the edges of the gate as if it was guarding the entrance.

What caught Kai's attention most were the dragon's eyes. They seemed to glow with a faint blue light, giving the illusion that the stone beast was watching them.

"Elder Feng," Kai asked, his curiosity getting the better of him, "does this dragon come to life if the sect is attacked?"

"Ah, Young Master, that's a question many have asked. To be honest, I don't know for certain. There are old stories that say it has awakened in the past to defend the sect. But it's been so many years since anyone has dared to attack us, I can't say I've seen it myself."

Elder Feng chuckled softly. "Who knows? Perhaps the tales are true. It certainly makes for an intimidating sight, doesn't it?"

Kai nodded. *It probably is true. It's such a typical xianxia trope after all, an idle statue turning out to be a powerful guardian beast.*

As they hovered near the massive gate, Elder Feng added, "Oh, and just so you know, only Legacy Disciples, Inner Elders, and the Sect Master are allowed to fly within the sect grounds."

With that, Elder Feng guided the sword downward, and they landed softly before the gate.

As the Outer Elder led them through into the sect, Kai's attention was immediately drawn to a group of white-robed disciples engaged in what looked like manual labor. Some were sweeping the pathways, while others tended to gardens or carried stacks of supplies.

Noticing Kai's interest, Elder Feng explained, "Those are our Outer Disciples. They handle most of the day-to-day tasks that keep the sect running smoothly."

"How many Outer Disciples are there?" Kai asked, curious about the sect's structure.

"Oh, about ten thousand or so," Elder Feng replied casually.

Kai's eyes widened. *10,000? That's like a small city!*

"And how many make it to the Inner Sect?" he asked.

Elder Feng's expression grew a bit more serious. "Every year, we hold an Outer Disciple Tournament. The top three disciples earn the right to enter the Inner Sect."

Only three per year? Kai thought. *Talk about fierce competition.*

As they continued walking, one of the Outer Disciples, a young boy with messy hair and dirt-smudged cheeks, approached them nervously.

A blue box appeared before Kai.

Name: ???
Cultivation: Qi Refining Stage 7 Strength: 53 Agility: 51 Durability: 55

Interesting. He's at the seventh stage of Qi Refining, which is pretty impressive for an Outer Disciple. His physical stats are decent, too. This kid's actually not bad.

But if this is the level of an average Outer Disciple, then the competition here is even fiercer than I thought. No wonder only three make it to Inner Disciple each year. If I didn't have the System, this could have been me . . .

"Excuse me," the boy said, his voice barely above a whisper. "Are you . . . are you the new Legacy Disciples?"

Before Kai could respond, Elder Feng snapped, "Show some respect to the young masters!"

The boy flinched, looking as if he might bolt at any second.

Kai's eyes narrowed slightly as he assessed the situation.

This is a perfect opportunity. If I play this right, building a network of loyal Outer Disciples could be incredibly valuable. They could gather information, run errands, maybe even help me acquire resources from outside the sect without putting myself at risk. And all it would cost me is a few kind words now and then.

Making a split-second decision, Kai stepped around Elder Feng to address the boy directly. "It's all right," he said with a gentle smile. "Yes, the Sect Master chose us. But we're all disciples of the Azure Sky Sect. Work hard, and who knows? You might stand where we are someday."

The boy's eyes widened. "Thank you, Senior Brother!" he exclaimed, bowing deeply.

Kai nodded, putting on his most benevolent expression. "What's your name, Junior Brother?"

"Chen Wei, Senior Brother," the boy replied eagerly.

"Well, Chen Wei, keep up the hard work. If you'd like, I'd be happy to give you a few cultivation tips here and there when I have the time. Just remember to pay it forward to your own junior disciples someday."

"Really?" Chen Wei's face lit up with excitement. "Thank you so much, Senior Brother! I'll work harder than ever!"

As Chen Wei turned to scurry back to his work, Kai noticed a sudden shift in the other Outer Disciples nearby. They began looking at Chen Wei with envy. One disciple, who had been sweeping the courtyard, quickly approached Chen Wei.

"Brother Chen," the disciple said, bowing slightly, "allow me to finish your sweeping duties. You must be tired after speaking with the Senior Brother."

Chen Wei looked surprised. "Oh, thank you, Brother Li. That's very kind of you."

Well, well, Kai thought. *It seems my words carry more weight than I expected.*

As they resumed walking, Shen Yu spoke for the first time since they'd left the plateau. "That was unnecessary," he said quietly.

Kai glanced at him, raising an eyebrow. "What was?"

"Giving him false hope," Shen Yu replied. "The chances of an Outer Disciple becoming a Legacy Disciple are astronomically low."

Ah, there's the cold, calculating xianxia protagonist I was expecting, Kai thought. But he didn't disagree, not really. The only reason he'd done it was to start building a positive image for himself within the sect.

In a righteous sect, reputation is probably the next most important thing next to raw power.

As they entered the Inner Sect area, Kai noticed a change in the disciples' attire. Instead of white robes, these disciples wore red.

"Elder Feng," Kai said, "could you explain the color scheme? I noticed the Outer Disciples wear white, but here everyone's in red."

Elder Feng nodded, seemingly pleased by the question. "Of course, Young Master. White is for Outer Disciples, red for Inner Disciples, purple for Core Disciples, and black for Legacy Disciples like yourselves."

It's like a visual representation of the faction system. Makes it easy to know who's who at a glance.

As they walked, Kai noticed Inner Disciples whispering among themselves, casting glances their way. Unlike the Outer Disciple from earlier, however, none approached them directly.

Interesting, Kai thought. *They're curious, but more cautious. I wonder if that's natural wariness or if there are unsaid rules about interacting with Legacy Disciples.*

Elder Feng continued his explanation as they walked. "Inner Disciples have more privileges than Outer Disciples, of course. They focus primarily on cultivation and advancing their skills. Every five years, we hold an Inner Disciple Tournament. Those who catch the eye of an Inner Elder during the tournament may be chosen to become Core Disciples."

The elder's tone grew slightly bitter as he added, "Even if a disciple comes in first place, if no Elder is interested, they remain an Inner Disciple."

Kai glanced at Elder Feng, noting the frustration in his voice. *Sounds like he's speaking from experience.*

Sure enough, Elder Feng continued, "When I was a disciple, I worked my way up to Inner Disciple. I even won the tournament once! But no Elder chose me. That's why my breakthrough to Core Formation has been delayed. I've been stuck at Pseudo Core Formation for fifty years."

Then, his mood suddenly brightening, Elder Feng smiled at Kai and Shen Yu. "But now, because I brought you both to the sect, my breakthrough is guaranteed!"

No wonder Elder Feng doesn't mind bootlicking us. The chance to break through has changed his entire life. Becoming a Core Formation cultivator won't just let him live longer—it'll hugely improve his status in the sect. After fifty years of being stuck, who wouldn't swallow their pride?

As they entered the Core Disciple area, Kai couldn't help but be impressed. The buildings here were grander and gardens filled with rare and exotic plants dotted the area, and Kai could feel the concentrated spiritual energy in the air.

Now this is more like it. I bet cultivation is much easier in an environment like this.

Suddenly, a young woman in purple robes approached them. She had long, dark hair and sharp features that gave her a fox-like appearance.

Wow, Kai thought, momentarily taken aback. *She's gorgeous. Like, protagonist's-love-interest level of beautiful.*

Then he mentally shook himself. *Focus, Kai. Remember, in this world, jade beauties like her usually bring nothing but trouble. Either they're secretly evil cultivators, or they have some kind of tragic backstory that ends up dragging the hero into deadly situations. Best to be on guard.*

The System immediately provided more information.

Name: Li Ying
Cultivation: Early Foundation Establishment Realm Strength: 110 Agility: 120 Durability: 105

Early Foundation Establishment, Kai noted, impressed despite himself. *I don't think I'm ready to take on a Foundation Establishment cultivator . . .*

"Welcome, new Legacy Disciples," the girl bowed slightly. "I'm Li Ying. I hope we'll have a chance to exchange techniques sometime soon. It's always exciting to see what new blood can bring to the sect."

She wants to test us, Kai tensed slightly. *Probably to establish dominance early on.*

He glanced at Elder Feng, surprised to see the normally talkative elder remaining silent. Then it clicked. *Ah, I see. Even though his cultivation is higher, his status is lower than a Core Disciple. He doesn't want to risk offending her.*

Before Kai could respond, Shen Yu spoke up. "We look forward to it. But right now, we have other matters to attend to."

Li Ying's smile tightened almost imperceptibly. "Of course," she said, bowing again. "I'm excited to see what Legacy Disciples can bring to our little exchanges."

As they walked away, Kai frowned slightly. *How transparent. She's only targeting us because we're new and our cultivation is lower. Classic bully behavior.*

A small, cold smile played at the corners of Kai's lips as he felt Li Ying's gaze on their backs, but he didn't turn around.

I've read too many xianxia novels to fall for this. I might not be able to handle a Foundation Establishment cultivator right now, but just you wait, Kai's eyes narrowed slightly. *Once I break through, I'd be happy to "exchange techniques" with you. And I have a feeling you won't like the outcome.*

Finally, they reached the Legacy Disciple area. Kai's jaw nearly dropped at the sight. Each Legacy Disciple had their own small pavilion, surrounded by gardens and what looked like private training grounds.

"Here we are, young masters," Elder Feng said proudly. "Your new homes. You'll each have servants allocated to you to handle day-to-day tasks, allowing you to focus entirely on your cultivation."

Kai nodded, trying not to show how impressed he was. *This is more like a luxury resort than a cultivation sect. But I can't let myself get too comfortable. I need to stay focused on getting stronger.*

After a brief tour of the available pavilions, Kai selected one that overlooked a small waterfall. Shen Yu chose a pavilion on the opposite side of the area, as far from Kai as possible.

Keeping his distance, huh? Kai thought. *Fine by me. The less we interact, the less chance of him figuring out my secrets.*

"I'll check up on you every now and then to see how things are going," the elder said, bowing once more.

Yeah, I bet you will. More likely you just want to create a connection so you can use our names to throw your weight around in the future.

As Elder Feng departed, Kai turned to Shen Yu. "Well," he said, "I guess this is where we part ways for now. See you around."

Shen Yu nodded, then turned and entered his pavilion without another word.

Not much for goodbyes, is he? Kai thought, shaking his head slightly.

Kai then entered his own pavilion, taking in the spacious main room with its polished wooden floors and elegant furniture. A staircase led up to what he assumed was a bedroom, and he could see a door that probably led to a private cultivation room.

Not bad, Kai thought, nodding in approval. *Not bad at all. But now, it's time to get down to business.*

He sat down on a chair, closed his eyes, and focused his thoughts inward.

All right, System. Let's see what rewards we've got waiting for us.

Name: Kai Thorn
XP: 1,100/4,000 Level: Qi Refining Stage 8 Qi: 300/300 Strength: 60 Agility: 63 Durability: 67 Intelligence: 30

Wisdom: 29
Titles: Novice Instructor Once in a Hundred Years Talent Azure Sky Sect Legacy Disciple
Elemental Affinities: Lightning: 20%
Skills: Qi Condensation (Level 4) Basic Cultivation Technique (Level 3) Unarmed Combat (Level 2) Deception (Level 4) Iron Skin Technique (Level 3) Swift Wind Step (Level 4) Flame Palm Strike (Level 3) Mental Fortitude (Passive) Spirit Beast Communication (Level 1) Qi Concealment (Level 1) Qi Detection (Level 1) Iron Rebound (Level 1) Rock Hard (Passive) Lightning Step (Level 1)

A small smile played on Kai's lips as he examined his status screen.

Not bad. That 1,000 XP boost from completing the "Join a Sect" quest was pretty sweet. And look at that qi increase—gotta love that "Once in a Hundred Years Talent" title.

He focused on the new title he'd gained, Azure Sky Sect Legacy Disciple. The effects were impressive. Sect techniques would level up twice as fast, and he gained five stat points to allocate to any physical attribute.

Now this is interesting. First time the System's letting me choose where to put points. Time to min-max this bad boy.

He began breaking down his options:

Strength, already decent at sixty. More power is always good, but I'm not aiming to be a brute force fighter.

Durability, sixty-seven is my highest stat because of the Rock Hard bonus. Tempting to boost it further, but I don't want to rely on tanking hits.

Agility, currently at sixty-three. With my Qi Condensation ability, I can create all sorts of constructs on the fly. The faster I can move and react, the more versatile that becomes. Plus, in xianxia worlds, speed is life. You can't hit what you can't catch.

All five points into Agility. Let's lean into that hit-and-run playstyle!

The System responded instantly.

Agility increased by 5!
New Agility: 68

With that settled, Kai turned his attention to the last notification, the option to accept three random cultivation resources.

Time to see what kind of loot drop I've got.

He accepted the offer, and information about three items appeared.

Root Grasping Vines (Rare) - A living plant that responds to the user's will, allowing them to control its growth and movement.

Mystic Jade Pendant (Rare) - A small, translucent green pendant that gradually purifies the wearer's meridians and qi.

Thunderstorm Essence (Very Rare) - A swirling, electric blue liquid that can be fused with a Foundation Establishment pillar to imbue the user's qi with natural lightning properties.

Kai raised an eyebrow at the Root Grasping Vines. *Huh. Not exactly what I'd expect for my build. This seems more suited for someone like Zhi-Zhi.*

Curious, he activated the skill. Immediately, thin green vines sprouted from the floor around him, swaying gently as if in a breeze.

Interesting, let's see what it can do. Kai focused, and the vines responded, weaving together to form a simple chair. *Not bad for crowd control. Maybe I could even combine it with my lightning qi for some shock value.*

He shook his head. *Getting ahead of myself there. That's way beyond my current abilities. File that away for later.*

Next, Kai examined the Mystic Jade Pendant. It was a simple design, a pale green disk on a silver chain. As he slipped it over his head, he felt a cool, soothing sensation spread through his body.

Oh, that's nice, Kai thought, closing his eyes to better focus on the feeling. *I can actually feel it purifying my qi.*

He nodded to himself. *Impure qi is bad news in cultivation. Makes breakthroughs harder, stunts growth, it can even cause qi deviation if it gets bad enough. Wearing this long-term could give me a serious edge and prevent issues from breaking through too quickly.*

Finally, Kai turned his attention to the Thunderstorm Essence. It looked like a small vial filled with swirling, miniature storm clouds. Occasional tiny flashes of lightning could be seen.

Now this . . . this is something special, Kai thought, a grin spreading across his face. *I've never heard of an essence that could be fused with a foundation pillar like this. Then again, my knowledge of this world's specific cultivation methods is pretty limited.*

His grin faded slightly. *I'm going to need to hit the library, do some serious research before I even think about using this. Can't risk messing up a major break-through because I didn't understand the process.*

After a moment's consideration, Kai carefully placed the vial into his inventory.

Better keep this one safe. A natural lightning effect to my qi would be a massive advantage. Can't risk anyone getting their hands on it.

Just as Kai finished securing his new treasures, a voice called from outside the pavilion. "Young Master?"

Kai stood, smoothing out his robes as he walked to the entrance. *Time to see what this is about,* he thought, keeping his expression neutral as he stepped outside.

Outside stood a middle-aged man in white robes, an Outer Disciple no doubt.

"Young Master, I've brought the list of candidates for your personal servant," he said, offering Kai a scroll.

Kai's eyebrows rose slightly. *That was fast. The sect doesn't waste time, do they?*

"Thank you," Kai said, accepting the scroll. "I appreciate the promptness."

The Outer Disciple bowed. "It is our honor to serve the Legacy Disciples, Young Master."

As Kai unrolled the scroll, the Outer Disciple continued speaking. "All candidates are from the Outer Sect, as is tradition. Being chosen as a Legacy Disciple's servant is a great honor and opportunity for advancement."

Kai nodded absently, his eyes already scanning the list. There were fifty names, each accompanied by a brief description of skills and attributes. Three, in particular, caught his eye.

Name: Huang Hui
Age: 18 Cultivation: Qi Refining Stage 5 Notable Skills: Talented herbalist, knowledgeable about medicinal plants

Background: Orphaned at a young age, raised by an eccentric hermit
who taught her herbal lore.

Zhao Feng

Age: 20
Cultivation: Qi Refining Stage 8
Notable Skills: Former city guard, skilled in basic combat and security
protocols
Background: Seeks to redeem family honor after his father's disgrace
in a corruption scandal.

Name: Chen Wei

Age: 16
Cultivation: Qi Refining Stage 7
Notable Skills: Exceptional memory, quick learner
Background: From a merchant family in a nearby town.
Joined the sect hoping to elevate his family's status.

Kai tapped his finger against the scroll, considering his options.

Apart from their role as a servant, each of these could be useful in their own way.

Huang Hui: Her herbal knowledge could be helpful, especially if I need to brew potions, but I really don't think it'll give me an edge. I could just hire an Alchemist instead . . .

Zhao Feng: Combat skills and security experience would be great for a bodyguard. And his background means he's likely to be loyal, eager to prove himself. But then again, I'm not leaving the sect anytime soon, and even if I did, I expect the Sect Master will provide at least a Core Formation elder if not a Nascent Soul elder as protection.

Chen Wei: I've already met him, and he seemed eager and respectful. His merchant background could be useful for gathering information or handling sect resources. And that exceptional memory could come in handy. Plus, he seems like a good kid, they're usually easier to use . . .

After a few more moments, Kai made his decision. "I'll take Chen Wei as my servant," he told the waiting Outer Disciple.

The man nodded, making a note on another scroll. "An excellent choice, Young Master. I'll inform him immediately. Is there anything else you need?"

Before Kai could respond, another figure appeared. This one was older, dressed in the robes of an Outer Elder. His face was narrow and pinched, reminding Kai of a weasel.

The newcomer bowed. "Young Master Kai, I apologize for the interruption, but the Sect Master has summoned both you and Young Master Shen Yu."

Already? Kai's eyebrows rose. *I thought I'd have more time to prepare.*

"I see. Thank you for informing me. We'll head there right away."

The weasel-faced elder nodded. "Very good, Young Master. I'll escort you."

CHAPTER FIFTY-THREE

Sect Master Luo Qiang sat in his private quarters, his mind replaying the events of the Disciple Selection Trials. A faint smile played on his lips as he contemplated the unexpected boon the heavens had bestowed on the Azure Sky Sect.

Two Immortal-Rank talents. What are the odds?

Talent was categorized into distinct ranks.

At the pinnacle stood the Immortal Rank, those rare individuals with the potential to ascend beyond mortal limitations and achieve true immortality. Below them were the Heaven Rank talents, capable of reaching the Enlightenment Realm. Earth Rank talents had the potential to reach the Astral Realm, while Mortal Rank talents could aspire to become Nascent Soul cultivators.

And anything below that, Luo Qiang thought with a hint of disdain, *is hardly worth the attention of a true cultivator.*

However, the Sect Master's amusement faded as he considered the harsh realities of the cultivation world. Potential was just that, potential. The path to immortality was fraught with dangers, both internal and external.

He leaned back in his chair, fingers drumming on the armrest. *How many promising disciples have I seen fall over the millenniums?* Luo Qiang wondered. *Some succumb to qi deviation, pushing themselves too hard in their quest for power. Others fall prey to their own arrogance, challenging opponents far beyond their capabilities. And then there are those who simply lack the will to persevere, giving up when faced with seemingly insurmountable obstacles.*

His face darkened as his thoughts turned to a more immediate threat. *Assassination.*

"With news spreading of two Immortal Rank talents, it won't be long before the Dark Moon Sect and other demonic cultivators send their assassins," Luo Qiang muttered to himself. "They'll want to nip this threat in the bud."

He shook his head, a bitter smile twisting his lips. "And it's not just the demonic sects we need to worry about. Even our so-called righteous allies will be eyeing our new disciples with envy and fear."

The Sect Master's thoughts turned to their most bitter rival. *The Crimson Phoenix Sect. We'll have to be especially wary of them.*

Despite both being considered "righteous" sects, the Azure Sky Sect and the Crimson Phoenix Sect had been locked in a blood feud for heavens knows how long.

Some say the founders were brothers. Brothers whose rivalry spiraled into this mess we're dealing with millions of years later. Hmph. Family.

While the exact cause of this enmity was lost to time, the consequences were clear.

As soon as one sect produces an immortal, the other's end is all but sealed. We can't allow the Crimson Phoenix to gain such an advantage . . . and they also know the same.

A soft tap at the door interrupted his brooding. A muffled voice called out, "Master, I have returned."

Luo Qiang straightened in his chair. "Come in," he commanded.

The door swung open, revealing a thin, middle-aged man. His features were sharp and angular, giving him a distinctly rodent-like appearance. Luo Qiang had long ago learned that such men often made the best information gatherers.

What was his name again? Luo Qiang wondered briefly before dismissing the thought. *It doesn't matter. Anyone below Core Formation without Heaven Rank talent isn't worth remembering. He likely won't last a millennium anyway.*

The Outer Elder bowed low. "Master, I have completed my investigation of the Misty Waterfall Village as instructed by Elder Tao."

"What have you learned?"

"Regarding the disciple Shen Yu," the man began, "his background appears unremarkable. His father is a simple farmer, his mother tends to their home. He has a younger sister who has shown no aptitude for cultivation."

The Outer Elder paused, as if gathering his thoughts. "The villagers speak well of the boy, though they find him . . . unusual. It seems he has rarely shown emotion since he learned to speak. Always the silent type, they say."

"Go on," Luo Qiang prompted.

"They describe him as intelligent, never causing trouble. A model child, by all accounts, if somewhat distant."

Luo Qiang nodded slowly. *The lack of emotion is a bit concerning, but not unheard of. Many great cultivators have . . . eccentric personalities. And the silent types often harbor great depths.*

"And what of Kai Thorn?" the Sect Master asked.

The Outer Elder's expression grew slightly uncertain. "That's where things become . . . interesting, Master. The boy seems to have appeared in the village out of nowhere. None could tell me of his origins or family."

Luo Qiang's eyes narrowed. "Explain."

"A former disciple of our sect, one Zhang Wei, apparently took the boy under his wing. He taught Kai the basics of cultivation." The Outer Elder hesitated before continuing. "Zhang Wei noticed something . . . unusual about the boy. A strange mark on his wrist that allows him to condense qi in ways Zhang Wei had never seen before."

"A birthmark?" Luo Qiang asked, his interest piqued.

The Outer Elder shook his head. "Zhang Wei didn't think so. He . . . he wondered if the boy might be a member of one of the Hidden Clans."

Luo Qiang's eyes widened fractionally. The Hidden Clans were a subject of much speculation and fear in the cultivation world. Five families, each led by an immortal cultivator, shrouded in secrecy and wielding techniques beyond the comprehension of most.

The Song, the Li, the Chen, the Wang, and the Zhao, Luo Qiang recited mentally. *Each clan a power unto itself, their true strength unknown.*

Of course, sharing a family name with one of these clans doesn't necessarily mean a connection. There are countless Songs, Lis, Chens, Wangs, and Zhaos throughout the realm with no ties to their secretive namesakes.

This fact often led to confusion and false alarms in the cultivation world. Many times throughout the years, ambitious young cultivators have claimed to be from the Hidden Clans, only to be exposed as a fraud and killed.

The converse was also true, genuine members of these clans often hid behind the commonality of their surnames, blending in with the masses.

It's a clever tactic. The very ubiquity of their names serves as both camouflage and smokescreen. But if the boy truly was from one of the Hidden Clans . . . Luo Qiang suppressed a shudder. *Offending such a group could see the Azure Sky Sect reduced to rubble before the night was through.*

Luo Qiang shook his head, forcing himself to consider the situation logically. "It's unlikely," he muttered.

"Sect Master?" the Outer Elder questioned.

"It's unlikely that one of the Hidden Clans would send a member to a medium-sized sect like ours, even for training," Luo Qiang explained. "They know we possess the Eye of Veiled Truth. It would have detected any duplicity in the boy's heart during the trials."

The Outer Elder nodded, visibly relieved. "Of course, Sect Master. You're right."

Luo Qiang continued his train of thought aloud. "Moreover, I doubt they'd give a clan member an immortal treasure just to infiltrate a sect of our size. It doesn't make sense."

He saw confusion flicker across the Outer Elder's face and sighed internally. Sometimes he forgot how limited the knowledge of lower-ranked cultivators could be.

"You see," Luo Qiang explained, slipping into a lecturing tone, "sects are generally categorized by the cultivation level of their leaders. Large sects are those led by true immortals. Medium-sized sects, like ours, are led by cultivators who've reached the Enlightenment Realm. Small sects have Astral Formation masters at their head."

The Outer Elder nodded eagerly, drinking in the knowledge.

Luo Qiang's lip curled slightly. "As for sects led by mere Nascent Soul cultivators . . . well, they're hardly worth mentioning."

The mark and the boy's ability to condense qi . . . that's precisely why I chose him as my disciple, Luo Qiang reflected. *During the trials, his demonstration was unlike anything I've seen in millenniums of cultivation. Such an unusual and powerful technique simply couldn't be overlooked.*

A plan began to form in the Sect Master's mind. "I need to inspect this mark myself," he said aloud. "The ability to condense qi in such a manner . . . it's not something even I can do."

For a brief moment, a hungry look flashed in Luo Qiang's eyes. The Outer Elder caught a glimpse of it and visibly flinched.

Luo Qiang quickly schooled his features back into a calm mask. "Go. Summon my new disciples."

The Outer Elder bowed hastily. "At once, Sect Master!" He turned and practically ran from the room, clearly eager to be away from the sudden intensity radiating from Luo Qiang.

As the door closed behind the retreating elder, Luo Qiang allowed himself a small smile. *Two Immortal-Rank talents. Each with their own mysteries. This could be exactly what I need to finally break through to the next realm.*

His fingers absently traced the patterns on his chair's armrest. *I must tread carefully. If the boy truly is from a Hidden Clan, I can't afford to act rashly. But if he's not . . .*

Luo Qiang's smile widened, taking on a predatory edge. *Well, there are many ways to nurture young talent. And many secrets an old master might . . . borrow . . . from his disciples.*

He rose from his seat and moved to stand by the window, looking out at the majestic peaks of the Azure Sky Sect. Clouds drifted lazily between the mountain spires, giving the impression that the sect really did float in the heavens.

How long has it been, Luo Qiang wondered, *since I reached the peak of the Enlightenment Realm? Millenniums of meditation, of seeking that final epiphany that would propel me to true immortality . . . and nothing.*

He clenched his fist, feeling the immense power surging through his body. To most cultivators, his strength would seem godlike. But Luo Qiang knew the truth. He was still bound by mortality, still subject to the ravages of time, albeit on a much-extended scale.

"Perhaps," he murmured to himself, "these new disciples hold the key. If I can unravel the secrets of that mark, understand how it allows for one to use a skill reserved only for immortals . . ."

Luo Qiang's thoughts were interrupted by another knock at the door. This time, a young voice called out, "Sect Master? The Outer Elder said you wished to see us."

A smile spread across Luo Qiang's face. "Enter," he called out as he closed his eyes, composing himself. It wouldn't do to reveal his eagerness to the boys. A Sect Master must always project an aura of calm wisdom.

Calm wisdom, and absolute authority.

ABOUT THE AUTHOR

Kalzara is the author of the Demonic Sect Elder series, originally released on Royal Road. He is an avid reader of LitRPG and cultivation novels so it was only a matter of time before he decided to write one of his own.

≋ Podium

RESPAWN YOUR CURIOSITY

follow us on our socials

 podiumentertainment.com

 @podiumentertainment

 /podiumentertainment

 @podium_ent

 @podiumentertainment

www.ingramcontent.com/pod-product-compliance
Lightning Source LLC
Chambersburg PA
CBHW032341310726
48973CB00007B/1804